Praise for Minerva Spencer's Outcasts series:

[DANGEROUS] *Booklist Top 10 Romance Debuts of 2018*

[BARBAROUS] *Bookpage 14 Most Anticipated Romances of Fall 2018*

"Minerva Spencer's writing is sophisticated and wickedly witty. Dangerous is a delight from start to finish with swashbuckling action, scorching love scenes, and a coolly arrogant hero to die for. Spencer is my new auto-buy!"
-NYT Bestselling Author Elizabeth Hoyt

"[SCANDALOUS **is]** *A standout...Spencer's brilliant and original tale of the high seas bursts with wonderfully real protagonists, plenty of action, and passionate romance."*
★Publishers Weekly STARRED REVIEW

Gareth clenched his jaw; his desire for her was unfortunate but he was a man who knew how to exert self-control.

Now that he was aware of the danger she presented to his concentration he would see to it that episodes such as this one— the two of them alone, thinly clothed—did not occur again.

Tonight he would leave her at her door and then strip and vent his sexual energy on his punching bags.

They came to the entrance to the grand hall and he reached around her to open the door. She reached at the same moment and their hands met.

"Oh!" she tried to move back and found her hand held in his. She looked down and so did Gareth, perhaps even more surprised than she was. His body acted without his consent and he drew her toward him. She came toward him without hesitation, looking up at him, her unbound breasts pressing against his chest. For once, she was not smiling and her lips were parted. Her pupils had flared; a sign of desire. Gareth knew his own eyes would be just as dark. He slid a hand under the curve of her jaw, his fingers skimming the unspeakably soft skin of her slender neck and then he lowered his mouth over hers.

Also by

S.M. LaViolette &
Minerva Spencer

THE ACADEMY OF LOVE SERIES

The Music of Love
A Figure of Love
A Portrait of Love

OUTCASTS SERIES

Dangerous
Barbarous
Scandalous

ANTHOLOGIES:

BACHELORS OF BOND STREET
THE ARRANGEMENT

A Figure of Love

Minerva Spencer

writing as S.M. LAVIOLETTE

Crooked
Sixpence
**CS
P**
Press

CROOKED SIXPENCE BOOKS are published by
CROOKED SIXPENCE PRESS

2 State Road 230
El Prado, NM 87529

First printing March 2020

ISBN: 978-1-951662-02-8
eISBN: 978-1-951662-03-5

10 9 8 7 6 5 4 3 2 1

Book design by Biserka Design
Photo stock by Period Images
Printed in the United States of America

For my wonderful readers

Chapter One

Kent, England
1817

G areth Lockheart looked down at the snuffling brown and white balls of fur in some perplexity. "Do I really need so many?" he asked the Honorable Sandford Featherstone.

The puppies stirred and whimpered at the sound of his voice and the mother dog—or bitch, Gareth supposed she was called—gave him a look of reproach for waking her sleeping brood. Or flock. Or whatever one called a herd of puppies; puppies with a finer pedigree than Gareth Lockheart could claim.

Featherstone's head bobbed up and down with an enthusiasm Gareth found exhausting. "Oh yes, this many and more if you are to hunt."

Ah, hunting. He'd forgotten all about the supposed need for hunting. Gareth frowned at the prospect but didn't bother arguing with the fussy, fine-boned aristocrat. After all, this was exactly the type of information he was paying Featherstone for: how to behave like a nob; how to build and furnish a house that looked as if toffs had been living in it for centuries.

Gareth had to pause for a moment in order to remind himself *why* he was doing this.

Ah yes, he recalled now: He was enduring all this upheaval and irritating discussion and excessive expenditure because his business partner—Declan McElroy—claimed they needed to present a civilized front if they were ever to gain credibility with the aristocracy and Gareth was more likely to be successful in such a venture. Gareth supposed the man had a point, although why he should trust Declan's judgement on anything English was beyond him. After all, Declan despised the English and took great joy in acting *more* Irish *than* Irish, even though he'd never stepped foot on the Emerald Isle.

"And about those hunters, Mr. Lockheart."

Gareth looked up from the sleeping puppies at the sound of Featherstone's voice; a grating voice with its clipped consonants and condescending cadence. The smaller man was watching him closely; his expression one of concern mingled with . . . *something.*

While Gareth might not be good at reading people he knew what aristocrats saw when they looked at him: an upstart cit with more money and influence than such a mongrel deserved. He found such an attitude neither offensive nor amusing; just irrelevant.

The truth was that the thick walls of the aristocracy had been breached by wealthy merchant princes like Gareth; the power of the peerage was leaking through that breach like water draining from a ship's scuppers.

But the change was happening slowly and England's ancient, landed families still wielded influence in government that was disproportionate to their numbers or wealth.

The resulting equation was simple: aristocrats needed men like Gareth as much as he needed them.

Featherstone shifted from foot to foot under Gareth's silent regard. "My cousin has a very well-respected stud farm in Yorkshire and—" words poured out of his mouth and filled the close air of the stables like a cloud of gnats. Words, words, and more words.

Gareth began to get the flying-apart feeling that invaded him whenever he was too long in Featherstone's company—or in the company of anyone who wasted his time with trivial matters that had already been discussed.

Controlling the unpleasant sensation required mental gymnastics and a great deal of effort on his part.

First, Gareth directed his attention away from his current situation. Next, he focused on the Goldbach Conjecture, an open mathematical problem dating from 1742, as yet unsolved. Pondering such a conundrum never failed to calm him.

Every even integer greater than two is the sum of two primes—

"Mr. Lockheart?"

Gareth forced his eyes to refocus on Featherstone's narrow, anxious face and recall what he'd been babbling about. Horses. He'd been talking about horses.

Gareth frowned. "I've already told you to purchase whatever stock you think fitting, Featherstone. I have entrusted you with such decisions so that *I* will not be taxed by them." *And yet you are taxing me with them,* he wanted to add, but didn't.

Instead, he pivoted on the heel of his boot and strode toward the exit. He'd hoped the other man might stay behind, but he could hear his footsteps struggling to keep up.

"But Mr. Lockheart, you don't even want to talk about your own hunters—"

"No." The sound of their footfalls echoed through the vast and, as yet, unoccupied stables like the sharp reports of a pistol. Gareth deliberately changed the subject. "When does Hiram Beech arrive?"

"Mr. Beech will be here late in the afternoon."

Gareth bit back the irritation he felt whenever he thought of Beech. He'd wanted Amon Henry Wilds to design Rushton Park but the famous architect refused to take a commission so far from his beloved Brighton. Gareth had not been able to lure him away even by offering triple his usual fee. A man without a price was singular in Gareth's experience and he discovered he did not like it.

Instead of Wilds he'd chosen Beech, who was highly recommended as an architect known to favor the Indo-Saracenic style; a style which

Gareth had been told was all the rage. He could not care less what style the country house was built in—he only wanted it to be built by the best. Otherwise, what was the point of all this?

To be honest, Garth had lost interest in the sprawling pile of bricks after the construction phase ended. He had no aptitude for design, décor, or furnishings and had only enjoyed the engineering aspects of the project.

Oh, he was pleased enough with the house, he supposed. Not that he spent much time in it. He'd hoped all the fuss and mess would be over last spring, when the structure had been completed. But now he'd been told he needed some sort of pleasure garden or ancient ruin or other such nonsense. It seemed Beech was the man to arrange the design and building of such things as he already knew the property, and to Gareth, employing him sounded like the least painful and time-consuming option.

They reached the steps to the front entrance—twenty of them, made of the finest breccia marble quarried and transported from the Continent, now that the War was over—and Gareth stopped and turned to Featherstone, eager to be shed of him.

"I have a great deal of work to do and will be in the library, I trust you will handle whatever arrangements need to be made for Beech." Even to Gareth's untutored ears his words sounded abrupt and uncivil. "I will leave you to your business," he added to soften the rude directive.

Featherstone nodded, his hands moving in the compulsive washing gesture Gareth found distasteful and annoying. The man was an unpleasant combination of condescending and unctuous, but Beech had recommended him. "Mr. Beech will be bringing—"

Gareth held up a hand. "Yes, you've already said. He will be bringing a stone-worker or sculptor or gardener or what-have-you. I will speak with both or all of them before we dine this evening." Gareth tossed the words over his shoulder, impatient to get back to work.

He strode through the great hall and then turned right to pass through the portrait-less portrait gallery on his way to the residential wing of the house. He spent most of his time at Rushton Park in the library, which was composed of three massive rooms linked together. The size seemed excessive to Gareth but the design apparently aped an ancient library from some place Gareth had never heard of. All he'd requested of Beech was that it be well-lighted and commodious enough to contain a desk, his journal collection, and a comfortable chair. And all Gareth had required of Featherstone when the man began stuffing the house with furniture and other frippery was that the library remain free of distracting clutter.

Two footmen stood at attention outside the double doors, waiting for nothing other than his arrival. Gareth ignored the unease he felt at such excess; after all, this was what he'd wanted, a country home that was as gratuitously sized and overstaffed as one of the royal dukes' residences. Actually, Gareth had more servants *and* a larger house.

Since coming down from London two days ago he'd had his correspondence delivered twice daily by couriers. The pile of letters was easily three inches tall. There would be reports from all his businesses, but most of the stack would be about the new pottery he was building in London, his most ambitious project thus far.

Gareth was only half-way through the pile when the sound of somebody clearing their throat made him look up. His butler, Jessup, stood in the doorway.

"I asked not to be disturbed."

The towering, bone-thin man gave a slight nod, but his expression remained as fixed as a totemic carving. He was, Gareth knew, utterly unflappable. Gareth had poached him from the Duke of Remington's household, where Jessup's family had been employed as butlers for two hundred years. Remington could not compete with the pay Gareth offered.

"You have a visitor, Mr. Lockheart, Mrs. Serena Lombard."

Gareth shook his head. "I am not acquainted with, nor am I expecting any such person."

"She is here at the behest of Mr. Beech, sir, about the gardens."

"Ah, I see." Although he did not. He cleared his throat. "You say Beech has engaged a woman gardener?"

"Yes, sir. Mrs. Lombard is a woman. And a gardener," Jessup agreed.

Sometimes—just occasionally—Gareth wondered if his butler made mock of him. He shrugged the thought away. What did he know of gardeners? For all he knew, they might all be females. Well, whoever she was and whatever she did, Gareth would find out at the appropriate time. He cut Jessup an impatient look. "Have Featherstone see to her, Jessup."

"Mr. Featherstone has gone to the village, sir."

Gareth stared at the man.

Jessup nodded, just as if he'd spoken. "I shall put her in the sitting room and offer her tea."

"Yes, very good. Put her in a room with tea." Lord knew there were enough rooms in the house—seventy-three—certainly one of them would be appropriate for accommodating unexpected female visitors.

Gareth's eyes and attention drifted back to the neat column of figures in front of him.

"Very good, sir."

He barely heard the butler, his mind already back on his numbers, the woman forgotten.

***

Serena eyed the generously loaded tea tray with approval and helped herself to three different types of biscuits and the loveliest fairy cake she'd ever seen. Such delicacies were rare these days. Even when she paid a visit to the home of her dead husband's parents, the Duke and Duchess of Remington, the offerings were rather thin; the powerful duke had suffered since the War ended, forced to retrench at his six houses.

Serena examined the huge sitting room—the gaudiest specimen she'd ever sat in—and enjoyed her delicacies. The butler returned after she'd been alone for about a quarter of an hour.

"Do you have everything you need, Mrs. Lombard?" The hesitation before her name was almost imperceptible, but she noticed it all the same.

Serena cocked her head and smiled up at him. "What? Are we no longer friends, Jessup? How are you? I have not been to Keeting yet this year, but I was there at Christmas. His Grace speaks fondly of you, you know." Keeting Hall was the country seat of the Duke of Remington.

The slightest dusting of color appeared on the butler's high, sharp cheekbones. "And I often think of His and Her Graces as well as the rest of the family." He looked as if he wished to say something else, but hesitated.

"His Grace does not blame you for leaving, Jessup," she said.

Well, that was a bit of a fib. Her in-laws *had* been devastated by their family retainer's desertion. But Mr. Lockheart—a man reputed to be among the ten richest in Britain—had offered a wage too high for Robert Jessup to resist.

Jessup's lips flexed in what passed for a smile. "You are very kind, madam."

"So, how do you find it here?" Serena glanced around the cavernous room, which evoked a seraglio with its bold fuchsia, gold, and green color scheme, opulent silk and velvet window coverings, and Egyptian-style furniture.

"I find my position suits me admirably, Mrs. Lombard."

Again she heard the hesitation before her name. She knew that Jessup, like her dead husband's family, were unhappy that she refused to use her honorific. Serena allowed them all to believe her resistance to aristocratic titles was because of her French Republican upbringing, rather than the truth; a truth they could never know.

She realized the butler was waiting for her answer. "I'm pleased to hear you are happy here, Jessup." And she was. It was too bad he'd needed to leave his home of many years, but—as she knew all too well—everyone deserved a chance at a better life.

Serena returned her cup and saucer to the massive tea tray. "Mr. Beech has asked me to work with him on the new gardens for Rushton Park." Jessup knew what Serena did for a living. He'd worked for the Lombard family when she had first arrived in England almost ten years ago. He'd been there when Serena—after living her first year under the care of the duke and duchess, who were very kind to their youngest son's foreign widow—had scandalized her new relations by moving to London to take up a position teaching art and sculpture at a girls' school.

Once again, her husband's family blamed her mad French blood—but, thankfully, hadn't tried to stop her—for taking her infant son from the comfort of Keeting Hall and moving them both to a town house with two other women teachers. It had been a difficult decision, but she did not regret it.

"If you will permit me to say so, madam, I have seen your work, and it is quite lovely."

The Jessup of old would never have offered an unsolicited opinion. Perhaps working in a Whig household had given him a more egalitarian outlook.

"Thank you, Jessup." She stood and smoothed down the skirt of her dark green traveling costume. "I'm refreshed and eager to see Rushton Park. Would it be possible to take a stroll around the grounds?"

"Of course, madam."

Serena opened the flap of the large leather satchel she was rarely without and took out her sketchpad.

She smiled up at him. "I'm ready."

As he moved to open the door for her, Serena studied his familiar narrow form and black-clad shoulders and decided she was more pleased than she would have expected to find an old family ally and retainer. Of course she'd known Jessup worked for the reclusive Gareth Lockheart, but the man kept houses in London, Edinburgh, and Bristol. If she'd given the matter more than a passing thought, she would have assumed Lockheart kept the unparalleled butler in his London house, where it was rumored he spent most of his time.

Jessup escorted her down a staircase wide enough to accommodate seven soldiers marching abreast and paused on the ground floor.

"Shall I take you out through the orangery, madam?"

"Yes, please. I didn't see it from the drive, but I've seen it on Beech's drawings."

The house resembled an Elizabethan "E" but with many modifications—some rather. . . unconventional.

"How long have you been here, Jessup?"

"I came down with Mr. Lockheart two days ago, madam. I have been at his London house but accompanied him here to see to some unfinished household matters."

Serena had never seen a house quite like it. It was a *corps de logis,* comprised of a central block with two wings that were three stories and curved to form a three-sided courtyard—or *cour d'honneur*—on each side of the central block.

Either Lockheart or Beech must have been very fond of onion domes, as there were no fewer than five of them. The blinding white façade was festooned with multitudinous cusped arches, minaret-shaped finials, and vacant plinths waiting for statuary. The mishmash of Orientalism and Indo-Saracenic styles was so like the Royal Pavilion that she kept thinking she must have taken a wrong turn and ended up in Brighton.

The interior lacked the chinoiserie so far as she had seen. Indeed, the décor was far less definite than the exterior and felt like the rather halfhearted result of a committee.

The hall flooded with light and ahead was a wall of leaded glass.

"My, how lovely," Serena said as Jessup opened one of the massive double doors to the empty conservatory, which was without even a stick, plant, leaf, or crumb of dirt. "When was this finished?" She turned in a circle, gazing overhead at the spectacular glass walls and canopy.

"Last spring, ma'am."

Serena couldn't help thinking of the orangery at Keeting Hall, which was perhaps a quarter of this size and so choked with plants it had felt like a jungle. It might be old and crowded, its glass hazed and cracked, but it was alive. Which was more than she could say for this empty glass box. Beech had not mentioned the orangery, but Serena couldn't help feeling a frisson of excitement as she imagined filling such a beautiful space with living things.

Jessup opened one of the French doors and they stepped out into the cool spring sunshine. She turned to him. "I will walk the immediate area until Mr. Beech arrives."

The butler's eyebrows arched.

"What is it, Jessup?"

"Mr. Beech is not expected until late afternoon, ma'am."

Serena frowned. "He told me it was to be a midday meeting. I have engaged the post chaise to return for me at four."

"Mr. Beech is to arrive at five o'clock and will stay the night."

Serena wanted to howl with frustration but it was hardly Jessup's fault. "I'm afraid Mr. Beech neglected to inform me of either the correct time or duration of our meeting." She sighed and glanced around her without seeing anything, her mind churning. The expensive journey out and back had been paid for by Mr. Lockheart, of course, so she was not concerned about that. But she had brought no change of clothing or any other items for an overnight stay. She also had not told Lady Winifred, her friend and housemate, that she would be gone overnight. And of course Oliver would be expecting to see her tomorrow morning.

She looked up half a foot to meet Jessup's impassive eyes and shrugged. "Well, Jessup, this is a bit of a muddle. I did not come prepared for an overnight stay, nor did I tell anyone I would be away that long." She caught her lower lip between her teeth and worried it. "You know the way of things here, what do you advise?"

His expression didn't change, but his dark brown eyes glinted with approval at her calm reaction.

"Mr. Lockheart is a gentleman who does not stay long in one place, ma'am. It is his plan to leave Rushton Park tomorrow. He will return to London for a few days but then I believe he is headed to the North. It may be some time before he returns to Rushton Park for another meeting."

That was his way of saying she should stay. "I see."

Jessup's mouth opened a crack, but then he closed it.

"What is it you are thinking? Don't be shy."

"Do you need to be back in London tonight?"

"No, but my son and the woman we live with will worry if I'm not back by this evening."

"If I could make arrangements to provide you with the items necessary for an overnight stay and send a message to reassure your friend and Master Oliver, would you have any objections to staying?"

It was not ideal, but she knew this commission would be worth a great deal of money.

"Thank you, Jessup, that would serve admirably."

"If you will excuse me, I will see to it. I will leave you to enjoy your walk and return for you in half an hour."

***

Gareth had the big rolls of plans for the new pottery spread out on the vast trestle table he'd had made for this exact purpose. He was examining it with a magnifying glass, studying the details for the massive kilns.

He was so enrapt he nearly jumped out of his skin when a throat cleared behind him. He ignored his rapidly beating heart and sighed. "Yes, Jessup, what is it now?"

"I am terribly sorry to disturb you, sir, but there appears to have been something of a misunderstanding."

Chapter Two

Serena stared at the immense book-lined room. Three rooms linked together, actually. A library unlike anything she'd ever seen. Of course the entire property was singular, from the lush countryside that surrounded the gargantuan house, to the vast suite of rooms she'd been given for her brief stay. Rooms that were twice as large as any she could recall at Keeting Hall.

Jessup had taken care of her as if she were a queen, sending one messenger speeding off to London and another all the way to Ayelford—the nearest town with a dress shop—to purchase a nightgown and dressing robe. These, as well as a selection of toiletries, combs, and brushes—all new—awaited her in her sumptuous chambers. Serena would have to wear her clothing to dinner and again tomorrow when she left, but Jessup told her Mr. Lockheart had been apprised of the matter and tonight's dinner would be informal.

All in all, she could not be unhappy to be staying an evening in such a house. The library alone was worth the inconvenience. Bookshelves began only a few inches off the floor and did not stop until the ceiling, which she believed to be at least fifteen feet high. The book ladder was precariously tall, and she could imagine herself scaling it and risking life and limb for the sake of a book.

She was examining a rather exquisite set of six volumes of illuminated French poetry when the door opened behind her. She turned to find Sandy Featherstone, her deceased husband's cousin, twice removed.

"Hallo, Serena, Beech told me you'd agreed to come." He came toward her with his arms outstretched and Serena submitted with resignation to his embrace. He was a sticky-handed man whom she had only ever tolerated because of his connection to the family.

Serena stepped away when it became apparent he was not going to voluntarily release her. He eyed her in a way that made her jaw tighten, his small-fingered hands moving in their habitual hand-washing motions.

"Hallo, Sandy." Serena forced a smile. "So, it appears I have you to thank for this." She made a gesture which encompassed everything around them.

He grinned, the sight somewhat alarming as he seemed to have twice the normal complement of teeth. "It was nothing, my dear—merely family looking after family. Besides, I told Beech we had better snap you up before your fees became exorbitant." He chortled, clearly tickled at the thought of such a thing happening.

Serena's smile became even stiffer. "Well, whatever the reason, I do appreciate it. I've just finished a series of small commissions and was at loose ends."

"What are cousins for, my dear?" He gestured toward a cluster of decanters sitting on a granite slab supported by massive gold lion's feet. "Would you like a drink before dinner, Serena?" His hand trembled slightly, making it clear *he* would like a drink.

"A glass of sherry, if you have it."

"Mr. Lockheart has everything." He smirked and then turned to fix their drinks. "Oh, and I'm afraid I've got some rather disappointing news," Sandy said over the sound of glass clinking against glass. "It seems Beech was delayed in London."

Serena closed the volume she'd taken down and replaced it on the shelf. Of course he was. It had been exactly that kind of day.

Sandy came toward her with their drinks. "Not to worry, though. He sent his plans down and we can study them after dinner."

Serena perked up. That was actually better than having Beech here as she'd noticed the successful architect had a tendency to talk over-much about himself and his achievements. The two times she had met with him it had taken him more than a half hour before he could come to the point.

Serena sat on a gilt settee that had been upholstered in a rather shocking chartreuse while Sandy took the chair closest to her, a gothic thing with dragons for armrests.

"So, what have you been up to since we last saw one another—Lord!" He examined the ornately coffered ceiling, as if it might contain the information he sought. "Was that five years ago?"

"Has it been that long?" But she knew it had. Sandy had done something to displease the duke and had not received an invitation to the famous house party the duke and duchess had every year around Christmas. She took a sip of excellent sherry and set down her glass on a side table that appeared to be a Sphinx.

"Yes, Oliver was towing around that wooden horse, if I recall correctly. You were on holiday from the school." He wore a sly smile, clearly amused by her method of supporting herself.

Serena was surprised he remembered her son's name. "The Stefani Academy closed last year."

"I'd heard that." His pointy nose quivered, putting her in mind of a rat. "I'd also heard the woman who owned it was rather dodgy and hared off abruptly—almost as if there was something scandalous she wished to leave behind?"

Serena felt a surge of distaste for both him and his characterization of her friend Portia Stefani. The school in question had been an oasis of friendship and security, and she sorely missed it. She changed the topic before she said something to Sandy she would regret.

"I have had a series of commissions since then. Most notably a project for the Mannerings.

"I heard about that, too—some rather ostentatious work on an undercroft in their private church."

It always amazed her how Sandy seemed to know everything that went on in *ton* circles, even though he was perpetually on the fringes of it.

"And you, Sandy, how have you been occupying yourself?" Besides drinking and gambling, she could have added.

"As you see." He waved a hand in the air, his other hand holding the glass which already held just half of what it had only a moment earlier. Sandy had always had too much of a taste for spirits.

"What exactly do you do for Mr. Lockheart?"

"This and that. In truth, I am no more than a well-paid secretary, although he does not use me for his matters of business." He smirked. "You might say I act as his wife, until he can buy one."

"Oh? Is he in that market?"

He gave her a smile that made her feel dirty. "You sound interested, Cuz."

"I am quite happy as I am, Sandy."

His raised brows told her what he thought of that claim. "I selected many of his servants, furnished all his houses except the London townhouse, and advise him in his acquisition of art. Right now I am busy with his stables, which he wants to have ready for use by the fall."

Serena suddenly understood the hideous furnishings. "Mr. Lockheart hunts?" She could not recall hearing much about the man, other than he was rich and rather odd.

"No."

The door opened before Sandy could explain, and their host entered the room. Serena was surprised—he was not only younger than she had expected, he was also elegantly dressed and strikingly handsome. Serena realized she'd given in to preconceived notions and had expected a brawny merchant or flashy cit.

He crossed the long expanse of carpet and Sandy leapt to his feet to make introductions.

"Mr. Lockheart, may I present Mrs. Lombard."

The tall, well-proportioned Adonis took her hand and made a perfunctory bow over it.

"I am pleased to make your acquaintance, madam." His eyes were slate gray and the most opaque Serena had ever seen, observing her without a hint of interest or any other emotion. His lips, sinfully lush and shapely, bore no trace of a smile.

He was perhaps a head taller than she, his dark blond hair on the longish side. Like Sandy, he was dressed informally to accommodate her lack of evening dress, in a bottle-green coat, rich brown waistcoat, and buff pantaloons tucked into coffee-colored Hessians polished to a blinding shine. His snowy white neck cloth was tied with simple elegance; he wore a plain gold watch with no fobs at his waist. His clothing had been made by a master and tailored to fit his form as snuggly as a well-made glove.

"Thank you for inviting me to Rushton Park, Mr. Lockheart."

He nodded abruptly and glanced at his watch, his sensuous mouth turning down slightly at the corners. "There are still seventeen minutes until dinner." He looked up, his gaze flickering over Serena's untouched sherry to Sandy's empty glass. "What are you having, Featherstone, I will refill it."

"Ah, thank you, sir. Brandy."

He took the glass without speaking and went to the sideboard.

Sandy smiled at her and gave a slight shrug. So, her prospective employer was a gloriously handsome man who was also brusque and without social graces. Well, she had heard he was different.

"I daresay Jessup has informed you Mr. Beech will not be here for dinner," Sandy said, his flickering eyes proclaiming his discomfort with silence.

"I received his plans by courier. We will proceed without him," Lockheart said. "After dinner we will examine what he has drawn up." His voice was as devoid of expression as his face. No irritation, regret, or anger at Beech's absence. He returned to where they were seated and took a chair across from Serena after giving Sandy his drink. A double, if Serena was not mistaken.

He fixed Serena with his rather unnerving cool gray stare and took a sip from his glass. His hands, like his person, were slim, elegant, and devoid of jewelry. Serena had expected the stereotype merchant, a beefy, bluff man in his later years. But Lockheart not only resembled a gentleman, he spoke like one, too. While his accent was not exactly aristocratic, it was refined and precise, definitely not that of a man said to have come from the stews of London. There was more here than met the eye.

"I understand you inspected the property this afternoon, Mrs. Lombard."

"Nothing so thorough as an inspection, but I did wander as far as the stream and then along the small wood."

"And did you have any ideas?"

Serena chuckled. "I always have ideas." She smiled at him, but he only blinked calmly back at her. So, he was lacking in humor. She tried again. "My understanding was Mr. Beech would submit a general design and I would see to the details and statuary."

"It is true I have engaged Mr. Beech to create a plan. Have you designed and laid out gardens yourself?"

"Yes," she admitted, surprised by the question. "But never anything as large as this."

"What would you do if it were yours?"

Now *that* was an interesting question, and one she had never been asked by any other client, most of whom had had their own ideas, many of them quite bad.

"I would lay out a parterre directly off the orangery. Beyond it, I would leave things as they are. I believe the terrain on the south side, with its gentle slope, is similar to Badminton and would be perfect for a Brown-like lake, which could be achieved by some clever damming of your stream. Right now there is an old wooden footbridge over the stream. I would replace that with something more interesting." She smiled. "Naturally I would recommend something in stone. If you wish for a folly there is a nice rise on the far side, and once you've created a lake it would be a lovely situation with the addition of a few trees. A rose garden, with a walk to the woods on the east side. You have the two *cour d'honneur* that face the drive and they could be given greenery, a fountain, more roses, intimate seating areas. Of course I did not inspect anything beyond the immediate area and could see more of the estate, more quickly, if I had a horse." She paused. "But those are my first impressions and what I would consider if it were mine." Serena took a sip of claret and never took her eyes from her host, whose expression had not flickered while she spoke. He was not an easy person to talk to; he gave no facial or physical cues to put the speaker at ease. He sat silently for a long, uncomfortable moment, as if considering her words, and then nodded.

"It sounds perfect." He turned to Sandy, who again had his glass raised to his lips. "Will you recall everything Mrs. Lombard said, Mr. Featherstone?"

Sandy gulped down a mouthful of brandy, coughed, and set down his glass. His eyes slid in Serena's direction and then snapped back to his employer. "If I do not, I'm sure Mrs. Lombard will be able to tell me in greater detail."

Mr. Lockheart turned back to her. "You have several ideas I approve of, ma'am. Would you be able to implement such plans without further consultation with Mr. Beech?"

Serena's eyebrows shot up. "Are you asking *me* to design your gardens and park, Mr. Lockheart?"

"Yes."

"But haven't you an agreement with Mr. Beech?" Serena would hate to gain a reputation for poaching commissions.

He continued to regard her with his flat, disorienting gaze. "I have not engaged Mr. Beech, but asked for his bid. He would not go uncompensated for the work he has done. Is Mr. Beech your only objection to accepting such work?"

"I have no experience with anything this large."

Still he did not speak.

And I'm a woman, or don't you care? Or haven't you noticed. Good Lord! Design an entire estate's grounds? Why, that would be—

"Do you think you could accomplish what you described, ma'am?"

Serena felt a flutter of anticipation at the thought of being paid to experiment with such interesting concepts at someone else's expense. It would be a creative endeavor that would be beyond her dreams—and also one that would be a glorious fit with her talents. She could design a garden to showcase her work, rather than the other way around.

She looked up at his impassive face. "Yes, Mr. Lockheart, I believe I could."

***

Gareth could hardly believe his good luck. He could dispense with Beech's irritating presence and deal only with the woman. True, he thought, spooning soup into his mouth and casting a glance across at her, she was rather *odd*. Oh, she was not odd looking. Indeed, she was attractive, if one discounted her wild mass of hair which seemed in danger of escaping its moorings and her worn, unflattering green gown. But it was not her appearance so much as the entirety of . . . well, *her*. She belonged to a type of person who had always mystified him: good-humored, quick to smile, laughing easily, but obviously not unintelligent for all her humor and easy ways.

And then there was the fact she was a woman who worked with not only plants, but stone. Gareth did not know of any other woman who did such a thing. Of course he did not know any other sculptors. He had, however, met more than a few stone-cutters in the course of his business dealings, and none of those were women.

She appeared to have no trouble readjusting her expectations according to a change in circumstance. In Gareth's experience such boldness—such fearless independence and fluidity of thinking—was not common in his dealings with women. Although Gareth would be the first to admit his dealings with women had been shockingly few during a life that spanned three and half decades.

Lastly, and this was something that he was realizing over the course of the meal, she was rather . . . opinionated. Right now she was bickering with his factor-cum-secretary as vigorously as any man in a pub, and on a subject usually considered a male purview: horses.

Featherstone was quite heated and his face had turned a dull crimson at something she just said. "You are hardly an expert on such matters, Serena, for all that you are willing to share your opinions so freely. Well here is my opinion: Leeland is one of the best breeders in Yorkshire."

Mrs. Lombard gave an unladylike snort and took another mouthful of soup before deigning to answer. "No doubt. But we are speaking of his horses, not the man himself."

Gareth froze, his spoon a few inches above his soup. Had she just said what he thought she said? He looked across at her. She met his stunned gaze, a tiny smirk curving her lips before she took another mouthful of food.

Even Featherstone couldn't help laughing, a braying sound as irritating as his voice. "You haven't changed a whit, Serena. You still have no governor on what comes out of your mouth."

She shrugged, unperturbed by what was obviously meant to be insulting.

Gareth looked from one guest to another, something occurring to him which should have occurred much earlier—if he paid attention to such things. He lowered his spoon. "You two have a prior acquaintance?"

"Yes, Mrs. Lombard and I are cousins." Featherstone punctuated this statement with a slurp of wine and a footman stepped forward to replenish his glass. Gareth had never noticed before what a prodigious drinker the man was.

"My husband was his cousin, twice removed," the woman corrected in her low, accented voice, daubing her wryly smiling lips with her napkin.

"You do not agree that Mr. Featherstone's cousin's horses are of good quality, Mrs. Lombard."

She turned away from Featherstone, who was openly glaring at her now. "Mr. Featherstone is correct, Mr. Lockheart—I am not an expert on horses of any sort. I should not speak so forthrightly of Leeland Bowles. I have not seen him for quite a few years and I have never visited his stud farm in Yorkshire."

"Where would you purchase horses?"

The woman slid an uneasy gaze toward Featherstone. Gareth looked at his factotum and noticed there was an uncharacteristic tightness around his eyes. This time there was no mistaking the look of hostility he shot the woman.

A suspicion was beginning to form in Gareth's mind, but he placed it to one side for examination later. He looked from his red-faced secretary to the woman and deliberately changed the subject.

"Tell me, Mrs. Lombard, how is it that you came to become a sculptor in addition to landscape gardening?" Even Gareth, with his woeful ability to read the expressions of others, could see the relief on her face.

"I was trained as a sculptor in France. My father, Peter Veryan, was an Englishman. He went to France before the troubles to work under a well-known French sculptor, Jean Favel. My mother was Henriette Favel, his daughter. My mother died giving birth to me, so I was raised in a rather unconventional household—two artists who saw no harm in teaching me their craft."

"And the landscape gardening? Did you learn that in France?"

She laughed. "No, I'm afraid neither my father or grandfather knew anything about plants or gardens. I first discovered my interest in gardening when I was living with my mother- and father-in-law. They wished to make changes and I happened to be living in their home at the time. They wanted a sculpture from me, and I was allowed to design the setting, as well. I worked with the man they employed, who said I had an aptitude for such work. When I moved to London, I took care of the neglected garden in the house where I still live." She shrugged and gave him a smile that made his stomach clench for some odd reason. "Next I helped a friend, and then their friends saw what I had done. Within a few years people seemed to find me and ask me to design their gardens. I'm sure you know how it is?"

Gareth had no idea how it was. Nobody had ever asked him to design a garden for them. But he thought he knew what she meant. She had slowly worked her way into her current position. A difficult thing to do for anyone, and probably doubly difficult for a woman.

Featherstone came out of his sulk and took charge of the conversation. For once, Gareth was glad of the garrulous man's empty natterings. He was content to look at the woman and consider the interesting tale she had told him.

Chapter Three

It had been an exhausting night, but Serena could hardly recall a more interesting one. The three of them had retired to the library after dinner, Lockheart apparently having no idea of the impropriety of skipping after dinner port.

Serena had looked at the plans Beech provided and realized that, here again, was another man intent on abusing Lockheart's trusting nature.

She'd never met anyone quite like the wealthy young merchant prince. He appeared to be completely without interest in human beings, without a sense of humor, and utterly focused on whatever business was at hand. Not only that, but the entire time she spent with him, she couldn't help feeling she only had a part of his attention. She suspected a greater part of his brain was churning away and functioning on some other—higher?—plane. Indeed, he had the appearance of an artist in the midst of a creative frenzy. Serena had seen the same expression on her artist friends' faces and felt a similar near-euphoria when visited by the muse, herself. Although Lockheart had not manifested any of the outward signs of artistic obsession—dishevelment, absentmindness, forgetfulness, irritability—he'd maintained the distant stare of a person whose mind was engaged elsewhere.

But, after dinner, that stare had sharpened quickly as they'd begun to study Beech's oversized sketch of the estate.

Indeed, Lockheart had proved to be a fascinating conspirator on the landscaping plan, even though he had no interest in the results themselves. No, what he had liked had been the mathematics and engineering aspects. Questions of water flow and volume had, in particular, seemed to fascinate him. They had spent most of their time examining the best place to dam and build the lake.

At least two hours had passed before they looked up from Beech's plans and noticed Sandy had fallen asleep in a chair by the fire.

Lockheart's silky brown hair stood in furrows, like a freshly plowed field. He ran a hand through his disheveled coif yet again as he surveyed the room—Sandy, the fire, his watch—through distracted gray eyes.

"I had no idea it had grown so late. I believe I have been very uncivil to not offer you tea."

Serena did not mind. "Perhaps we might order some now and continue with our plans?"

He nodded abruptly and strode to the double doors, his voice a low murmur as he spoke to one of the footmen she'd seen stationed outside the room. His house was staffed like a duke's. Better than a duke's actually. Serena's father-in-law had not enjoyed the luxury of footmen outside his study in several years.

When he returned, Serena was studying an inset drawing of a temple. "They will bring our tea to the document room." He gestured to a part of the library she had not yet seen. "I should hate to disturb Mr. Featherstone."

Serena chuckled, and then realized Mr. Lockheart was not laughing. Instead, he was regarding her quizzically, as if wondering why *she* was laughing. "I daresay artillery could not wake Mr. Featherstone."

"Ah," he said, as if suddenly enlightened.

"Do you dine with one another most nights?"

"Not if I can avoid it."

Serena bit back a smile as she followed him toward a room lined with glass-fronted cabinets. He was dreadfully honest and blunt. She could not imagine the havoc he would wreak in a London drawing room or a room full of debutants, if what Sandy had said about him being on a hunt for a wife was correct.

Serena forgot all about Mr. Lockheart's awkward manner when she stepped into his document room.

"My goodness." Her voice naturally dropped to a reverential whisper. Dozens of cases filled the room and huge candelabra hung from long chains above each to illuminate the contents. The room blazed with light. She approached the largest case, which sat on a pedestal in the center of the room. Inside the beveled glass case was a very ancient looking leather-bound journal. The writing was in a language Serena knew to be Latin—not that she could read it. But the drawings—oh, they spoke for themselves.

Serena turned to Lockheart who was watching her with an impassive stare, his hands clasped behind his back. "Is that . . ?"

His cool, flat gray eyes swung from her open-mouthed face to the journal and back. "It belonged to Leonardo da Vinci. It is one of his many journals."

Serena's breathing had become difficult, as if she was inhaling hot steam.

"Good God."

He blinked.

"You have Leonardo's journal—in your *house*."

"Yes, that is what I said."

"But . . . how?"

"I bought it."

"Who would have sold it to you? Why would anyone be so mad as to sell such a thing? Why would anyone part with such a treasure?"

"For money, Mrs. Lombard." He said the words with a certainty which gave her a chill. They also put her back up.

"You say that as if money can buy anything, Mr. Lockheart."

"Everything has a price."

"That is what I said."

"No, you said you thought I believed money can buy anything. That is not what I believe. Some things require a different currency, but everything has its price and everything can be bought." The expression in his eyes was as cool, hard, and knowing as that of an executioner. "What is your price, Mrs. Lombard?"

"My price?"

"Yes. I wish to employ you to design my gardens and supervise and manage all aspects of its construction."

Serena had believed there was nothing that could have surprised her more than finding Leonardo's journal. "I thought you only wished me to design it?"

"But then I should need to employ another person to carry out your designs. And, in the process, some of what you have created would be altered. There will be misunderstandings, mistakes made." He shook his head, a moue of distaste on his beautiful mouth. "No, that all sounds very . . . untidy, very cluttered."

Serena thought his words were an odd choice.

"So," he continued. "I should like to hire you to manage the entire process. As well as any stonework and statuary you deem necessary."

A small, breathless laugh escaped her gaping mouth. "Do you have any idea how long that would take?"

"I am in no hurry."

The door opened and a maid bearing an enormous tea tray entered.

"Please put the tray on the table nearest the fire, Mary." Lockheart turned to Serena. "Would you do the honors, ma'am?"

"It would be my pleasure." She walked toward the tray in a trance, her mind awhirl.

Serena took comfort in the predictable ritual, her hands making tea and arranging biscuits on plates with no help from her mind. Only when the tea was ready did she look up. Lockheart was watching her with the steady, flat look she was beginning to understand was characteristic of him. He appeared to be a man utterly devoid of emotion.

"How do you like your tea?"

"Strong, with milk."

She poured her own and let the tea steep a little longer before pouring his and preparing it. He came to take his tea and plate. "Thank you, ma'am."

Serena watched him furtively as he seated himself. He really was gorgeous, his legs in their buff, clinging pantaloons long and muscular and his shoulders surprisingly broad for his slim build. He wore no jewelry, no seals, and his clothing was almost starkly elegant. Unlike his flamboyant house, he seemed to choose his garb and accouterments only to please his own tastes. For all that he had built this cathedral to wealth and excess, he did not come across as a man who took much personal interest or pleasure in the trappings of wealth. Why, then, *did* he work so hard, if not for money and what it could buy?

"You mentioned the project would take a long time. Can you be more specific, Mrs. Lombard?"

She took a sip of tea and considered the question. "I would have to sit down and give it a great deal more thought, but the grounds themselves I believe could be done in under a year, and that would be with trips back and forth to London and also with—"

"I would wish you to remain here if you accept the commission. I do not live here and I believe a project of this magnitude would require full-time supervision."

She put down her tea cup and saucer with a rattle. "You mean *live* here?"

"Would that present a problem for you? I would only come to consult and observe progress at various intervals." He frowned, as if an unpleasant idea had only just that moment occurred to him. "You mentioned your in-laws. I suppose your husband would not care to have you away from him for long periods of time."

"I am a widow, Mr. Lockheart."

His eyes flickered slightly, but his expression remained bland. He did not, like everyone else she had met, offer any words of condolence.

"So you might relocate here for the duration of the project without overmuch upheaval."

"I have a child."

He cocked his head. "A child?"

"Yes, a son."

"He is away in school?"

"He has grown up in a houseful of teachers. But he is ten now, and I am undecided as to whether he will go away to school or I will have to engage a tutor." Yet another subject of dissention between Serena and the duke and duchess, who insisted all male issue of the family go to Eton.

"You could bring him here. I believe country air is said to be quite beneficial for children."

"Is that so?" she teased, eating a biscuit to hide her smile.

The question gave him pause and his smooth brow wrinkled. "It seems I have read that, although I cannot think where." He fixed her with his cool stare. "Is this something you would wish to have confirmed before you-"

Serena couldn't help it, she laughed.

His eyebrows shot up, making his handsome features look haughty and almost regal. "You disbelieve me?"

She shook her head, still smiling. "Not at all, Mr. Lockheart, I, too, believe children thrive in the country." She hesitated. "Did you spend time in the country as a boy?"

He looked up from his plate, which she saw was largely untouched. "I was raised in an orphanage in London. I have never lived anyplace other than a city."

She'd heard a variety of rumors about his past but had hardly expected such a naked admission. In her experience, people did not admit to negative aspects of their lives. At least not so unequivocally. Serena could think of nothing to say. An orphanage? What must that be like? Dozens of questions popped into her mind, none of them the kind she had any right to ask.

"You have never done so until now, you mean?"

He gave her a questioning look and she gestured around them. "You live in the country now."

"Ah. No. I do not. I have spent less than a month here, in total, since construction was completed, and I have no plans to reside here on any permanent basis."

She shook her head. "Less than a *month*? Why did you build it?"

This time, when he looked at her, she felt as if he *really* looked. "Why did I build this house?"

Again she nodded.

"Because one must have a country house in order to conduct business with the aristocracy."

Never had she heard such a thing put so baldly. She would have given a great deal to hear him say such a thing to the duke or duchess.

"So that is the only reason for," again she waved, "all *this*? This enormous house, these grounds you wish to shape, the sculptures you want to fill them?"

His sleek brows rose only half-way this time. "Yes."

He appeared to find nothing odd in expending hundreds of thousands of pounds for something that was only a tool. "Do you like your house?"

He frowned slightly.

Ah, finally a reaction.

"I'm afraid you misunderstand me, Mrs. Lombard. It is not a matter of liking or not liking. It is whether it will prove efficacious."

Serena decided she needed more tea to pursue this conversation. "More tea?"

**

Gareth shook his head at her offer of tea and studied her closely as she refilled her own cup. His opinion of her had altered subtly in the course of the evening. While he still found her hair in need of proper management and restraint, he had come to the conclusion that something about her drew the eye. At least it drew *his* often enough. Gareth tended to avoid women's company as he usually had no idea what they were thinking and therefore tended to either insult or disappoint them when they realized he was abysmal at either conversation or flirtation. Mrs. Lombard seemed not to mind at all. In fact, he found conversing with her to be not so different from speaking with Declan, his only real friend. Not that Declan was always easy or direct, mind. There was also the slight smile both Mrs. Lombard and Declan seemed to wear as a matter of course. Gareth was not sure they weren't amused by him, but at least they kept any such observations to themselves. At least Mrs. Lombard did. Declan would often chide him for this or that.

But what he *liked* about both of them was the fact they did not belabor him with uninteresting and cloying bits of information and social affectations. They both possessed clean, logical approaches he found refreshing.

"When you say efficacious, what do you mean, Mr. Lockheart?"

There. Yet another example of what a wonderfully direct female she was. Gareth couldn't help congratulating himself on having the perspicacity to recognize such a gem when he saw it and offer her employment. He had no doubt she would accept his offer, even though she had not yet done so—and on his terms, as well. Everyone had a price, even her, even though she did not believe it.

"I am pleased you have asked this question. You are a woman who works for her bread, Mrs. Lombard. Perhaps you might not be aware of the habits of the upper class?" She smiled and nodded rather than clutter up their conversation. "I was not aware of it myself, you see. But I began to notice a certain point beyond which I could not progress when it came to business negotiations. The barrier was invisible to me and, I will admit, as a man who is often incapable of recognizing nuances, I was unable to discern the problem. It was my business partner Declan McElroy who explained it to me."

"I see. And Mr. McElroy speaks as a representative member of that class you wish to, er, penetrate?"

Gareth stared. "What? Declan? No, he is Irish and possessed of a great dislike for the landed classes of both Britain and Ireland. However, having spent a great deal of time in close proximity to such people he advised me to purchase land and construct a suitable house and also acquire a wife from the ranks of the aristocracy if I wished to penetrate the invisible barrier."

"That seems a sound plan."

Gareth liked this woman more and more. He had half-expected some fatuous exclamation as to the cold-hearted nature of his decision.

"You have built a fine house and the setting will soon flatter the house. You have only to acquire your bride. Tell me, Mr. Lockheart, if I were to take on this commission would I find myself joined by a Mrs. Lockheart within the next few months?"

Ah, that was the question. Gareth picked up a biscuit, a sandy looking thing studded with bits of nuts, and then put it back down. "No, I have not yet begun my foray into the area of matrimony. I had thought to begin such a search when Rushton Park was completed and I might have something to offer a wife."

"Why, Mr. Lockheart, that sounds almost romantic."

Gareth blinked. "It does?"

She chuckled at his perplexed response and set down her empty cup and saucer.

"Ah, I see. You are jesting. I'm afraid I lack a sense of humor, Mrs. Lombard, or so my friend McElroy often claims."

"If that is indeed the case I must point out it has not held you back."

Gareth couldn't help feeling pleased by her indirect praise. "That is an interesting observation, Mrs. Lombard. I believe I will repeat it to Mr. McElroy when he next laments the fact." She laughed and he permitted himself a small smile, not that he believed he had said anything witty. Still, it was a rarity to converse with a woman and even rarer to make one laugh.

He cleared his throat. "Now, if I might lead matters back to our original conversation."

***

Serena could not recall ever sleeping so well in her life. She could only assume it was the mattress, which appeared to be made from some substance similar to clouds of silk. She lay in her heavenly bed and stared up at the shirred celestial blue canopy above, slowly reconstructing the events of the prior evening.

Once she'd realized, a bit belatedly, that Sandy's plans involved bilking Gareth Lockheart, she refrained from commenting on anything other than gardens and statuary. Who could have guessed that Lockheart—for all his renowned prowess as a shrewd businessman—was no better than a babe-in-the-woods when it came to those matters nearest and dearest to the aristocracy's heart: estates, country houses, and horses.

Serena shook her head, her stomach tight with shame. Sandy must truly be below the hatches to be behaving in such a dishonest, unscrupulous fashion. Buying hunters from their cousin Leeland—Landy, as they mockingly called him—was disgraceful. Landy's "stud farm" in Yorkshire was a once-prosperous property he had destroyed in the decade since inheriting it. Serena had heard of Landy's current embarrassment, a liaison with one of his tenant farmer's daughters that had resulted in a child that Landy wasn't supporting. He had no money, certainly he had no bloodstock. She supposed he and Sandy would procure some broken down nags and sell them to Mr. Lockheart for many times their value.

She glanced around her room, which was so stuffed with furniture and gewgaws she could only assume Sandy had done a similar thing when it came to filling Rushton Park—spent money in ways that ended up lining his pockets. Mr. Lockheart was ripe for exploitation and it seemed there was no shortage of people willing to take advantage of him, some her relatives.

"Lord," she muttered, pushing back the heavy silk and velvet bedding and—with great reluctance—leaving her pleasurable bower.

She rang for hot water and considered the result of last night's meeting. She had decided to take a week to consider Lockheart's proposition—that she both design and implement his landscaping project. He had already informed her she would have *carte blanche* when it came to all aesthetic considerations. Not only could she create the *piece de resistance* and as many of the works she deemed necessary, but she would also be in the position to share commissions with other sculptors and artists.

The door opened and a maid entered bearing a steaming ewer.

"Good morning, ma'am."

"Good morning. Am I the last one up?" Serena poured water into the basin.

"Mr. Lockheart is at breakfast, ma'am, but Mr. Featherstone has not yet come down."

Serena would go down to the breakfast room and see about her return journey.

"Mr. Jessup had me slip in earlier and take your gown ma'am. I sponged it and gave it a pressing, it looks nice and fresh."

Serena smiled. "Thank you so much. Mr. Jessup thinks of everything."

"That he does, ma'am. The breakfast room is on the first floor, in the family wing. Shall I send up a footman to guide you down when you are ready?"

"Thank you, but I can find my way."

Serena washed, combed, and dressed with her usual efficiency and was down in the breakfast room within the half hour.

Mr. Lockheart stood when she entered the delightful, sunny room, his tall, well-proportioned person attired in fawn pantaloons, Hessians, and a navy coat that made his gray eyes more blue than gray. He was quite devastatingly handsome in the stark light of morning, his dark brown hair and pale skin striking against his crisp white linen. Beside his half-eaten plate of food were several large books, open. It pleased her to know his fancy library was not merely for show.

"Ah, Mrs. Lombard. You are an early riser?"

"I usually wake even earlier than this but the bed in my room is the most comfortable I have ever slept on."

"I am pleased to hear it. The mattresses are made in a small manufactory just outside Manchester."

"A pot of tea, please," Serena said to the footman, her eyes flickering to the vast number of dishes arrayed for only two people.

"Please, help yourself to breakfast, Mrs. Lombard."

"Thank you. Don't let your meal get cold, Mr. Lockheart, it may take me a few moments to make my selection."

He resumed his seat. "Jessup insists that serving oneself is done in all the best houses, but only for breakfast."

Serena smiled at his naïve comment as she studied the selection of meats, egg dishes, and pastries spread over the massive sideboard. It was unlike anything she had seen in a long time—since her childhood at Monsieur Favel's, where food had been a religion. Serena and Lady Winifred usually had simple breakfasts of porridge and the duke and duchess lacked a chef of Lockheart's caliber. Breakfast had been her favorite meal as a child and she heaped food onto a plate in a manner that should have left her ashamed, but did not.

She took the seat across from him and buttered one of the warm croissants—a rare treat. "You have a French cook, Mr. Lockheart?"

He glanced up from his food, which he seemed to be eating according to food group, much the way her son liked to do. "So Jessup tells me. He is new to Rushton Park. Do you approve of his cooking?"

Since he asked the question while Serena had her mouth full of flaky, buttery pastry so light it might float away, she could only nod and hope her eyes hadn't crossed with bliss. She decided to try one of the four jams arrayed on the table next.

"Have you given our discussion any further thought, Mrs. Lombard?" Serena looked up from her feast and he lifted a hand. "I know it is not done to discuss business matters at the breakfast table but I'm afraid I will be leaving later today. I will be away from Rushton for some weeks and hoped to leave any necessary instructions with my man in London before I depart."

Serena ate a bite of eggs coddled with heavy cream and chunks of ham and wanted to weep. Breakfasts like this were almost enough to make her jump at his offer. She swallowed and wiped her mouth with an exquisitely embroidered napkin. The door opened and the footman deposited her tea.

"May I have a week to consider your offer and draw up a complete proposal?"

"That sounds reasonable. If you accept the work, when would you anticipate beginning?"

"I would move myself and my son here by the end of the month." That would give her three weeks to make her arrangements.

Lockheart nodded. "I will be in Leeds a week from tomorrow. If you have any questions you may give them to my man of business in London and he will forward them."

"Excellent. One way or another, you will receive something from me by the end of next week." Serena looked at the books beside him. "What were you reading when I came in and disturbed you?"

There was a hitch in his expression as he accommodated her change of subject. She had noticed that in their discussion last night. His concentration, when he focused, was total.

He turned the open book around and slid it across the table.

Serena looked down on a two pages filled with utterly incomprehensible mathematical problems. Symbols and formulas of a type she had not imagined could exist. She looked up.

"What is this?"

"These are calculus problems which are published in a journal four times a year. I have them bound into books and study them when I have the time. This is from 1812."

Serena shook her head, her gaze moving from his face to the numbers, both of them oddly similar in their inscrutability. "You . . . *read* these journals?"

"Yes."

She gestured to the pages and then pushed the book back toward him. "Will you tell me what these pages say?"

"Say?"

"Yes, what information do these numbers and symbols communicate to you?"

He took the book and turned it right-side up and gazed down at the page, his eyes flickering rapidly beneath his lowered lids as he surveyed the enigmatic contents.

When he finally looked up, his face was taut, his eyes a bit darker. It was an expression Serena had seen on her father's face before he tackled a new project or when he found the perfect piece of marble. It was controlled, creative passion and it was the first real emotion she had seen him display.

"They make order out of seemingly random events. This," he tapped the page but did not take his eyes from hers. "This explains *everything* if you can unravel its mysteries." His voice was soft, but his gray eyes burned. So, here was a subject that excited him. Not money, not possessions, not the taking of a wife: numbers.

He looked at his hand, which was resting on the table and clutching his napkin hard enough that his knuckles had whitened. He frowned and tossed the wrinkled napkin onto his empty plate and stood. "I am sorry to leave you so abruptly but I have an appointment shortly. I have instructed Jessup to have my coach made ready for your return journey to London whenever you wish to leave. Inside it you will find Beech's sketches and any other information I have about the estate grounds. I wish you a safe journey and look forward to hearing from you." He bowed and was gone. It was like a whirlwind had swept through the room. Not a restful person at the breakfast table.

Serena pulled his open book toward her, flipping through the pages as she ate, looking for something that might help her understand the man who'd just left.

***

Gareth left Rushton Park in his curricle shortly after Mrs. Lombard departed in his coach and six. He didn't see Mr. Featherstone before leaving and decided the man must have still been abed—even though it was after noon. He made two stops along the way and did not reach town until after eight o'clock

He bathed, changed his clothing, and ate his evening meal while examining the latest correspondence. After his dinner he sent for Partridge, his man of business in London, even though it was after ten in the evening. Gareth felt no qualms about such a summons; he paid the man several times what any other factor earned and called on him but infrequently.

He forewent port or whiskey and took tea in his study while examining two new proposals Declan had sent to him. One was a faltering shipbuilder in Liverpool, whose holdings, contracts, and prospects Gareth determined to be unpropitious, but the other was a canal scheme which had faltered before ground could be broken and was seeking fresh investors.

Partridge presented himself just as Gareth had finished scribbling a note to Declan to acquire more information on the canal project.

"Good evening, Mr. Lockheart."

Gareth nodded at the elderly, spindle-shanked man and gestured to the chair across from him. Partridge was old enough to refuse the new style of dress and sported garments even Gareth—with his utter lack of interest in fashion—knew to be at least fifty years behind the times. His skirted frock coat was a brown brocade threaded with gold and his black shoes had buckles as big as teacups.

"Would you care for something to drink or eat, Mr. Partridge?"

"No, thank you, sir." He cleared his throat, a sign he was prepared to move on to business. Gareth liked the older man and his no-nonsense style, which fit perfectly with his own manner; a manner people often considered awkward, unfriendly, or cold.

"I would like you to investigate Mr. Featherstone and his cousin Leeland Bowles. Specifically, Bowles's breeding operation in Yorkshire." Gareth paused and pushed his hair back off his forehead, mentally reminding himself it was time for a haircut. "I should have investigated him before I engaged him, but he came highly recommended by Jonathan Graves, who used his services while setting up his property in Surrey." This last bit was more to himself than his employee. He had behaved foolishly and now it seemed he had paid the

35

price. Not only was the man engaging in some chicanery, but he had virtually ceased working on Gareth's behalf. Except for the hunting dogs he had acquired, of course. Still, before he took any action against Featherstone he would acquire proof.

"Very good, sir. I'll use Mr. Steele"

Steele was a man who did work for the Runners but remained a free agent. Like his name, he was tough and impervious, a monstrously big man whose slow, plodding manner in no way reflected his mental agility.

"Tell him time is of the essence. I will be off to Yorkshire by Thursday and should like to dispose of the matter before then." He put the matter of Sandford Featherstone out of his mind. "Now, have you those plans I commissioned for the new brewery in Leeds?"

Gareth and Partridge worked through the remarkable number of business matters that had accumulated in less than a week and when Gareth looked up he realized it was after two in the morning.

"That is all for tonight, Partridge. I will not need to see you tomorrow, but come to me the day after."

Partridge straightened the new stack of papers he would take away with him and stowed them carefully in his large leather satchel. "I will tell Steele to contact you as soon as he has any information. Goodnight, sir."

Gareth nodded and looked down at the papers on his desk, not looking up until the other man had left the room. He hated leave-takings and always felt uncomfortable with them. He found it less arduous to simply ignore people when it came time for them to leave. Likewise, when it was his turn to depart he usually left without making a fuss. Declan, a man who treated every coming and going as if it were a state occasion, felt it was not only his place, but his duty, to chide and scold Gareth for his odd behaviors.

"It is bloody disconcerting to be speaking to you one moment and the next realize I'm speaking to myself," he'd said on more than one occasion. Since Declan's mouth rarely seemed to stop moving it would have been difficult to find a time to depart when he was *not* speaking.

Gareth found it expedient to ignore the gregarious, loquacious Irishman when he rode rust on him for his dismal lack of social polish. According to those who kept track of such things—Declan, for one—

A Figure of Love

Gareth was one of the ten wealthiest men in the country. As such, he no longer needed to worry about his odd behaviors and how they struck others. It was acceptable that he did not—could not—seem to fit in.

That realization should have been soothing. Instead, it left a gnawing hunger in its wake: a hunger to not always be on the outside.

Gareth pushed up from his desk and strode to the sideboard where he poured himself a glass of whiskey. He took his drink to the window and looked out over the quiet square. This house was his favorite even though it was by far the smallest. He had purchased it—complete with furniture, art, and servants—from a man who had played too deeply at one hell or another. He had, essentially, moved in to another man's life. Declan told him there was something wrong with him for feeling so comfortable surrounded by somebody else's trappings.

Gareth sipped his drink as he considered his friend's accusation, the fiery liquid like a soothing balm over a raw, stinging wound. He realized his hand was balled into a fist and unclenched his fingers, stretching the taut soreness from them before resting his forearm against the window frame and sighing as he leaned against it for support. He should not be thinking of such things—certainly not right now.

It was late, and he often found the time between three in the morning and first light to be the worst time of the day. The protection of logic and numbers and mathematics was at its weakest point and emotion rose to the fore. It did not help that he suspected Featherstone of dishonesty. No, that suspicion drained him and made him wonder what the point was to all of this; this accumulation of wealth and possessions and the need to protect it from those who wanted a piece. It made him feel like a rat protecting a big cheese.

For some reason, the word *estate* brought the woman—Mrs. Lombard—to mind. Would she accept the position? Did he want her to? He had believed she was the most expedient choice for a problem that had been taking up entirely too much of his time, but something in her eyes made him wonder. She was not dishonest—no, it was not that—rather she might be *too* honest.

***

Two days later Sandford Featherstone stood in front of Gareth's desk in his London study.

His eyelids had the loose, stretched look of a man who was burnt to the socket. His skin had an unhealthy yellow tinge and his hand trembled when he set it on the arm of his chair and heavily lowered himself into the seat in front of Gareth's desk.

It vexed Gareth to realize he had missed these signs of dissipation. That was what came of being such an unobservant dolt. He could only imagine the chiding he would have to endure from Declan about this.

Featherstone's eyes darted from Gareth to the neatly stacked documents he was preparing for his journey north. "Leaving for Yorkshire today?"

"Tomorrow morning." Gareth turned to the two men filling boxes with ledgers and papers Declan had asked him to bring. "Will you please come back in one half hour?"

The men nodded, got to their feet, and left without another word, closing the door quietly behind them, accustomed to Gareth's odd ways.

Gareth took the two-page report Mr. Steele had prepared and handed it to Featherstone, watching his face as he read. His face turned red and splotchy. Guilt and, surprisingly, fury vied for control of his narrow features. His mouth twisted as he read, until his face resembled an angry prune. He did not bother to read the second page.

He glanced up, his blood-shot eyes flashing. "So, she set you to snooping, did she?"

It was not what Gareth had expected him to say and it took him a moment to discern who "she" was. Ah. He thought the Lombard woman had exposed him. Gareth briefly wondered whether she had known of the man's duplicity and then decided it did not matter. Nor did he feel disposed to contradict the other man or explain how or why he had decided to investigate Mr. Featherstone's background and criminal behavior.

Gareth drummed his fingers on his desk, the staccato *one, two, three, four* soothing. He did not care for such emotional encounters and could see the other man wished to draw out this ordeal and make it more unpleasant than it had any need to be.

"What you have done is legally actionable, sir. It is lucky for you the amount is too insignificant for me to be bothered with. I have decided I will not have you brought before a magistrate." *One, two, three, four, one, two, three, four.* "I've sent word to Rushton Park and your possessions are already on their way to London." He ceased his drumming only long enough to push a cheque across the uncluttered surface of his desk. "Here is your pay for the last quarter." *One, two, three, four, one, two, three, four.* "You will take this money and the possessions from your chambers here—which have been boxed and are waiting in the foyer—and you will leave my house immediately." *One, two, three, four, one, two, three, four.*

Featherstone's chest was rising and falling rapidly, but he had not moved, his eyes flickering wildly from the cheque to Gareth and back again and again. For a moment Gareth thought he might leave without a struggle or fuss and his fingers paused their drumming.

But then Featherstone sprang to his feet faster than Gareth thought possible for a man in his diminished condition. He flung Steele's report onto the desk and leaned across it, his face an ugly mask. Gareth could smell his sour breath and stale body odor and felt revulsion.

"You ignorant, upstart *mushroom*, you *pushing cit*, you. . . you—"

A speck of spittle flew out of his mouth and landed on Gareth's clean, smooth desk. Neither of them learned whether Featherstone would come up with yet another epithet. Gareth's left hand, his dominant one, shot out and grabbed the other man's wilted cravat. He stood at the same time, pulling Featherstone's body across the desk while he struggled.

Gareth twisted his fist and the motion tightened the cravat like a tourniquet until the other man choked, his hands clawing at Gareth's, but gaining no purchase.

"You will take the cheque and leave immediately. I will have your possessions delivered to your lodgings. If you speak even one more word to me, I will be forced to take action. You may nod your head if you understand and agree."

Featherstone nodded, at least as best as he could with his toes barely touching the ground and his throat in a viselike grip.

Gareth released him and he slumped almost to his knees, catching himself on the edge of the desk to hold himself up. Gareth watched to make sure he did nothing foolish. He found it upsetting to touch the other man but would touch him with considerably more violence if he did not keep his word.

But Featherstone scrabbled for the cheque and thrust himself to his feet. He made his way to the door unsteadily and turned, his hand resting on the knob. His jaw worked as his eyes locked with Gareth's. For one moment Gareth thought he might be compelled to live up to his own threat and deliver a thrashing. But Featherstone only sneered and flung open the door hard enough that it bounced against the wall before striding out, his gait lurching.

Gareth watched until he turned the corner toward the stairs and then looked at his watch: it was one twenty-three, he had seven minutes until the men would return for the books. He resumed his seat and rested his left hand on the smooth wooden expanse of his desk.

Methodically, he purged his mind of the events of the last twenty-three minutes.

One, two, three, four, one, two, three, four, one, two, three, four.

Chapter Four

That night, after Serena returned to London, she sat with Lady Winifred Sedgwick, her housemate and closest friend, and Lord Miles Ingram, in the cozy parlor on Albermarle Street to have what Miles called a Counsel of War.

"We will discuss this in detail and assess the objective and potential strategies," Miles said, a grin spoiling his serious words. He was so beautiful he made even Mr. Lockheart appear plain. His golden curls, sleepy blue eyes, and patrician features made him resemble a playful god who'd come to frolic among mortals.

Winifred, or Freddie—a cool, winter blonde to Miles's sunshine and warmth—shook her head. "This is not a military campaign, Miles. Serena is merely considering whether or not to accept a position."

"A position with one of the richest men in Britain. More importantly: a bachelor in pursuit of a wife."

"Serena is not marrying the man, she is considering a position as his landscape gardener." Freddie gave the beautiful, but impoverished, lord a look of fond frustration as she chided him. The two behaved toward each other with the casual ease of a long-married couple. Not for the first time did Serena wonder if her two friends carried more in their hearts for each other than friendship. Not that she had ever seen any sign they were lovers.

Serena turned to Freddie, the more serious—and knowledgeable—of her two friends. "Come, Freddie, you know everything about everyone, what do you know about Lockheart?"

Freddie earned her living launching the daughters of wealthy industrialists into society, an activity she loathed, but was perfectly suited for. Her lineage went back to the Conqueror and she was related to every aristocratic house in Great Britain. She somehow managed to maintain a reputation as a paragon of society even though she had worked at a girl's school and took money from cits.

"As Miles has already noted, he is very wealthy. Unlike other titans of industry he does not specialize in one area. Instead, it seems his talent lies with numbers rather than machinery or manufactories."

Serena recalled the book of equations and symbols and could well believe this was true.

"I have not met him, or seen him in society, but he is said to be comely of person and remarkably well-spoken, nothing at all like the general run of men who have fought their way up from places like St. Giles."

"Yes, he speaks with no regional accent or particular inflection."

Miles grinned. "And is he *comely of person?*"

Serena pursed her lips and gave him a severe frown, the one she usually kept for badly behaved students. But her hot, red cheeks worked to undermine her.

Miles slapped his thigh and hooted in a most un-lordly manner.

Freddie huffed with disgust. "Really, Miles."

"What? You are a matchmaker, Fred, surely you can agree a marriage of convenience need not exclude the possibility of attraction or love?"

Freddie's full lips thinned into a pale pink line. "You know how much I dislike that vulgar word, Miles."

"Love?"

Serena laughed at Freddie's withering stare. "Come, you two, play nice. At least until I decide what I should do."

Miles shrugged and stretched his long, muscular legs before him. Faded pantaloons and scuffed Hessians did not diminish the beauty of his perfect person in any way. "I suppose I don't think there is really much to discuss. An attractive wealthy man has offered you an opportunity you admittedly wish for, and probably for pay you can hardly imagine. What is there to consider?"

"You are forgetting Oliver, Miles. She will have to uproot and move him to a new home."

"Yes, a new home in a lavish house in the country. The owner of said house has virtually agreed to abandon it for Serena and her son." He feigned a look of horror, "Oh, the hardship!"

Freddie gave Serena a look of resignation. "He is a man, there is no reasoning with him."

"Oh, bosh Freddie. I only speak what is patently obvious."

Serena sighed. "I wish the others were here." By *others* she meant their friends from *The Ivo Stefani Academy of Music and Art for Young Ladies*, where they'd all met.

"If they were here they would weigh in behind me quickly enough," Miles assured her.

"Not Lorelei," Freddie pointed out.

Miles and Serena looked at one another.

"All right," Miles agreed, "Not Lorelei."

Lorelei had taught literature and poetry at the academy and was a self-proclaimed bluestocking and vociferous opponent of marriage, viewing *any* marriage as a prison for women.

"But Portia and Honoria would certainly support me," Miles insisted.

"And how do you come to that conclusion?" Freddie asked.

"Well, neither of them is *here* right now, are they? They've both accepted positions that have taken them far away from London and their lives here. And look how well it turned out for Portia."

Serena considered Miles's words. Portia, who'd owned the failing academy where they'd all met, had been left deeply in debt when the school closed. She'd needed money so desperately that she'd behaved in a deceitful way to secure a lucrative position in Cornwall, even though Freddy, Miles, Honoria, and Serena had all tried to convince her to abandon her dangerous plan. In what appeared to be a fairytale ending she'd married her handsome employer and was expecting her first child.

As for Honoria—who owned the house they were currently sitting in—she'd rarely been home in months because she accepted painting commissions that took her all over the country.

So, yes, Miles was right: her two friends had stepped away from the comfort of what they knew to earn a living, and perhaps make a name for themselves or find happiness in the process.

"As for Annis," Miles said when Serena didn't answer, "We all know what she would say."

Serena chuckled. "Fine, I will grant you Annis's support without any argument."

Annis, the language mistress at the academy, was a sensitive dreamer who believed even spiders and insects fell in love; she would likely think an industrialist seeking a wife was a perfect opportunity for romance.

"Well if you were to ask *me* what you should do," Miles said, although nobody had. "I would send him my proposal along with an astronomical fee. I would charge enough that you and Oliver would not have to worry about money for a very long time." The teasing glint in Miles's eyes had been replaced by something far grimmer.

Like Serena and Freddie, Miles had to work for his living. He was the younger son of an earldom that was so impoverished his family couldn't afford to give him an allowance after Miles left the army three years ago. Serena didn't know why Miles chose to work as a dancing master—rather than take up a government post or something more respectable for a man of his class—and she didn't feel like it was her place to ask. After all, there were plenty of things about her past she chose not to share with anyone, not even her dearest friends.

"What of your sculpting?" Freddie asked, pulling her from her thoughts. "I know you find the notion of designing a garden exciting, but your true passion is your art, is it not?"

Serena considered her friend's question. Was it? Oh, she loved it when a work progressed according to her internal vision. But Serena knew, deep inside, she would never be a great artist. She would give enjoyment to those who saw her work, but she would not be admired and emulated by generations of sculptors to come.

She realized the other two were waiting for an answer. "He has a brand new stable block, and there is a stall in it that is enormous with doors that open on two sides to provide wonderful light. He said I might take it for my workspace while I live there." She looked from one friend to the other. "I will be busy with laying out the various parts of the estate to begin with, but once the projects are underway I will have ample time to work."

Miles nodded. "And he wishes to commission sculptures in addition to the gardening." It was not a question. "All jesting about the man himself aside, I do not see how you could turn down such an opportunity, Serena—or why you would want to. You might have work for years to come even after the gardens are finished."

"I know. He has told me I can either do the work myself or choose artists whose work I approve of. It is a great opportunity for me to forge some much needed alliances in the London sculpting community."

They all knew what she meant—with such patronage power she could enter the ranks of sculptors who had excluded her, both because she was a woman and a foreigner.

Serena looked at Freddie, who had taken up her tambor and was plying her needle. Freddie hated to be idle and her flawless needlework was yet another way she made her money—although nobody was supposed to know she sold her work.

"Am I foolish to be dithering about this, Freddie?"

"It is never foolish to consider all the angles. As much as I hate to admit it, I agree with Miles." She looked up from her stitching, her fawn-colored eyes serious. "I believe this is an opportunity you cannot pass up. You will uproot Oliver, but to good purpose. I also think it will be excellent for the two of you to be together in the country. I will miss him—and you—terribly, but it will be such a pleasant holiday away from the filth and noise of London." She hesitated and then asked, "And you say Mr. Lockheart will not spend much time there?"

"He does not care for the country and spends a great deal of time running around Britain, meeting his business partner in various places to assess investments. No, I do not think we will see him often."

"Mr. Lockheart contacted me, you know," Freddie said.

"He did?" Serena and Miles spoke at the same time.

Freddie nodded, but did not look up from her work. "I was engaged with the Wandsworth girl at the time and had yet another engagement after that. I told him I was not available just then but I sent him a letter indicating when I might be free. He did not respond."

Miles raised his eyebrows. "When was this, Freddie?"

"Not long after the school closed."

"We never let you finish telling us what you knew of him," Miles prodded.

"I told you all I know. He appears to have come from nowhere perhaps fifteen years ago. Other than the fact that he emerged from London, nothing else is known. He belongs to several clubs but almost never steps foot in them. His friend Declan McElroy, by all accounts a far more gregarious man, seems to be his only point of contact with society." Freddie gave them a wry look. "I suppose he wrote to me in the hope I could simply deliver a bride to him, the way he probably orders everything else. Since I've heard nothing about him moving in society I can only assume he's put the matter aside."

Serena wondered if it was significant that he'd told her about the orphanage and decided it was not. It was probably that nobody knew about him because he was a man of so few words rather than a man intent on obscuring his past. After all, he had told her of his origins and they were not well-acquainted. No, he seemed the sort to rarely engage in small talk. She must count herself lucky at having lured him into such an indiscretion.

Miles leaned forward, his face suddenly eager. "I understand he utilizes mathematical formulas to determine his investments."

"I cannot speak to that, but it would not surprise me. He was reading mathematical journals for pleasure while I was there. They were quite. . . incomprehensible. He is a very clever man whose greatest priority is leaving the mundane demands of day-to-day life in the hands of somebody else." She turned to Freddie. "You knew he hired away Remington's butler?"

Freddie chuckled. "Yes, it was quite a scandal, wasn't it? The inestimable Jessup. And you saw him there?"

"He appeared quite contented. He also hired Sandy Featherstone—I saw him there."

Freddie's head jerked up and Miles frowned. It was Miles who spoke, "What was he doing there?"

"He claims to be helping Lockheart play the country gentleman. But I think he is playing some game with Landy, his cousin. I'm afraid they are engaged in fleecing Mr. Lockheart."

Miles shook his head. "The infamous duo—Sandy and Landy Featherstone. Landy was at Eton, a year below me. He was a weasel even then. I am surprised a man as astute as Lockheart would allow himself to be the victim of such obvious schemers."

"Mr. Lockheart, I think, does not wish to be bothered with trifles. I daresay he engaged Sandy on somebody's recommendation—much as he is engaging me on Beech's—and put the matter out of his mind. Unfortunately, Sandy has taken the opportunity of such trust and unlimited latitude to bring Landy into the picture."

Serena had thought about whatever Sandy was up to almost as much as she'd pondered accepting this unusual employment from an unusual employer.

"Are you going to say anything to Lockheart?" Miles asked.

"I will speak to Sandy first, and warn him to cease whatever chicanery he and Landy are up to. If he does not, I will tell Lockheart, when I go to work for him."

Freddie looked up at her words and Miles grinned. "So, that's settled."

She smiled at her two friends. "Yes, that is settled.

***

Serena took three days to work on her proposal after making her decision. She would provide him with a more comprehensive plan once she was settled at Rushton Park, but for now, she wished to comply with their agreement and send him word of her acceptance within the week.

She could have simply sent the plans and proposal to Mr. Lockheart's secretary by messenger, but she had a curiosity to see his London residence, which apparently also served as his place of business. The distance was too long to walk so she made the journey from Albermarle Street to Russell Square in a hackney.

Mr. Lockheart lived in one of the newish houses built on the grounds of the Duke of Bedford's old London house. The residences were quite elegant and Russell Square had been landscaped by Humphry Repton, a man many considered the successor to Capability Brown. Serena had visited Repton, a few years back, when she had commenced her interest in landscape gardening. He had been generous and had shown her several of his famous "red books," the extensive illustrated plans he made for most commissions.

A housekeeper greeted Serena and took her rather rough "red book" and the proposal she had prepared.

"I will take these to Mr. Partridge, ma'am, who will wish to see you. Will you be so kind as to wait a moment in the sitting room?"

Serena declined an offer of tea and the woman left her in a second floor room with a pleasant view over the square. The furnishings bore no resemblance to those of Rushton Park, but were simple, tasteful, and almost stark. As at the country house, no pictures hung on the walls, the occasional tables held no knick-knacks on their highly polished surfaces, and the attractive mantelpiece held only one item, an unusual clock with its workings exposed.

Serena was examining it more closely and thinking how much Oliver would enjoy it—he had taken apart the schoolroom clock without permission, but had been clever enough to reassemble it—when the door opened and a tiny man entered.

He swept her a gracious, courtly bow. "What an honor to meet you, Mrs. Lombard, I am Richard Partridge." When he stood, he came no higher than her nose, his clothing that of at least a half century past.

"I am sorry to come without notice, but Mr. Lockheart indicated he wished to proceed as soon as possible."

Partridge chortled, taking the smaller of two chairs across from her. "Yes, he is a man who does not let the dust settle. He left strict instructions regarding the matter. I merely glanced at your proposal before coming to let you know it is acceptable."

Serena blinked. "But. . . won't Mr. Lockheart wish to look at it?"

"Oh no. He was most specific in his instructions. I was to accept any proposal you presented."

Serena was stunned. The amount she had requested was scandalous—thanks mainly to Miles's urgings. He'd advised her to come up with a shocking amount, and then double it for good measure. When Serena had demurred he had, for once, been quite serious.

"Don't undervalue your work, Serena. He is expecting you to uproot yourself and your son and to manage the entire, huge project. Humphry Repton himself does not handle such matters. This is going to take up your life for a long time to come. In fact triple the amount—he is said to be among the five wealthiest men in the entire country."

So Serena had, against the qualms of her conscience, tripled her original amount. And Lockheart had not even looked at it before approving it. She realized Mr. Partridge was still waiting.

She gave him a somewhat embarrassed smile. "I beg your pardon. I was just a little . . . surprised."

"Oh, no need to apologize. I quite understand. I had the same reaction myself when I first came to work for him." Partridge removed a folded rectangle of paper from his coat. "Mr. Lockheart instructed me to issue the first quarter in advance, I have just written out a bank draft for you."

Serena looked down at the amount on the draft and swallowed. This was now real.

"Mr. Lockheart has also left his coach and the servants of this house at your disposal if you should need assistance with your packing or moving."

She nodded, dazed. "Thank you, that is very kind."

"I am also at your disposal, Mrs. Lombard. Please direct any bills or requests to me and I will see they are handled promptly."

She stood and he made his way to the door to open it.

"Mrs. Hazelton indicated you came by hackney, ma'am. I took the liberty of having Mr. Lockehart's town carriage brought around to take you home."

Serena soon found herself ensconced in yet another of Lockheart's luxurious carriages, clutching a check for more money than she had ever had in her entire life, her head in a whirl.

***

Only Mrs. Brinkley, their housekeeper, was home when Serena arrived. "My lady is out shopping with her newest young girl and Oliver and Madam have gone to the park."

Serena nodded, disappointed she had nobody to share her news with.

Well, she might as well begin packing.

"I will be out in the carriage house, Mrs. Brinkley."

Serena changed into older work clothes before making her way to the mews beside the house. As they kept no carriage or horses she used the big empty space as her workshop.

There was no piece in progress just now but she was a messy worker—much to her chagrin—and she had to spend a good deal of time cleaning up the room before she could locate the tools she would take with her to Rushton Park.

She'd just put the last of her chisels in her battered wooden tool box when a voice behind her made her jump.

"Packing for a trip, are you?"

Serena turned to find Sandy leaning against one of the double doors, the sun behind him hiding his face.

"Sandy!" She raised a hand and lowered it over her pounding heart. "You startled me."

He sauntered toward her, his gait unsteady. She gasped when she could finally make out his face. One eye was blackened shut, his lip swollen, and purple bruising up and down his jaw.

She took a step toward him. "What happened?"

His hideous face turned even uglier with a sneer. "*You* happened, my dear cousin."

She flinched back. "What do you mean?"

"You know damned well what I mean!" He stalked toward her, the menace in his slim form shocking. Serena took several steps back, but he kept advancing. "You said something to him, didn't you?"

She shook her head, her feet stumbling over something on the cluttered floor. She reached out to steady herself against the splintered wood of a horse stall. "If you mean Mr. Lockheart, no, I did not say a word."

"You are a liar!" His screech was high-pitched and piercing.

Serena stopped, refusing to move back another step. He pushed against her, needing to look up to meet her eyes. Revulsion, fear, and anger surged through her at the feel of his body against hers, but she stood her ground.

"Only an idiot would not have seen through your scheme with Landy." She let all the distaste she felt for him show on her face. "Your behavior was disgusting. Lockheart is foolishly generous with his pay, but that was not enough, you had to cheat him."

"And who are you to act so high and mighty? You and your *cousin* and whatever it is you are hiding between you."

Fear froze her in place. "I don't know what you are talking about," she lied, her voice hoarse.

"You're a bloody liar. If Bardot is your cousin, then I'm your grandmother. He is your lover or conspirator or both and the two of you are up to something." He grinned, the act exposing an empty tooth socket and bleeding gums. "I am going to find out what exactly that is, and I am going to wipe that sanctimonious expression right off your face with it."

A shadow appeared in the open doorway and Featherstone turned.

"Featherstone, what a surprise seeing you here," an amused, cultured voice cut across the space. Miles's large, powerful frame filled the doorway.

Serena felt weak with relief.

Sandy sneered, but he stepped away. "Why, if it isn't Viscount Ingram," he said the courtesy title—which Miles never used—in a tone that dripped with loathing and gave a nasty laugh. "Come for a little afternoon tussle with the widow, have you?"

Miles stopped a few steps away, his eyes flickering to Serena to check that she was all right before moving back to the other man. He wore the same charming smile that always graced his beautiful face, but Serena knew him well enough to know he was angered by Sandy's crass question.

"It looks like you've fallen from your horse and landed on your face, Featherstone." His lips quirked. "Or perhaps you asked rude, disrespectful questions of the wrong person?" His sky blue eyes were as hard as glass.

Featherstone swallowed at the unspoken threat and turned to her. "I apologize for my disrespectful comment, Serena."

She nodded. "You should go, Sandy." Serena couldn't look away from Miles, whose smile could not hide the danger that rolled off him like waves of heat.

Sandy limped from the carriage house without another word.

Serena heaved a sigh. "I am always happy to see you Miles, but never quite as much as I am today."

His lazy, amused look was back on his face, a mask he took off and put on so quickly she hadn't even seen the switch. "I'm hoping it was you who did that to his face?"

Serena gave a weak chuckle.

Miles took her arm, "Come on, darling, I came by to scrounge some tea and a few of those lemon biscuits Mrs. Brinkley makes just for me. I had no idea I'd have to rid the place of rats first. I'm parched."

She laughed and they went inside, but Sandy's threats about Bardot continued to ring in her ears. He might have left today, but he was not gone for good.

Chapter Five

Oliver slept on the seat across from Serena, his curly brown head on Nounou's lap, the old Frenchwoman's head against the squabs, her jaw sagging as she snored. Although Oliver was too old to require a nurse Serena had kept the older woman on because she had nowhere else to go. Besides, she also served as a chaperone for Serena to those sticklers who thought such things necessary.

It had taken her son a good hour and a half to stop bouncing on the well-sprung, soft leather seat and pelting her with questions. Even three weeks had not been long enough for him to become jaded by the notion of a new home.

He had lived most of his ten years at the house on Albermarle Street, no matter how much the duke and duchess had tried to convince Serena to move into one of their houses, or, barring that, to let them raise their grandson. No, Oliver was hers. In spite of what her relations seemed to believe, she was not raising him in squalor, but with love in a perfectly stable home—albeit a bit more unconventional than most children of his class. He spent late summer every year and Christmas with his grandparents and family at Keeting Hall. But the rest of the year he lived with his mother. He was growing up too fast and she enjoyed his company too much to yield to their wishes to send him away to some barbaric English boarding school, where the other boys would taunt and torment him for his plebeian mother, a woman who actually *worked* for her living. No, he would stay with her until they, together, decided how he wished to spend his life.

Serena opened the sketchbook she was never without. It contained both the sketches she had made of Rushton Park as well as, for some reason, one she had made of its odd owner. It was Gareth Lockheart as he had looked that morning at breakfast—when he had described the appeal of numbers and symbols. In her sketch his hair was wilder, his cravat untied and his coat loose and flapping, as if he were in a cyclone. The drawing made her smile and she shook her head. Oh, she was such a predictable female, attracted to his handsome face and body and intrigued by his remote, untouchable manner. In her saner moments she told herself numbers were the only thing that would bring such a cold man to life. But in the night, when she was alone and remembering the hours they had spent together planning and creating beauty for the grounds around his house, she pictured herself as the key that would unlock him. Like a princess kissing a frozen prince.

She closed the book and her eyes with it, laying her head back against the plush upholstery. She would not have believed such romance remained in her after so many years alone. When was the last time she had looked at a man as a man? Her friend Miles's face flickered into her mind. It was true Serena could hardly look at anything else when her handsome friend was in the same room, but that was true for most women. But Serena's initial infatuation with the beautiful man had quickly grown into warm, sisterly affection. It was lucky for Serena that Miles was not the type of man to excite her romantic interest. Oh, he had his share of deep, dark secrets, but he was—by and large—open, social, and sunny. For whatever reason—most likely just sheer stubbornness—Serena had always gravitated toward the shy, inscrutable, or wounded men. Freddie said it was a strong mothering instinct.

"You are the type of woman who should have many children, Serena." Freddie had told her on more than one occasion, most often when Serena was offering excuses or coming to the rescue of some student who had neither the ability nor enthusiasm to complete a project.

That might be true, but Gareth Lockheart was not a child, and she was not being paid to rescue or save him.

***

It was near dusk when their coach rolled down the long drive that led to Rushton Park.

Oliver had woken up a short time earlier and they'd been staring out the window together. He'd been properly impressed by the mansion.

"*Il n'est pas si vieux que la maison du grand-père?*"

"No, this is a far newer house than your grandfather's." Serena glanced from Nounou to her son. "I think it would be best if you spoke English with me while we are here, Oliver. You may continue to speak French with Nounou when you are in private. However, it is quite rude to speak a language those around you do not speak."

"Hurray!" he yelled, as if speaking English was a treat.

Nounou, a cranky old woman who had come to England with a family of refugees who had not been able to continue paying her, had no patience for the language of the country that gave her asylum. She snorted and rolled her eyes at Serena's dictum, clearly determined to continue on in any manner she chose.

The carriage rumbled smoothly over cobblestones and Serena looked up to see they had arrived. To her surprise, a long row of servants stood waiting. And, she squinted through the gloom, there was Jessup at the head of them.

"What is *he* doing here?" Nounou demanded, her eyes fastened to the butler as the carriage came to a halt.

"In English, Nounou. He works for Mr. Lockheart now." She cut her willful, surly servant a sly smile. "I'm sure you will enjoy becoming reacquainted with him." She couldn't help the gentle teasing. Jessup and Nounou had been at loggerheads since the first time they'd met years ago, at Keeting Hall. Serena thought they behaved like lovers. Well, now they would get to spend months in the same house together and be something to entertain her of an evening.

"Gather your things, Oliver," Serena said as the carriage shifted, indicating the groom had disembarked. The coach was the same massive, luxurious thing Mr. Lockheart had sent her home in three weeks earlier. Serena worried she was now spoiled for any other kind of vehicle.

Jessup stood outside the door, waiting. "Welcome back, Mrs. Lombard, and Master Oliver, I have not seen you since you were just a—" He stopped, his face turning to stone. "Ah, you are still in England, Madame Petit."

"And so are you, *Monsieur Jessup.*" Nounou's posture was regal as she allowed the handsome footman to assist her from the carriage. The two older servants surveyed each other like cats with twitching tails before Jessup turned to the line of waiting people and began to make introductions.

Once Jessup had led her down the long line of servants and Serena had greeted each of them, aware she would forget half the names already, he turned to her. "I've taken the liberty of having the schoolroom equipped and two rooms made ready. Would you care to see them before I show you to your quarters, ma'am?"

Serena looked down at her son. Oliver's eyes were heavy, no matter how excited he was. "Yes, I shall see he is situated and perhaps take a light supper with him in the schoolroom."

Although Serena had not been to the schoolroom during her last visit it was easy enough to guess where it was located. Like the rest of the house, the rooms had been furnished and decorated. Unlike the rest of the house, somebody had done so with sense and good judgment. The furniture was all of good quality and sturdy. Oliver's room had large windows that would let in a nice amount of light, as did the schoolroom itself.

"And this is Madame Petit's room," Jessup opened a door that led out of Oliver's small dressing room.

Both Serena and Nounou paused in the doorway. The room was small but cozy, luxuriously decorated in shades of rose, gold, and rich chocolate brown. The bed's canopy was a lovely garden tapestry and the entire suite was far beyond what a nurse or governess could expect.

Nounou remained uncharacteristically silent so Serena spoke. "Why, this is a charming room, Jessup."

Jessup's heavy lids were too low to see the direction of his gaze, but Serena would have sworn he was watching his French nemesis.

Serena left Nounou and Oliver to settle in and followed Jessup back to a suite of rooms not far from the ones she had occupied before. Her trunks already awaited her and a young girl was unpacking them.

"Susan will see to your personal needs while you are here, Mrs. Lombard."

Serena could tell by the infinitesimal tightening of Jessup's mouth that he'd noticed her lack of a lady's maid and would not permit such a thing to stand while he was in charge.

"Thank you, Jessup. Hello, Susan."

The girl flushed and bobbed a curtsy.

"Would you care to have a bath before you eat, madam?"

"I'll just change and freshen up. I don't think Oliver will be awake much longer, so perhaps I will bathe after we have eaten our evening meal."

Jessup bowed and took his leave.

***

Later that night Serena realized she was far too anxious and excited to sleep. After tucking in Oliver and reading him a story she decided to do a little exploring. In spite of the house's rather fantastical external appearance the layout was quite logical: a central section containing a grand entryway, a wing with kitchens, laundry, and servant quarters, and another wing for family.

Every part of the house she had seen was scrupulously clean and ridiculously well-lighted. When she had asked Jessup about the excess of candles, he'd said it was on Mr. Lockheart's explicit instructions.

"But there are even candles in the rooms people rarely use."

"Yes, madam. And they are to remain lighted all night when he is here. He has indicated I might extinguish whatever candles I choose in his absence. His London house is lighted thus at all times—in case he might make an unexpected appearance." He'd hesitated a moment before continuing. "Mr. Lockheart is a very easy master, but there are a few areas in which he is rigid. He is excessively fastidious about his person and surroundings. I have found it best to always leave any items exactly where he places them."

Serena had understood his meaning. She was to live here, but not to treat it as her own property.

As if he had heard her thoughts Jessup added, "He is only so precise about his own quarters and the area in the library he uses as his study."

Yes, Serena had seen his desk and the area around it; it had been an oasis of calm. So, his own tastes were naturally elegant. Serena thought his house would have been far more appropriately decorated if he had trusted his own neat and simple style rather than Sandy's.

She decided to explore the common rooms first and then investigate the family quarters.

The library she had seen and would explore in far greater detail in the months to come. Her heart actually palpitated when she thought about Leonardo's journal and all the other treasures yet to be discovered.

In addition to the library there were three sitting rooms, although one was small enough to deserve the name parlor. Serena decided it would be the room where she would spend her evenings with Oliver. The thick carpets and fireplaces at both ends of the room ensured it would be warm and cozy in the fall and winter months.

There was a music room with a piano her friend Portia would salivate to play and Serena made a note to herself to mention it in her next letter to her friend.

The dining and breakfast rooms she had already seen. To the rear of the house was a billiard room, compete with untouched accouterments. Serena had a difficult time imagining Mr. Lockheart engaging in anything so frivolous as billiards.

On the upper floor were only bedchambers. The first four Serena looked were pristine and untouched in appearance. The fifth door opened to a room different from all the others. This could have been the cell of a monk. She closed the door behind her and lighted three of the candles on a large branch beside the door. The room was utterly stark, no artwork, no tapestries such as hung in her room and even in Nounou's.

The room's only furniture was a bed and two nightstands. The bed was a massive four-poster with no canopy, its four posts giant squares with no decoration other than inset metal rings. The bedding was white linen. The floor was entirely without rugs, the wood so dark it was almost black. In the dressing room the clothes were stored with such precision it looked as if a person had measured the gaps and spaces with a ruler. Footwear and folded garments were likewise exactly placed. The room seemed to contain an entire wardrobe and Serena realized he probably did the same thing in all his houses, eliminating the need to do a great deal of packing other than nights he might be forced to spend in hotels or inns.

Every item was flawless and new-looking, four pairs of top boots, two pairs of Hessians, all polished to a blinding shine, not so much as a speck of dust to be found.

She fingered the exquisite silk of a dull pewter banyan, easily imagining him garbed in such a garment. Either he or his valet had impeccable taste, and every waistcoat and coat had been chosen to complement his coloring and physique.

The massive dressing room had an adjacent bathing chamber, as did hers, but the floor was a black marble shot through with striking bolts of white, the tub a dull gray metal in front of a fireplace whose mantelpiece matched the bold, stark lines of the rest of the room. The walls were hung with the same pale, patternless silk as the rest of the chamber, their pristine surface not disturbed by art of any kind.

There was another door off the other side of the main chamber which Serena assumed would be a sitting room. But she opened the door to find the strangest room she had ever seen. There were no pieces of furniture—at least not of a sort she recognized. Instead there were leather and canvas bags hanging from different heights, a few vertical circular wooden bars, perhaps the diameter of a handrail, and thick padding covering all about the perimeter of the room's floor. Serena went to one of the bags, this one slightly above the level of her head, pear-shaped and made from leather. When she tapped it, it swung back and forth. The other bag was far larger, perhaps the size of a human torso.

Ah, so that's what it was: this was a room to train for pugilism, a violent, ugly pastime which men of all ages and classes seemed to adore. She pushed the big bag and it swung pendulously, hard to the touch, as if filled with sand.

So, Mr. Lockheart had at least one pastime besides reading obscure mathematical texts and making money. Such exercise would account for his trim physique.

On her way back into the main chamber she stopped to examine the contents of the dressing table: a brush and a comb.

On each side of the bed were heavy, squat nightstands that matched the design of the dark bed. Each had two drawers, all four were empty of even a stray hair.

Serena stood in the center of the room and turned in a slow circle. This was undoubtedly Mr. Lockheart's room. She knew she should feel a twinge of shame for prying, but what had she seen? Nothing. Although perhaps the stark nature of his living quarters told her more than a peek into a journal. She told herself he spent so little time here it was unlikely he would have many possessions. Yet something told her she would find the same arrangement in any place he inhabited. He was a solitary man, a man who appeared to enjoy his own thoughts and company better than any other. He was, she believed, the most self-contained person she had ever met.

It was a good thing he would not be here often. Such a man was exactly the kind of puzzling enigma Serena was drawn to—a man with secrets.

Chapter Six

Serena's mind was still on the work at the dam when she came around the corner into the stable block and almost collided with a stranger on a horse. A rather magnificent horse, she noticed right away, not to mention its rider, who was quite magnificent in his own way.

"I beg your pardon, ma'am!" The man said, deftly sidling his mount out of her way and touching his whip to his hat, which sat at a jaunty angle on his vivid auburn curls. He looked her up and down in a manner that made her face heat, his expression of surprise quickly shifting into a grin. "You must be Mrs. Lombard," he said in a voice that had more than a trace of an Irish burr.

Serena couldn't help smiling back at him. "And you must be Mr. McElroy."

He feigned a look of surprise. "And how did you guess *that* I wonder?"

Serena ignored his question and guided her job horse toward the stables. The Irishman fell in beside her.

"That's a rather nice hack you've got, Mr. McElroy."

He glanced down, as if surprised to find himself mounted. "Is it?"

Serena laughed and gave her reins to the groom before dismounting. "Mad for horses, are you?"

He slid from his horse and handed the groom his reins as well.

Serena raised her eyebrows. "I thought you were heading out for a ride?"

He fell into step beside her, his broad, heavily muscled shoulders only a few inches above her own. "I was going down to the lake site, but it was you I was in a fever to see, Mrs. Lombard, not a load of sweaty blokes shoveling dirt."

"Me? Whyever would you be in a," she hesitated, *"fever* to see me."

"'Cause Lockheart hasn't stopped talking about ye these past five weeks."

Serena stopped and turned to him. His eyes sparkled as they looked down into hers.

"Mr. McElroy, I find that very difficult to believe. Would you perhaps be spreading a bit of the, er, *blarney*?"

He threw back his head and laughed. "Ach, ye caught me all right."

She shook her head and resumed walking. "Tell me why you've really come all this way, Mr. McElroy."

"We've come to bring you some decent horseflesh, since Jessup complained you'd hired a horse fit for the knackers." His Irish accent had miraculously departed. "Lockheart himself picked out old Kestrel." He jerked his chin back toward the stables.

"Jessup misspoke. I am quite satisfied with Honey. I'm afraid you've come all this way for naught."

He reached in front of her to open the door to the sunroom, which was the most convenient entrance to the house when coming from the stables.

"Oh, we've come to look at a brewery down south of here."

Serena halted by the double doors to the great hall. "We?"

McElroy leaned unnecessarily close to reach for the door. "Aye, me and Gareth, both." He opened the door and there was the man in question, crouched low in the middle of the black and white tile looking at something with her son.

***

Gareth had wanted to merely send the horses along, but Declan had convinced him it was his duty to check on the progress at Rushton Park.

"You don't want another incident like Featherstone, Gare. The way to avoid that is to have some oversight."

Gareth had shaken his head. "You just want to see this woman sculptor, Declan. You couldn't give two pins about the progress of my park."

The Irishman had laughed, not denying his curiosity.

"We need to see to Kennelworth's Brewery and it's only a short ride from Rushton."

"Yes, but hardly direct."

"Humor me, Gare."

So Gareth had let himself be talked into an unnecessary journey. He'd left Declan to whatever schemes he had devised about the horses and had gone to the library, only to find a boy spread out in the middle of the smaller reading room, several large books open on the floor, along with an automaton in half a dozen pieces. He had looked up at Gareth, his eyes vague as his mind was obviously still on his work. Of course Gareth knew who he was: the sculptor's child. He looked like a miniature of his mother, his complexion rosy, his cheeks round, and his golden-brown hair a riot of unkempt curls. Only his eyes were a different shade than his mother's, a calm blue gray rather than hazel.

"Who are you?" the boy asked, quite justifiably, in Gareth's opinion.

"I am Gareth Lockheart."

The boy's jaw dropped and he scrambled to his feet and executed a hasty bow. "Oh, Mr. Lockheart. I'm sorry, sir. Mama did not tell me you were coming. I am Oliver Lombard."

Gareth was momentarily nonplussed by the lad's pronunciation of his name, which he'd spoken in the French style. He remembered the boy's name, of course. He never forgot anything, an ability that was sometimes helpful, sometimes not.

Oliver Lombard shifted from foot to foot. "I beg your pardon, sir, but Mama told me I might use the library if I were to treat the books kindly and return them to their places. It will take me only a moment to put them back and—"

"You have taken apart your automaton?" Gareth asked as the boy's nervousness and embarrassment began to settle over him like the faint, difficult to remove threads of a spider's web. Society and its strictures made Gareth restless, as did apologies for things that weren't bad or wrong. Gareth did not care if the boy used the library. In fact, it quite pleased him to have somebody using it.

The lad pushed a tangle of hair off his forehead, his expression becoming perplexed as he looked at the pile of tiny metal pieces scattered on a white handkerchief. "There is a problem with the tension in the spring, but I do not know how to fix it. I have rewound it, to tighten it, but that does not seem to work."

Gareth crouched down, his eyes moving over the various parts, his mind already putting the pieces in their proper positions. He had a fondness for automata and had taken apart more than his fair share of clocks and other mechanisms with moving parts.

The boy knelt beside him and pointed to the book, which showed a schematic of a clock-winding mechanism. Oliver Lombard was a clever lad; he'd found Gareth's well-thumbed science journals and then searched the indices until he found something appropriate.

Gareth looked from the spring in the palm of the boy's grubby hand back to the drawing and picked up a metal plate from the small pile of parts. "I believe the problem lies with this small pin. Here," he pointed to the drawing and then to the piece in his hand. "There is still a piece inside this dimple but it is bent almost in half. It will not catch the spring and hold it." He looked at the boy, who was nodding his head, comprehension dawning in his sea-colored eyes.

Gareth gestured to his desk. "Go fetch the letter opener from the top right desk drawer and we will see if we can bend it back."

After Gareth had carefully straightened the bent piece he turned to the boy. "Do you know how to put it back together?"

He shot Gareth a look of boyish scorn. "Of course, sir."

Gareth watched in silence as Oliver deftly fit tiny pieces together with his dirty, but slender, agile fingers. The toy was some type of big cat with wheels beneath the lower panel hidden by the clever placement of the animal's four feet. The key location was, naturally, just below the cat's tail, a scandalous placement sure to please any young male.

Once he'd fully reassembled the toy they both stood and—without any need to consult on the matter—left the library to test the toy in the hall, which had carpet but only a runner, leaving a perfect strip of black and white tile down each side that was perfect for metal wheels.

Oliver put his hand on the key and then hesitated. He looked up at Gareth. "Would you like to do the honor, sir? You were the one to find the problem and fix it."

"I will do the next one."

Oliver's smile was one of relief and he twisted the key with great care and then bent down, holding the toy in both hands before turning his head to look at Gareth. "Ready?"

"Ready."

The metal cat shot down the hallway, emitting a high-pitched mechanical whirring sound and skidding almost all the way to the second library entrance before sliding to a halt. The boy leapt into the air, both arms raised in victory. "Hurrah! Hurrah!"

Gareth smiled. "It is my turn."

Gareth heard a small clicking sound as he wound the mechanism, as if the spring were slipping. He looked down at the boy, who was waiting with barely restrained impatience. "I think it will require a new pin. The metal has been stressed and is no longer stable." He finished winding the mechanism and handed the cat to Oliver, who held it with both hands to stop it from prematurely beginning its cycle. "You can release it. I think you will find it cannot be wound too many more times."

"Do you know how to make a pin, sir?"

"I do not possess the necessary equipment for such fine work. But I daresay a clockmaker could fashion what you need."

The spring had begun to slip badly by the time Mrs. Lombard and Declan found them a quarter of an hour later.

The sculptor looked at her son—who was in the process of crawling on hands and knees toward the cat—and then at Gareth, who was following behind him, but on his feet.

"What a pleasant surprise, Mr. Lockheart." The smile she gave him seemed authentic, as far as he was ever able to gauge such things. "I think you will be happy with the progress we are making with the dam."

Her riding habit was a dark green that made her even prettier than he recalled. Her hair, as usual, had come loose around her flushed cheeks and softened her round face, making her appear younger. Gareth looked at Declan, only to find the Irishman watching him, an amused glint in his eyes that Gareth could not like.

"What do you think of the project?" Gareth asked his friend when he realized they were waiting for some response—any response—from him.

"I never got so far. I met Mrs. Lombard in the stables and decided to accompany her back here."

Oliver came up to his mother, holding up his toy. "Mr. Lockheart fixed it for me, Mama, but it will not stay fixed. He says we must take it to a clock maker."

She brushed his hair from his forehead, the love on her face as she looked at her son blatant enough even for Gareth to notice and identify. What must it be like to be the recipient of such undiluted affection?

"I believe there is one in town, Oliver. We shall take it with us the next time we go. Now, it is time for your tea. Nounou will be waiting for you."

"Yes, Mama." He turned to leave and then pivoted back around. He grinned at Gareth and held up the toy. "Thank you so much, sir."

Gareth nodded and the boy sped down the corridor.

Mrs. Lombard began pulling off her gloves. "Would you gentlemen care for tea?"

"No," Gareth said.

"Yes," Declan said at the same time.

The woman's lips twitched. "Perhaps we might leave the hall and discuss the matter more comfortably in the small drawing room?"

Declan gave Gareth an ingratiating smirk. "That would be lovely. Wouldn't it, Gare?" He offered Mrs. Lombard his arm and they headed toward the small drawing room, leaving him to trail behind.

Gareth did not like what he saw on his friend's face. Not at all.

***

Serena could not envisage a less likely pair of friends: McElroy would not shut up and Lockheart was all but mute. And then there was the awkwardness of acting like a hostess in a strange man's house. But Lockheart appeared either uninterested in, or unaware of, his duties as a host.

When the tea tray arrived even before they sat down Serena recognized the invisible hand of Jessup at work. No doubt he'd been prepared with a tea tray even before his master's carriage rumbled into the front drive.

While Serena prepared the tea, McElroy, a man bursting with energy, paced the room and fired off questions.

"I see they are laying out something directly behind the center section of the house."

"Yes, that would be the parterre gardens." She looked at Lockheart, who was watching her with the silent, opaque look that made her feel self-conscious. Was her hair a mess? Was there a dirt smut on her nose? "Milk or sugar, Mr. Lockheart?"

"Milk, please." He came to claim his cup and saucer. "No biscuits for me, thank you."

"Gareth is an ascetic, Mrs. Lombard. But I will have both milk *and* sugar in my tea and a couple of those delightful looking fairy cakes as well." McElroy paused in front of her and waited for his cup and plate, his smile making her feel just as self-conscious as his friend's brooding stare.

Serena poured herself a cup and added a little milk, selecting one of the cream-filled cakes even though she had promised to exert some restraint when it came to her teas. In the weeks she had been here the magnificent food had begun to tell and her gowns were all a bit snug, even with all the activity that took up much of her days.

She looked up to find both men watching her. "Mr. McElroy tells me you have returned to the area to inspect a brewery?" she asked her employer.

"That is correct. It is possible we may consider investing in it."

"Do you consider *any* kind of business?"

"Our decisions are based on a variety of factors that all contribute to the health of a business."

"We also bury a potato on the west side of a building during a full moon before we make up our minds," McElroy added.

Serena had a mouthful of cake and almost choked on it. Mr. McElroy winked at her.

Mr. Lockheart sighed. "I came to see how the work was progressing and bring the horses."

"Horses?" She glanced from man to man, "I saw only the one."

Lockheart sipped his tea before answering. "We brought six in all. One among them should be suitable for your son."

"You brought a horse for Oliver? But—"

"Jessup informed me you had rented two horses from the livery stable in the village. He indicated that," there was a slight hitch, "your son was an accomplished rider."

Serena realized her mouth was open and shut it. She looked at the Irishman, who was managing to smirk and drink tea at the same time. Lockheart's eyes were as unreadable as the moon and not dissimilar in color. He had cut his hair since last she'd last seen him and she would have sworn his face was slightly thinner, as if he had been ill or not eating well. She shook her head to dismiss the thought. The horses, she reminded herself.

"That is *very* kind of you, Mr. Lockheart. I assure you, you needn't—"

He waved one hand and a flicker of something that looked like irritation crossed his face. "It is something I wished to do, so I did it. There is no need to thank me."

Serena blinked at his rather abrupt tone.

The silence was so loud it clanged like a bell.

McElroy's chuckle broke it. "You're doing it again, Gare."

Two bright strips of red appeared like slashes over Lockheart's high, sharp cheekbones.

He sighed. "I apologize, Mrs. Lombard. It was not my intention to be discourteous." Lockheart's shapely lips flexed into a frown. "I'm afraid you will find my manners are often . . .wanting."

"Quite savage, really," the Irishman added, popping an entire cake into his mouth and managing to smile around it.

Serena could not decipher the look Lockheart cut his friend. But when he turned back to her, he wore the same undecipherable expression. "Yes, savage is perhaps more accurate. Fortunately today I have Mr. McElroy nearby to apologize or translate for me."

Unabashed, the Irishman nodded. "Mr. Lockheart just made a joke, Mrs. Lombard. You may laugh now."

Serena couldn't help laughing and the tension drained from the room.

"I believe I'll need another of those fairy cakes, ma'am." McElroy presented his plate and Serena transferred a delicate pastry onto it with two forks.

The Irishman raised his eyebrows at the method of serving but made no comment.

"Would you care for more tea, Mr. Lockheart?"

His response was to bring his cup to her. She refilled it, handed it back, and smiled up at him. His disconcerting eyes were on her, serious and unreadable, his handsome features bland. Serena swallowed and wondered if he noticed the hitch in her breathing, which to her was as noisy as the rasp of a saw.

"Thank you."

"I understand this is a first for you, Mrs. Lombard?" McElroy's question seemed to come from a long way off.

She assumed he did not mean having tea with two men who'd grown up in an orphanage. "You mean designing a garden of this size?"

He nodded, his smile encouraging but the glint in his green eyes unsettling. *What a pair these two were!*

"Yes, it is. Until now, the only gardens I've had the pleasure of designing were in the city. And most of those were done according to the owner's rather particular plans."

"And Gareth is giving you free rein, I hear."

Serena felt there were more to his words than was obvious and could only nod.

"How do you find it thus far?"

"I'll admit I was anxious before actually commencing work." She glanced at her employer to see how he received such information, but saw his attention was on her sketchbook, which had slipped out of the large satchel onto the settee beside her.

Serena set down her cup and saucer. "Would you like to see the sketches I've made since returning? There are more formal plans that should be here by the end of the week."

He set down his own tea and came to sit beside her, his presence on the small sofa making her aware of how tall he was. He was slim but sleekly muscled. Serena thought of the room off his bedchamber and realized he must visit it frequently. She swallowed at the thought and opened the sketchbook to the section in question and handed it to him.

Lockheart took the book in his long, sensitive fingers, and held it lightly, as if it was valuable. McElroy had come to stand beside him, his hand resting on the arm of the couch as he leaned over his friend's shoulder.

"As you know, Mr. Lockheart, I commissioned a draughtsman to come and help me once you approved my original drawings."

The first sketch was one as she imagined the property would look like from above.

"That is interesting," McElroy, murmured. "How were you able to get the correct perspective?"

"We spent four days, most of that time pacing out the various sections." She looked up at Lockheart, but his attention was on the sketch. "I know that might seem excessive, but I felt it was called for as this is so new to me."

When she realized he had no response, she leaned closer to turn the page. She could feel his warmth, and he smelled of some wonderful cologne, clean wool, and warm male.

"Here is my plan for the east courtyard."

McElroy leaned closer. "What are these rectangles?"

"Those that are vertical are sites for statuary, these three here," she gestured to three horizontal rectangles, "Are benches."

Serena kept waiting for her employer to ask questions or make comments, but he seemed contented to let his friend do the talking.

***

Gareth did not care if the woman decided to erect bent lamp posts as sculptures and plant brambles and thistles on every square inch of land; he just wanted to sit beside her and breathe in her scent. And enjoy her nearness—the heat of her body inches away from his own—something he had only sought with one other person, also a woman.

He vaguely heard Dec's questions and her answers. His friend would be curious about Gareth's proximity to the woman. He knew his preference for space between himself and others, his dislike of being touched by strangers, which, for him, meant almost everyone.

She smelled of the outdoors, with a hint of whatever female soap it was she used. He detected the not unpleasant odor of leather and horse mingled with a more feminine scent. Her hands were what one would expect from a woman who did manual labor. The backs of them were square and broader than the rather delicate bone structure of her face would have suggested, the skin a bit chapped, callouses evident on her thumbs, a writing bump on her right middle finger that mirrored the one on Gareth's left hand. They were not pretty, dainty hands, but he found them mesmerizing.

The last time he had been this near a woman was with Venetia, a woman who could not have been more different.

"And here you see how the lake will follow the contours of the gentle hillside." Gareth looked at the picture she was referring to, the geometry of her drawing the first thing he noticed.

"Where is the berm you are constructing?"

He felt her jolt beside him.

"It is here," she traced her thumb nail over a line. "But you can see it better in this drawing." She flipped the page. "Here."

Gareth looked at the orientation of the berm and turned back the page, and then looked at the berm again.

"What is it?"

Gareth could hear the anxiety in her voice.

"If the degree of elevation is as you have indicated in this drawing, you will need to shift your berm perhaps fifteen degrees to get the support necessary." He looked up and found her face only inches from his, a deep notch between her green-gold eyes. This close, he saw fine lines around her eyes, perhaps from squinting, and parentheses around her plump, coral-pink lips. The texture of her skin was quite fascinating. She was golden brown—unfashionably so, he knew—a sprinkling of freckles over the bridge of her straight, small nose. Her lips were small but shapely, the corners of them invariably curled up in a smile. But not now. Now they were moving, and Gareth had not been paying attention. Instead he'd been imagining his own lips on hers, his tongue delving between them.

"Mr. Lockheart?"

He blinked. "Mrs. Lombard?"

71

She gave him an uncertain smile. "Will you come down with me tomorrow?" She looked at the watch pinned to the left side of her bodice. "It is too late now, but perhaps we might go in the morning, before they commence work and you could look for yourself?"

Gareth supposed he should. After all, he had never even seen this part of his property before.

"We can leave our trip to the brewery for the day after, Gare."

Gareth looked up at the sound of Dec's voice. The Irishman was no longer smiling, which was almost more frightening. He'd known Dec since they were boys—far longer than anyone else in his life—but Declan was an amazingly complex human being and Gareth still could not read or interpret all the other man's expressions. Except to know he was scheming or planning some sort of mischief.

Gareth knew he had dug a hole for himself, so to speak, and now he would need to see the site. "I will send a message to Mr. Fowler and reschedule our tour of the brewery." He turned back to the woman, who was waiting for his answer with obvious interest. "We can walk the area and see if the berm will need to be moved." He already knew it would, but he guessed it would not be politic to declare such an opinion so baldly in the face of her mistake. Her smile told him he had guessed correctly for a change.

They looked at the rest of the drawings without incident.

Chapter Seven

The only meal Serena could recall being odder than the one she'd had tonight was her last dinner at Rushton Park. Oh, the food and service were impeccable, as usual. But Lockheart and McElroy were not the most restful of dinner companions. The Irishman seemed to delight in prodding and poking not only his friend, but Serena, and—she suspected—anyone else who had the misfortune to enter his orbit. He was a sharp man with a rather thin, brittle façade of charm and she did not trust for a moment.

Mr. Lockheart remained as mysterious as ever. Although he rarely spoke, he seemed articulate and comfortable when he did. Which made her wonder what it was he enjoyed inside his own head enough to ignore the discussions and people around him the rest of the time.

By the time the sumptuous dessert course had been cleared from the table Serena had endured quite enough prodding by McElroy and Lockheart's quiet, measured looks.

"I will leave you gentleman to your port. I'm afraid I've had rather a long day and will turn in unfashionably early." She stood and they with her.

"Good night, Mrs. Lombard." McElroy said bowing. "I'm afraid I'm something of a late riser, so I'll leave matters of earth moving and dams to you and Gareth."

Lockheart met Serena at the door, even though a footman hovered nearby to open it.

"Will six be too early, Mr. Lockheart? It is when I usually breakfast and then head to the site." She had hoped to see him recoil or at least wince at the early hour, but he merely nodded.

"At six, madam." He bowed and opened the door. "Good night."

Serena breathed a sigh of relief as the door closed behind her. She would have liked to be a fly on the wall in the dining room—especially to see how the two men interacted while on their own. Over the course of dinner McElroy had shared the general details of their history. Two boys dropped at the same orphanage. McElroy was older than his friend, although he behaved in a far younger and more carefree fashion. In any event, she was glad he was staying away in the morning. She wanted to speak with Mr. Lockheart without wading through witticisms and double entendres.

She went up to Oliver's room, which was on the third floor of the family wing. There was a light beneath Nounou's door so she tapped softly.

"Entre!"

The older woman was in bed reading. She raised her eyes when she saw who it was and lowered her book.

"So," she asked in her native language, "How was a dinner with those two?" She used a word for "men" that had untranslatable connotations in English.

Serena smiled. "Much as you would expect. They will be staying for at least one more day. Mr. Lockheart believes there is some problem at the dam."

Nounou's dry smile showed what she thought about that.

"Is Oliver asleep?"

She made a sound that was entirely Gallic. "That boy! He will burn us in our beds. I have decided it is safer to let him read all night if he wishes. He will be sandy-eyed and sleepy, but that is the only way to learn. He is like his mother that way—a head like a stone."

Serena chuckled. "It won't hurt him, Nounou." She stood. "I will go and see if he is awake. Either way, I will extinguish the light, so you may go to sleep without worry of immolation." She bent over the bed and kissed her on the cheek. "Good night."

Her son was indeed still awake and reading, not one book, but two spread across his lap while a single candle burned in a holder on his nightstand.

"Mama." He grinned up at her, unabashed to be found awake at almost eleven o'clock.

"You will go blind reading in such light." She nudged one of the books over and sat on the side of his bed. "You are driving poor Nounou to distraction. I want you to promise lights out by ten from now on. It is good to think without a book in front of you. That is when I have my most creative thoughts."

He nodded and closed the books. "All right, Mama. I will try it." He shot her a furtive glance. "But maybe we can discuss the matter after I have done so for a while?"

Serena laughed and ruffled his hair. "Very well, a negotiation. How long?"

"A week?"

She shook her head at his hopeful look. "A month. And then we can reassess."

He gave a heavy sigh but nodded.

"Good," she said, leaning forward to give him a loud smack on his cheek and chuckling at the "Aw, Mama!" her action elicited.

She stood and picked up the candle.

"Mama?"

"Hmm?"

"How long will Mr. Lockheart stay?" His voice had a hopeful note in it that made her pause.

"Do you like him?"

His vigorous nod set his hair flopping and reminded her he needed his hair cut.

"He likes automata. He has *built* one of his own, Mama."

"Has he?" She smiled at her son's enthusiasm. She'd been disappointed that he'd shown no interest in sculpture, but she would be just as pleased if he had a passion for another subject.

"He said I might build my own, too." He gave her a shy look. "I like him, Mama."

"So do I," she said, and then extinguished the light.

***

Two hours later Serena was still awake. She had tossed and turned, trying to force sleep on herself, but it had not worked. She needed to walk, to think. She put on her dressing gown and found a fleecy scarf.

It was a half moon and the south side of the house looked magical in the silvery light. Pine stakes had been hammered into the rough turf where the parterre garden would go, its shape defined by twine. Dew had already begun to collect on the shaggy grass and her ankles were damp by the time she'd walked the perimeter of the garden twice. Her mind, however, was down by the river. She was anxious about what Mr. Lockheart had found with her dam and hoped it would not require a great deal of money and time to repair, although she could not see how it could not.

She bit her lip. She'd been foolish to take on such a commission. Three weeks of studying the work of Capability Brown and looking at gardens were not enough training to take on a job of this magnitude. She had let the promise of money—riches to her—lure her out of her area of expertise. She was arrogant and foolish to resist the notion of moving back to her in-laws' house.

Her feet had led her away from the main block and toward the west. She could walk around the wing and enter through the arcade that ran along the northwest side of the building. As she came around the corner of the building, she saw light coming from one of the second floor windows. Her own rooms had the ninth through fourteenth windows and these were. . . she counted to herself. . . part of the last block, the master suite. She was too close to the building to see so she walked toward the small stand of trees until she had a clear vantage point. It was Mr. Lockheart's room, the one with the padded floor and odd hanging bags. The room blazed with light but she saw nothing but the smaller of the bags, the one shaped like a pear. Shadows flickered in the background meaning there was somebody—Lockheart, most likely— moving about. She was just about to turn away when he came into view.

Serena sucked in a noisy gasp of air. It was Mr. Lockheart, and he was without a shirt. Serena looked away, staring at her clenched hands in the darkness. What she was doing—spying, there was no other word for it—was wicked. She was intruding on his privacy. How would she like it if he were to do the same?

Her eyes moved back to the window, as if they'd been dragged there by a team of oxen.

He was hitting the bag with his fists, alternating hands, the movement so rapid it was a blur. Even from this distance she could see his nude torso was slick from exertion, the muscles so distinct they might have been graven upon metal. His body, for all its musculature, was too thin—hard and devoid of any fat. Even though she was a female, her father and Monsieur Favel had seen to it that she'd had many opportunities to sketch nude models, men and women chosen for their superlative physiques. But never had she seen such definition.

"It is like watching one of your sculptures come to life, isn't it?"

Serena screamed and jumped at least a foot, her heart thudding against her ribs to get out. She whipped around, her hand clutching her chest.

"I apologize, Mrs. Lombard. Did I startle you?" McElroy did not sound sorry. He sounded amused. "I must admit I was surprised to find *you* out here at this time of night. Especially after such an arduous day."

She did not hear only humor in his voice, but skepticism. What could she say? He had caught her gawking at a half-naked man.

So she stated the obvious. "I could not sleep."

He took a step closer. "Perhaps I might help you with that."

Serena could scarcely believe she had heard him correctly. But his arrogant smirk and hooded eyes told her she had.

She gave him a freezing look.

"Ah," he said, his smile growing harder. He turned his gaze back to the window and she was glad to follow. They watched Lockheart pound the bag without ceasing.

"This is some sort of pugilistic training?" she finally asked, deciding to forget his lapse in manners.

He nodded but did not look away from the window. "It is the type of thing men of your class play at in places like Jackson's Salon, except this is the real thing."

The derision in his words made her bristle. "What do you know of my class, Mr. McElroy?"

This time he did turn to her, his smile as mocking as his words. "Oh come now, Mrs. Lombard, your husband was the son of a duke. You can scarcely marry much higher."

Serena supposed it was arrogance that had led her to believe men of the merchant class would not know of her lineage.

McElroy chuckled, as if she'd spoken out loud. "Oh yes, I make it my business to know who Gareth associates with, even if he doesn't."

"Mr. Lockheart knows of my connections."

"Connections like your cousins Leeland and Sandford Featherstone?"

Serena ground her teeth. "Cousins by marriage."

"By marriage," he agreed.

"Yes, he knows." Serena found his smug, knowing tone annoying. "If *you* are so keen on keeping up with your business partner's associates, why didn't you warn him about the Featherstones?"

"I said I made it my business to know about his associates, not to make his decisions for him." He shrugged. "Featherstone is a small-time operator. He was skimming from Gareth, but he was also providing a service Gareth believed necessary. I'm afraid my friend has a bee in his bonnet about the need for a genteel setting in which to wine and dine the men who make the laws the rest of us are supposed to abide by."

"Mr. Lockheart told me it was *you* who put the bee in his bonnet, Mr. McElroy."

His eyebrows arched high and the look he gave her was speculative, rather than just accusing. "Did he? It is unlike Gareth to confide such matters—or even have them in his head to discuss them. It would seem he has taken an uncommon shine to you."

"And you believe that is unwise."

"Tut, tut, Mrs. Lombard—or I suppose I should call you Lady Lombard—don't put words in my mouth."

"Trust me, Mr. McElroy, I don't wish to go anywhere near your mouth. As to your other comment, no, you should not call me that." She no longer bothered to keep the disdain from her tone. "Not only because it would be inaccurate—you would refer to me as Lady Robert Lombard—but also because I have stated my preferred title, and it is *Mrs. Lombard*".

A Figure of Love

"Come, *Mrs. Lombard,* no need to come the ugly with me. I must admit I do not understand why you would feel the need to hide your light, or your rather grand connections, under a bushel—especially around Gareth."

"I can't tell you how much comfort it gives me to know the workings of my mind are beyond your comprehension, Mr. McElroy."

He chuckled. "You have a remarkable facility with English to say you are a Frenchwoman."

"My father was English, as I am sure you are well aware—being a man who does such a thorough investigation."

"You are correct, yet again. But I will continue to be perplexed about your attitude to your august connections. I've not met one of your kind yet who hasn't felt the need to rub it in my face. I'm sure you must be wondering what Gareth makes of your connections. And let us be honest with one another, isn't that your true object in burying yourself in the country and messing with dirt? Marrying a very, very wealthy man you believe you will be able to easily manipulate?"

Serena snorted. "You sound like you speak from experience, Mr. McElroy. Do *you* enjoy manipulating your friend?" She did not give him any time to respond. "I refuse to dignify your aspersions by defending myself to you, Mr. McElroy. I will say, however, that I believe you might not know your friend as well as you think you do. Or perhaps your own desires color your judgement."

His eyes lost their amused glint. "Just what the devil do you mean?"

"I mean I have not spent a lot of time around Mr. Lockheart but certainly long enough to realize he has *no* interest at all in those things which others might value. He appears to treat society and his own wealth with equal disdain. Perhaps it is your *own* social aspirations you speak of so passionately. You speak on the matter with such heat I can only assume you have some personal axe to grind on the matter."

To her surprise, he laughed.

"I am glad I amuse you," she lied.

He shook his head, still laughing. "Thank you, Mrs. Lombard, you are certainly very . . . imaginative. But I am afraid it is *you* who misunderstand me. Gareth is not in search of an aristocratic bride because he wishes to acquire an arm ornament who will spend his money, sneer at his lineage, and stoop to warm his bed only so far as to provide him with an heir. No, my dear widow, it is for another reason entirely that he would suffer the condescension of your *crowd*. You see, unlike me, Gareth is concerned about more than just money. He wants influence with the people who wield it. He wants change—safer working conditions, shorter hours, age limits, decent wages. In short, he is concerned about the wellbeing of workers. To that end, he is willing to shackle himself to a spouse who has as much interest in him or chance of caring about his happiness as she might in flying to the moon."

Up in the lighted window Mr. Lockheart paused, stilling the swinging leather bag with one hand and holding it while he dropped his head onto his forearm, his deep breathing obvious even from this distance.

"Perhaps you might take take a leaf out of your friend's book and state your point in plain words, Mr. McElroy," Serena said, not bothering to look at him.

Mr. McElroy moved until he stood between Serena and her view of the window, his face as hard as a granite carving, his eyes glittering dangerously. "Gareth Lockheart is the smartest man I have ever met. But, in a lot of ways, he is like a child. Because he is not motivated by greed or jealousy or envy, he does not take those emotions into account in his dealings with others. In addition to being the smartest person I know, he is also the most honest, generous, and kind." He reached out and ran a finger along her jaw. "I, Mrs. Lombard, am quite another kettle of fish."

Serena jerked her head away from his hand and took a step back. "What exactly—"

"I am good at reading people and can spot a liar or somebody who is hiding something from twenty paces. You, *Mrs. Serena Lombard*, are hiding something. I can smell it on you like other men might smell your perfume. If it turns out it is this blasted garden or some other scheme you have cooked up with Featherstone, I warn you, Mrs. Lombard, your august connections will not save you from me if I find out you are manipulating my friend. Good evening, ma'am." He turned and walked away, leaving Serena feeling as if she had been slapped in the face.

How dare he?

She spun around to ask him just that, but he had disappeared into the darkness without a trace. Serena slumped against the closest tree, her mind whirling. What did he know? How could he know *anything?* Even Sandy didn't know, although he suspected, with his own aptitude for lies and deception, that something was not quite right.

Should she leave? If she did, where would the money come from for the next payment? If she didn't, would McElroy make good on his threat and she would find herself in an even worse bind? She had meant no harm to Mr. Lockheart, but it was hard to remember that with all the guilt and fear that surrounded her.

And if she had briefly entertained the thought of marrying Mr. Lockheart, and giving him the connections into the aristocracy he needed, could she really be blamed? Her first thought was for her son. She would do anything to protect him. Anything.

She looked up at the window, foolishly thinking there might be answers there. But it was now dark, just like all the others.

Chapter Eight

Mrs. Lombard was in the breakfast room before him, a roll of plans laid out across the large table while she ate her breakfast.

"Good morning, Mr. Lockheart." She gestured to the drawings. "I will bring the plans with us today."

"Very good." Gareth didn't need plans to know there was a problem, but he did not demur. She still had more than half a plate of food and had just poured a cup of coffee so Gareth ordered a pot for himself and proceeded to fill a plate.

He saw she was wearing a different riding habit—this one an unusual shade of burnt orange with dark gold piping, the style and cut somewhat old fashioned. Gareth had dressed in the clothing his valet, Chalmers, set out for him after learning of today's plans: leather breeches, a dark brown clawhammer, and green waistcoat with narrow brown stripes. Chalmers was responsible for choosing and caring for his clothing, two chores Gareth found beyond fatiguing. His only stipulation was that the fabrics be comfortable and that the cut did not hamper his movement beyond good sense. His memory, all but faultless in most matters, seemed to develop a selective amnesia about clothing and the correct suit of clothing for different occasions. Chalmers did not dress or shave him, but the dour valet did administer Gareth's haircuts, which seemed to be necessary ever more frequently.

She looked up from the plans when he sat across from her. "Mr. McElroy did not change his mind and decide to join us?"

Gareth paused in the act of opening his napkin. "Did he tell you he had changed his mind?"

Her cheeks, already somewhat rosy, turned an even redder shade. "No, I just thought he might have."

Gareth had prepared for today by composing a list of conversational gambits and rehearsed responses. He'd found such lists helpful for those occasions when he expected to be in prolonged company with a person who was not Declan or a servant, the only people with whom he felt no social compunction to make pointless comments or idle conversation. Today's list had been easier than usual as he seemed to have developed an actual curiosity about Mrs. Lombard and her son, an unusual development for him. It was not that he did not *like* people, of course, but he rarely wished to become any better acquainted with them.

"Your accent is very slight, Mrs. Lombard."

She gave him a look of such surprise he wondered if he'd erred once again. Were accents—like bodily functions—yet another taboo subject? But, no, she did not appear scandalized. More than likely she was stunned that he would generate a question of this sort.

"My father spoke English to me when I was growing up. He wanted me to be fluent in his mother tongue."

"How long have you lived in England?"

"It will be ten years soon. I came just before my son was born, in 1807."

Her answer spurred a new question, one that had not been on his list. "You told me the last time you were here that your father groomed you to become a sculptor? Is that not unusual in France?"

"It is just as unusual as it is here." She smiled, the same genuine, open look she had given to her son. Gareth thought the expression transformed her face from merely pretty to beautiful. He was, by no means, immune to feminine beauty, but he'd never considered it quite so closely before. "My father, like most men, had wished for a son, but my mother died having me. I was perhaps five when he realized I had an aptitude for clay modeling as well as sketching. He began to take me into his studio. At first I only watched and played with my bits of wax or clay. I made my first piece from terracotta, and he was so pleased he purchased some rather fine marble—a softer grade of stone than he would normally use because I was still young and did not have the strength for the more durable types. When I was fourteen I began to help him in the studio at Monsieur Favel's chateau. He was a very old sculptor who no longer worked but employed several sculptors and stone cutters to complete commissions he still received. It was a pleasant, if somewhat unconventional childhood," her smiled wavered. "Or at least it was before the War took its toll." She shrugged and cut a piece of ham. "So I am an artist by a fluke of nature. If my father had had a son, I would more than likely be married to a sculptor by now."

He watched her lift the fork to her mouth and realized he possessed a rather unexpected desire to see her wield a hammer and chisel. Her hands were not beautiful in the accepted feminine sense, but they were shapely and dexterous.

"And you, Mr. Lockheart, how is it that you learned to do—" her hand fluttered as she sought the correct word. "Whatever it is you do?"

How to explain what he did? He had tried, once, to Dec, but had given up at his friend's mystified look. Did she really want to know? Or was this polite conversation?

As if he had spoken the words aloud—which he knew he had not—she answered. "I am asking because I know you are knowledgeable about mathematics and its applications and my son seems to have taken an interest in those areas."

Ah, so she *was* interested. "He does not wish to sculpt?"

She chuckled. "No, I'm afraid his talents lie elsewhere. He dislikes any form of artistic rendering but seems to enjoy drawing when it involves solving a problem, as with his automaton."

Gareth could sympathize with the boy. Art often made him uncomfortable with too much emotionalism, or inexplicable tangents and lack of uniformity or logic. But machinery? Even something as simple as a toy? There was a certain type of poetry in things that worked. And numbers? Well, there was something about the precision and beauty of mathematics that made his soul—if humans indeed possessed such a thing—sing.

"I have always found patterns—mathematical patterns—in even the most mundane of things. They existed before I could understand them. And when I was exposed to my first lesson in the simplicity and power of numbers, I knew I would need to keep seeking until I could know the whole of it." He paused, considering his foolish words. "Of course the more you learn the more you realize that is not possible." He could not recall the last time he'd spoken so much to a stranger. Luckily, Mrs. Lombard did not seem to find his words odd.

"That is how you were able to look at the drawing and know there was a problem, wasn't it?"

"Yes, if the drawing is properly to scale."

She nodded, her eyes wandering back to her plans.

"Do you have a tutor for your son?" That was a question that had not come from his list, either.

"Not yet. I have been teaching him myself, but I have reached the end of what I can offer when it comes to many subjects. He is of an age where he should go off to school, but that is not," she hesitated, "possible."

Gareth wondered why that was. Money? Emotional attachment? Naturally he did not ask.

"He will meet us at the stables after finishing his breakfast in the schoolroom. I've told him this is not a holiday, but an opportunity to learn. I believe he will greatly appreciate the calculations that go into building a dam. Besides," she smiled, "he was delirious with joy when he heard there was a horse waiting for him."

Gareth looked down at his plate, his stomach tight. He was glad to have pleased the boy—he had liked his quiet, thoughtful way immediately. But he did not wish to be the recipient of effusive gratitude from either Oliver or his mother.

He pushed back his chair with a loud scrape. "If you will excuse me, I've forgotten something I meant to take care of." He bowed. "I will meet you at the site." He turned before she could answer, nodding to the footman who opened the door and facilitated his escape. He knew his behavior was rude, but he did not wish to be trapped in the stables and forced to endure an emotional scene. Just the thought of facing such a situation made him feel ill. He realized he hadn't eaten much and knew that might be part of it. He tended to forget food when either immersed in thought or some other interesting activity. How interesting that he'd forgotten about eating in the woman's presence. He could not recall that happening before.

***

Serena half-expected Mr. Lockheart not to be at the dam when they arrived. She couldn't help wondering if she had said something to drive him away. But she'd gone over her words a dozen times in the past half hour and had come up with nothing—at least nothing rude or offensive. And she knew he liked Oliver, so it couldn't have been that he would be joining them. No, the man was an enigma.

The horses he'd brought for Serena and her son were by far some of the finest they'd ever ridden. Thanks to the generosity of his grandparents, Oliver had been riding since before he was breeched.

Serena had ridden a lot as a girl, mostly her mountain pony and astride. On a side saddle she was an adequate rider, but she took no great joy in the activity, only in the sense she was able to get from one point to another that much quicker.

And so they'd headed out, Serena and Oliver on their new mounts, followed by the nine young dogs they had found living in the stables on their arrival. The stable master, Horrocks, had told them Oliver was welcome to them—if he would train them. The dogs had gone from a half-mad hoard to reasonably obedient companions over the past five weeks and she was proud of her son. So when he'd asked this morning if he might bring them along, she had assented.

"You may take the dogs today, Oliver. But I want you to take them for a run and exhaust some of their enthusiasm before you come to watch the workers."

Her son nodded, but she could tell his head was elsewhere—flying across the hillside on his new steed, which he had immediately named Starling because of his unusual mottled coat.

Her own horse, a pretty chestnut mare with a sweet disposition, suited Serena's abilities to the ground. She must thank Jessup, who had apparently paid close attention to both her and Oliver to be able to make such a report.

Her son's voice broke into her thoughts. "Mama?" Oliver was twisted sideways in his saddle, looking at her with a mournful expression.

Serena laughed. "Go on, already, and ride. But be careful." He was gone before the second word left her mouth, his pack of hounds like a noisy tail to his comet. She had ceased worrying about his horsemanship several years ago, when she learned he raced the countryside unattended by adults with his herd of cousins.

It took her only a few minutes on horseback to reach the worksite. At first she'd thought not to need a horse, but after two weeks of making five or more trips a day, she'd realized that was foolish—and not efficient.

She saw Mr. Lockheart's horse before she saw him—that was because he had taken off his coat and was down in a ditch, using a stick to draw something for a group of men standing about watching.

She dismounted and left her horse beside his. He looked up as she approached.

"I hope you don't mind, Mrs. Lombard, but I have taken the liberty of showing the men how they might save part of this work and only re-dig a small section."

"Of course I do not mind. I am only glad you came before we had positioned the entire berm."

The foreman chuckled. "Aye, as much as we like the work, doing a job twice ain't something to be wished for."

Lockheart turned back to the drawing with his customary abruptness, not interested in banter. "The only problem I foresee with this new path is that boulder."

"Aye, sir, that be why we thought to move the berm up here." He looked at Serena, "Yon gent that walked the land with Mrs. Lombard argued it made no matter."

The foreman, Mr. Flowers, was right. She had drawn her initial plans very near to where Mr. Lockheart was moving the berm. She was pleased that Flowers, a stout Kentish gentleman who worked with his group of laborers more than merely overseeing them, had pointed this out to their employer. Serena had earned his respect in the weeks since coming to begin the job and they had an excellent understanding and working relationship. And now, she realized, she had earned his loyalty, as well.

Not that Lockheart appeared to care. His mind seemed stuck on the boulder. "Do you have the necessary means to remove it?" he asked her.

She shook her head. "I'm afraid I didn't pursue the matter when it seemed it would not be an issue." She cocked her head as she mentally measured the dimensions of the rock in question before turning to the foreman. "Have you moved something of this size before?"

Flowers scratched his head and then shook it. "Not this size. I suppose we could dig it out enough to roll it down into the lake."

"That would be the easiest, but. . ." Serena bit her lip.

The two men waited.

Serena shook her head. "Never mind. That would be the easiest."

"What were you going to say, Mrs. Lombard?" Lockheart sounded intrigued, rather than resigned or skeptical, as many men would do.

"It would make a lovely feature beside the lake. It just seems a pity to submerge it."

He looked from her to the rock to the hillside. His stared at the rock again, but now Serena knew he wasn't seeing it. Somehow, she knew this was one of those times where he saw the numbers and symbols he spoke of.

"I have read the great stones on Salisbury Plains come from many miles away." He spoke the words to the rock.

Serena looked at Flowers, who looked back at her and gave a small shrug.

They waited.

Lockheart turned to Flowers, "Do you understand the changes to the grade?"

"Aye, sir."

"How many days will the digging take, not including the area the rock occupies?"

"If the weather stays like this I'm thinking we'll be done by the end of the week."

Lockheart nodded. "I will have a way to move the stone by then." He glanced at something over Serena's shoulder and she turned to see

Oliver dismounting. The dogs, she was pleased to see, were staying put at his command.

When she turned back it was to see Lockheart still staring, his brow furrowed.

Serena waited until the men had moved off toward the new dig site to speak. "I hope you do not mind, Mr. Lockheart, but there were these pups in the stables when we arrived. Horrocks seemed to think you were building a hunting pack, but as there was no kennel master, he said Oliver might train them."

Oliver arrived beside her. "Good morning, Mr. Lockheart."

Lockheart looked from Oliver to Serena and back to her son. "I am pleased to see you have taken care of the dogs. I'm afraid I did not take care of hiring a kennel master, so I'm glad to see they have found somebody who wants them. I daresay they are quite ruined for hunting now?"

Serena nodded. "Horrocks seemed to think so. But Oliver has been training them to behave."

He looked at her son. "Have you?"

Oliver nodded. "They are *good* dogs, sir. But Mama says they must live in the stables. They have a stall, where they sleep and stay when I cannot be outside with them." He hesitated. "Mama says they may not live in the house."

Lockheart appeared intrigued by this piece of information and Serena could see the man did not realize he was in the process of being manipulated by a master at the art. He looked at Serena.

"You do not approve of animals in the house, Mrs. Lombard?"

"It is not that."

Lockheart took his coat off the handle of a shovel which was jammed upright into a pile of dirt, and shrugged into it, his perfect cravat disheveled and his lovely, expensive boots covered in mud.

"What is the reason?"

In the sunlight she could see his eyes had a dark gray ring around the paler gray of his iris. His lashes were dark brown like his hair and were unfairly long.

"It is not my house, Mr. Lockheart."

He merely looked at her.

89

"I would not wish to take such liberties with bringing pets into the house," she explained.

"I have never had a pet. Do most other people keep them in the house?" As was usual with this man, he managed to say words she was not quite expecting.

"Well—"

"My grandpapa, His Grace of Remington has over *twenty* dogs. And they all live in his chambers, some even sleep on his bed," Oliver offered, pointedly avoiding Serena's glare.

Lockheart appeared to find this intriguing. "Is that so?"

"They are not, however, hunting dogs, Oliver."

"Neither are these, Mama."

Serena sighed.

"I have no objection to dogs in the house, Mrs. Lombard, but the decision is yours." He continued with hardly a pause. "I have something in mind to move this stone and also to position it where you would like it. It will take me a few days to assemble the necessary materials. I hope you will not mind if we extend our visit a few days more?"

Serena was about to remind him that it was *his* house when her son took the issue out of her hands.

"You mean you will stay, Mr. Lockheart?"

He gave Oliver his characteristic blank stare. "Until the stone had been moved."

"Will you show me how to build an automaton?"

This time Serena got the first word in. "Mr. Lockheart is here to work, Oliver, not play." She spoke gently, but with the firmness she knew he required once his high spirits had taken charge. Because Oliver had been raised in so much love and showered with so much affection that he believed everyone wished to spend their time with him. Serena usually allowed him the comfort of his assumptions. After all, life would come along soon enough and deal him its share of pain. She wanted him to know only joy for as long as she could contrive.

"When are your studies over for the day?" Lockheart asked, walking up the hill with them.

"Three o'clock. Except Sunday, which is a day of rest. Except we have to go to church."

"Come to the library at three every day and we will work on it." His lips twitched. "Except Sunday, of course."

"Hurrah! Hurrah!" Luckily Oliver was already halfway up the hill when he began shouting, the dogs leaped and danced around him, not caring what they were celebrating.

She smiled up at her employer. "That was very kind, Mr. Lockheart, but you don't need to indulge him."

"It is something I will enjoy."

Before she could thank him, he asked a question about the position of the pavilion. It wasn't until they were riding home that she realized he'd once again deflected any words of thanks or gratitude.

Chapter Nine

Gareth was in the cellar again. The darkness was total; not even a pinprick of light. The floor was damp, cold, and slimy and the sound of things skittering and slithering around him was deafening in the suffocating closeness. He screamed, but he knew nobody would come; they never came. His voice was gone, his throat hurt and his mouth was flooded with the metallic taste of blood. Something heavy and furry brushed past his naked ankle and teeth like needles sank into his big toe.

He screamed.

The hoarse, terror-filled yell was like a catapult flinging Gareth upright in his bed. He couldn't get enough air; it was like breathing water. His hands fisted the covers on both sides and the darkness that had shrouded his eyes cleared, burned away by the single candle he always kept burning, no matter where he slept. It was across the room, hidden by a blue glass shield, but it provided enough light to keep him from drowning in the terrifying blackness.

Afraid of the dark; he was afraid of the dark. The taunting voices of children floated through his mind like fragments of clouds across the moon. Children liked to find and exploit weakness, and none knew that better than Gareth.

His heart ceased its mad flapping against his ribcage and his breathing slowed. The fine Irish sheeting was twisted and wrapped around his torso, soaked with sweat and telling him the dream had been of long duration.

He untangled his legs and swung his feet to the floor, more exhausted than when he'd gone to bed—and he'd been plenty tired then, having spent the day either in a carriage or examining a brewery that had been run into near ruin by the current owner's feckless speculation on the 'Change.

He might be tired, but he also knew there was no chance of getting back to sleep after one of these nightmares; dreams which plagued him at least several times a month. As always, he was famished—as if he had lived the dream and actually spent days in the dark without food or water.

He put on the heavy silver silk banyan Chalmers had purchased for him and slid his always cold feet into his sheepskin slippers.

He would go to the kitchen and hunt for food. He'd not yet done that at Rushton Park, but Jessup was familiar enough with his nocturnal habits in London that he would know to have pies or bread and cheeses and such always waiting for him.

The journey to the kitchen was a substantial one but it gave him a chance to look at his house without the presence of the dozens of servants he employed, people who were always at hand during the daylight hours to see that he never went without. While Gareth appreciated efficient servants, he sometimes felt like a visitor in his own house.

He passed through the great hall into the corridor that housed the kitchen, laundry, servant quarters, and everything else that made the huge house run—usually for him alone. Which made him think of the woman and her son.

Mrs. Lombard and Oliver, he reminded himself. It was a bad habit of his to refer to people by labels, rather than their names: the woman, the brewer, the architect. Something about putting names to faces always struck him as intrusive and overly familiar. Just one more of his hundreds of quirks and foibles, like the wall sconces he kept burning all through the night, which made his bill for candles probably greater than that in St. James Palace. Of course Gareth probably had more money than the King and could actually pay his bills.

The candles burned everywhere, in every part of the house. Even those parts he rarely entered, and some—one part at least—which he would never enter: the cellars. It was a small price to pay in his opinion.

One candle burned in the vast kitchens and Gareth lighted two more branches to banish the shadows to the fringes of the big room. In no time he'd located a loaf of bread, a large wheel of the crumbly white cheese he liked so much, and a small pot of pickled beef. He set out his feast on the sturdy wooden table beside the banked fire and went to the cold room to fetch a bottle of ale.

Gareth munched his food and examined the massive, modern kitchen. It lacked the coziness of the cramped galley kitchen in his London townhouse, but there was something about kitchens that he liked; something that gave him comfort. Perhaps it was the proximity to food, and the knowledge he could eat as much as he wished. He had no need to go hungry ever again. Yet every time he came to feed he found himself oddly full, and had to force himself to take sustenance.

Declan knew of Gareth's odd food habits, mainly because he had a few of his own.

"Those bastards fucked us up for good, Gare. Our only revenge is to live well." Well, that had not been their *only* revenge, but Gareth knew what his friend meant.

For years Declan had lived up to his promise, but Gareth thought his debaucheries had developed an air of forced desperation lately. How much drink, food, wealth, and women could one man pursue? Gareth had noticed even Declan's appetites had withered over the past few years. His friend also hounded him far less now, which Gareth was greatly relieved about. For years the Irishman had battered and nagged him about drinking and gambling and whoring.

"You need to *live* my friend! Live in any and every way you can. We know better than most how it can all be snatched away in the blink of an eye."

But Gareth had no taste for spirits, gambling of any type had been poisoned for him long ago, and women? Well, even the ones you hired cost more than their stated price. With people, there was always more than met the eye, which was as true—or more—with prostitutes as it was with anyone else.

Not that Gareth didn't have the sexual urges of any normal man—at least he thought he did, although Declan's behavior in that arena had often astounded him. He certainly had no desire to engage in the orgies Dec had been so fond of a few years back. The very last thing he wanted was to have sexual relations with a large number of women, or even a small number, at one time. One woman at a time was more than adequate. Nor did he feel compelled to sample a broad spectrum of body types as Declan had advocated so many times. Gareth did not think the fact he'd had sex with only one person meant there was anything wrong with him.

He snorted and popped a chunk of beef into his mouth. He *knew* there were many things wrong with him. But he did not think sex was one of his problems. Now *women*. . . well, that was—

"Mr. Lockheart?"

The chunk of beef went down the wrong hole when he sucked in a mouthful of air. His throat convulsed as his body tried to expel the foreign object from his airway without any conscious order from his brain. His eyes strained until he felt like they were popping out of his head—which felt like it had doubled in size.

A sharp *whack* on his back slammed his chest into the table and sent the half-chewed chunk all the way across to the opposite chair.

Gareth filled his lungs with blessed air, breathing convulsively in between coughing.

"Oh, I'm so sorry for startling you. Don't try to speak," she added, not that he'd been either considering it or capable of it. The food was gone but his body seemed determined to make certain and coughing wracked his chest and his eyes, no longer bulging, teared profusely.

It was all extremely mortifying. Thankfully, he felt her move away, which took at least half the stress and strain away. He collapsed on his forearms on the table and focused his attention on breathing deeply and evenly.

When he felt capable of looking up without gasping, coughing, or weeping, he found a glass of water beside his plate. She was standing across from him, her face a mask of guilty concern.

"Better?"

He nodded, for once equipped with an excellent excuse for his characteristic taciturnity.

"I couldn't sleep and came down to make a pot of tea, which I often do. Would you like some tea?"

He shook his head. She gave him an embarrassed smile and went about the business of brewing tea.

Gareth drank the water and the beer and was considering getting up to get more when she put another full glass of water on the table and removed the two empties.

"Thank you." The words came out a ragged croak.

Because he couldn't think of anything else to do, he ate the remainder of the bread and meat on his plate. He was feeling back to normal by the time she returned to the table bearing a plate filled with biscuits and more of the cream cakes she seemed to favor.

"Fairy cake?" she offered.

For a change, Gareth took one. The cool cream felt good on his raw throat.

They ate in companionable silence. When she'd finished her cake and had a sip of tea she looked up at him.

"I often cannot sleep. I believe Jessup knows that and makes sure there are tasty tidbits waiting."

"Jessup knows everything."

She laughed even though Gareth had not been jesting, a not unusual occurrence for him. The butler was considered the best of his breed. Gareth had overheard some toff discussing him as a nonpareil and lamenting his inability to poach him from Remington. So Gareth had poached him instead.

"How did you find the brewery?"

Now that he was not occupied with struggling for breath he noticed she was wearing a dressing gown, her masses of curly hair tucked beneath one of the improbable bonnets some women insisted on wearing even when they slept. Gareth could not abide wearing a head covering to bed.

Her raised eyebrows and enquiring look told him she was waiting for a response.

"It is in need of a good deal of money and work."

"Is that what you hoped for?"

"I believe it will suit our needs admirably. Mr. McElroy thinks otherwise."

She rested her chin on her hand, her brow furrowed. "And why is that?"

"He believes the structure is past the point of retrieval." Dec's exact words had been that the old brewery, "had gone to shite" but even Gareth knew that was unacceptable language in front of ladies.

"What will you do?"

"We have purchased the operation."

Her eyebrows jumped up. "Just like that?"

"Just like that."

Gareth could have told her more—how the owner's son, a well-regarded brewer whose livelihood had been all but decimated by his father's gambling, had wept openly at learning they would keep both he and his employees on—but he was finding the subject of the brewery slippery and elusive, like a piece of silk that kept sliding from his hands. He usually had the ability to concentrate with a fixity that made him deaf and blind to anything else. But right now he noticed her nightgown. It was buttoned up to her neck and was a gauzy white fabric that looked soft, fine, and was probably almost translucent. The dressing gown over it, which buttoned only slightly less high, was a practical garment of some fabric that looked rough enough to chafe if worn against skin. Gareth had a weak spot when it came to fine, luxurious materials; he was far more interested in the composition of his clothing than the cut. The fabric of her robe offended his sensibilities. It looked neither comfortable nor sumptuous. His hand, which lay on his thigh, twitched and he was contemplating leaning forward to test the texture with his thumb and forefinger when her voice brought him back to the present.

"Mr. Lockheart? Do you feel well?" She leaned closer, bringing both her person and the unpleasant robe nearer. He caught a whiff of her: a clean soap smell with only a hint of the fresh grass smell he had noticed before. She must have bathed but not washed her hair. The faint salty tang of female sweat sent a jolt up his spine and an undeniable message to his brain: he wanted her.

It was time for him to leave.

Gareth cleared his throat and looked away from her distracting person. "Did you have enough to eat and drink?"

She sat back a little at his cool tone but gave him a smile he was beginning to crave. "More than enough, thank you." She stood and made as if to clear their dishes.

"It is late, Mrs. Lombard, the servants can see to this in the morning."

She nodded. "You are correct, of course. No doubt they would prefer a mess to me mucking about with their system." She preceded him from the room and he carried the candle he'd brought with him. She had come without one as there were so many in the halls.

He kept a little behind her and could see the shape of her body beneath the ugly robe, which was more form fitting than either her habit or her morning dress. She had full, generous hips and it was easy to imagine them under his hands, his fingers gripping her soft flesh, holding her steady while he penetrated her and rode her to their mutual pleasure.

He was hard and *had* been almost since he'd recovered from his bout of coughing. His imagination—which had a will of its own tonight—visualized bedding her, watching her eyes darken as he brought her to crisis. He imagined experiencing the particular fulfillment that only came from pleasuring one's partner—making her scream and writhe—right before he brought himself to completion inside her.

Gareth clenched his jaw; his desire for her was unfortunate but he was a man who knew how to exert self-control. Now that he was aware of the danger she presented to his concentration he would see to it that episodes such as this one—the two of them alone, thinly clothed—did not occur again.

Tonight he would leave her at her door and then strip and vent his sexual energy on his punching bags.

They came to the entrance to the grand hall and he reached around her to open the door. She reached at the same moment and their hands met.

"Oh!" she tried to move back and found her hand held in his. She looked down and so did Gareth, perhaps even more surprised than she was. His body acted without his consent and he drew her toward him.

She came toward him without hesitation, looking up at him, her unbound breasts pressing against his chest. For once, she was not smiling and her lips were parted. Her pupils had flared; a sign of desire. Gareth knew his own eyes would be just as dark. He slid a hand under the curve of her jaw, his fingers skimming the unspeakably soft skin of her slender neck and then he lowered his mouth over hers.

***

His body was hard and warm, like stone made hot from the sun.

Serena knew she should have turned around the moment she found him in the kitchen. She could have left without him ever knowing. Indeed, he would not have suffered a painful and embarrassing coughing episode if she had. But his back had been to her when she'd entered and the sight of his body pressed against the heavy silk of his robe had caught at her. The fabric had flowed over his sculpted backside like molten silver and had drawn a throb of want from her that almost brought her to her knees. Her hands had ached to feel the texture of his body, the heat and shape of him.

His cool, speculative stare had not prepared her for this—for lips that were firm, soft, and hot and his slick, skilled, and determined tongue. He held her in a light grasp that did nothing to disguise the power in his sinuous frame. Fingertips teased and stroked the skin of her throat while he pushed closer, his hardness thrusting against her belly.

Serena closed her eyes and sighed at the feel of raw male arousal, sagging against the muscular column of his body. It had been a long, long time since she'd taken a lover, and never one as beautiful or unknowable as this.

He slid a second hand around her waist, his fingers kneading and massaging her uncorsetted body as he delved more deeply into her mouth, his rhythmic strokes making her hips buck against his. It would be so easy to simply give in to the long-repressed sensations he was drawing from her body without effort. She leaned in closer, her own hand snaking around his corded, narrow waist to rest at the top of his deliciously hard buttocks.

This is a mistake, Serena. You will not be able to stay here after this. The voice was shrill and annoying, and Serena ignored it.

He walked her slowly toward the wall, rubbing the stiff length of his erection against her as he pushed, until her shoulders hit the wall, but he kept coming.

Stroke.

Stroke.

Stroke.

His stiff length drew an answering pulse from her sex and she imagined his strong, insistent body entering hers, plunging into her with all the strength she knew he possessed. She could feel the struggle of will and desire that raged inside him. The slightest sign from her and he would take her right here, against the wall.

I can have him right now. Her inner muscles clenched and tightened and she pushed back against him the next time he thrust, her body already preparing to welcome his, her thighs slick with desire.

He made a low growling sound and bit her lower lip, sucking it into his mouth, pulling her so hard the pain was exquisite. His knee nudged between her thighs and she opened to him.

You will need to leave this place. It will be a disaster, for you, Serena, but especially for Oliver.

Her son's face—wearing a tragic expression—rose up in her mind and her eyes flew open; never had her ardor been extinguished so quickly.

She laid her hands on his upper arms, that part of her mind that wanted him thrilling at the feel of hard, sculpted body. But her son's face remained with her.

She pulled back and his lips left hers immediately. When she looked up, she saw he was staring at her, his chest rising and falling rapidly, his heart strong, steady, and fast against her hard nipples and sensitive breasts.

"Mr. Lockheart?" She sounded just as he had after his coughing fit.

He dropped his arms to his sides and stepped back, putting empty space between their bodies.

His eyes never wavered from hers. "I apologize, Mrs. Lombard."

She shook her head, unable to come up with anything coherent to say.

He turned away and opened the door, waiting until she'd gone through. The silent journey to the family quarters took a hundred years.

They stopped at her door and he bowed his head. "Good night, Mrs. Lombard."

"Good night, Mr. Lockheart." But he'd already turned away and his silk robe receded down the hall and disappeared around the corner in a flash of silver.

Back inside her room, Serena couldn't help wondering if it had all been a dream. But when she looked in the small mirror that hung beside the door her eyes sparkled and her lips were swollen and bruised, just as if she'd been thoroughly kissed.

Chapter Ten

Serena went down to breakfast almost three hours later than usual. Part of that was because she'd not gone back to sleep until dawn. The other part was because she hoped to avoid encountering Mr. Lockheart, a foolish impulse as she would have to see him again eventually.

But the breakfast room was empty when she arrived and Jessup was examining the contents of the chafing dishes when she entered.

"Good morning, Jessup. I am sorry to keep you waiting. A pot of coffee, please," she told the footman—Raymond—before going to fix herself a plate.

"Only Mr. Lockheart has been down and he left just after first light."

She looked up from the fresh dish of eggs Jessup must have just brought. "Oh?"

"He will not be back until tomorrow. He said to inform you he has gone to acquire some necessary materials for next week."

"Ah." Serena felt the relief of a prisoner who has received a temporary reprieve.

"He informed me Master Oliver is to have his dogs with him wherever he chooses and requested I advise as to the best place to feed them."

Serena grimaced. "Oh, poor Jessup. It's like the duke's house all over again."

Jessup permitted himself the ghost of a smile. "If I may say so, Mrs. Lombard, I have quite missed having dogs underfoot."

102

Serena laughed. "You lie majestically, Jessup. But thank you for your offer. I will send Oliver down to the kitchen later and you must feel free to instruct him."

"Very good, ma'am."

The door opened. Instead of the footman bearing coffee it was Mr. McElroy. Serena had to force a smile. She'd not been alone with the Irishman since that night outside Mr. Lockheart's window.

"Good morning, Mr. McElroy."

He grinned and bowed, as if they'd never been anything but the most cordial of friends. He was a dangerous man and Serena doubled her intention to avoid him and his friend.

"Coffee, if you please, Jessup."

The butler left the room and McElroy slumped into the chair across from her.

"You are not hungry?" she asked.

He gave a mock shiver. "Coffee first, food later. That is the civilized order of things." He glanced at her plate. "I see you subscribe to a different theory?"

She blushed, suddenly aware of her more than healthy appetite. "I'm afraid I have a weakness for food—especially when it is as well-prepared as it is here."

"We all have our weaknesses." His eyes slid down her torso and her face became hotter. He was a very attractive man but an air of dissipation clung to him that diminished his good looks and charm. Not to mention the memory of his behavior two nights ago.

The footman arrived with her coffee first and Serena poured them both a cup.

"You are kindness itself, madam." He raised the cup in a toast.

"I understand you are the owner of a brewery, Mr. McElroy." Too late she realized the error of her words. When would she have learned such a thing other than last night? *Late* last night, as the men had not returned from their journey until long after dinner.

His eyebrows rose and he looked arrested. "Do you now?" He glanced around the room, as if Mr. Lockheart might be lurking someplace. "Did Gareth just leave?"

The door opened and the coffee the Irishman had ordered arrived, followed by Jessup bearing a dish of something or other.

"Black pudding, sir."

McElroy rubbed his hands together. "Ah! And just in time, too." He cut Serena a sly look, and she knew that he accurately read the relief on her face. "Shall I dish you up a plate?"

Serena shivered. "No thank you, I'm afraid it is not a taste I have developed."

"Blood pudding is not popular where you are from?" He wore a smile but it did not reach his eyes. He would want to know what she was doing up in the middle of the night with his friend. He would want to know about *her*.

"Certainly not in the part of France I lived in, Mr. McElroy."

"Ah." He proceeded to fill his plate, but Serena knew this was only the beginning of his probing. She ate, hoping to finish her meal quickly. While she no longer had an appetite, to leave any food on her plate now would be to show weakness, which the sharp-eyed Irishman would not miss.

They ate in silence, until Serena was beginning to think she might be wrong, when he struck again.

"Tell me, Mrs. Lombard, how did a half-French sculptor's daughter come to meet the Duke of Remington's youngest son? That must be quite a story."

Serena almost laughed at the harmless look he tried to assume. She was not worried, she had told this particular version of her history many, many times.

"Robert, my husband, was part of the diplomatic corps and had been entrusted with information intended for British allies. He encountered a small group of men who'd deserted the *Grand Armee* and had established their own fiefdom in the small town not far from where I lived."

He nodded encouragingly.

"They attacked him and he was injured, but he managed to slay two of them before getting away. He lost consciousness in the forest and I found him and brought him back to the small chateau and hid him."

"What a remarkably romantic tale!" He sat back in his chair and daubed his full, sensual lips with his napkin, his eyes wide. "You must have placed yourself in grave danger—and in the face of your countrymen."

Even after all these years anger surged strong and fast at his words. "They were nothing but roving bands of thugs who raped and stole and terrorized the populace. Our region had been traded between warring nations for hundreds of years. It was not uncommon to hear four languages spoken of an evening in our tiny village."

"You will have to forgive me, Mrs. Lombard. Like so many people raised in England I suffer from a vast ocean of ignorance when it comes to the greater outside world."

Serena doubted this man missed anything—either in his world or outside of it. His disingenuous response was just another part of his act. He simmered with anger, no doubt a butt of many Englishmen for his Irish background, which was even more despised than her French heritage.

"I understand your husband was killed while spiriting you and your child to safety."

Serena was not surprised he knew her story, the details had been noised about widely enough almost a decade ago. Although she suspected he'd gathered his information far more recently than that.

"Yes. The man who was to ferry us across the Channel betrayed us. Robert gave his life so that I and our child might live." Perhaps he actually felt as abashed as he looked by the abrupt ending of her tale, but Serena doubted it. Either way, she was spared having to endure more of his probing by Jessup's arrival.

"I'm sorry, Mrs. Lombard, but the gentleman is here with the shrubs."

Serena swallowed back her sigh of relief and gave McElroy a cool smile before pushing back her chair.

"Please excuse me, Mr. McElroy."

He bowed, his hard green eyes crinkling. "Of course, of course—you have a job to do. No matter, I shall have plenty of time to get to know you better at dinner tonight."

That was exactly what Serena was afraid of.

***

105

Gareth hadn't needed to go all the way back to London for the supplies he wanted. But he *had* needed to go for his peace of mind. Even an hour beating the bags had not mitigated the woman's—*Mrs. Lombard's*—distracting influence on his body and mind. He had experienced this level of obsessiveness before, but always in relation to a mathematical problem or new project. Never a woman. He'd hoped relieving himself would have quenched his desire, but it had been an empty release.

He could not function this way, not with the new brewery, the impending canal project, and half a dozen other matters that required his undivided attention. He needed to see Venetia. She would help him assuage the nagging urge that was clouding his usually sharp brain.

He'd first gone to his London house, which had been waiting and ready as it always was, his servants well-trained and well-compensated to expect their employer at any hour of the day or night. He'd taken care of a few domestic matters and then gone out to a shop he knew specialized in automata. After spending an hour inspecting the new kiln at the pottery he was building—in a part of town so dangerous the land had been bought for a song—he'd gone home and bathed and changed into his evening clothing.

He left instructions to have his bed chamber prepared but ordered no dinner. He would dine with Venetia tonight if she was available. If she was not, he would eat somewhere on his own. Either way, he always slept in his own bed, never at the White House, Venetia's place of business.

The door to the inconspicuous white building opened before Gareth reached the top step. A footman garbed in sumptuous green velvet and gold lacing greeted him.

"Good evening, Mr. Lockheart."

"Good evening. I have come to see Mrs. Hensleigh."

The servant took Gareth's hat, gloves, and cane. "I will see if she is receiving. Will you have a seat in the parlor?"

Gareth stepped into the small, opulent room just off the foyer. He was struck, as he always was, how the brothel had all the appearance of every other house he'd ever entered—be it the home of a well-to-do merchant or proud, destitute aristocrat.

A Figure of Love

The ancient wood floor was polished to a high gloss and covered with rugs that glowed like jewels. Delicate furniture was arranged around a marble-clad fireplace that generated the exact amount of heat necessary to combat the damp chill of the building without being stifling. Paintings of idealized landscapes hung on cream-silk covered walls. All in all, it was the kind of room he had striven to replicate in his country house, but failed miserably.

The door opened and he turned.

"What an unexpected pleasure, Gareth." Venetia Hensleigh was one of the smallest women he had ever seen. From across the room she looked like a human doll with her guinea gold curls and wide blue eyes. But as she approached him, her hands outstretched, the look in her eyes and sensual curve of her bow-shaped lips was enough to make a man begin to harden. Or at least she had always done so before. But tonight, he was not aroused, merely relieved to see her.

"Venetia, thank you for seeing me on such short notice." He took her delicate hands in his and gave them a gentle squeeze before bowing over them. He had learned to accept and enjoy her touch, not an easy task for a man who avoided human contact the way others avoided angry hornets or rabid dogs.

"Come," she said, taking his arm before he could offer it. "Let us go somewhere more private."

Gareth knew he was the only man she invited into her inner sanctum because she'd told him so, years ago, when he'd first approached her. He was not unaware of the honor she accorded him and knew many of her patrons had offered outrageous sums to spend only one night with the notoriously private madam of the most exclusive brothel in London.

Venetia led him through her private study, where a panel concealed a door to her quarters.

"It has been some time, Gareth. Where have you been keeping yourself?"

"Business in the north and also the new estate in Kent."

"Ah yes," she said, cutting a glance up at him, her head not reaching his shoulder. "I should tell you that Sandy Featherstone has been noising your name about."

He gave her a look of surprise. "He came here?"

She chuckled. "Lord no, he doesn't have two shillings to rub together. Keller saw him at Beacon's new hell. I gather he was playing deep while in his cups." She shook her head. "If I had known you'd employed him I would have warned you. Who recommended him?"

"Beech."

She groaned. "That man is a delightful architect but a fool in every other way. If you are looking for help at your country home I would be happy to recommend somebody."

She stopped and Gareth opened the door that led to her library, the room that had inspired his at Rushton Park. Venetia Hensleigh was a notable collector of first editions and had knocked the ceiling out of the building to construct a library that rivaled that of any great house.

She released him and went to a sideboard laden with decanters. "Would you like to try a new whiskey? I've only managed to latch on to one barrel."

"Please."

Venetia was the only woman he knew who smoked and drank hard spirits. She was considered a connoisseur of both. She brought two glasses and then moved toward the oxblood leather couch that occupied a place of honor in front of the mammoth fireplace. Gareth had a fondness for this particular item of furniture as they had enjoyed several very memorable evenings on it. But tonight it did not send blood coursing to his groin, nor did his breathing quicken with anticipation of the evening ahead.

"Sit," she said, grinning up at him and shoving him onto the couch, but—oddly—taking the chair beside it instead of sitting next to him. "You have come to say goodbye."

Gareth should not have been surprised by her insight; Venetia had always read him as easily as any of the thousands of books that lined her walls.

She warmed her glass between her hands. "Tell me about her."

To his horror, his cheeks heated—as if she were rubbing his face between her small, wickedly skilled hands.

She chuckled, a laugh far too low for a woman her size. "I do not think I have seen you blush before, my friend. At least not unless it was from exertion."

Gareth smiled at her teasing reminder of their many—and adventurous—sexual encounters.

"Ah, and one of your very rare smiles, as well. I am fortunate this evening."

Gareth took a sip and considered her words. It was true that he rarely smiled. Each time he did he was immediately struck with terror, as if he would be made to pay dearly for such an indulgence.

"I did not know I was coming to say goodbye, Venetia. As usual, you are aware of my desires and needs before I am."

"I have been sensing it for some time. It is seven years we have been lovers, Gareth."

He nodded. It was a long time, yet that first night was as fresh in his mind as if it had been yesterday. He felt an ache of something—regret? Sadness?—as he looked in her blue eyes. Eyes that shielded their contents from the world as skillfully as his. They were two of a kind, able to give affection but not love.

"Her name is Serena Lombard."

As usual, Venetia knew everything. "Ah, the sculptor."

"You have seen her work?"

"Not only that, I have commissioned her work, not that she knows where it went." Venetia gestured to a sculpture that was perhaps three feet tall. He had noticed it before, but never looked closely. He stood and went to it.

It was a woman, the stone grainy, rather than smooth, the eyes heavy lidded and long; she wore an odd headdress with a serpent crown.

"It is Seshat, the Egyptian scribe of the gods."

Gareth saw a sticklike item clenched in one hand. "What is she holding?"

"A palm-leaf rib, which the ancients were said to use as quills."

He brushed the back of his knuckles across the statue's shoulder. "Limestone?"

"Yes."

The statue was alien and had an odd kind of potency that drew one's eyes. It took some effort to pull his gaze away and resume his seat.

"Why did you engage her?"

"Need you ask? A woman sculptor? Naturally I had to champion her cause. Why did *you* hire her?"

He shrugged. "Featherstone or Beech chose her; I do not know which. I have engaged her to design the pleasure gardens around Rushton Park."

"I knew she occasionally designed small town gardens but nothing so vast as a country estate."

"She initially resisted, saying the project was too large. But something must have changed her mind."

She raised her eyebrows. "Indeed."

Gareth frowned. "Why do you say it like that?"

"Do you really not know, Gareth?"

"I can only assume—based on your sly expression—you believe her decision has something to do with me."

"You sound skeptical."

"She is the daughter-in-law of a duke, and an accomplished and attractive woman." She cocked her head and Gareth sighed. "I can see you are intent on teaching me a lesson, Venetia, and employing the Socratic Method to do so. Why not just spell it out for me, I am a simple man."

"Oh, bosh! Shame on you for trying to sham me, Gareth."

He shrugged and took a sip, too unsettled to play games with her. Games she was far better at playing in any case.

"She is an exceptionally vibrant woman, and . . . demonstrative and loving—at least with her son." He gave her a pointed look. "You know how it is with me—you are the same. I cannot give her those things, nor can I be a proper father to her son."

"You are a wealthy, powerful, and attractive man, Gareth. You are also loyal and caring, as much as you deny it. That is an assessment from a woman who knows men. Perhaps I am jaded, but I do not think much of romantic love. Love is selfish and, unlike passion, has expectations beyond the moment. I know you are a good friend, and friendship—in my opinion—is far more valuable than what you think of as love."

Gareth wanted to believe her, but it was not his way to accept any conclusion without proof. But Venetia had an answer for that, as well, as if she knew his mind. Which he thought she might, at least better than anyone he'd ever met, and that included Declan.

"Even if you reject that argument, there are others that are equally, if not more, persuasive. She is a widow who I believe supports herself and her son without the assistance of her husband's family. It is not inconceivable she would like a husband to share her burdens—or remove them entirely. She would give you the connections to society you have long wanted and you clearly find her attractive. What is the problem?"

Gareth didn't know. The same logical arguments had crossed his own mind, yet there was a part of the equation that was missing. And it was more than a little frustrating.

"I don't know," he finally said, shaking his head.

Venetia's eyes narrowed and her expression suddenly became very knowing.

"What?" He leaned forward. "What is it? You know something, I can see it."

She smiled and shook her head.

"Venetia . . ." he let his tone speak for itself, but she just laughed.

"This is a side of you I have never seen."

"What side?" She was beginning to irritate him.

She set her glass on the table beside her chair and unwound her small, sinuous body and came toward him.

He swallowed at the look on her face. He had not come here for carnal pleasure, but this woman was considered one of the most sexually skilled females in London and he realized, quite suddenly, he would regret the end of their association—because that was what tonight was: the end. Not just because of the sex, but because she knew him. He had a moment of regret that he did not know her half as well, but she had put a wall between most of her life and him, and he was not the kind of person to force his way in. At least he wasn't with her.

She placed a hand on each of his knees, her white skin very pale against his black pantaloons. "I will miss you, Gareth, more than I would have expected possible when you came to see me that evening so long ago." She pushed his unyielding thighs wide and slid to her knees between them. His breathing roughened and his eyes fastened on her

111

plump lips, which she wet with her wicked pink tongue. "I was honored to be the one you chose to give your virginity to, Gareth. And, in a way, you were my very first. Certainly not the first man to have my body, but the first and only lover I have taken voluntarily." Her hands slid up his thighs but stopped short of the hard ridge. His eyelids fluttered and it took monumental effort to keep from thrusting into her hands. His body wanted her even as his mind knew her clever mouth could only offer temporary relief.

"I know you did not come here for this tonight, but I am not good at saying goodbye, so I will let my actions speak for me." Her lids were heavy as her hands kneaded and massaged his taut thighs. "Close your eyes, Gareth, and let me ease your mind, at least for a little while."

Gareth laid his hands over hers, the gesture staying her actions. "Perhaps it is time we moved our association to another level, Venetia." He patted the cushion beside him. "I may not need the same things from you, but I value our acquaintance more than ever. Please, sit and talk with me, help me understand this new, puzzling development."

She hesitated, but somehow Gareth knew it was not because she didn't wish it—but because such intimacy frightened her.

She finally smiled and sat beside him, her small hand still in his. "What would you like to know, Gareth?"

Chapter Eleven

Sometime in the night before the event those in the village were calling "Boulder Day" it began to rain. Not a gentle summer rain, but a torrential downpour that began just before dusk and continued on through the night.

It was still raining when Serena woke just before dawn and parted the heavy velvet drapes to peek outside. Her room, like most of the big suites that comprised the family wing, had windows overlooking the south side of the house. The parterre gardens, which they'd just begun to lay out with shrubs this past week, were below water, the freshly turned dirt a brown slick sheet that seemed to be sliding slowly down the gentle slope.

Serena let out a few choice French words under her breath and quickly dressed. She was headed for the servants' wing when she encountered Jessup already talking with half a dozen grooms and other servants.

"Good morning, Mrs. Lombard, I was just instructing the men to spread the waxed tarps you had delivered."

Serena smiled. "You are too good, Jessup. That was exactly why I was coming to find you." She turned to the assembled men. "The clusters of plants will be fine, but I'm afraid our trenches may already have washed away. Please cover what you can."

The men dispersed and she turned to Jessup.

"You really *do* think of everything, don't you?"

His eyelids lowered slightly to show her words pleased him. "I know you would probably like a hot cup of coffee."

"I would do murder for a cup. Don't bother bringing it up for me, I'll take it in the kitchen."

"Mr. Lockheart is in the breakfast room, ma'am."

"He is?" she asked, stupidly.

"And I must confess it was he who recommended the tarps."

"You fibber, Jessup! Very well, I shall join him. Thank you." She'd seen Lockheart since his return from London, of course, but they'd managed never to be alone together. She had taken to coming to breakfast a little later and she believed he accommodated her by dining even earlier. That way they'd managed to only see each other in the company of either McElroy or Oliver, with whom she'd found Lockheart closeted three nights earlier when she went to visit her son in the school room.

"Mama!" Oliver had shouted, "Look what Mr. Lockheart brought." Spread out on the table were a number of automata, more than a few of them in parts. Oliver answered before she could ask.

"Mr. Lockheart and I are taking them apart so that we might study them."

Serena risked a look at her employer, who was regarding her with the cool look she now knew could hide any number of things.

"Look, Mama," Oliver grabbed her hand and pulled her toward the table, interrupting the awkward tableau. "See, this one uses a different type of spring, and this one—"

She'd spent a bewildering hour being lectured about the internal workings of toys. Since then, she'd seen him every evening, as he came to supervise Oliver's work as it progressed.

And of course she saw him at dinner, where McElroy dominated the conversation and made sure Serena was aware of his continued observation and investigation into her background.

Mr. Lockheart also came out to the work site every day, looking and observing, but rarely making any comments. And once, he'd wandered into the stall she used in the stables, and then quickly excused himself when he's seen she was working. Naturally that had been the end of her efforts for *that* day.

She stopped not far from the breakfast room to check her hastily dressed hair in a large hallway mirror. Strands had escaped and were curling in the extreme humidity, but it was not an embarrassing wreck. Yet. She straightened the lace fichu she wore tucked into her old green morning dress and smoothed down her skirt. She would do.

Mr. Lockheart rose when she entered the room. "Good morning, Mrs. Lombard."

"Good morning, Mr. Lockheart." She smiled at Raymond, who was already heading toward the door in anticipation of her order. "Jessup is bringing me coffee, Raymond." She turned back to the other man. "Please, do keep eating."

Serena absently piled food on her plate, imagining his eyes burning into her back. But when she turned, he was looking at a newspaper laid out beside his plate.

When she sat, he folded the sheet and pushed it aside.

"Thank you for having the foresight to spread the tarps."

"I wish I had thought of it last night."

Serena buttered a hot roll. "I didn't realize it was raining until three or four o'clock." She heaped preserves onto her bread, marveling at the insipid conversation when all she could think about was how luscious his body had felt. She swallowed, alarmed by the way she was salivating, like a jungle predator eyeing a tasty morsel. Oh, she was revolting.

"This is showing no signs of letting up," he said, clearly unaware of the turmoil taking place inside her.

"No, it is a dark sky. I daresay it will be some days before it dries out enough. Obviously the moving of the rock will need to be postponed. Will you stay?" She couldn't decide what she wanted his answer to be. Her body rejoiced when he was near but her mind—as willful as it was—alternated between celebration and terror.

"There will be no traveling in this weather, at least none that I care to do." He nodded to Jessup, who'd entered with a fresh pot of coffee. "I have plenty to occupy me indoors."

So did Serena. She'd run behind on her current sculpture, too distracted by her brief clutch with her employer to risk working on expensive marble. Instead, she'd studied the submissions she'd solicited for the other four sculptures. While she would have liked to provide *all* the work, she knew it was not only unrealistic and unwise—variety in art was always to be desired—it would also be selfish. She'd sent her ideas to the Royal Academy, as well as to several of her fellow sculptors. It was good to spread the wealth.

"And will you sculpt, Mrs. Lombard?"

This unprecedented display of curiosity from the normally uninterested man surprised her. "I may, it depends if the muse cooperates." She could see her words intrigued him and she explained. "It is best not to work unless I am able to give all my attention to the piece at hand. Anything less than total concentration is a recipe for disaster, and lots of ruined, expensive materials."

"I have recently seen one of your pieces."

"Oh?"

"An Egyptian piece."

"You saw Seshat?"

He nodded.

Serena could hardly believe it. "That was an anonymous commission. I was paid in advance," she gave him a wry smile, "which is very unusual in the art world." She bit her tongue, dying to ask him where he'd seen it.

"I found the piece to be. . . mesmerizing."

Again he had surprised her—and pleased her. Her cheeks burned as she looked up, shy at his praise. "Thank you. It was a difficult commission because I never knew how the owner felt about the piece." It was as much fishing as she felt comfortable doing.

"I do not think she would mind me telling you that she treasures it."

She? Twin flares of pleasure and jealousy burnt inside her. Was it his lover? And why would a person wish for such anonymity? How was it that everything about this man seemed to be shrouded in mystery?

"If it is not too—" he paused, as if searching for the correct word, the hesitation not characteristic of him. "Intrusive, I would like to know something of the process of sculpting."

The degree of pleasure his question generated should have frightened her, instead, she was just gratified by his show of interest.

"My father trained me as his father had trained him, which is to say in the manner of most sculptors. You begin with years of molding and casting and then move along to some of the less-critical parts of a master's work." She smiled. "I am more of a craftsman than artist, I'm afraid. I have never seen the spark of genius in my work." She shrugged. "But it gives me joy all the same."

"How does one recognize a spark of genius?"

"Ah, that is the question. I could not describe it, but I know it when I see it." She thought how she might communicate what she meant. "The sketchbook you have in the glass case—the one belonging to Leonardo, do you recall his drawings toward the back of the journal?"

His eyes went vague, as if he were inspecting the contents of his memory. When his vision cleared, he said, "There are several of an old man and one of a young woman. Those?"

"Yes, those. He is able with a few lines to elevate the ordinary to the sublime."

He paused, moving his uneaten piece of ham from one side of the plate, and then back to the other. This was interesting. Was he fidgeting? She had never seen him act anything less than cool and composed before. Why now? What could—

"Your sketches do not elevate the ordinary to the sublime?"

"There are some very good ones of Oliver when he was a boy, but—by and large—I am far more expressive with stone or even clay. I am not, like Leonardo, a Renaissance genius, able to dabble gloriously in any medium."

He nodded but made no response. So, that was that. A brief burst of conversation with a man who was on her mind far more often than was healthy.

***

By that evening it seemed as if it had been raining for days. Gareth spent a large part of the afternoon with Oliver in the schoolroom. Mrs. Lombard did not appear and Gareth wondered if she was avoiding him on purpose.

Oliver was a very clever boy with an aptitude for science and math and Gareth relaxed in his presence more than he did with anyone else other than Dec. The boy was not a chatterbox and spent a good deal of his time on solitary pursuits. Gareth believed that was by choice rather than circumstance. He was as Gareth might have been, had his life taken a different path.

As Gareth dressed himself for dinner, he considered Dec's question from earlier in the day.

"How long are you planning to stay here, old man?"

The nervy Irishman had sought him out hours after breakfast, making Gareth wonder—not for the first time—how his friend spent most of his days. He knew how he spent a good part of his nights, having learned Declan had already made conquests in the village and carried on with his normal enthusiasm at the local inn.

He'd been working on the brewery ledgers when Dec had interrupted. He put his quill in the standish and leaned back in his chair. "I plan to stay until we complete the berm. And you?"

Dec shrugged, tilting back his head until he was facing the ceiling. "It would be hell to travel in this," he waved to the windows without looking down. "I can't even be arsed to drive into town." He brought his head down slowly, his sharp green eyes focusing on Gareth. "You've taken to the boy."

"I have," Gareth agreed.

"And his mother?"

"What of his mother?"

Dec's mouth twisted, but he said nothing.

Gareth felt a frisson of irritation at the knowing look in his eyes. Why was it that the people he knew best—all two of them—seemed to think he was some sort of child or village idiot when it came to the opposite sex?

Probably because he was.

"Out with it, Declan."

Dec shrugged hugely and his eyes widened. "What?"

"You do not like her."

"That is not true."

"You will parse words with me even though you know how much I dislike the pastime. Very well, you do not *trust* her."

Again he shrugged. "I don't trust anyone. Except you."

Gareth knew that all too well. He believed his friend was suspicious to his own detriment. But it was possible he himself was not suspicious

118

enough. It was tiresome to think of such matters, and ultimately unimportant. What could people take from him other than money? And he could always make more of that, as his history had shown over and over.

Gareth straightened the already straight pile of ledgers that rested to one side of the open book before looking up. "I will be staying here until I have seen to the shifting of the rock."

Dec nodded his head slowly, his eyes no longer laughing. "Very well. I shall remain until it is decent to travel, and then I will see to some business in London."

"The pottery or the docks?"

"Something new," he said, his smile mysterious.

Gareth knew better than to ask what he meant when he was in one of these moods. He would give his life for Declan McElroy, but that did not mean the man didn't often make him positively murderous with his moody and unpredictable behavior.

***

The last plate had been cleared away and Serena stood. "I will leave you gentlemen to your port."

"Perhaps you might share our port with us tonight, Mrs. Lombard?"

Serena looked across at the Irishman with more than a little surprise. "I beg your pardon?" She glanced at Lockheart, but he appeared happy to spectate.

McElroy gave her a grin she knew was meant to disarm women. It did not work with her. "It is a wretched night yet still early." His grin grew. "Not a good night for evening strolls. Why don't we retire to somewhere more comfortable and keep one another entertained? Isn't that the way of things in the country?"

He'd already let her know he did not like her. What was he up to now?"

Serena gave him a smile laced with false regret. "I hope you are not looking to me to play the piano or sing. I'm afraid my accomplishments do not lie in that direction."

He laughed. "I had something less elevated in mind. Do you play cards, Mrs. Lombard?"

Mr. Lockheart gave his friend a sharp look, which he ignored.

What was going on here?

"I play Cribbage and Piquet. Is that what you mean?"

His mobile mouth tilted up on one side. "Something like that." He turned to Lockheart. "What say you, Gare? It's been a while since we have pitted our wits against one another."

Lockheart gave his friend a long, silent, and not very friendly look. Serena thought it was the equivalent of another man's version of telling him to go to hell. But in the end, he nodded.

"If you wish."

McElroy clapped his hands together and rubbed them enthusiastically. "Excellent! I believe I saw a smallish table in the library that could be put to the purpose." He nodded to one of the footmen lining the wall. "Have the port brought to the library. And one of you fetch a deck of cards from my room. Pierson will show you where one is." He offered Serena his arm and she laid a hand on his sleeve, glancing at Lockheart.

McElroy grinned at his friend. "Sorry, old chap, you walk alone tonight."

The next few hours were some of the oddest in her life—a life that held no shortage of odd moments. There was a tension between the two men she had not noticed before, and there were uncomfortable currents in the room she did not understand.

Once in the library, a table was moved closer to the fire, a shawl was fetched for Serena, and cards arrived.

McElroy broke the seal on a new pack and commenced to shuffle them in a manner that proclaimed his familiarity with gambling louder than words would have done.

"How would you feel about learning a new game, Mrs. Lombard. It is called *vingt-et-un*."

Mr. Lockheart crossed his arms but made no sound.

"Oh, I've heard of that."

"Ah, I thought you might have." His smirk reminded her of a serpent.

Serena had no idea what his aggressively knowing look meant and couldn't help wondering if he was foxed. She hadn't noticed how much he'd drank during dinner, but, then again, she hadn't been paying attention to him. Why would she when Gareth Lockheart was in the room? He looked like a statue, as usual, but she would have sworn he was furious.

"The rules are very simple—you wish to accumulate *vingt-et-un*, but nothing greater than that. I will give you two cards, and you may ask for more. The ace has a special role in that it can represent either one point, or eleven." His hands, which had been shuffling the cards nonstop, halted. He glanced around. "But wait, we have no stakes."

"No."

McElroy and Serena both turned to Lockheart.

"What's that you say, Gare?"

"I said no stakes. There will be no gambling. Deal the cards, Declan."

The men locked eyes and it was the Irishman who first broke away. He chuckled and shrugged, his hands resuming their rhythmic motions. "I will abide by the will of our host, Mrs. Lombard. You will just have to image the excitement, the air thick with tension as men—and women! —wager their fortunes, their ancestors' homes, their very lives." The fire was not the only thing crackling in the room by the time he ceased speaking.

"Now," he said, his voice back to its normal tone and register. "There are many variations of the game, but I will play the one I prefer. The first card face down," he dealt three cards, "and you would look at it—oh, but do not let anyone else see," he chided when Serena picked up her card, a four of tiles. "Now, put it down." She noticed Lockheart had not uncrossed his arms or looked at his card. His eyes were fixed on his friend. "At this point," McElroy continued, "You would place a bet and I, as the dealer, would be responsible for covering your money. If you did well, *you* might become the bank later in the evening. Here is your second card." He dealt three, these face up. Serena was dealt a seven, giving her eleven, and Lockheart a ten, and McElroy a two.

"Would you like another card, Mrs. Lombard?"

"Yes, please."

He dealt her an ace. She frowned: twenty-two or twelve.

"Another?"

"Yes."

121

He dealt her a ten.

"Oh, bother!" she said, laughing.

"For shame, Mrs. Lombard. I would now be raking your coins across the table to my pile." He turned to Lockheart. "Gareth?"

A vein jumped in Lockheart's temple, but he finally uncrossed his arms and looked at the bottom card. He shook his head.

"Ah," McElroy grinned. "What is Mr. Lockheart's hidden card? That ten of his makes me nervous. I must assume the worst, Mrs. Lombard— that Mr. Lockheart has a second ten. That means I must take another card."

He flipped over his hidden card, which was a ten, for a total of twelve. Serena would have thought he'd wanted another card in any case.

His next card was a six. "Eighteen." He looked from Serena, to his friend. "What do you think, Mrs. Lombard? Does he have a ten hidden? Or a five?"

"A five? Surely he would have taken another card if he had only fifteen."

McElroy smiled, his eyes never leaving Lockheart's. "Is that true, Gareth?"

Lockheart sighed and McElroy laughed. "I will stand."

Lockheart flipped over his hidden card.

"Twenty!" Serena clapped her hands, happier about his victory than was entirely warranted. Lockheart himself did not seem to care one way or the other. Of course there was no money at stake, which might have accounted for his lack of reaction.

McElroy scraped up the used cards and deposited them in a pile face down. "I shall deal the remainder of this deck and then *you* will be the dealer, Mrs. Lombard."

Serena found she was enjoying the game by the third or fourth hand, even though she had only won once. Lockheart, on the other hand, seemed to win each time, and look just as happy about it as he had the first time.

McElroy chatted almost nonstop as he dealt, easily able to do three or even four things at one time.

"I see you have a large block of marble in the stables, Mrs. Lombard but have not yet commenced carving?"

"That is correct. I am still making sketches."

He gave her a wicked leer as he dealt the first round of cards. "Do you need a model to commence your work, by any chance?"

She slid Lockheart a look and saw he finally appeared interested.

"Are you volunteering your services, Mr. McElroy?"

"I would not be averse to donating my time—in the interest of art, of course."

She tilted her head and studied him with exaggerated care. "Yes," she said after a long pause, "I think you would be perfect."

He preened, shooting his friend a not-so-subtle look of triumph. "I understand it is to be a classical piece. Perhaps Apollo? Or maybe Bacchus?"

She lifted the bottom card up enough to see it: an ace, and then gave him a sweet smile. "Actually, it is to be a rendering of Judith beheading Holofernes."

The expression on his face was priceless, but not as priceless as Mr. Lockheart's reaction. He threw back his head and laughed, the sound deep and rich and utterly enchanting for being so extremely rare. He looked . . . radiant, like a younger man. and Serena could not tear her eyes away.

McElroy gave him a wry smile, taking his friend's laughter with unexpected good grace.

"I suppose I deserved that."

Lockheart nodded and wiped his eyes. "Yes, I suppose you did, Dec."

The look the Irishman gave Serena was, for the first time, one of respect.

***

The only reason Gareth was tolerating Dec's behavior was because he wanted to see where he was leading.

Actually, that was a lie. He was also far too fascinated by Mrs. Lombard to leave her alone in the infamous rake's company. It had been Gareth's experience that women could not resist the big, charming Irishman; the thought of Mrs. Lombard being unable to resist Declan displeased him.

123

Since returning from London, he'd felt an odd, enhanced awareness of her that felt almost instinctual. He knew animals sensed each other that way but had never expected such heightened sensitivity of himself. It was invigorating and enervating at the same time. It led to lots of sessions in his private boxing arena. And right now it was making him think of going a few rounds with his best friend.

Declan knew how much he hated cards and he certainly knew how much he hated to be reminded of the part such games had played in his life. Cards were pain, and his friend was not usually so cruel as to rub it in his face. So why he'd orchestrated this evening was a mystery. Gareth supposed he should have asked him earlier in the day exactly why he did not trust Mrs. Lombard. But he'd not wanted to give him what he'd been seeking: a dust up. Yes, he recognized when Declan was spoiling for an argument or fight and he refused to indulge him.

Some of the tension in the room dissipated after Mrs. Lombard's master stroke about her sculpture and the subsequent hands passed without incident.

When Dec got to the last six or seven cards he spread them out face down on the table.

"Not enough for a hand," he said, "but there are other games." His eyes slid from hers to Gareth's and back. "Do you know what these cards are, Mrs. Lombard?"

"What do you mean?"

"Do you know what is hidden, which cards were not played?"

Her forehead wrinkled in a manner that charmed Gareth. He had noticed that happening quite a bit of late: finding even her smallest mannerisms and characteristics charming. She shook her head after considering Dec's question. "No, I do not know—how could I?"

Gareth envied her innocence in this matter.

She looked from him to Dec. "Do you know?" she asked him.

Which of course was the question Dec had wanted all along. He closed his eyes. "A king and nine of hearts, a three, seven, and ten of spades, and an eight, nine, and ace of clubs." He opened his eyes and turned to Gareth. "Am I close, Gare?"

He hated his friend in that moment. "A nine of clubs, not hearts, and a six and eight of spades, not clubs."

McElroy flipped the cards over and Mrs. Lombard stared.

"But, how?" She looked up at Gareth, her stunned expression forcing an answer out of him.

"I have a good memory."

Dec chuckled as he scraped up the cards and handed her the deck. "Mr. Lockheart has a *very* good memory."

"But you were almost correct, too."

"I am good enough with a single deck." He smirked at Gareth. "We've tested Gare and he's accurate up to six decks."

Serena shook her head. "I don't understand."

"It's simple. You see—"

Gareth rarely raised his voice, but he wished to do so now—not that he yielded to that wish. Instead he spoke even softer than he usually did, savoring the control he had over his emotions and how he chose to display them, lamenting the fact he could not control Dec's behavior as easily.

"Do you have any reason for showcasing my freakish abilities this evening, Declan?"

Dec grinned and shrugged. "Not any that I can think of."

"But that is a *wonderful* skill, Mr. Lockheart. Whyever would you call it freakish?" She looked at him with the same wonder people had always displayed when they learned of his ability. Well, not *everyone* had looked at him that way. Certainly not the card players and hell-owners he had sharped.

She cocked her head in a way that was . . . he struggled for the word, and then avoided it when it came slamming into his brain: adorable. It was a word he'd never used before, not even for small animals or children or neat and tidy columns of figures. He wanted to slap his forehead with his palm, the way he did when he'd made a foolish mistake with some formula or equation and then suddenly saw the light. Except he had not seen the light. In fact, he was more in the dark than ever. Not only that, but he realized she'd spoken while he was experiencing his non-epiphany.

"I beg your pardon, Mrs. Lombard?"

"I wondered if this game might not be tedious for you?"

He almost laughed. Tedious? No. Evocative of hateful, terrifying memories? Yes.

"Not at all, Mrs. Lombard. Please," he gestured to the cards she held clasped with two hands.

And so it went, until the enormous longcase clock behind them began to boom midnight.

"My goodness," she said, looking up from the hand on the table, yet another she would overbid and play with absolutely no concept of strategy, but a good deal of cheer and open enjoyment. Gareth had made himself numb to her playing long before, or he would have gone mad. "I had no idea it was so late." She glanced at the windows, which were covered by drapes. "Do you suppose it is still raining?"

Declan went to peer out the closest window. "It has slowed, but not ceased."

She heaved a sigh, and Gareth couldn't help appreciating its effect on her bodice.

"I should have known we'd been too lucky with our weather." She stood. "I do hope you will excuse me, but it is well past my bedtime."

Gareth preceded her to the door and opened it, memories of the other night, and another door, assaulting him. "Good night, Mrs. Lombard."

When he closed the door, he turned to his erstwhile friend. Declan was in front of the fireplace, jabbing at a log with the toe of a very expensive boot.

"What was that about?" The fury he'd held in check all evening began to break free of its bindings.

Declan shrugged. "What? Playing games and cards and such are all there is to do out in the middle of this cow pasture."

"You, of all people, know how I feel about such a pastime."

"Yes, well, it's about time you got over that."

"Who are you to say what I should get *over*?"

Declan turned away from the fire, his face red from more than the heat. "*I'm* the one who keeps you from making a fool of yourself."

"Since when? You are not my keeper or my conscience and I have not needed your protection or advice arranging my affairs for many years. And if I *were* to seek a moral compass it most certainly would not be you." He snorted, giving free rein to his anger. "You have never been a beacon of morality and social responsibility and have only become worse with each passing year. As a matter of fact, your appetites seem to have overwhelmed every other part of you. Have you saved any of the money that has passed through your hands, Declan? You own no house, no land, nothing of any value. Everything you have earned goes directly to drinking, gambling, whoring—"

"And what bloody business is that of yours?" Declan's voice was so loud Gareth thought they could probably hear it in the kitchen. His eyes had become wild and his face a dangerous crimson. "Just what are you saying? That I do not do my part?" His ginger brows plummeted like twin comets, until they formed an auburn 'V'. "Is that what this it is all about?"

The conversation had developed into an obscurantist's fantasy. Gareth had not felt so frustrated in years, and managing frustration was not his forte. "Good God! Just what the devil *are* we are talking about, Declan?"

Declan blinked as his pickled brain translated Gareth's words. That was when Gareth realized just how drunk his friend was, and he probably should not even be speaking to him when he was in such a condition.

"I'm saying that I know you don't need me—I serve no purpose in this business."

Gareth gave a huff of disgust. "You are cupshot, Declan. Go to bed and sleep it off."

"You're off, are you?" Dec's expression was sly and ugly. "Where to, I wonder?"

Gareth closed the gap between them in one long stride. "Say it."

Declan sneered. "You say it! Say the real reason you have no time for this discussion. Not because I've had a little to drink. It's because of her."

Gareth's head pulsed. "What about her? Just what is it? Why do you dislike her so?" A thought hurtled from the dark recesses of his mind and exploded like a fireworks display. "You're angry because she might prefer *me* to you."

Declan's face became even redder, which Gareth hadn't believed possible. He appeared to struggle to find the breath to speak. "I am *not* angry," he yelled. "But if I *were*, it would not be about a bloody woman! It would be about *you*, and how you are too fookin' naïve to know when a woman is using you."

"Using me? She is my employee, Declan. How is that using me?"

Dec gave him a look of loathing; a look he'd not turned on Gareth in over two decades.

"You're the one whose brains are addled and you're behaving like a dog in rut and her—well, she is like a bitch spreading—"

Gareth's fist made the decision all on its own, connecting soundly with the right side of Declan's jaw. The heavier man reeled back, his arms wind milling for balance and not finding it. Instead, he staggered drunkenly and collapsed, luckily, into the chair a few steps behind him. Pity and anguish surged inside Gareth for his friend. His hand hurt like hell, but not as badly as his conscience. Declan had put back the better part of a bottle of port during their play, not to mention the wine he'd drunk at dinner and the whiskey right before. Not only that, but he was bigger and slower and far less fit than Gareth.

He was also out cold.

"Declan?"

A loud, raspy sigh greeted his question.

Gareth went closer, but not too close. Declan fought dirty and Gareth wouldn't put it past the other man to lure him close and then attack. But the Irishman's head lolled in a way that was too boneless to be feigned, and his stertorous breathing was that of a man deep in a drunk.

Gareth kneaded his throbbing temples, the chaos of his thoughts more painful than the headache he felt brewing. He could not recall the last time he'd fought with Declan—surely back when they were both in short pants—nor could he recall the reason. Not that he knew the reason for *this* argument. Could the other man really believe he was not an integral part of their mutual success? Had Gareth done or said something to make Declan feel less than valued? He could not think of anything, but, then, dealing with others was not an activity he was comfortable with, even when the person was his best friend.

He wished now that he had told the other man how *Declan* was the one who held it all together, that without him—his strength of character, wit, charm, and foresight—Gareth and all their bloody enterprises would fly apart, just as Gareth's thoughts were prone to doing. It was true Gareth saw the potential in the businesses they rescued and resuscitated, but he often lost interest after the endeavor was sleek and healthy, and it was Declan who saw to such matters as selling or operating the resultant businesses. No, Gareth was not the one responsible for their success, they were a team. And without each other? Gareth did not want to travel down that path.

"Bloody hell, Dec, what has happened with us?" Gareth whispered, shaking his head.

But there was no answer.

Gareth filled his lungs with as much air as they would hold and then slowly expelled it. His friend was in trouble—in pain—and for whatever reason, Gareth seemed to be at the heart of it.

Chapter Twelve

Gareth was reading the last of the ledgers when there was a light knock on the door. Actually, he was *staring* at the pages but seeing Declan's face again as it had been the night of their argument—the last time he'd spoken to his friend, who'd left without warning early the following morning. Gareth's concentration—usually as solid as the Rock of Gibraltar—had been non-existent in the days since.

"Come in," he called.

The door opened a crack. "Mr. Lockheart?"

Gareth removed the spectacles he used in order to read the cramped columns of numbers. "Come in, Oliver."

The boy entered and closed the door. "I hope I'm not interrupting, sir."

Gareth closed the ledger. "No, you're not interrupting anything—at least nothing important. What can I do for you?"

"I wondered—" he broke off, his round cheeks—so like his mother's—darkening. "Well, sir, I was wondering if you might wish to go fishing."

Gareth's eyebrows shot up. "Fishing?"

Oliver seemed not to hear the incredulity in his voice. Instead, he nodded, his face wreathed in eagerness. "Yes, there is a pool just upriver from where you and Mama are making the lake. It is my favorite spot to fish. And to swim, when it is warm enough." He cast a yearning look out the window, which showed the pale sunshine of a spring day, and a blue sky with scudding clouds. Gareth repressed a shiver.

Fishing. He thought about what he knew about the pastime: nothing. He glanced down at the stack of legers and frowned. He was tired of his frustrating inability to concentrate. He looked up to find the boy bouncing nervously on the balls of his feet, waiting.

"I've never fished before," he confessed.

Oliver could not have looked more surprised if Gareth had confessed to being a girl. "*Never?*"

"Not even once. I grew up in London," he paused, "Although I suppose I could have fished in the Thames." But not for fish.

Oliver grimaced. "Mama says the fish there are not fit to eat. She says they are not even fit to touch."

Gareth could well believe it. The boys he'd known—the mudlarks— who'd worked the filthy river had lived in dread of infection and wounds that could end in death.

"It's not difficult," Oliver said, breaking into Gareth's unsavory memories. "You can learn quickly. And I have two fishing poles, one is Mama's."

"Your Mama fishes?"

Oliver gave him a variety of smile Gareth would categorize as 'from-one-man-to-another.' "She gets impatient and usually gives up and sketches. Girls do not, in the main, care for fishing."

Gareth felt his lips curve into a smile. "It is a manly activity, then?"

"Oh, yes," Oliver assured him.

Gareth stood. "Well, I had better give it a go."

Oliver smiled at him in a way that could not but please him. "I will wait for you in the stables, where Horrocks lets me keep my poles."

"Wait for me?"

"Yes," his eyes flickered over Gareth's clothing. "Don't you wish to change your clothes?"

Gareth looked down at himself. He wore his usual country rig, which Chalmers had selected, assuring him it was the preferred garb of country gentleman: buckskins, top boots, and a wool coat—green today—over a colored waistcoat, narrow green and brown striped. He looked at the boy, who was dressed similarly, although his clothing looked oft washed and patched.

"I have no other clothes."

That was good enough for Oliver.

They went first to the stables, where Horrocks, Gareth's stablemaster, gawked, but quickly recovered and sent a stable lad to fetch the poles from the tack room.

"Goin' fishin', aye? In the deep blue hole up the river?"

Oliver nodded.

"You watch out for Old Harry, lad. He'll steal your bait and the rod along with it if you don't keep your wits about you."

Oliver chuckled. "Oh, Mr. Horrocks, you say that every time. But I have never seen such a fish." He turned to Gareth. "Mr. Horrocks says Old Harry has been there since he was a boy and that he is this big." He spread his arms as wide as they would go.

Horrocks gave a rusty laugh. "No, he's *this* big." He spread his own arms.

Armed with advice, poles, nine leaping, panting dogs, and an old tin for bait, they made their way on foot toward the east-northeast part of Gareth's property.

"It's not a long walk, only a quarter of an hour. We can dig our bait by the water."

"Tell me about the bait and how one fishes in such a way as to catch a specimen like Old Harry." Gareth knew worms were used, but he enjoyed listing to the boy talk. His enthusiasm was soothing and made him feel more optimistic. Already he was glad he'd decided to come. The day was clear and warm after such a long streak of rain. The ground was slow to dry up, but he would be able to remove the big rock before too many days were out.

The thought sobered him. He would have to leave after he'd completed that task. After all, what other reason did he have to stay?

***

Foolishly, Serena had stopped worrying and thinking and dreading Etienne Bardot, so when he arrived—unannounced and unexpected—

it was a nasty surprise, not unlike finding a fly floating in one's tea *after* one had already taken a sip.

He showed up two days after the horrific rains ceased, when the roads were still boggy with mud but no longer impassable for a carriage. He came when she was finally beginning to make some progress on the sculpture.

The muse had slipped in the door not long after Declan McElroy went away.

Something must have happened between the two men the night they'd all played cards, because McElroy was gone the following morning. He'd left on horseback, taking one of the hacks Mr. Lockheart—or Gareth as she'd been calling him, at least in her mind—had brought to Rushton Park. His journey must have been hellish indeed and Serena wondered at his sudden haste. Naturally she did not ask Gareth and he did not volunteer anything. Not that he had appeared any different than usual. At least not during the day. But at night—every night since his friend had left—he went into his odd room and punched his bag until his lean, muscular body ran with sweat.

She did not know if he made any late-night forays to the kitchen because she avoided that part of the house after dark, no matter how strong the pull to venture out and see him. Oh, yes, she wanted more. More of what they'd done all too briefly that night.

Serena was not blind, she knew Gareth Lockheart was intrigued by her. She knew he would consider her an appropriate candidate for a wife, her connections to the Duke of Remington as prestigious and well-regarded as any. She also knew his friend would do everything in his power to stop such a union from happening—not that it ever could. Even if McElroy left the issue alone, she could just imagine the glint in Etienne's eyes upon discovering he could extort money from one of the wealthiest men in the country. No, she could not immerse Gareth Lockheart in such a dangerous web of lies. He'd been too kind to her, to Oliver. His friend was right about one thing, at least: Gareth Lockheart was a kind, caring man, even if he concealed his true nature behind an impenetrable mask. She would simply need to manage her unfortunate physical reaction to his handsome and intriguing person.

It was to avoid those thoughts and sensations that she'd returned to work. Until the ground dried out, they could not extract the rock and complete the berm. It behooved her to keep on task—or at least to keep busy. She changed into her working clothes and went to the stables. Nobody was around when she made her way to the stall at the rear of the building, but she could hear male voices and the sound of metal being pounded and guessed the men were in the forge.

The stall she was using was the largest in the stables and the one kept for foaling. It had been constructed with huge double doors that opened out into a small enclosure. With the doors open the light was perfect; the doorway was also large enough that there had been no problem bringing in the stone, which meant—in theory, at least—taking the statue out would be equally simple. Not that transporting a block of stone and finished sculpture were anything the same. She would not finish it completely but would leave in a few sections of rock that supported the more delicate parts of the statue.

This was her most ambitious project to date. While she'd worked on statues of this dimension and complexity for Monsieur Favel, she'd not designed one from its inception. But she was a skilled sculptor and knew this was not beyond her ability.

She'd made several wax figures, not stopping until she'd produced exactly what she wanted. Her samples were perhaps a foot and a half high, just large enough to provide her with a ready reference while she worked. Because she could not use a pointing machine, which she had used often for Favel when he wished to make multiple copies of a popular statute, she had divided the block of marble into a grid. She'd also copied grids onto paper, and from each angle, and had reduced the sculpture to one-eighth its size. These were not methods Favel had used but she'd seen other sculptors employ a variety of tricks to work on projects that were larger than life.

She'd been teasing Mr. McElroy about the classical theme she'd chosen to carve. She was not sculpting Judith and her notorious trophy—not that the notion had no appeal. Instead, she'd chosen something that would suit the parterre, in which the statute was destined to be on display. She'd thought about Mr. Lockheart and his unusual house, about the man himself, and what it was he represented. She'd chosen, after much consideration, the under-represented Greek Titan Coeus, a son of Uranus and Gaia, one of the four pillars that held Earth separate from the heavens. Coeus was often associated with inquisitive minds and intellect.

Among the Titans he was best remembered for having been banished to the underworld, breaking his chains, but remaining in Hades as the eternal companion of Cerebus. Serena had decided to represent him in his "pre-fall" state.

She'd spread out her drawings and was examining the placement of his right foot when a loathsome voice penetrated her concentration.

"Ah, here you are, sweet cousin!"

Serena swung around, even though she knew who the voice belonged to.

Etienne Bardot stepped out of the shadowy corridor into the big stall, his eyes darting about her person. "What is that? Are you going to hit me and dump my body down a hole?"

Serena glanced down, surprised to see her hand has seized the bigger of her mallets from the table.

"I must admit your idea is not without a certain appeal." She spoke to him in French, as she always did. It was the only thing she could do to protect herself from eavesdropping servants, not that it would protect her from members of her husband's family, who all spoke French. Serena tossed the heavy hide mallet onto the workbench where it landed with a dull clatter. "What do you want?"

"Tsk, tsk, tsk. So rude. I've been looking for you for weeks, my dearest Serena."

"For what, Etienne? I told you I would receive my pay at the end of the quarter. I have nothing now." She held out her empty hands, hatred that threatened to choke her pulsing through her body.

"You would reduce our relationship to nothing but pounds and pence?"

"I would rather reduce it to nothing at all," she shot back.

He merely laughed at her heated words and hate-filled glare. "We are bound by ties that are much stronger than money. I have come to see how my son goes on."

Serena let out a string of curses in three languages.

He came toward her, his fashionable Hessians and expensive, but somehow tawdry, clothing enflaming her even more.

"Don't act like you care about him." She raked him with a look that held every ounce of loathing she felt. "If you did, you would not be dressed like a peacock while your own flesh and blood wears patched and too-small rags."

He reached out a hand to caress her chin and she jerked back. His mouth hardened and he moved with the lightning speed she recalled from all those years ago, knocking her against the workbench and pinning her against the wall.

"You've forgotten who holds the whip hand, Serena. Do you need me to remind you?" He lowered his mouth over hers, stabbing into her cruelly and repeatedly. She did what she'd always done and remained still and limp.

He pulled away and grabbed her jaw in a crippling grip. "Serena the Statue, eh?" He squeezed her until her eyes watered, but she refused to make even a whimper. His dark gray-blue eyes, so like Oliver's, glared down at her. He wanted to hit her, but love of his own hide and comfort held him back. After all, how could she go about fashionable society and get the work she needed to pay his crushing blackmail if she looked like a battered serving wench?

"Bah!" He shoved her away, slamming the back of her head against the wall and leaving her ears ringing. "I want nothing from you—you are old and haggard." He spat, but she could not see where it landed as her vision danced with black spots. "Women *love* me here. All kinds, rich, poor, beautiful . . ."

Serena didn't care, as long as he kept well away from her. Not that he would. No, she was the goose who laid golden eggs, and he took them without remorse and without ceasing.

She heard his boots on the wood planking and blinked rapidly, until she could see his shadow flickering as he paced.

"You flatter yourself that I came here to see you. I'm on my way to Dover, where I have business."

Serena knew what that meant: smuggling. Etienne Bardot was a criminal from a long line of criminals and she rued the day that misfortune had led him to her little corner of the world. A Parisian by

136

birth, he'd run from the city after an unfortunate incident that left an influential member of the local government dead.

He'd joined the army and quickly found his level, assembling a group of like-minded criminals and deserting at the first opportunity. They'd gone from village to village, until they found one so ill-defended, so lacking in men—men who were either dead from the endless fighting or off preparing to become cannon fodder—they could set up a private fiefdom.

Her vision cleared enough to see he was not looking at her, but at the block of marble. He shook his head and gestured to it before turning to her. "Why do you do this? You could live off the duke; he would care for you and the boy." He snorted, "Oliver is the only child of his dead, beloved son."

Serena pushed back her hair, which had shaken loose at his manhandling. "What? And live with you always lurking about? Do you think these people are stupid just because they are wealthy? And now that the War is over, do you think you will not see people who will know who you really are? *What* you really are?"

He waved a hand, dismissing her worries. "People of that class rarely travel."

"*You* did."

He'd returned to his usual, unflappable mood and merely smiled at her rude baiting. "Yes, but I am the odd one. I am, eh, how do you say it? On my way up the social ranks?"

He was filth, and lower than pond scum, but he was smart enough to know that. Which made him even more dangerous.

"Well, I have just come to pay my respects. It is unfortunate I do not have time to stay—meet your employer, see the boy. But perhaps on the return journey?"

Serena hoped he was run over by a wagon or shot by his criminal conspirators, but his type was hard to kill.

He gave her a mocking bow, tipping his hat, and then left, his footsteps echoing in the empty building.

She collapsed back against the wall when she could no longer hear him, her entire body shaking, her teeth chattering. She wrapped her arms around her body and tightened them, hugging herself as she would Oliver if he woke from a nightmare.

Oliver. What if Bardot hadn't really left, but had gone to find him?

She ran from the room before the thought was even fully formed, her mind like a crazed animal, trapped in a snare.

Oliver. Where was he?

Stop. Think.

She obeyed the voice that had guided her out of France and away from Bardot and dozens of others who would have killed her for what she'd carried with her.

Fishing. He'd come to her room this morning to tell her Nounou had agreed to let him fish, in reward for being so good during the days when he'd not been able to step foot outside.

She returned to her impromptu work room and took her cloak, hat, and satchel from the peg where she'd hung them. In addition to her ever-present sketchbook, the satchel contained all her money, a miniature painting of Oliver in a leather case—an item she'd traded a piece of sculpture for with another artist—her marriage lines, and Robert's signet ring, gold and emerald with his initials graven in the stone.

Serena took the satchel with her everywhere—a lesson she'd learned to her detriment over a decade ago, when she'd been caught and forced to flee and leave behind the information that had led Etienne Bardot to her door.

Oliver favored a bend in the stream where the water collected in a deep pool. They'd walked there together and she'd promised to come and bathe with him when the weather was warmer. There was a particularly alluring rock that hung over the stream and she'd told him—under *no* circumstances, was he to dive or swim alone. He was a boy who honored his word, so she was not concerned.

She half-ran, half-walked the distance to the stream, her breath coming in sharp, ragged gasps—especially after she saw the impression of far larger boots beside Oliver's familiar footprints.

Oh God, she begged, please let her be mistaken. Even Etienne would not do such a thing—he would then have to care for the boy and she knew he had no regard for anyone other than himself.

But then she recalled his threat of six months past, when she'd refused to pay him—chiefly because she'd had almost no money: "I'll take him from you, Serena, and I wager you'll find the money to get him back,   won't   you?"
She crested the rise that overlooked the small river and skidded to a halt. Two figures were down below, and neither of them was Etienne Bardot.

Serena quickly moved into the shade of a nearby grove of Scots Pines.

Oliver was down below and laughing, his skinny little body clad only in wet drawers. He was on top of the big rock and Gareth Lockheart, hip-deep in the pool and bare-chested, was calling out something in an unmistakably taunting masculine tone.

Oliver responded by leaping off the rock and clasping his knees with his arms, sending a great gout of water over his spectator.

Serena clutched her throat, where her breath had become stuck, her eyes flickering wildly.

But Oliver burst out of the water like some manner of fish, his characteristic, "Huzzah!" clearly audible.

The two males consulted one another, shook hands, as if completing some deal, and her almost nude employer turned in her direction and waded toward shore.

She swallowed as he emerged from the water, the fine linen he favored as translucent as a dragonfly's wing.

"Oh. My."

Serena had learned her art at the foot of a country sculptor who had no patience for the delicate sensibilities of his city equivalents. When he'd trained her in anatomy, he'd had every kind of body type as a model. Women, men, young, old—she'd seen dozens of bodies. But never had she seen one quite like Gareth Lockheart's. She'd seen his torso in the window night after night, but she'd not seen the rest of him.

Narrow, powerful hips attached to legs that would have done a statue of Atlas proud. He moved with the athletic grace she'd admired in him more than once but could now fully appreciate. He slid a hand down the front of his drawers to pull the clinging fabric from his private parts,

139

whose dimensions were quite impressive even considering the effect of the cold water.

He climbed the big rock, his actions affording her an excellent view of his backside, which her hands had so briefly caressed.

He strode to the end of the rock, said something to Oliver that made him laugh, and then launched himself into the air, making a splash that caused her son to hoot with joy.

Serena realized she was smiling so hard her face hurt. She unclasped her cloak and dropped it to the ground before sitting, and then she took out her sketchpad.

**

Gareth's jewels had contracted up into his body. The water was beyond cold and he'd been mad to let the boy talk him into it. Even with all their diving and splashing his goose-pimples had goose-pimples. But he had to admit—as they both lay on the grassy bank letting the pale but surprisingly warm sun dry their bodies—that he felt a sense of peace he'd never experienced before.

"Mr. Lockheart?"

He turned his head and shaded his eyes with one hand. "Yes?"

"Did you go away to school when you were a boy?"

Gareth considered his question, and how honest he should be in his answer. A child should not know that a thing like orphanages existed—and certainly not the nightmarish things that often occurred in them—but also, he deserved to know some of the truth.

"You could say I grew up in a school. I lived in an orphanage."

Oliver turned on his side, his eyes alight with interest—and sympathy. "You mean you do not know who your family is?"

Gareth nodded.

Oliver's brown wrinkled with concern. "But you had friends there, didn't you?"

Gareth could see that was important to the boy. "I did. Mr. McElroy was my best friend, and still is."

Relief rolled off the boy in waves and Gareth marveled at his capacity for empathy.

"I like Mr. McElroy. He showed me how to carve a conker into a dog."

Gareth looked up at the sky. "Yes, Mr. McElroy is very good with a knife." An image of Dec's hands covered in blood flashed through his mind and Gareth closed his eyes.

"All of my cousins have gone away to school. I'm the only one who hasn't." He paused and Gareth turned back toward him.

"What school?" Gareth asked, although he could guess.

"Everyone but Julian goes to Eton. *He* goes to Harrow."

"Oh, why is that?"

"His mama is the duke's daughter and she married the Earl of Synott and *he* went to Harrow."

As Oliver went on to describe his other cousins Gareth considered the boys august connections. Serena Lombard might work for her living, but she clearly did not have to. Venetia, for all her wisdom, had not assessed the situation correctly, in his opinion. A woman like Mrs. Lombard would never consent to marry an awkward, inarticulate bastard from a London orphanage. And that is what he was, a bastard. At least that's what Herbert Jensen, the man who'd run the orphanage as well as half a dozen less savory operations, had told him.

"You might have a skill, boy, but you're still a bastard and don't you forget it." How many times had Jensen said that same thing to him? All the way up to the night Dec and Gareth finally told him they would no longer do his bidding—bastards or not.

The sound of a growling stomach pulled him back from the abyss and he turned to find Oliver blushing furiously. "I guess I'm hungry."

"Me too. Shall we head back?"

"But we haven't caught any fish."

"I'm sure Cook will feed us even so."

They dressed, the sun-warmed clothes feeling good on his cold, clammy skin. Chalmers would no doubt wonder what the hell he'd been up to, he thought, looking down at his mud-caked boots and grass-stained buckskins.

"Do you want to go back a different way? I can show you the old mine."

"If you wish." Gareth slung his cravat around his neck but made no effort to tie it.

Oliver led him up the river and away from the proposed lake. Gareth had a general idea of his property boundaries and believed they could continue in this direction for some time before they'd be in danger of trespassing on his nearest neighbor, the squire who'd sold him the acreage.

After about ten minutes they passed through a tight clump of trees and into a clearing.

"See," Oliver pointed to the rock ridge that was partially hidden by some tree—Gareth had not even the slightest knowledge of botany— to a dark hole. He followed Oliver, his steps heavier the closer they got. It was a small cave-like opening, no more than three and a half feet high and maybe a little wider.

Oliver dropped to his hands and knees and crawled toward it.

"Oliver!" The word was like an explosion in the quiet glade and both he and the boy jumped at the sound.

Oliver swung around, his eyes wide.

"Come away from there," Gareth ordered, aware he was speaking too sharply, but unable to do otherwise with the boy so close to the pitch-black maw, which seemed to broadcast malevolence.

He was an obedient child and immediately came back. "I wasn't going to go in, Mr. Lockheart."

"Good. Such a thing is most likely unstable. I will have it seen to— blocked off. You have not gone in it?"

"No sir, my mother told me never to enter such a place, that it might come down on my head."

"That is sound advice." Gareth swallowed back the panic he felt just looking at the black cave, forcing himself to speak more calmly. He was frightening the boy.

"Come, I'm suddenly ferociously hungry."

Oliver smiled, the tension of the moment before already a thing of the past.

As they walked away from the cave, Gareth couldn't help feeling something was watching them; something that wasn't happy to see them leave.

A Figure of Love

Chapter Thirteen

Gareth determined the ground would be dry enough to move the rock in three days if there wasn't another torrential downpour. That meant he had only four more days.

They were eating dinner—a part of the day Gareth had come to enjoy, even though he felt guilty for being so pleased that without Dec around he was able to take more part in the conversation. Mrs. Lombard had just asked him about his pulley system and how long it would take him to set up the device.

"I'll only need a day, and most of that just to move the logs into position."

"Things have reached a fever pitch in the village. I believe you will have quite a number of spectators."

He looked up from his soup, his eyebrows arching. "Is that so?"

She laughed. "Surely you've heard the talk whenever you are there?"

"I'm afraid I've only visited the forge in town."

"Well, if you'd gone into the King's Head or Mrs. Cooper's Emporium, you would know it is the talk of the town."

Gareth had no idea what that meant. What possible interest could people from town have in the moving of a rock at least three miles away?

Mrs. Lombard opened her mouth and then closed it. And then opened it again.

It was clear she had something to say but didn't know how to say it; Gareth waited.

"I should not like to overstep," she said, her cheeks tinting and reminding him very much of her son.

"Mrs. Lombard, if you know something I should hear about, please tell me."

"I was going to suggest you have a little celebration around the event."

"A celebration?"

"Just something informal. A way for you to meet your neighbors."

Gareth doubted it would be politic to tell her he'd gone to a great deal of effort to avoid meeting his neighbors and had actively dodged them when they'd come to call in the early days.

"There is a good deal of curiosity about you, Mr. Lockheart. The squire, who would have provided a social core for the area, is old and fragile and has divested himself of a good deal of his property. I believe you purchased a large section of it?"

"Yes. He has no immediate heir and holds his entire family in great dislike. I believe he is considered something of an eccentric." It amused him to speak of somebody *else* being eccentric, for a change. "The squire was eager to sell it all so I bought the entirety of his land, including the house. He resides there by virtue of a life estate I granted him."

"You own *all* the land that surrounds the village?"

"Yes."

"My goodness. And the squire's tenants?"

"They are now my tenants."

A look of understanding bloomed on her face.

He could not resist asking, "What is it?"

"That explains the new roofs, drainage project, and other improvements. The villagers talk of little else—when not discussing the Great Rock Moving. But they believe the squire is responsible, which has confounded them as he has been notoriously clutch-fisted since taking possession of his estates."

"I've kept the transfer from the people who live here. The squire is old; although he is neither a kind nor generous man, I believe it would make his final days unpleasant should it be known he is nothing more than a tenant, himself." Gareth glanced from Mrs. Lombard to the two footmen standing in front of the sideboard. He stared hard at them, until he was sure he'd communicated his message. He paid his servants twice what any other employer in the area paid; he expected the extra money to purchase their discretion.

The look on Mrs. Lombard's face made him uncomfortable, so he changed the subject. "Tell me more about this celebration you have in mind."

**

One of the other aspects of life without Declan was that Gareth no longer had to drink port every evening. He loathed the beverage and had only fiddled with a glass of it to keep his friend company. He'd learned, after attending more than his fair share of business dinners, that men of business did not trust a man who would not drink with them.

But now he could join Mrs. Lombard in the library after dinner, where they'd taken to spending a couple of hours together before she went up to bed. He had no idea whether she'd wandered the halls since that night in the kitchen since he'd kept to his quarters to avoid finding out. Indeed, his nights had assumed a rather tedious pattern after she excused herself. He would do work for another hour and then go to his chambers and expend his pent-up frustration on the unfortunate bags. Already Chalmers had needed to repair the smaller bag when its seam split one night.

And when that didn't serve to calm him, he'd relieved himself in his fist. Not since he'd been a youth had he abused himself with such frequency. And even that did not serve to send him to sleep some nights. But at least it freed his mind for a few hours to think. He'd begun bringing his work to his chambers and drawing up his plans and recommendations in the early hours of the day.

Declan had been gone a week now and Gareth still had no word from him. He had told himself that he was not allowed to begin fretting about his friend until *after* the rock moving, which would make Dec's absence ten days. He would leave here the day after he'd completed the project and go to London first. He knew Declan's habits almost as well as he knew his own. He would be in London, most likely in a whorehouse. Possibly even at the White House, although he tended toward earthier establishments. Wherever he was, Gareth would find him.

***

It wasn't until two days before Mr. Lockheart was to leave that Serena realized she was more than just infatuated with him.

As a special treat, Oliver had been allowed to stay up later than usual and join the adults in the dining room for dinner.

It was Gareth who'd asked her, making a special trip out to her workshop to make the request.

Serena had commenced working on the statue the day after Etienne's visit, and the work was coming along quite nicely. She was looking at the sketches she'd tacked all around her when she heard something behind her. Her heart jumped into her throat and a hundred thoughts raced through her mind in the time it took to turn: was it Etienne? Had he returned like he'd threatened?

But no, it was not.

"I'm sorry to disturb you, Mrs. Lombard." His light gray eyes studiously avoided the dozens of overlapping, messy drawings covering the walls. "I understand many artists do not like their work viewed before completion?"

Serena smiled. "I am not so high strung, Mr. Lockheart. If I'd had such reservations, I never would have survived in the studio I was trained in, which had three or four apprentice sculptors working at all times." She paused. "Would you like to see what you have commissioned for the centerpiece of your garden?"

He stepped into the room. "I already know—Judith holding a likeness of Mr. McElroy's head."

Serena laughed. "That was bad of me, was it not?"

Rare amusement glinted in his eyes. "I would like to see what you are really sculpting."

She turned, intensely aware of his body as he came to stand beside her. She pointed to the first of the drawings. "These represent all sides starting from the front. I've chosen an unusual classical figure."

She turned in time to see a tiny, but wry, smile flex his lips. "Ah, for an unusual house and it's unusual owner."

"Something like that." She gestured to the first drawing again. "This is Coeus—have you heard of him?"

"My knowledge of the classics is not strong. A Greek deity, perhaps?"

"Close, he was one of the Titans, and is associated with intellect and inquisitive minds."

When he didn't speak, she turned. That's when she realized he wasn't looking at the wall at all, but at her sketchbook, which lay open to a nude picture of his body, from the rear. Before she could gather her wits and pounce on the book, he leaned down and turned the page. This picture was of the front, and there was no mistaking who it was.

He continued turning pages, only stopping when he reached a blank one. Thirteen sketches in all; she'd never counted them before.

Serena's body was hot all over; a mixture of shame, embarrassment, and arousal flooded her anew with each page he turned.

He looked up at her, his gray eyes wintry, like an ice-covered lake. "It seems you have the advantage of me, Mrs. Lombard."

Serena tried to smile but failed miserably.

"I would say these are from your imagination, but the details," he shook his head and glanced down, flipping the pages rapidly before looking up again. "Well, this is undoubtedly what I see when I look in the mirror. You are quite a draftsman. When?"

"At the river."

His eyebrows arched over his frosty eyes. "You were there?"

"I came to see Oliver. But when I arrived, you were both swimming and enjoying yourselves. If I had interrupted you? Well—" she shrugged.

"So instead you spied and sketched me." It was not a question.

She took a deep breath. "I'm sorry, Mr. Lockheart. I never should—"

He raised a hand and she stopped.

"I don't want your apology, Mrs. Lombard."

"Oh?" The single syllable was more of a squeak than a word.

"No, I want an opportunity to make my own sketches."

"*What?*"

He nodded, his expression as serious and unreadable as ever.

"I—" she cleared her throat and tried again. "I'm afraid I don't know what you mean."

He glanced out into the small corral area, his pupils narrowing against the sun. It was a warm day, the warmest yet this spring.

"It is a nice warm day for swimming."

"No," she said, suddenly seeing what he meant with painful clarity. "Absolutely not."

"Yes." He took out his watch and glanced at it. "It is just past eleven. I have a few matters to attend to but should be finished in an hour." He replaced his watch. "It will be warmer in an hour, as well. Let's say twelve o'clock, sharp." He turned and strode from the stall.

Serena stared; he expected her to swim with him? The man must be mad!

***

As it turned out, Mr. Lockheart had no intention of going swimming with her. When Serena arrived at the appointed time it was to find him seated on a blanket under a tree, with something that resembled a sketchpad beside him.

He turned as she approached, once again taking out his blasted timepiece. "Excellent, you are right on time."

"I only came to tell you I have no intention of going swimming with you."

"I have no intention of swimming with you, either."

Her shoulders sagged and she gave a relieved laugh. "You kept such a straight face I could not tell that you were jesting. I should have guessed."

"I wasn't jesting, Mrs. Lombard. I never jest."

"I beg your pardon?"

"It is true. I'm afraid I don't have the turn of mind required for humor. I only spoke the truth: *I* have no intention of swimming. I've come to sketch." He gestured to the book, which she saw was a ledger, all he could find on short notice, she supposed.

"I cannot believe you are serious."

"I'm very serious."

"This is rather . . . *biblical*, isn't it? An eye for an eye, and all that?"

149

He cocked his head, as if considering the matter. "Yes, I suppose you could call it that."

She placed a fist on each hip. "What would you call it?"

"Not revenge, certainly. Payment, perhaps."

"*Payment?*"

"I understand sculptors employ models, do they not?"

"Well. . . yes, but what does that have to do with *this?*" She gestured around them.

"You took my likeness but did not pay for it. I should like *your* likeness as payment."

"Why don't I simply pay you the standard hourly rate for models?"

His lips flexed into a slight smile. "Oh no, Mrs. Lombard, that is not the way this works."

Serena was speechless, a condition she'd rarely experienced. She glared at him, and he stared coolly back.

Her eyes narrowed. "Very well. You want to see me swim? I will swim." She marched toward the stream, waiting every second for him to call her back. But he didn't. She stopped at the edge of the water and spun around. "Are you going to force me to do this?"

He gave an exaggerated shrug. "If you wish to wet your clothes rather than remove them, that is your prerogative."

Serena closed her eyes and laughed.

Take them off; you know you want to. You want him to see you.

Serena had to agree with the taunting voice. She had, after all, posed more than once for Monsieur Favel when he or one of the others had needed a female form. Replicas of her body fairly littered Europe, armed with shields, winged helmets, and breast-exposing togas.

She *wanted* him to see her. Her body, although that of a mature woman, was lush and appealing and men found her attractive. She had nothing to be ashamed of and lacked an Englishwoman's ingrained shame when it came to nudity.

She glanced around, her eyes moving to the hillside where she'd watched from when he was bathing.

He saw her look. "I instructed Jessup that I wished to be alone and to advise the servants I have placed this portion of the river out of bounds. And the men are not digging today, as they have done all they can until after tomorrow. I believe the chances of discovery are less than eleven percent."

She wanted to ask him how he'd come to such a ridiculous figure but there was no point in delaying the inevitable.

The gown she was wearing was the type of day-dress a woman of limited means wore. It tied at the neck and beneath her breasts, where the bodice was gathered to adjust to any changes in size or to allow for a new owner with no alteration. She removed her fichu first and tossed it onto the ground. His eyes flickered down to it and he frowned, reminding her of his penchant for neatness. Well, that was too bad. She untied the ribbon on her bonnet and tossed it a foot in the other direction, enjoying the way his forehead creased, almost as if the scattering of garments made him physically uncomfortable.

She crouched to remove first one sturdy ankle boot and then the other before standing and kicking them in two directions.

Gareth shot to his feet. "*Mrs. Lombard.*" He did not raise his voice, but he spoke far more emphatically than usual.

She paused and gave him a look of wide-eyed innocence. "Yes, Mr. Lockheart?"

He made a vague, restless gesture with one hand. "Perhaps you would like to place your garments here, on the blanket. Neatly."

"No."

"No?"

She almost laughed out loud.

"You wished me to disrobe and bathe, sir. I am doing exactly that. Now, shall I continue?"

She could see his jaw moving from side to side and could almost hear his teeth grinding over the din of the running water.

He sat down, his back ramrod straight this time, his expression one of grim determination. Serena began to feel sorry for him and the obvious torment the garment tornado was causing him. But then she recalled this had been his idea and reached behind her neck and pulled the tape.

***

The events of the past hour and twenty-seven minutes were something of a blur. In fact, nothing was quite clear starting from the moment he'd seen the nude representations of himself in Mrs. Lombard's sketchbook.

His brain, usually the most reliable of organs, had utterly deserted him. Instead, it was as if some devilish stranger had taken control of his body and began to issue cool and shocking commands. Commands he heartily agreed with, by the way, but which he could hardly believe he was capable of uttering with such mastery.

He'd been having one of the best days of his life, right up until the moment she began to clutter up his enjoyment by distributing her garments in a way that was surely unnatural to any man or woman.

Now, his mind seemed to have fractured. The imp that had engineered this afternoon of unparalleled pageantry was mightily enjoying the display, as was evidenced by an erection that belonged somewhere between nine point nine and ten on the Mohs scale of mineral hardness.

But the total *disarray* around her!

Her lips curled in a way he could not recall seeing before. . .almost as if she were . . . *mocking* him. But that was not possible. After all, *he* was the one wearing the clothing.

She reached behind her neck and everything in life narrowed to that one moment. Their eyes locked as she pulled the tape loose and her neckline sagged lower. She reached her other hand behind her back, her movements sinuous and studied, like the steps of a sensual dance. The second tape made no appreciable change to her garment until she gave it a slight tug and the fabric opened the dress to a wider diameter, until it slid off her arms and down over her hips.

His chest hurt and he realized he'd forgotten to breathe. He inhaled deeply as she stepped out of the puddle of dress, toward him.

His eyes darted from the messy pile of fabric to her plain buckram corset in the shape of an hourglass. Beneath the corset was a whisper-thin chemise, tied around her waist a single petticoat made of undyed muslin.

He looked up at her face when he realized she'd stopped disrobing. She smiled and then reached for the waist tie of the petticoat and released it with a single pull. Again, it slid to the ground with nary a sound.

She left it behind as carelessly and callously as the gown, but his eyes saw nothing except *her*, now. Like a ship locked in ice, they remained fixed on her stockings, garters, the hem of her chemise—blessedly short—and the snug garment that compressed her into the ultimate manifestation of male desire.

Her garments were modest, threadbare (*Thank God! Thank God!*) in the case of her chemise. But he'd never been more aroused, not even when Venetia had sported the finest lace or silk.

She leaned down far enough to offer a flash of magnificent bosom, pulling the garter loose and tossing it behind her.

Gareth groaned, an animalistic sound that shamed him to his core. She smiled and released the second strap, tossing it directly into his tented lap.

The stockings slipped, and she rolled down first one, and then the other wadding them into a ball that made him briefly close his eyes, before hurling them somewhere off to the left.

She reached behind her back to get at her laces, her shoulders arching in a way that sucked all the moisture from his mouth. She plucked the laces open and then used both hands to alternately loosen the constricting garment until it, too, slid to the ground.

The sun was behind her and he saw immediately the corset had merely molded to her natural figure, it had not created it.

She took one last step and her foot touched the blanket.

Gareth swallowed, his face eyelevel with the apex of her long, shapely legs. The hem of her chemise fluttered mid-knee, the wind toying with it as if to taunt him.

She nudged the fresh ledger he'd brought with him with her toe. "You'd better get to sketching, Mr. Lockheart, I'll want to inspect the results." She turned without waiting for an answer and daintily picked her way not toward the shore, but to the big rock that hung over it. She was going to jump.

Remorse seized him like a fist and he opened his mouth to tell her he had changed his mind, but it was too late: she jumped, one hand on her nose and the other holding down her hem.

Gareth was already beside the water's edge when she came sputtering to the surface. He'd taken the blanket and held it before him.

"Mrs. Lombard, come and let me put this blanket around you, before you catch your death of cold."

She pushed water from her face, but more streamed from her hair. "What?" she demanded through chattering teeth. "Where is your sk-sk-sketchbook, Mr. Lockheart?"

"Don't be stubborn, come and put this around you."

Her face was blue and stubborn, but she came toward him.

"Good God."

She stopped at the sound of his voice and followed his eyes. She looked more nude than nude with the gauze thin garment molded to her glorious curves, limning the dark triangle between her thighs and the hard, pink nipples that tipped her high, full breasts.

Gareth realized he'd dropped the blanket and picked it up without removing his eyes from her.

Her face had become rosy somewhere during the brief walk and Gareth draped the blanket over her shoulders like a cape and then pulled her close, cupping her face and tilting it toward his.

Chapter Fourteen

Serena had never been so cold in her life, but when his eyes swept over her, she burst into flames. And when he lowered his mouth to hers, she forgot all about the cold and slid her arms around his taut waist, this time resting both palms on his bottom. He made a muffled sound of approval and pushed closer, the soft leather of his breeches cool and smooth against her belly.

He kissed as if he wanted to devour her, his lips demanding, his tongue invading, his teeth grazing and nipping as long, powerful fingers massaged their way down her neck, until they rested on her shoulders. He pulled away and rested his forehead against hers, his breathing labored.

"If you wish me to stop, tell me now."

She pushed her hands beneath the edge of his breeches and pulled out what felt like yards of shirting before she could reach his hot, hard flesh.

He inhaled sharply as she explored the shape of him, his thumbs stroking her collarbones while he backed away from the river. "Not out here. Come, beneath the trees."

Serena snatched at the blanket hanging from her shoulders and held it with one hand at her neck, taking his hand and following him beneath the tree canopy. He shrugged out of his snug-fitting coat.

"Take off your shift and put this on, you will be warmer."

She released the blanket and thrilled at the tightening of his facial muscles and the flaring of his pupils which turned his eyes from harsh gray ice to enveloping black pools of heat. Ever so slowly, she lifted the wet chemise over her head.

He muttered something emphatic sounding beneath his breath and a triumphant smile curled her lips as she freed herself from the wet garment.

She was about to toss it to the side but he took it from her, shaking his head.

"No." He handed her his coat and watched her slip it on with eyes as sharp as a raptor's. His coattails—which hit him just at the knee—tickled her ankles. When she was covered, he took her thin, wet chemise into the sunshine and stretched it out on the grass to dry.

The coat dwarfed her and the clean scent of him was dizzying. She closed her eyes and shivered in anticipation.

"Are you cold?" His voice came from beside her ear, hot breath on her temple and soft, soft kisses beneath her ear. "I will warm you."

His hands, strong and hot, pushed between the coat flaps and settled on her hips. He spanned her waist and squeezed her lightly, the gesture making her feel small and dainty, two things she knew she was not.

"Mmmm," he hummed against her, his kisses moving down her jaw, forcing back her head, until he nibbled and licked at the underside of her chin. He took his time, his focus on her pleasure rather than his own. It was an onslaught unlike any other she'd experienced and her arms hung uselessly at her sides while his hands roamed her torso. He licked, kissed, and tasted his way down her throat, grazing her strangely sensitive collarbones on the way to her breasts.

Serena cried out when he flicked a cold, hard nipple with the hot tip of his tongue, and then was gone. She pushed herself against him. *More.*

He took her in his mouth and suckled her until warmth radiated out from her breast. "So beautiful," he whispered into the hollow between her breasts, and then moved to her other nipple and tormented her until she had to bite her lip to keep from screaming.

Suddenly, the heat of him disappeared and she opened her eyes.

"Come." He took her hand and pulled her down beside him on the blanket. His hands slid between the flaps of the coat she wore—*his* coat—and he cupped her bottom with strong hands, molding her body to his. Lips and teeth drifted over her throat, jaw, and ear while his hands—his wicked, wicked hands—stroked and teased and kneaded.

"Unbutton me."

A rush of pleasure shot through her at the sound of his command, spoken in such hushed passion. She pushed a hand between their bodies, tracing the hard length of him thrusting against the soft leather.

He groaned and tightened his hold, his fingers sinking into her soft flesh. She stroked him again and again and again, until his powerful body vibrated with need, and then, with a few deft flicks, she opened the flap of his breeches and released him.

He hissed in a ragged breath at her touch and rolled onto his back, pulling her with him, his gray eyes heavy-lidded as they gazed up into hers. "The ground is hard and I don't want to hurt you." He explained in a lust-roughened voice she hardly recognized. "I want you to ride me, Serena."

She shivered at his raw words, her fingers working on the buttons of his waistcoat as she pushed up onto her knees. He watched her straddle his hips with a heavy-lidded, sensual stare, an expression of bliss on the hard, taut planes of his face.

Serena shoved up his shirt once his waistcoat was open, groaning in amazement at the latticework of muscles beneath her hands. His ridged abdomen shifted and tightened when he sucked in a breath, his hands holding her still as he flexed his hips and rubbed his hard ridge against the most sensitive part of her body.

It was too much and Serena's eyelids fluttered shut. She sucked her lower lip between her teeth as he ground against her, hard, insistent, and slick.

When she opened her eyes it was to find him watching intently, his jaws clenched tight as he stroked, the slight curve of his lips that of a man confident in his ability to bring her pleasure.

"Touch yourself." He spoke the shocking words in an even more shockingly normal tone. At her look of disbelief he nodded, "Yes, touch your breasts—your nipples. Tease them for me."

She swallowed loudly enough to be heard over their heavy breathing and the distantly chuckling river. Her hands moved slowly up her ribs

157

until she touched one finger to the tip of her breast. His hands tightened painfully on her hips and his thrusting motions became jerky.

"More," he forced the word through clenched teeth.

She put a finger in her mouth and slicked it before swirling it around her other nipple. His lips parted and his breathing roughened as he strove to control the rhythm of his thrusts. Serena tipped her head back, surrendering to the sensation building inside her. She was drowsily aware that he'd not entered her body and yet he was driving her steadily and relentlessly toward her climax, stroking and grinding against her sensitive core until her entire body hummed with delicious tension. Until she could not bear another second without coming apart.

Serena came hard, the waves of pleasure pummeling her, overlapping and receding, only to crash again and again. She realized, vaguely, that he'd stopped moving and she looked down to find him watching her with rapt hunger.

"I want to be inside you."

She nodded shakily and raised up off him.

His hand moved to where they touched and he positioned himself against her entrance. When he raised his hips, she impaled herself—hard. They gasped as he sheathed himself fully, the echoes of her climax contracting around his thick shaft. His body jerked and arched, the muscles of his stomach, chest, and shoulders so defined they looked as if they'd been carved from the finest alabaster.

Serena leaned forward until her breasts grazed his chest, her hands fisting the blanket on each side of his shoulders as she tilted to take him even deeper. Barely an inch separated their faces and this close to him she saw the fine, icy gray shards that made up his irises. She tightened her inner muscles and his eyes widened, his hands like butterflies on her waist.

She swiveled her hips and his nostrils flared. His grip tightened on her waist, but he did not take control of their lovemaking. He let her dictate the pace and depth and rhythm, the pale skin of his face flushing with passion as she rode him inexorably to his crisis, her own body tight with anticipation, her attention on his pleasure after he'd given her so much.

And when he stiffened and cried out, his beautiful face no longer under his tight control and his body pulsing inside her, Serena felt as triumphant as if she'd just completed a fine piece of art.

***

Gareth only gradually became aware of the rock jabbing his neck and the stick or twig digging into his lower back; he did not care. The warm, soft body lying on top of him was worth a thousand times more discomfort. He was still inside her, his cock too delirious with joy to have completely softened. Indeed, he began to want her again even before he'd emerged from the pleasurable fog that suffused both his body and brain.

She shifted slightly, the round firmness of her naked breasts against his chest making him harden.

She shook slightly and he realized she was laughing.

Gareth leaned back as far as he could—not much—and tilted her chin up, until he could see her flushed face and wicked smile.

"You find my condition amusing, Mrs. Lombard?"

She laughed outright and then buried her face in his chest. "Very."

"Hmph."

That only made her laugh harder. Which made him smile. It *was* amusing when one considered it. Men were just as much appendages to their breeding organs as the other way around.

Gareth flexed his rapidly hardening cock and felt her tighten in response. He grunted as ripples of pleasure washed through his body.

She propped herself up and crossed her arms on his chest, looking down at him with a quizzical look. "You made no sketches."

Gareth smiled at her unexpected words and she stared down at him with wide eyes. "You *can* smile!"

"Yes, I can." Gareth pushed a wet rope of hair back from her forehead. "But I cannot sketch."

"Everyone can draw."

He shook his head. "Not me."

Her lips quivered. "I think you are trying to make me cry, Mr. Lockheart. That may be the saddest thing I've ever heard. I believe I shall have to prove you wrong."

"Oh?" Gareth found he could not keep his hands off her body and he stroked from her slim waist to her lush bottom, his cock jumping on its own this time.

Her eyelids lowered and her sheath tightened.

Gareth swallowed. Would she let him—

She leaned down and kissed his chest where the 'V' of his rucked up shirt hung open. "You have very little hair on your chest."

His hands froze.

She *licked* him. "You are not unlike a sculpture."

Gareth cleared his throat, which seemed to crowd with foreign objects with each stroke of her tongue. "And is that good, or bad?" His voice was an unrecognizable croak.

She chuckled against his damp skin, her tongue and mouth headed toward his right nipple.

Gareth moaned and turned them both onto their sides. She slid a leg over his hip and continued her distracting licking and sucking while he began to move, his hand dropping between their bodies.

"Mmmm, yes please," she whispered when he thumbed her slick, swollen pearl.

He moved slowly this time, his motions languorous and thorough, his muscle memory cataloguing her responses and storing them for future use, his mind hoping such knowledge would again be necessary.

***

Gareth gathered her clothing and then wandered down to the river while Serena dressed.

She finger-combed her damp hair, twisted it into a heavy rope, and pinned it down with the few pins she could find. She told herself she looked much the same as usual when she tied her bonnet over the wet, tangled mess.

She'd just finished shaking out the blanket and folding it when a voice called down from the hillside.

"Hallo, there!"

Serena's head jerked up and a vile word escaped her mouth. She shot a glance at the river and saw Gareth was too far away to have heard her. But he *had* heard Etienne, and his face wore the first scowl she'd ever

160

seen. He looked. . . menacing as he strode up the bank, intent on reaching the stranger trespassing on his land.

"Mr. Lockheart!"

He stopped immediately and turned.

She gave him a rueful smile that probably looked more like the grimace it truly was. "That is my cousin, I'm afraid."

"Your cousin?" He glanced from Etienne—who was wearing clothes more suitable for a bordello than a day in the country—and back to Serena.

She went toward him, her eyes on Etienne, who was grinning from ear to ear and waving his walking stick as he staggered down the hillside in Hessians.

"His name is Etienne Bardot. I may have told you my mother was French?"

"Yes, you mentioned that." His gaze, once again, as distant as the moon. "And does he live in these parts?"

"No, he stopped by several days ago on his way to Dover." She could see he thought it odd nobody had mentioned a visitor and hastened to add. "It was only a brief visit, he had business waiting for him but mentioned he might stop by on his return." She looked into his veiled eyes—so different from a few minutes earlier—and wanted to weep. The little bit of ease that had developed between them had disappeared. "There is no reason to—"

"I was told you'd come this way, Serena, but I didn't know you were not alone." Etienne's sly smile and glinting eyes made her want to slap him.

"Mr. Lockheart, this is Etienne Bardot, my cousin. Etienne, this is my employer, Mr. Lockheart."

Etienne dropped a creditable bow. "A pleasure, sir. My cousin has told me much about you," he lied.

Although Gareth's expression did not flicker, Serena knew this was unwelcome news to the intensely private man.

"I've told my cousin about my commission here, Mr. Lockheart." She shot Etienne a venomous look that he ignored.

"So, you must be down here surveying the river for beautification?"

Serena did not trust herself to respond to his insinuating smirk and innuendo.

"We were on our way back to the house when you arrived." Gareth's voice was as chilly as his hard gray stare, and even Etienne's good humor dimmed under the other man's cool tone.

"Of course, of course. I will join you, if you do not mind."

They made their way up the hill, Etienne's inappropriate footwear slipping and skittering.

"You've just returned from Dover, Mrs. Lombard tells me."

"Ah, yes." Etienne grimaced down at a glob of mud on the toe of his once shiny boot.

"You had business there?"

"Yes, I did." He swatted at the mud with the cane and only succeeded in cracking his toe. "Damn!"

Gareth cleared this throat and Etienne looked up, his eyes swiveling to the other man's raised brow and Serena's scowl.

"Oh, I beg your pardon for my vulgar language, cousin." He left the boot alone and smiled at his host. "I have several interests down that way."

"So do I," Gareth said, "perhaps we share more connections?"

Etienne's guilty conscience made him look apprehensive. "More?"

"Yes, besides our mutual acquaintance with Mrs. Lombard."

"Ah, I see." He chuckled, clearly relieved. Serena had not before realized just how stupid he was. And what a poor actor. Gareth Lockheart would scent the lies on him like a hound scented a fox.

"Er, no, I doubt that is so. I am new to England, as Mrs. Lombard may have told you."

"Mrs. Lombard has told me nothing about you."

Again, Etienne chuckled. "I am crushed to hear it." He smiled at Serena, but his eyes were as hard as iron. "Especially when I consider her my *favorite* cousin."

"You have many cousins, Mr. Bardot?"

Although Mr. Lockheart's voice sounded the same as usual, the sheer volume of words he'd spoken since leaving the river betrayed his suspicion to anyone who'd spent any time around him. Serena prayed her *cousin* would shut up, but Etienne had always considered himself the smartest man in any room.

"Only the one in England."

"Two."

"I beg your pardon?" Etienne asked.

"You have two cousins here—Mrs. Lombard and her son."

Etienne laughed, even though Mr. Lockheart had said nothing amusing. "Yes, that is true. How foolish of me. Now he would be my second cousin? Or first cousin, once removed?" He waved his lavender-gloved hand. "I can never recall such distinctions."

"You have come to visit your cousins for a few days, Mr. Bardot? Tomorrow we will have something of an event, followed by celebrations in town. Mrs. Lombard has organized it all—a dinner and small dance at the King's Head, our local inn."

Etienne was momentarily rendered speechless by his offer. So was Serena. Not only at Gareth's uncharacteristic effusiveness, but at the sheer horror of having Etienne anywhere within a hundred leagues of her son.

Etienne's face flushed—most likely in anticipation of what he could steal if he was allowed to run tame in Gareth's house.

"Why thank you, Mr. Lockheart, I should be delighted to stay for a spell. Tell me, what is this event you speak of?" The remainder of the walk was given over to Etienne's disingenuous interest in the rock moving and Gareth's strangely comprehensive explanations.

Meanwhile, Serena's mind spun and whirled trying to figure out a way to get the man who'd raped her, fathered her child, and was now blackmailing her, out of the house before he did something stupid and exposed her lies, as well as his own.

Chapter Fifteen

Gareth did not know what was between Serena and Etienne Bardot, but he suspected it was not cousinly affection.

While he couldn't identify exactly *what* he sensed, he wasn't willing to dismiss his keen perception when it came to subjects that interested him. And nothing had ever interested him as much as Serena Lombard.

Gareth knew he should feel ashamed at the relief that had washed over him when Bardot arrived and saved him from having to make sensible conversation with a woman whom he'd just mounted not once, but twice. But his relief had overwhelmed any shame or remorse.

Right or wrong, Dec's words had taken root into his mind the way lichen penetrated brick and mortar: "You've let your wealth soften your brain; you are from the London gutter and she was the husband of a duke's son. Trust me Gareth, fine women might come to men like us for a bit of rough, but they will *never* do more than take us to their beds."

Venetia's observations couldn't have been more different than Dec's.

So, he had two friends with completely different opinions of his situation. Which one of them should he believe?

Gareth told himself the answer was irrelevant. He would ask for her hand in marriage no matter which of his friends he decided he believed. If she did not want him, he would be disappointed, but he'd weathered disappointment many times and survived. Still, he did not wish to offer for her if it would only put her in the unpleasant position of having to decline her employer.

In any event, he had time to decided; he could not speak to her on the subject with her cousin present.

Etienne Bardot was a man who liked to hear himself talk. He might rival even Dec on that score. But while Declan McElroy was amusing, witty, and—ultimately—kind, Bardot was self-centered, vain, and uninteresting. He also clung to his cousin like a limpet.

Not until Serena had excused herself—close to midnight—did Bardot leave for his own chambers.

Gareth heaved a sigh of relief when he had the library to himself. He'd hardly had a second away from Bardot since meeting the man. When he'd gone to the lake to deliver the specially made rope net he'd had made, Bardot came with him. When he came down to dinner early, hoping to catch up on some correspondence before dining, Bardot was waiting to play a game of billiards with him.

He'd talked non-stop through dinner about his activities in London—gambling, shooting, and boxing at Jacksons—his excursion to some friend's hunting box last fall, the warm reception he'd received from Serena's housemate, the lovely and distinguished Lady Winifred Sedgwick—and on and on. When Serena left them to their port Bardot consumed the better part of a bottle in thirty minutes.

Gareth had half worried, half hoped that Serena would have already gone to bed when they returned to the library, because then he'd have felt entitled to go up to his chambers, as well.

But she'd been waiting for them.

She'd listened to her cousin talk, served tea, and finally begged they excuse her, her usually sunny face tight and drawn.

Gareth had extricated himself from Bardot's clutches soon after, leaving him alone in the library.

***

Serena paced like a cat in a cage. It was past one o'clock, and she knew Gareth had returned to his room not long after midnight because she'd heard his distinctive step as he'd passed her door.

Etienne's room was directly across from hers. Serena knew that because she'd asked Jessup to put him there. The old butler had not shown any interest by even a flicker of his eyelid, but she'd known that her request surprised him. No doubt he believed they were lovers. People tended to think she had looser morals, being French. It didn't matter that the reality was the opposite; French women from her class would never have been allowed the liberty she had in England. It was unfortunate Jessup would now question her morals, but that was far better than him knowing the truth.

She'd heard Etienne's door open and close a half hour after Gareth went to bed, so she'd pulled a chair close to her door and sat, preparing to spend the night at her vigil. But her legs and feet had twitched so badly she'd had to pace, her ears straining to hear movement outside.

Sure enough, the nearly inaudible sound of a door clicking shut reached her ears just as the clock out in the hall struck two.

Serena opened her door and caught him headed toward the staircase, garbed in his night clothes.

"Etienne!" Her whisper was like the crack of a pistol in the dead silence of the hall and he jumped and gave a gratifying squeak of surprise before whirling around.

Serena opened the door wider and motioned for him to come inside. She shut the door soundlessly behind him and turned; Etienne's color was high and his chest was heaving.

"What do you want?" he demanded, his fists resting on hips covered by a ridiculously gaudy purple and gold-trimmed robe.

"Where were you going?" she demanded in French.

His eyes flickered over her, his lips twisting when he saw she was still dressed in her clothes from dinner. "Waiting for me, were you?"

"Please tell me you are not planning to steal from this house."

He lifted a shoulder and dropped his arms before spinning on his slippered heel, prowling her room with deliberation. "What is it to you?"

"It is my *job,* Etienne. A position that is paying me well—which means I can pay *you* well. But not if I get sacked because my cousin has light fingers."

Again he shrugged, lifting the lid of her jewelry cask with one finger and then letting it fall again when he saw the cheap paste jewels it contained.

"The shipment I was expecting in Dover was lost. One of the men who worked for me was captured by excisemen, two of the others killed."

Serena's fingers itched to strangle him. "What did you expect? The English have been patrolling the coast in ever-increasing numbers, even I know that."

"They know who I am."

Serena covered her face with both hands and sagged against the door. "Please tell me you did not use your real name."

He turned on her, all the fear he'd been hiding now evident on his face. "Don't be a fool! But they know what I look like, and it will not be long before descriptions of me circulate the coast."

"So stay in London."

"It's not so simple."

"Why not?" Serena had to fight to keep from yelling.

He grimaced and shoved a hand through his carefully disheveled hair, disheveling it further. "I owe money."

Serena could not have heard him correctly. "I beg your pardon?"

"You heard me, dammit!"

"I cannot believe this."

For once, he had nothing snide or witty to say. "I had a run of bad luck, on top of another run of bad luck. If the shipment had come in this week, I would have been fine. But now?" He heaved a sigh of self-pity that made her want to take his head off.

"I have another delivery scheduled for next week."

"*What?*" She didn't wait for him to speak. "You must get word to them—they must not come or more people could die."

"If I don't get that shipment I will be ruined."

He was even more loathsome than she'd always suspected. Serena marched to the cheap looking jewel box and dumped it out, its pitiful contents spilling over the dressing table. She took a hat pin and jabbed it into the bottom of the box, prying it up. Underneath was a necklace given to her by the duke's mother. It was worth thousands, or at least it

167

had been before she'd sold several jewels. She picked it up and hurled it at his head.

He ducked, but the clasp grazed his cheek.

"Are you mad?" he demanded, running a finger over the small bloody scratch and holding it out for inspection. When she didn't answer, he bent and picked up the necklace, his eyes widening. "You have been holding out on me," he accused.

"Take it. Tomorrow you will leave, and I will not see your wretched face again. This is the last time I will allow you to squeeze even a pence from me, Etienne. I promise you, if you come to me again, I will have you arrested for blackmail, which is a crime. I will leave the country and go back to France. Unlike you, I can earn my own way in life. Now, tell me how to get word to the men risking their lives to bring you goods."

He swept her with a look that oozed scorn. "Why do you care about those strangers? Besides, what can you do about it?"

Then and there, Serena decided she would kill him if he did not leave tomorrow. Maybe he saw something in her eyes, because his hand tightened around the glittering jewels.

"Fine, do what you want—do something stupid and get yourself killed for a handful of strangers, for all I care. Get a quill and paper. You will need to write this down."

Serena wrote down directions to a smuggler shack, names of three men—if you considered Pickaxe, Longfoot, and Derby to be names—and the nonsense phrase which would get their attention: fresh mackerel for a song.

"How can they even think of getting a message through with the channel crawling with excisemen?"

"You don't understand these men; they are like rats, they need only the tiniest gap to squeeze through."

"And why would they agree to perform this service?"

"Because they get part of the shipment. Also, if the men coming over are caught it's possible they might give up their names to the excisemen."

She nodded. "Very well. How much time do I have?"

"I would not leave it beyond the end of the week." He caught her wrist and squeezed. "Why are you doing this?"

"Can you really be so stupid?" She wrenched away. "You *know* why. If they find you it is only one more step to me and Oliver. If the man they have now doesn't talk, the next ones they get might." Her voice shook with anger at his stupidity and the danger it had put them all in.

"What will you tell them?"

"I'm going to tell them you're dead."

He flinched away from her. "That's a bit severe, is it not?"

"Do you wish to evade capture or not? If *they* think you dead, the word will spread. You may be lucky enough to avoid their interest altogether."

A slow, ugly smile curved his lips. "You would have made a fine criminal, Serena."

"Thanks to you, I *am* one."

He laughed and sauntered toward the door.

"Wait!" she hissed, but he'd already opened it and stepped into the hall. "Etienne!"

He turned and leaned close. "Yes, my dear?"

"Don't forget. You will be gone in the morning."

He grinned, and with lightning speed lowered his mouth over hers, giving her a big, wet kiss before she could pull away.

She cursed him in the silence of her mind, watching until he entered his room and closed the door before closing hers and then collapsing against it.

Would it never end?

***

Gareth was tired of waiting. And what was the point, anyhow? For whatever reason, he felt sure she was awake and wishing to speak with him, perhaps even as badly as he wished to speak with her.

He pushed back the bedding and donned his robe and slippers, his body already responding to thoughts of finding her in the kitchen, alone.

He smiled to himself as he left his room, not realizing he'd forgotten to bring a candle in his haste to see her. His smiled widened—perhaps he was overcoming his fear of the dark at the same time he was overcoming his fear of women?

He turned the corner that led to the long hall and froze in his tracks. It was Bardot, and he was leaving Serena's room, dressed in his banyan and slippers, his hair standing out in all directions. He took a step toward his door and then turned back, as if beckoned. He smiled and leaned into the doorway just enough to take hold of Serena and deposit a smacking kiss. Chuckling in a way that made Gareth want to smash his skull, he turned and swaggered across the hall to his room and went inside. Not until his door was closed did Gareth hear her door click shut, as if she'd not been able to tear her eyes away from him until the very end.

Gareth could not have said how long he stood rooted to the plush carpet as his mind, like a well-oiled piece of machinery, ran through the possibilities. It was always ill-advised to jump to conclusions. Perhaps Bardot had suffered a headache and had gone to his cousin for a powder? But a man would not intrude on a woman—even a relation— at such an hour. Bardot would have rung for a servant. Gareth knew his valet, Chalmers, kept every remedy known to man at hand. That was the duty of a personal servant.

Besides, it was impossible to deny that he'd not come from her room like a man with an aching head; he'd looked like a man who'd come from his lover's bed, mussed and wearing a dressing gown.

And then there was that kiss, and that swagger.

When one removed the improbable, one was left with the most likely answer.

The unease he'd felt from the moment he'd met Bardot began to shift and take a different form. Gareth might go through life missing out on its subtleties, but if there was one thing he knew about, it was men who made their livelihoods by manipulating and cheating others. After all, such men had taken his youth and innocence and made him what he was today.

So, Dec had been right. She was not at all what she seemed: the eccentric widow of a duke's son. No, she was a woman forced to make her way using her talents and wits. Her acknowledgement of Featherstone first—a shyster, albeit a clumsy one—and now Bardot, a slightly less obvious criminal—was no coincidence. She was involved with these men and he could only guess that plucking *him* was at the heart of it.

It took him a moment to recognize the alien emotion that seized him. His breathing—regular only an instant before—grew rough and rapid, as if he'd been running. His heart pounded percussively in his chest, which suddenly felt very hollow. And a hard, cold ball of something formed in the pit of his stomach.

Gareth was angry. No, this was cold, murderous fury—an emotion he'd not felt since the night he and Dec had escaped from the home. The thought momentarily diverted him from the rage blooming inside him. Nineteen years ago his rage had been as sharp and as deadly as an arrow, directed at the man who'd used and exploited and terrorized him for years.

But tonight?

Her face rose up in his mind with the clarity of an oil portrait. He saw her as she'd been this afternoon, when she'd taken him inside her body not once, but twice. She'd smiled at him as if . . . as if it had been *him*, Gareth Lockheart, that she'd wanted, not his money. *Him.*

And tonight she had taken another man—her real lover—into her room, into her body.

Gareth hated Etienne Bardot for having what he'd hoped to make his. And he hated Serena Lombard—a woman who'd toyed with him as easily and heartlessly as a cat played with a mouse. And she had done so with a deceptive sweetness that made him want to smash every stick of furniture in the entire house.

But the white, hot core of his hatred? *That* he saved for himself, for the fool who'd convinced himself that people were not all the same. He hated the idiotically optimistic voice in his head that had caused him to strike his best friend when the man had only been trying to save him from humiliation, pain, and disappointment.

Gareth's first impulse was to march down the hallway, fling her door open, and discharge her this very night.

But then he remembered the boy.

She might be a virtuosa manipulator and fraud, but there was no ten-year-old boy in existence who could behave with as much innocence and sweetness as Oliver.

Gareth swallowed his hot rage, unwilling to stoop to her level and inflict pain on somebody who'd done nothing to deserve it.

His forte had always been patience, inhuman concentration, and a relentless drive to solve any problem that faced him. He would plot, plan, and wait until he had a punishment that would fit the crime. And then he would exact his revenge.

Chapter Sixteen

Gareth had already gone to the work site when Serena woke the next morning. When she asked a servant about Etienne, she learned her 'cousin' had left at first light.

She'd not really expected him to comply without a struggle, but no doubt he'd been eager to take the necklace to whomever he used to fence his stolen goods. Serena had picked at her breakfast, her mind sifting through the issue of the Dover trip until she thought she'd go mad. There was no way around it—nobody she could send in her stead. Oh, it was not *her* responsibility, except it was, if she could do anything that would stop it. Every step the authorities took toward Etienne was a step toward her, too. She'd bluffed him when she told him she would confess the truth. No, her plan was different. At the end of the month she would receive her first quarter payment. It would be enough to get her, Oliver, and Nounou to Paris. Once there, she could look for commissions. There were people who would remember Favel and her father and they would give her work. It would be little things at first, but she would be able to keep them fed and housed with the money from this job.

She gave up trying to eat and went to find Oliver. They were to walk over together, since Nounou had no interest in gathering for what she called "foolishness."

Oliver was practically leaping out of his skin and didn't complain even when she told him he could not take the dogs with him.

173

"I believe there will be a lot of people and they will end up underfoot. Besides, you don't want to have to look after them and miss all the excitement?"

"Mr. Lockheart says this might be how the great statues on Salisbury Plain were moved. Mama, did you know that?"

She did, only because he had told her at least six times. "Is that so?" she asked, glad to listen to his excited chatter rather than her own thoughts.

It occurred to her, unhappily, that Oliver had become quite attached to Gareth Lockheart in the weeks he'd been at Rushton Park. It was good he was leaving tomorrow. Already it would be heart-breaking to pull Oliver away from a place he was beginning to think of as home.

She'd been a fool to take this job and believe they could live a normal life. With Etienne always nearby they could never live normally. His constant blackmailing would ensure they never had enough money to live anything other than a hand-to-mouth existence. And while killing him had more than a little appeal, she'd known—once her temper cooled—that she could never kill another human being. Not even one who deserved it.

Although they were early, there were already a surprising number of people milling around, admiring the dimensions of the rock, looking at Gareth's simple mechanism for moving it, and generally enjoying the holiday-atmosphere of the sunny, warm day.

Gareth was standing with Mr. Flowers and the two men were looking out over the area that would soon be covered with water.

Oliver took her hand. "Mama, there are Robbie and Tom." He pointed to the two young boys she knew to be Cook's nephews.

"Go ahead and play. Just make sure you stay well away from the workers once the work begins."

He was gone, the other two boys already running to meet him.

"Mrs. Lombard?"

Serena turned to find Mrs. Cooper, the owner of the little shop of all needs in town. She smiled. "Hello, ma'am. Have you run away and left Mr. Cooper in charge today?"

The older woman chuckled. "Oh no. 'Tis a holiday for him as well. Besides, there is nobody in town to buy anything today. 'Tis like a ghost town." She stepped a little closer. "I hope it's not forward of me, but I've brought some lemonade and a cask of ale. The other ladies have brought a few things as well." Her round cheeks flushed. "We don't often have a day like this, all together, and we thought to make a small picnic."

"What a wonderful idea, Mrs. Cooper." Serena noticed that blankets were being laid and the beds of the few sturdy wagons to have made their way from Rushton Park's drive were serving as impromptu buffet tables. "I don't know why I didn't think of that and we might have had a tent and tables."

Mrs. Cooper waved her hand. "You've had enough to do what with organizing tonight's dance, as well."

Serena laughed. "Now *that* I cannot take credit for. Mr. Jessup, who is a wizard when it comes to such things, made all the arrangements for this evening's festivities."

Another lady, this one a stranger, approached, and soon Serena was surrounded by happy, chattering townsfolk.

***

Gareth felt her before he saw her. He was not a mystical person—quite the opposite, but he knew, without a doubt, when she arrived. The fine hairs on the back of his neck lifted and his skin prickled with awareness. And then Mr. Flowers had looked over his shoulder, smiled, and said, "Ah, there is Mrs. Lombard."

Rather than feeling gratified at being correct, Gareth was unnerved at his body's response. *He* was in control of himself, not his flesh. Or was he? Yesterday flashed through his mind and he frowned. Thinking of the scene at the river made him cringe; she'd manipulated him as skillfully as she'd sketched him.

Fortunately for his sanity, his anger had cooled during the night and the result was a more stable emotion, like ore that had been forged in fire, impurities burnt away until only cold, hard iron remained.

Gareth would not discharge her; why should he? She meant nothing to him. Just a temporary disarrangement of his thoughts. Nor would he waste any time plotting some elaborate revenge. He would simply ignore her, which would probably do enough to hurt her pride.

Satisfied with his decision, he tucked the unproductive thoughts away and turned his attention to the task at hand.

Gareth's pulley, net, and log system ended up moving the big rock up the hill in almost half the time he had planned for it. He believed the entire village and more than a few farmers had taken the day as a holiday and come to watch the event. Women had brought food, children ran wild, dogs barked, and the sun shone its benevolent rays over all of it.

Had he not felt so . . . muffled, he would have enjoyed immensely the sight of the big rock rolling out of its hole as if it had wanted to move all along. The pulley had shifted it with admirable smoothness, the uniform logs he'd chosen rolling as surely as the finest crafted carriage wheels. When the rock reached the summit of the small hill a cheer went up. Mr. Flowers clapped him on the shoulder and then realized what he'd done when Gareth flinched.

"Ah, beggin' your pardon, sir, Mr. Lockheart."

Before Gareth could respond, another hand touched his other shoulder and gave a light squeeze.

"Congratulations, Mr. Lockheart!"

He turned at the sound of *her* voice, his face schooled into the same expression he always wore: an expression that gave nothing of his thoughts away.

"Thank you, Mrs. Lombard. It went far more smoothly than I anticipated." Because he was watching her with the intensity of a scientist monitoring an experiment, he saw how his cool, civil response surprised her, and not pleasantly.

Her smile dimmed a little and she took an almost imperceptible step back. "Our neighbors have provided food and drinks for the festivities." She gestured toward the wagons and blankets on the opposite side of what would soon be the lake. "Would you care to join me?"

He looked down into her hazel eyes, searching for some sign of her duplicitous nature, but they were clear and bright, although the slight dent between them spoke of her nervousness at his distant behavior.

He offered her his arm. "It would be my pleasure."

***

A Figure of Love

Serena took a last look in the mirror. Because it was a country dance, she was wearing the simplest evening gown she possessed. All four of the dresses she'd brought with her from London were gifts from the duke and duchess. Because they were kind and thoughtful, they'd always given her the garments on her birthdays, so that it would not appear to be charity.

Serena knew they believed her to be foolishly proud for refusing the portion they'd reserved for their youngest son, but she felt guilty enough for the deception she perpetrated each time she brought Oliver to see them. She could not bear to take their dead son's inheritance on top of everything else.

The gown she wore was a glorious teal silk that gave her plain brown hair a burnished glow and made her eyes look green, rather than hazel. It was low cut—perhaps scandalously low for the country—but it suited her lush figure and the gauzy fabric of the skirt clung to her, even though she had added a second petticoat to the scant one that had come with the gown.

Around her neck she wore a simple chain and cross. It had no sentimental value but was something she'd purchased so that her neck did not appear naked at the grand functions she attended whenever she visited Keeting Hall. She'd once had a pretty cross of her mother's but like everything else of value—including Robert's letter—it had been left behind when she'd been forced to flee the Continent.

The young maid who often waited on Serena had dressed her hair high with loose curls, a style that flattered her face and made it seem less round and cherubic. She decided to wear her heavy velvet cloak as the nights could be cool. She knew nobody in London would be caught dead in such a practical wrap, but this was the country and she'd always valued comfort over fashion, in any case.

She was to ride with Gareth in his carriage; her body had hummed with excitement all day at the thought. They would finally have a chance to talk, alone. Perhaps they could get past the awkwardness that seemed to exist between them today.

But when she arrived in the great hall, she found only Jessup.

"Good evening, Mrs. Lombard."

"Hello, Jessup."

"Mr. Lockheart has been detained, ma'am. He asked me to tell you that he would join you later at the King's Head." He gestured to the door. "The carriage is waiting for you."

Serena felt as though all the light had gone out of the room. She opened her mouth to ask just what could be detaining him but wisely caught herself. It would be impertinent to ask another employee such a question about their employer. And that's what she was: Mr. Lockheart's employee.

She thanked Jessup and the footman who handed her into the luxurious carriage. Once inside, she slumped against the soft leather seat, her mind churning and her eyes sheening with sudden tears. She blinked hard, stunned by her body's response. Why was she acting like such an emotional fool? How mortifying to show up in front of the entire town without Mr. Lockheart, red-eyed and crying?

In the ten minutes it took to get to town she relived yesterday afternoon a hundred times, sifting every conversation and every look for hidden meaning. But the truth was, he'd behaved much the way he usually did—except for proposing she take her clothes off, of course. But even that had been done in his serious, businesslike fashion.

But his lovemaking? Serena shivered as she recalled his skill with her body and the tender but confident way he'd touched her. He'd been a generous lover who'd made certain she experienced fulfillment before he'd taken his own pleasure. But did it follow that he had any deep feelings for her simply because he was a thoughtful lover?

Serena had very little experience with men. There'd been Etienne, of course, but that had been against her will. She'd taken a few lovers in her early years in England, mainly in the hope she could wipe the vile stain of Etienne from her mind.

The first one had been a fellow sculptor, a selfish, competitive man both in bed and out.

The second had been a sweet, impressionable architect, a man younger than herself who'd quickly become infatuated. That had ended badly and she'd been convinced lovers were just not worth the risk. Indeed, those two experiences had made her wonder what the fuss was all about. The only good thing she had taken from the affairs was that Etienne had not ruined her for physical love.

A Figure of Love

And now, here she was with this mess. In love—or at least infatuated—with her employer, a reclusive, private man who was notorious for avoiding women—or at least she had never heard of any liaisons while he'd lived in London. And she was certain he'd entertained no women while in the country these past weeks. Well, other than her.

The carriage rolled to a smooth stop and she sighed. It was time to go and be social, an activity she usually found pleasurable. But tonight, she only wanted to be alone with her thoughts. Or him.

**

Gareth was both pleased and annoyed by the message. Pleased because it proved Dec was still alive, annoyed because of the reason for the note.

The message was from an inn perhaps one hundred miles from Rushton Park. The note was written by an innkeeper named Trencher, of all things. It appeared Declan had rented a room and enjoyed the 'appurtenant benefits'—Gareth was pretty sure he knew what that meant—but had run out of the means to pay for any of it. Gareth read between the lines for the rest of it. Dec had emerged from his stupor long enough to argue but finally capitulated after negotiating a stay of ejection, giving Gareth's well-known name as a guarantee of payment.

"Damnation."

"Sir?"

Gareth looked up. He'd forgotten Jessup was waiting. The imperturbable butler looked surprised and Gareth realized he'd probably never spoken an angry word in the man's hearing before.

"Shall I tell the messenger to wait?"

"Yes. Put him in the kitchen and feed him. By the time he's done I'll have what is needed ready to go."

"Very good, sir. And Mrs. Lombard?"

"Mrs. Lombard?"

"You are escorting her to the King's Head in six minutes."

Oh, that.

He reached up to scrub a hand through his hair and saw Jessup wince. He lowered the hand and left his hair untouched. "Have the carriage take her. Please tell her I shall be along shortly."

The butler bowed and left.

Gareth's mind bounced between Declan's condition and Mrs. Lombard. He would go to this town, wherever the hell it was, and fetch the idiot home. But he did not think he need do so in the middle of the night. He would go to the dance and leave at first light. Leaving tomorrow had been part of his plan, in any case. He would simply be going to a different destination.

He wrote a brief message and included a draft for an amount well in excess of the standing bill, indicating he would consider it payment toward adequate discretion. Although he doubted there was a person between Rushton and Bicklesfield or Bigglesworth, or whatever the hell it was called, who wasn't aware of Dec's debauch.

Gareth went to the kitchen himself, his appearance causing the skeleton staff to leap to their feet and fidget. He'd given all his employees the evening off to go to the dance and most had taken him up on the offer. The only ones who remained were Cook, Horrocks, one of the gardeners whose name he'd never heard, two scullery maids who could not have been older than ten, and a wiry man with the look and build of a postillion.

"You are waiting for a message?"

"Aye, sir, Mr. Lockheart." The man pulled his forelock and dropped a clumsy bow.

"Sit and finish your meal," Gareth instructed. He tossed the sealed missive on the table when the man had complied. "I've written a letter for your master and included a draft. See to it that it ends up in the correct hands."

The postilion half rose, recalled himself, and then sat, nodding. "Aye, sir. I'll be off in a tick."

Gareth paused on his way to the kitchen door. "Not on the same beast, I presume?"

"Oh, no sir, I changed in town 'afore coming here."

Gareth passed Jessup in the corridor and ordered the curricle brought round. He'd have rather walked but wouldn't make it a mile in the ridiculous dancing slippers Chalmers had insisted he wear. He suspected his black pantaloons, tailcoat, and whites would make him vastly overdressed, but could not be bothered to argue with his valet, whom he had never disputed before. He wondered at this sudden concern for appearances. Surely it was not some foolish worry about what *that woman* would think? He'd schooled himself to think of her only as *that woman*—not Mrs. Lombard and *certainly not* Serena—in the privacy of his own mind.

Gareth had decided to avoid her company as much as possible tonight. That decision was sorely tested half an hour later when he found himself cheek by jowl with every person in the county, watching *that woman* dance with a strapping young farmer and give every appearance of having the time of her life.

The *de facto* head of the town, in the squire's absence, was a Mr. Pillsbury, a farmer of some importance, whose land ran continuous with Gareth's on the western side, not that the man knew it, of course. Mr. Pillsbury and his wife, a woman a head taller and half the girth of her rotund spouse, had trapped Gareth beside the punch bowl, making it impossible for him to get out and dance with *that woman*. Not that he wished to, of course.

"And will you be having entertainments up at Rushton Park this year, Mr. Lockheart?" Mrs. Pillsbury asked, fluttering her eyelashes in a way that was distracting, but not in the way she probably intended.

Gareth realized he'd been staring. "Entertainments?" he parroted the only word he could recall hearing. It was bloody hot in here and there was not a window in sight.

"Yes, balls, dinner parties, and so forth."

"I had not planned on it." His words were met by a sighing sound, making Gareth notice they'd been surrounded by townsfolk—primarily women—without him being aware of it. *Frowning* female townsfolk.

"Er, that might change if the gardens are completed on time," he lied.

A sigh of relief swept through the room, the ripple of air cooling his neck. Mrs. Lombard was now chatting with the bull-necked farmer, while a group of other, equally healthy-looking men hung back a respectful distance, like supplicants awaiting their turn at a shrine.

Gareth put his untouched cup of whatever on the table. "If you would excuse me," he murmured, not realizing Mr. Pillsbury had been speaking until he stuttered to a halt.

"Oh, of course, sir."

181

Gareth wove his way through the bodies, his eyes flickering between her laughing face and plunging neckline, both of which seemed to beckon him like a false lighthouse beacon luring a ship toward hidden rocks. He vaguely recalled his intention of ignoring her but could no longer recall *why* he'd thought that was such an excellent idea.

Well, there was no shame in adjusting one's plan, not that he'd ever done such a radical thing before.

She looked up just as he eased past a clutch of young girls dressed in pastel shades and resembling a cluster of flowers.

"Mr. Lockheart."

A half dozen male heads swung toward him at her words. Gareth nodded vaguely, without making eye contact with any but her. He positively *despised* meeting people in clumps.

"Good evening Mrs. Lombard. I would like to apologize for abandoning you to a solitary carriage ride."

Her smile was as carefree as ever. "No harm done. I hope everything is all right?"

"Oh yes."

She waited with an expectant look, as if he might say more. As if it were his practice to broadcast his personal business like a town crier.

She gestured to the man nearest him, the strapping man without a neck. "I'm sure you recall Mr. Paget."

He looked at the neckless stranger, who smiled broadly, and then back at her. Was she being sarcastic? Laying a trap? Gareth had never seen this man in his life.

"No doubt you've seen the lovely walkway he's been laying out for the past week." She paused and then added helpfully, "In the east courtyard. At Rushton Park." Her carefree smile had become strained.

Gareth had never seen the man, of that he was certain. Yet there was nothing to be gained by belaboring the point.

"I was very impressed with the walkway," he told Mr. Paget, who beamed at him. He turned back to *the woman*. "Would you like to dance, Mrs. Lombard?"

She looked behind him. "Oh, the next set, you mean?"

Gareth glanced over his shoulder and realized all those females he'd pushed past were engaged in a dance and not just milling about.

A Figure of Love

He turned around and caught her biting her lip, her eyes once again sparkling.

"Yes, perhaps the next set would be best."

***

Serena hadn't realized how socially awkward Gareth was until tonight, which was the first time she'd seen him interact with strangers. After all, a dinner with her and his best friend hardly qualified as a social event.

He gave her the same fixed, discomfiting stare in a crowded room that he gave her at home. They might as well be alone for all the notice he took of the hundred or so people milling about, most of them staring at him, waiting to be noticed, wanting to be introduced.

And his blank reaction to Mr. Paget? The man had been working at his house for *weeks*. His obvious lack of recognition had been mortifying. Serena suddenly recalled a comment—one of thousands—Mr. McElroy had made during his stay: "Gareth is not like regular men."

She'd thought he might have meant his looks, which were certainly well above the herd. Or perhaps his intellect, which was keener than any she'd ever encountered. Now she realized McElroy had meant *this*. This . . . imperviousness.

The way he was standing beside her, for example, staring at the dancers in rapt fascination and ignoring the conversation. Why, he was looking at them as if he'd never even *seen* a dancefloor before.

A horrifying thought struck her. She leaned closer to him. "Mr. Lockheart?"

"Hmm?" He could not seem to pull his gaze from the dancers.

"I do not wish to be impertinent, but have you ever danced before?"

That got his attention. He arched his brows in a manner that made him appear lordly and haughty. "Not as such."

"Not as such?" she hissed between smiling lips. "What does *that* mean?"

He shrugged. "I've been watching them. It doesn't look difficult."

She couldn't help laughing. "It is unfortunate that the next one will be quite different."

"Yoo-hoo, Mr. Lockheart!" Coming toward them, and trilling her fingers, was Mrs. Pillsbury.

183

Serena laughed at his horrified expression and he cut her a wounded glare.

"Tell her you have a sore ankle," Serena said out of the corner of her mouth.

"What?"

"Sore ankle," she said, hiding her words with a cough.

"Mr. Lockheart, I would like to introduce you to my cousin Ephraim Plunkett's oldest daughter, Lily."

Gareth acquitted himself with an elegant bow. "A pleasure to meet you, Miss Plunkett."

Mrs. Pillsbury seemed to have something stuck in her eye, or perhaps a tic. Either way, she never stopped fluttering her eyelashes. She nudged the beautiful young girl closer to Gareth, taking a step nearer herself, her elbow accidentally jabbing Serena in the process.

"Oh, Mrs. Lombard." The older woman looked at her as if she'd only that moment noticed her standing there. "I did not see you there."

Her unlikely admission caused the object of her interest to glance sharply from Serena to Pillsbury to the young girl. She waited for comprehension to dawn, but she was to wait in vain.

Serena had not encountered Mrs. Pillsbury in town before, but she'd heard her mentioned as the area's leading light. What had not been mentioned was Mrs. Pillsbury's militant desire to see her younger female relation engage in the most felicitous of matrimonial connections. She remained undaunted in her task, even in the face of Gareth Lockheart's obvious indifference to the lovely young woman standing mere inches away.

Although she'd come to introduce her niece, and no doubt secure at least a set for her, Mrs. Pillsbury's voice droned non-stop on a variety of subjects.

Gareth first stared at her, and then began to shuffle and shift, and finally turned his back on her and stared at Serena.

Mrs. Pillsbury's voice ground to a grudging halt at his unprecedented display of disinterest.

"I've given some thought to the trees you recommended for the drive, Mrs. Lombard."

184

A Figure of Love

A disgruntled clucking sound came from Mrs. Pillsbury's direction, but Gareth appeared not to notice, his gaze fixed, his beautiful—and she knew, soft and skilled—lips compressed into a severe line that made her think he was not talking about trees, at all.

***

The Pillsbury woman was like some kind of large burr. That talked. And could move.

Just when Gareth had managed to block her incessant voice from his head and concentrate on something of worth—like *that woman*—Mrs. Pillsbury came up with yet another scheme.

"I'm afraid Lily has a rather delicate constitution, Mr. Lockheart. Perhaps you might escort her someplace where she might rest and fetch her a glass of lemonade?" The diabolical woman placed a hand on her niece's shoulder and gave her a push in his direction.

Gareth glanced at Serena, who was looking up at him with a slight smile, her expression expectant and curious. Almost as if she were *enjoying* his persecution.

"It would be my pleasure, eh, Mrs. Pillsbury." He'd forgotten the girl's name. That *never* happened. He could not recall ever forgetting anything before in his life. He shoved aside the worrisome thought and led the girl toward a vacant chair, her aunt chattering non-stop in their wake. After depositing them both and seeing to their comfort he ventured toward the refreshments table, which was on the opposite side of the room from *that woman,* who, in any case, had rejoined her admiring horde and appeared to have forgotten all about him.

Gareth had just taken a glass of lemonade from the flunky dispensing it when he felt somebody beside him. He turned to find Edward Poundsworth, a fellow member of the London Mathematical Society, grinning up at him.

Gareth gaped at the unexpected sight; it was like finding one's dentist plowing a field, or one's tailor shoeing a horse.

"Poundsworth," he said stupidly.

"Fancy seeing you here, Lockheart!" Poundsworth clapped him on the back and Gareth caught his wince before it slipped out. He'd been manhandled so much this evening he was all but numb.

"What are you doing here?" he asked rudely.

"Visitin' my uncle, Sir Richard." Poundsworth removed his glasses and began polishing them on the cuff of his ill-fitting coat. He was always doing this, yet his spectacles—the thickest Gareth had ever seen—never looked anything but thumb-printed and smudged.

"*You're* one of Squire Nelby's relatives," was all Gareth could think to say, only aware of how ill-mannered his question sounded after the words were out.

But Poundsworth, a jovial sort, just laughed. "Yes, one of his many nieces and nephews. Here to do the once-a-year pretty, although I missed it the last few years." He replaced his spectacles and Gareth tried not to grimace as he peered up at him through glasses that looked as if they'd been licked by a cow. "I understand you've bought all the old gent's property." Gareth must have made some expression without being aware of it. "Oh, I say, don't chaff yourself, old man." Poundsworth raised a hand to give him a reassuring pat on the shoulder but seemed to recall Gareth's dislike of being touched at the last minute. "I missed the rock-moving today, which was a great disappointment. Heard it was a jolly good time. By the way, did you go to the last meeting?"

There was only one *meeting* he could mean: the monthly London Mathematical Society meeting.

Gareth had not gone, but he'd read of the discussion in the minutes that were printed and disseminated after each meeting.

"Have you seen what Congreave proposed for the Bexam Equation?"

Gareth set the lemonade down on the refreshment table. "Did he make some recommendation?" He frowned. "It was not in the minutes."

"No, he proposed this just last week at an impromptu meeting at Sheffles." Sheffles was one of the few remaining coffeehouses in London. It was a ratty looking hole in a dangerous part of town; the sort of place whose owner didn't seem to mind members of the LMS commandeering tables and arguing mathematics all day.

Poundsworth grinned up at Gareth. "Let me show you what the fool proposed."

A Figure of Love

An indeterminate amount of time later, Gareth and Poundsworth were crouched over a corner of the refreshments table they'd cleared off. The shorter man had brought a small notepad with him because *his* valet would not sigh and cast his eyes skyward because such a thing would distort the fine line of his coat. He'd also had the presence of mind to bring a graphite stick, which Gareth was currently using to debunk Congreave's latest quack theory.

"See here, Poundsworth . . ." but when his companion did not comment on his formula, Gareth looked up.

Serena Lombard smiled down at him.

Gareth stood.

"I thought you should know that it is time for supper."

Poundsworth blinked owlishly through glasses now smeared with graphite powder.

Gareth glanced around and realized that, indeed, the dancing had ceased.

Poundsworth was the first to recover. "I say," he laughed, his round cheeks bright red. "We're in the doghouse now, old chap."

Gareth shook himself. "Mrs. Lombard, this is Edward Poundsworth."

"It's a pleasure, Mr. Poundsworth." She gestured to a table across the now empty dancefloor, where Mr. and Mrs. Pillsbury and their niece sat glaring in their direction.

Gareth looked down at the empty glass on the table; he must have drunk the lemonade during their heated discussion.

"I'm afraid you will have to make up to Mrs. Pillsbury for your neglect, Mr. Lockheart."

Gareth heard the amusement in her voice, confirming his suspicion that she *had* been taking pleasure in his discomfort, and was continuing to do so.

Chapter Seventeen

The short ride back to Rushton Park was largely silent. Gareth seemed to be focused on some internal matter—no doubt the mathematical problem she had caught him and his friend Poundsworth debating in the middle of the dance.

Serena smiled as she recalled their expressions. She'd felt as if she'd disturbed two boys robbing birds' nests or filching sweets from the kitchen. Gareth's face had been lively and flushed, his usually perfect hair in rows and peaks, as if a very small farmer had plowed some of it and made hay-cocks with the rest.

She studied his face in the lamplight that illuminated the carriage. He was staring out the window, or at his reflection in the glass, his strong, angular profile toward her. A flash of memory from yesterday swept over her: Gareth with his eyes burning into hers, his jaws tight and nostrils flared as he held her body against his, stroking into her with deep, controlled thrusts.

She swallowed and looked down at her lap. Why wasn't he speaking to her? She'd just determined to say something to him when the sound of cobbles beneath their wheels told her they were already home.

Gareth opened the door before the carriage had even come to a stop, flipping down the steps and handing her out. They gave their things to a waiting footman and walked in silence to the foot of the stairs. She was about to ask him if he cared for tea when he turned to her.

"Thank you for a pleasurable evening, Mrs. Lombard."

A Figure of Love

Before she'd even opened her mouth, he strode down the hall in the direction of the library.

Even for Gareth Lockheart, this was strange behavior.

Serena continued to contemplate his odd actions as she undressed herself and changed into her nightgown and dressing gown.

She was still mulling it sometime later when she heard someone talking in the hall. When she peeked out the door, she saw the backs of Gareth and his valet just turning the corner.

She closed the door and looked at the clock: it was after one. Country entertainments ended early and they'd left the King's Head before midnight. She'd been pacing and dithering for almost an hour. Already she knew she would not sleep.

She should go to him, ask him directly what was wrong. He was the sort of man who appreciated directness, she'd noticed that almost immediately.

Serena groaned. Respectable women did not approach men in their chambers at one o'clock in the morning. Respectable women did not approach men in their chambers at *any* time of the day or night. Respectable women did not strip naked in front of men in the middle of the day, either.

She flung herself into the wingback chair beside the fire and took her sketchbook out of her all-but-empty satchel. She'd put the other items—the miniature, wedding lines, and money—in the reticule she'd carried tonight, keeping those few things with her, as always. But there'd been no room for a sketchbook. She had dozens of sketchbooks, but this one—with the sketches of Gareth—had now become an item of value. She flicked through the book until she found her favorite. He'd been looking at Oliver, who was on the shore. His face wore a smile she'd never seen before and she'd known they were trading taunts about manliness or lack-thereof.

She carefully tore the page from the book and folded it, tucking it in with the marriage lines. There, now she would not have to worry about losing all trace of him should she and Oliver need to run.

***

Gareth beat the leather bag with a savagery that popped one of the seams loose and sent sand flying across the padded floor. He seized the bag with both hands and stilled it, resting his head on his forearms while he caught his breath.

His mind seemed to have arranged itself into two distinct camps. On the one side was reason and calm and mathematics—he was still annoyed to have been stopped before he and Poundsworth could finish their counter-proof. On the other, was *that woman*. She had taken possession of a full half of his concentration. Perhaps even more than fifty percent?

Gareth shook his head at the pointless thought.

He told himself he'd done the right thing—the *gentlemanly* thing—when he'd left her standing alone in the hall. He had to confess that when he'd woken this morning he'd not entirely abandoned his plans to ravish her and then callously leave her. But sometime during the evening, without him even being aware of it, he'd come to realize such petty, childish revenge was beneath him. It was beneath anyone—or at least it should be.

So instead of ravishing her, he'd taken his bruised sensibilities to the library and made preparations for his departure in the morning. Yet here he was, at two o'clock in the morning, beating this infernal bag.

He'd sent Chalmers to bed after the man had driven him half-mad with questions about where they were going and for how long and so forth.

"*You* are going to London and will await me there, Chalmers." The last thing Gareth needed was more spectators to Dec's bad behavior. Not that his dour valet hadn't seen most of it before. Still, Gareth decided he wanted to take the journey alone. He'd dressed himself for years without a valet, he could do so again.

Once he'd sent Chalmers packing, he'd stripped to his drawers and begun to exorcise whatever possessed him. He should have wrapped his hands, he realized, looking down at his grazed, swollen knuckles. He heard a sound behind him and sighed.

"Chalmers, I was—" he stopped. It wasn't Chalmers, but *the woman* who stood in the doorway.

She swallowed so hard he could hear it all the way across the room.

"I'm sorry. I knocked. I thought your valet was in here. I heard you both talking as you passed my room. I thought maybe nobody heard me because of all the activity. I didn't—" she broke off as he strode toward her, her eyes sweeping his naked chest and dropping lower, to where his body had begun rejoicing at her unexpected arrival.

He stopped a foot away from her, not bothering to put on his robe or conceal his sweaty body or growing erection. If she insisted on invading his privacy, she could deal with the consequences.

"What can I help you with, Mrs. Lombard?"

She licked her lips in a way that made his cock throb, her eyes making the journey from his hips to his face with tortoise-like speed.

Again, she swallowed, her chest rising and falling in little jerks. "Your bag is beside the door. Are you leaving?" Her voice sounded strained and it pleased him to know he could at least discountenance her with his body.

"In the morning."

"But you said you'd stay until we'd begun filling the lake?"

"I changed my mind."

She nodded slowly, her expression oddly . . . stricken.

A ball of anger rose from his stomach and momentarily choked him. She was an impressive actress; she should not be playing with stone and dirt but treading the boards. How *dare* she act as if she cared what he did or where he went? Did it mean nothing to her to take her lover to her own bed one night and go to Gareth's bed the next?

He took a step closer, for once shedding his obsessive fastidiousness and not caring that he was sweaty and no doubt smelled like a barnyard animal. "You still have not told me what I can do for you, Mrs. Lombard."

She had to crane her head back to meet his eyes.

"Are you angry with me?"

The question stopped him like a stone wall. Before he could think of an answer, she touched him, her hand on his chest as light as a soft breeze.

Gareth's control snapped and he crushed her mouth with a ferocity that left the metallic taste of blood flooding his mouth. His blood, her blood, both, he didn't know or care. Her fingers plunged into his hair and she yanked him down, meeting his violently ravaging tongue with her own.

She pushed her hips against his and his mind went blank as they ground against each other like rutting beasts. Vaguely, he heard the tearing of fabric and realized it was her dressing gown. He pulled away from her throat, which he'd sucked hard enough to mark—and looked down at her. It was her hand that had torn the fastenings off her dressing gown while trying to open it. Gareth took the fragile nightgown she wore beneath it with both hands and tore it open with a long, soft hiss.

She shrugged and clawed at the garments until both fluttered to the floor. When she would have pulled off his drawers, he stopped her, taking both wrists in his hand and lifting them above her head.

"What?" she demanded, her eyes, so drowsy with passion only an instant earlier, widened in shock as he held her in a cruel grip. Gareth paused to admire the musculature in her arms, which was that of a woman who worked with her hands, connected to the lush, ripe body of a woman made for pleasure.

"Stop struggling," he ordered.

She stopped, her lips parted, her breathing shallow and ragged.

He drew her hands higher without any resistance, stretching her until she stood on her toes. He drank in her taut, vulnerable form, the high position of her arms raising her breasts until the stiff peaks pointed up. He walked her back the short distance to the door.

"I am going to release you, Mrs. Lombard. You may either take my dressing gown and wrap it around yourself and return to your room, or you may grasp the door frame with your hands and do exactly what I tell you. Those are your choices."

He let go of her hands, expecting them to drop. Instead, they remained where they were, clasped together.

He watched her throat move, as if it was a struggle to find the words and push them all the way out.

"I want to stay."

Gareth's jaws clenched and his body hardened as unbearable anticipation thundered through him. His brain shrieked at him to take her, plunge into her, quench the fierce need he had for her. But he took himself as firmly in hand as he'd just held her.

A Figure of Love

"Take the doorframe with your hands."

She did so, and he nodded. "Keep your position." His hand went to the tape of his tented drawers, her eyes following. He released the string and pushed down the fine lawn, stepping out of the cloth and then picking the garment off the floor. He took his time folding it before placing it on a chair, a leisurely activity that was only to test his control over her, since Chalmers would merely stuff them in a laundry bag when he found them.

He approached her but did not let their bodies touch. Her eyes were riveted to his erection, which pulsed and slickened under her stare. He moved close enough that the sensitive crown rested against the skin of her midriff. A satisfying noise came from deep in her throat and she shivered and closed her eyes, her head tipping back.

"Look at me."

She swallowed convulsively but opened her eyes.

He flexed his hips, the action lightly rubbing his cock against her soft belly. Gareth thrilled at the sight of her pounding pulse and hard nipples—signs of desire for him she could not feign. She might be using him, but at least she wanted this—his body, and what it could do to her—as badly as he did.

"I want to bury myself deep inside you." He ground his length against her, making her gasp while he whispered in her ear, "But I think you know that, don't you?" He stepped away, until their bodies were no longer touching and raised his hands, palm out, barely grazing the erect tips of her breasts, caressing them with light, circular motions.

She jerked and bucked against him, her back arching, the impressive muscles of her arms like the taut strings of a bow as she clutched the wooden door frame above her head and strained toward him.

Gareth would have liked to bind her wrists and then tie her arms to restrain her, but he did not have the patience for such games tonight, nor did he have Venetia's impressive array of equipment. He decided he liked this even better: making her voluntarily provide her own bondage. He stroked her sides with feather touches, her body shaking, her eyes hot and wanting, the pulse at the base of her neck racing.

He took his time, avoiding her small, pebbled nipples and tracing the sensual curve of a hip, the soft, velvet swell of her stomach, and the quivering flesh of her thighs. A small, angry, growl came from deep inside her body.

Gareth could have told her the teasing was worse for him. His body *hurt* with desire but she was a banquet and he had only this one chance to savor every part of her.

He flicked her breast with his tongue, making her jump. And then the other, and back to the first, alternating and sucking now, pulling and nipping her tender flesh. She writhed beneath him, chasing his mouth with her body when he moved away.

He stopped as abruptly as he'd started. "Arms above your head, Mrs. Lombard."

Gareth memorized her look of stunned disbelief and stored it carefully in his mind, like a greedy squirrel storing nuts for the lean times to come.

Her hands slid back up the frame.

"Higher," he said, when she stopped, nodding when her elbows were straight. "Good. Keep them there." He dropped to his haunches, the sudden motion again causing her to jump. When he looked up, he saw her head had come away from the wall, her hands had sagged.

This time he had only to raise his eyebrows and her arms straightened. But her eyes stayed fixed on him.

Reveling in his power he leaned forward and tongued the golden down that dusted the gentle swell of her belly. She gave a sharp gasp, which he ignored, his tongue circling the shallow depression of her navel before dipping into her.

"Oh."

Gareth smiled against her velvety skin, probing the sensitive dimple while his hands slid from her hips to her ankles, tracing the delicious shape of her legs. Up, and then back down. Up and down. Until he circled each of her delicate ankles with his hands and gently pulled.

Her feet slid apart without resistance and he lowered into a more comfortable crouch. This time, when he stroked up her legs, he stopped at the apex of her thighs. Her hips trembled beneath his hands as his thumbs moved toward her mound. Gareth wrenched his gaze away long enough to make sure she was still obeying. Her eyes held a mixture of raw desire and curiosity that told him she'd never had a man's mouth on this part of her body before.

That knowledge sent a bolt of lust straight to his cock and he parted her lips and took her tight little bud into his mouth.

***

Serena bit her lower lip *hard* to keep the animals sounds from slipping out, but it didn't work. It was all she could do to keep herself upright. The rest of her faculties had decamped, casualties of the transcendent pleasure emanating from between her legs.

The view of him alone had been enough to send her body hurtling toward release: broad, sculpted shoulders, powerful hands moving up and down her thighs, biceps rippling with leashed power as he worked her toward madness.

She wanted to see his face in the worst way, but his brown tousled locks hid what his wicked mouth and tongue were doing.

She'd believed his hands on her body yesterday—was it only yesterday?—had been the most erotic sensation possible. She'd been wrong.

He nudged her thighs wider and she opened for him eagerly. Some distant part of her mind said she'd feel ashamed later. But for now. . .

His mouth was hot and clever and it felt like he had half a dozen tongues. Her climax came fast and hard, surprising a cry out of her as her hips bucked beneath his lips. She was still shuddering from the aftershocks when he surged to his feet and lifted her off hers all in one powerful motion. Her legs went around his waist as his hands slid beneath her bottom. His lips were red and slick, his eyes as black as coal.

"You can release the door frame now."

Triumph and amusement echoed in his words but she didn't care. She'd do whatever he asked of her to feel that way again.

"Touch me."

She fell on his mouth like a starving person, consuming him as he'd just done her, tasting herself on his tongue. He lifted her higher while they kissed, until she felt his hot, insistent crown nudging against her sex.

He leaned away from her, just far enough that she could see between their bodies. His stomach, lean, ridged, and sweaty, hers flushed, soft, and trembling.

He lifted her higher, until she could see his erection. "Guide me inside you."

Serena reached for him, reveling in his harsh hiss of breath and the feel of him against the sensitive skin of her palm. She stroked him, spreading the moisture from his small slit all over his silky hardness before placing him against the entrance to her body.

A low sound of pleasure rumbled up from deep inside him and he began to lower her onto his shaft, inch by rock hard inch, not stopping until he was fully sheathed.

She tilted her hips, taking him a tiny bit deeper; the action making him groan.

The sound of this composed man coming apart was almost as pleasurable as the feeling of his thick length filling her body.

Almost.

Serena kissed his jaw, chin, cheek, neck—anything she could reach—while he began to move. He pulled out slowly and then savagely slammed back in.

They both grunted with pleasure.

"Gareth," she whispered in his ear. "Yes."

He spread his feet shoulder length apart to stabilize himself while he worked her, penetrating her deeply with each brutal thrust. The power he was expending caused him to breathe like a bellows, his muscles flexing and stretching and as hard as iron beneath his slick skin. The sight of his exertion was almost as arousing as what he was doing to her.

Almost.

Even now—when he'd already brought her to climax—he managed to rub that exquisite part of her body every time he pumped into her, driving her over the edge before him.

The pleasure consumed her, and she was only vaguely aware that he'd began to breathe more harshly—his muscles less coordinated with every thrust. She forced her heavy lids open, desperate to watch him come undone.

A Figure of Love

His eyes were closed, his jaws clamped tight and his nostrils flared with each snap of his powerful hips. He began to shake—to lose that last scrap of control—and with a hoarse yell, he drove himself deep and emptied himself inside her.

Serena clung to him, listening to the pounding of his heart against her chest, reveling in the feeling of his strong arms around her; she never wanted to let him go.

***

Gareth left his body for a moment, the shudders that wracked him gradually diminishing until all that was left was a heavy lethargy and sense of contentment.

But there would be no falling asleep in this position.

He hefted her a bit higher before straightening his legs with a groan and carrying her into the next room, where he gently laid her down on his bed.

She smiled up at him, made a soft sound of contentment, and then curled up and proceeded to fall asleep. Gareth shook his head in amazement and pulled the blankets over her body. By the time she was covered, her eyes were closed and she was already breathing in a deep, regular rhythm.

Gareth left her sleeping and padded naked to the bathing chamber that was off his dressing room. Like all the suites in the house there was a fireplace that heated a tank of water above it. The tank was concealed by a wooden panel, on which some enterprising soul had painted a pastoral scene. He turned the valve that sent hot water gushing to the tub.

Once he'd submerged himself, he lay back and relaxed. On the outside. On the inside, his usually organized mind was like a ship that had been seized by mutinous sailors.

He should have told her nothing was wrong and sent her away. He should have told her he'd never intended for their interactions to go beyond a business relationship. Instead, he'd acted out a sexual fantasy.

At the thought of said fantasy he began to stiffen again. Venetia had engaged in anything Gareth had dreamt up, and a lot more that he hadn't. It hadn't surprised him that he enjoyed restraining his lovers. He knew enough about himself to know he valued control above all else: control over events, his person, his surroundings—over anything that mattered. Controlling his lover's pleasure had been the logical next step.

He'd always enjoyed his nights with Venetia, but these two explosive incidents with Mrs. Lombard? Gareth shook his head; he had no words for what he was feeling right now.

The women themselves were very different, of course, but it wasn't just that. With Venetia, he'd bedded her and left her, forgetting about her until the next time he needed sexual release.

Right now he was further away from forgetting Serena Lombard than he'd been *before* he'd sated himself. As far as he could discern, each encounter with her seemed to leave a deeper imprint on his brain and diminish his ability to control his thoughts, which was something he usually did with merciless rigidity.

And speaking of rigidity, never had his body been so demanding and insatiable in the past. He'd spent himself less than an hour ago, and he wanted her again. And again.

He shook his head and applied himself to the business of washing his body, ignoring his insistent erection the way he ignored any other time-wasting diversion. By the time he'd finished with his bath he'd taken the reins and steered his brain in a different direction.

Declan.

It was getting on for four in the morning. It would be light soon, at least light enough to ride.

He was shaved and dressed for riding at half-past. When he went into his bedroom, he saw she was still asleep, but had turned. She'd exposed one delicious breast in the process, her hair streaming across the pillow, half up, half down.

He could crawl right into bed with her. Fasten his mouth on her rosy nipple and explore her in the comfort of his own chambers, horizontal. Not on a rocky river's edge or showing off his strength for her against a wall, but in comfort.

He was fully hard and halfway to the bed, his hand on his cravat, when he recalled another man who'd swaggered because of this woman barely a day before. Something ferocious and cold twisted in his gut and Gareth put his hand to his midriff, feeling as if he'd been knifed. But there was no puncture, no gash, no blood. No wound at all, in fact—at least no injury the human eye could see.

***

Serena was having the most delicious dream. She was with Gareth, and he was making love to her, holding her tight in his arms. So tight she could not move. Too tight, in fact. She cracked an eyelid and felt a moment of terror when she did not recognize her surroundings.

And then it all came back, like a deluge from a rainspout. She pushed herself up clumsily, hampered by bedding, which seemed to have coiled and twisted around her body from neck to toe.

The first thing she noticed is that she was alone. Candles burned in the wall sconces and the room next door—the room where they'd—

She looked away from the doorframe, blushing hotly even though there was nobody to see.

He had seen.

She covered her burning face with a cool hand. Lord. He had seen *everything.* Certainly more of her body than Serena herself had ever seen.

She pushed back the bedding and heard something crackle. A piece of paper, her name—Mrs. Lombard—written on the front in writing so perfect it looked like the printing in a book.

When she unfolded the missive a second sheet of paper fell out: it was a bank draft, but for the remainder of her work rather than the agreed upon quarter.

She opened the letter with shaking hands.

"Mrs. Lombard:

Enclosed is the agreed upon payment for the entirety of the work. I have paid you the remainder rather than a quarter as I do not anticipate returning to Rushton Park for some time."

Serena's hand shook so badly she could not read the small, neat writing. She swallowed, and then spread the letter out on the bed.

"Please send any questions or requests for funds through my factor in London. I took the liberty of entering your chambers only to select an undamaged nightgown and dressing gown. Both are on the bench at the foot of the bed. The servants have been instructed that you are not feeling well and to avoid both the family and guest wing until later in the day.

Your servant,
Gareth Lockheart"

Serena stared at the letter as if it were a live asp; how dare he treat her this way—like some kind of prostitute? She grabbed the piece of paper and tore it to shreds. "You—you—*fiend.* You heartless *snake!* No, snake is too good for you; a snake has a heart." Or at least Serena thought they did. She shoved the pointless thought away and grabbed the pieces of paper and ripped them into even smaller pieces. "You cad! You-you *poltroon!* You automaton!" This last bit she yelled in English.

She launched herself out of bed and snatched the—neatly folded, of course—nightgown from the bench and threw it over her head, her eyes sweeping the unhealthily tidy, sparse room with a scathing glare. She yanked on her robe and stormed from the room, making no effort at stealth.

She told herself she was *glad* he had sneaked off like a coward, slinking away in the dark of night like a cur with its tail between its legs. She'd had lovers, he was just another. Albeit a lover unlike any other. Serena uprooted that thought—and any other positive ones that might have sprung up—like noxious weeds.

When she got to her room she washed her face with freezing cold water, raked her hair back into a bun so tight her head hurt, and donned her work clothes. The only thing to do in a mood like this was work with unbreakable items like shovels and dirt.

She went first to the schoolroom, dreading what she would have to say to Oliver. But when she arrived, it was to find him happily completing the mathematics homework she had assigned him the day before the festivities.

"Hello, Mama! Guess what Mr. Lockheart left me?"

Serena bit her tongue.

"Look." He held up a handful of metal bits. "They are the parts he had made according to my schematic." Oliver rose and went to his worktable, which was arranged in neat piles, each one marked clearly and beside clearly drawn mechanical drafts. He stopped in front of the project on the far end. But when Serena tried to look at it, he shook his head. "It is a surprise, Mama. You cannot see it yet."

"What if I sneak in here and peek while you're sleeping?"

He laughed and shook his head. "You wouldn't do that." His forehead furrowed. "Would you?"

It was her turn to laugh. "Come here and give your mother a hug."

He complied and she closed her eyes while she pulled him tight. "You are getting taller," she accused the top of his head. He nodded and pulled away, too old to submit to hugging and cuddling without a struggle.

"Nounou made only a tiny mark on the door frame. I have grown almost a quarter of an inch since coming here."

Serena wondered if she would ever be able to look at a door frame again without getting a rush of heat between her thighs.

"I am almost done with my math work and then I will work on my story." He did not sound nearly so enthusiastic about his English and French studies as he did math and history.

"When you are done come down to the parterre garden and you can help me. I will even pay you for your work."

"You will?"

Serena felt terrible at his excitement. She gave him so little money, even pennies for sweets were hard won. Thanks to Etienne. Recalling the thieving pig made her remember Dover. She closed her eyes for a moment. Well, at least she would not have to explain her journey to her employer, would she?

***

Biddenden was the name of the town Declan had chosen for his rustication and the Biddenden Twins was the name of the inn where he was ensconced.

Gareth had taken his time, having to force himself to do so. Why rush? After all, what awaited him would be anything but pleasant. Even though he had made several stops and gentled his mount, Thunder—a ridiculous name Oliver had given the horse when he'd learned Gareth had failed to do so—was tired and so was he when they rode into the small agricultural town.

The first person Gareth saw when he entered the courtyard was the postilion who'd brought the message.

The small man darted forward to take Gareth's mount. "Good afternoon, Mr. Lockheart."

Gareth nodded, pulling off his gloves while looking around the neat and tidy courtyard with approval. At least it did not appear to be the type of place to have damp sheets and bugs.

"Ah! Welcome, welcome—Mr. Lockheart, I presume?" A stout man wearing an apron was barreling toward him, his blinding smile proof that the extra money had been well-conceived.

"You are Mr. Trencher?"

"Aye sir, at your service. Willie, take Mr. Lockheart's bag and have it brought up to his rooms." He turned to Gareth. "I've put you right beside Mr. McElroy, thinking that would be the way you'd want it."

Gareth thanked him for the dubious honor and followed his bustling person into the inn.

"Is Mr. McElroy out?" He peered around the darkened interior of the taproom, thinking this is was probably the most likely place to find him. But only two farmers sat in the cool near darkness.

Trencher motioned for Gareth to follow him out into the hall, where he stopped, and glanced up at him with a flushed, uncomfortable look.

Gareth sighed. "I will have the words with the bark still on them, Mr. Trencher."

"Ah, yes, as to that. Well, Mr. McElroy has not left his room in some time. We've given up sending girls to clean—they are my daughters, you see, and—"

"Yes, yes of course. I understand keeping any females away from him well enough. Is he ill?"

"Oh, no, nothing serious. Just a bit too much elbow bending, if you take my meaning."

Gareth frowned. It was as he thought: drunk.

"How has he been getting his spirits?"

He could see the question surprised the innkeeper. "Why, we deliver 'em, sir."

"You shall cease that immediately. When he rings, bring him ale, and nothing stronger." He paused, considering the next few days and how unpleasant they would likely be. "You said you put me in the rooms adjacent. Are there other rooms?"

"Oh, aye, two more there and another two in the garret."

"And are they occupied?"

"Which, sir?"

"*All* of them."

He scratched his forehead, clearly confused by the direction and pace of the conversation. "Not as yet, sir. It is a slow time, the spring being—"

"I wish to engage them."

Trencher squinted up at him. "I beg your pardon? Did you say—"

Gareth was aware of a great tiredness rising in him. This kind of transaction or discussion, where so many more words were expended other than what was necessary, made him wish to crawl into bed and hide.

"Yes, I will pay for every room here. Do not rent to anyone else."

"Uh—"

Gareth tossed his gloves in his hat and handed the innkeeper both, along with his crop. "My man will not be joining me. Do you have somebody to see to my needs?"

"Ah, yes sir. My daughter's husband is—"

"Please send the gentleman up with my things and direct me to Mr. McElroy's room."

Declan's room was at the end of the hall, which was dark and narrow and poorly lighted. Gareth made a mental note to order more candles. He rapped on the door and waited. When no sound issued from within, he rapped again, harder.

"What the devil do you want?" a recognizable voice roared.

Gareth opened the door and had to duck as a boot sailed past his head and landed in the hall.

Declan lay on the bed, the sheets tangled around him, empty bottles on the floor, and the foul stench of body odor and vomit hanging over the room like a cloud.

Declan had leaned down to scour the floor by the bed for more projectiles. He came up with an empty bottle in his hand and froze in the act of throwing it.

His shoulders slumped. "Oh, it's you."

Gareth breathed through his mouth. "Did you expect somebody else?"

Dec tossed the bottle onto the bed beside him, where it clinked against something. "I knew there would be no money without a lecture."

Gareth shut the door and picked his way across to the window, which he opened, filling his lungs with air that did not smell like a sewer.

He turned and propped himself up on the sill, not wishing to get too far from the source of air. "If I recall correctly, it was *you* who was lecturing *me* the last time we spoke."

Declan didn't answer. He looked worse than Gareth had ever seen him; gaunt, unshaven, skin yellow and unhealthy.

Gareth looked at his best friend in the world. The only person who knew everything about him, and still stood by him.

"I don't want to lecture you. I want to help you."

The Irishman turned on him like a rabid cur that had been kicked. "Well you *can't* help me, Gareth! I am beyond it."

"Nobody is beyond it. What happened?"

"What the bleeding, fucking hell do you think happened?"

"You lost a packet in some hell?"

"I lost it *all* in some hell."

Something cold crawled down his spine. "All? What do you mean, all?"

"You're the goddamned genius, *you* figure it out." He shot him a poisonous glare. "Don't worry, I didn't touch anything belonging to you or the company. Everything I lost belonged to me."

Gareth hadn't even considered the possibility that Declan could have gambled away everything he had. But it was true, the other man had signing rights on all Gareth's accounts. Still, the amount of money Dec had gambled away must have been in the hundreds of thousands. Half of everything they had ever made, in point of fact. How long had this been going on? How could Gareth have been blind to it?

He rubbed his temple, which had been dully throbbing for a good part of the day; the ache had suddenly turned sharp.

"So, it's not all gone."

"Your half is yours. I won't take your bloody handouts."

"I couldn't spend all the money I have in a hundred years, and there is more coming in every day. According to my calculations, our new pottery may be our most successful venture yet. With the contracts Mister—"

"I don't care."

"Declan, you have always been the one who understands other people, their foibles, nuances, expressions, wants, desires, machinations. It is a great weakness in me that I cannot see to the heart of any problem that involves people." Serena's face flashed into his mind and he ruthlessly banished it. "Even you, the one person who knows *me*, a person closer than a brother, I do not truly know. I look at you and am mystified by what drives you, what interests you, what would make you happy. I trust you with my life, with everything I have, and I would give my life to save yours." He shook his head, his fear deeper and more chilling than any he could recall since they were both boys. Since that night when everything had changed. "I know you feel the same. I know it. As surely as I know the Fibonacci Sequence or the Pythagorean Theorem."

He looked up from his clenched hands to find his friend staring, his eyes blank and dead.

"Let me help you Declan, please. Because if you die, you will be killing both of us."

They sat in silence for so long Gareth thought he would never answer.

"I don't know what ails me, Gare. I don't," he said, as if Gareth had argued. "I could not believe it the first time we bought a company, turned it on its end, and made money." He shook his head as he stared into the past, the ghost of a smile on his lips. "I felt rich—*so rich*." He looked up. "But the hole inside me—you know?"

Gareth *did* know.

"The money didn't fill it. It just seemed to make it bigger."

Gareth nodded. He had no better words for what Declan was describing, but he knew the feeling as surely as he knew his reflection in a mirror. He'd quickly figured out money wouldn't fix the problem. For him it had been the quest for knowledge that had filled the void—at least as long as he stayed buried inside the quest. Any time he ventured into the wider world—any occasion without a book or formula or journal—he would look down to find the hole had advanced, that he was standing on the edge looking down into something worse than the dark.

"I had to do it, didn't I?" It was a question Declan hadn't asked him for nineteen years.

Gareth nodded. "It was me or him, Dec. And after me, he would have come for you. You defended us—you saved my life."

"I know, I know," the words came out on a moan. "I've told it to myself a thousand times. But a murderer is a murderer."

Gareth did not believe that, but his friend needed something more. "I don't think the hole can be filled with money, or drink, or gambling, or an endless string of women." Dec opened his mouth but Gareth raised his hand. "Let me finish. I'm not lecturing you; I'm saying something out loud that is true about both of us. I don't gamble or drink, but I bury myself in numbers and the clarity and numbness they give me. When I can't, I am . . . well, you have seen what I am. I could not function in society; I cannot talk to the people with whom we are partners or investors." He shook his head, "I cannot go to a country dance without making an ass of myself. But recently I've noticed times when I do not feel this ache. When I help the boy, when I try to do something for somebody else, I am somehow—" He shrugged, frustrated with his inability to describe the contents of his own head. "I don't know. It is just—*better.*"

Declan spread his hands on the dirty sheets, looking at them as if he'd never seen them before. "Somedays, it all seems so pointless. Getting out of bed, even." He looked up. "Do you think it's this way for everyone?"

Was it? Gareth opened the door in his mind where he kept the things he didn't want to think about. The woman was the first of those things to sneak out, flooding his mind with the sight, scent, and feel of her. Was she restless and miserable and only part of a person? He didn't think so, although he had often sensed that something dark lurked beneath her laughing eyes and light-hearted ways. But what did he know? When had he ever applied himself to the emotions of others and how to read them? Or to his own emotions, for that matter.

"I don't know," Gareth admitted. "But I do know I don't want to live that way—hating my life so badly I will hasten its ending—not if I can help it." His words didn't surprise him, even though he'd never thought them so clearly before.

"Gare?"

Gareth looked up.

"About the woman—"

"Never mind about that."

"No. I want to say I'm sorry. I never should have said the things I did. I was wrong."

As clear as painting in a museum Gareth saw Serena kissing her lover, as he'd done countless times since. He shook his head and looked away. "You weren't wrong about her, Dec. About her, you were dead on."

Chapter Eighteen

Serena wished, not for the first time, that she was in Gareth's sumptuous carriage rather than the mail coach. But using his coach all the way to Dover would have been outrageous, even for a person who was still very angry with Mr. Gareth Lockheart.

But she *had* used his carriage as far as Sittingbourne; she'd had no other choice. She'd told Jessup she would arrange a post chaise for the return trip, even though that would eat up a chunk of her wages. The mail coach had cost her a half guinea each way, which was—to her way of thinking—highway robbery, especially as they'd already had to get out once to walk over a wretched section of road because the coach couldn't get over it.

When she'd purchased her fare and inquired as to the schedule the innkeeper at the posting inn had boasted the coach would make the trip in five hours, his eyes dismissing her as unworthy to travel on it in any case, being a woman on her own.

But Serena had not been able to take Nounou and leave Oliver unprotected. Already it had been difficult to leave him. More than once she imagined Etienne arriving at Rushton Park, either to check on her progress in Dover, or to squeeze more money out of her. Travelling alone was a risk but she could not afford twice the fare and Nounou would have slowed her down.

The coach left Sittingbourne at seven o'clock, which meant she would need to pay for lodgings in Dover, if there was any respectable place that would take her.

A Figure of Love

As it turned out, after two hours stuck in a ditch and another hour to fix a problem with a wheel, they didn't arrive at the Dover posting inn until after three in the morning. Serena was bone-tired, every muscle and nerve abraded and jostled from eight hours either crammed cheek-by-jowl or clambering over ragged and steep terrain.

On top of her physical exhaustion, her anxiety over Etienne's incessant demands, Gareth's inexplicable behavior, and the prospect of confronting a group of English smugglers, had all combined and taken its toll.

The inn was accustomed to odd comings and goings and the preparations were already being made for the outgoing coach, which departed Dover at four every morning—a delightful trip Serena hoped to be making tomorrow morning.

For once, she'd not brought the full contents of her satchel. She'd left her marriage lines and the precious miniature tucked beneath the tools in her big wooden toolbox, which she kept locked in the tack room. She'd brought her sketchbook, in which there were dozens of pictures of Oliver, and, of course, all but one of those she'd drawn of Gareth. Jessup had advanced her money from his housekeeping money on the bank draft, which she'd had no time or opportunity to take to a bank. As a result, she carried only so much as she'd estimated she would need for this journey.

She ordered a hearty breakfast and ate in the common room, which was bustling with passengers showing up to claim a spot on the next coach. The inn was far too busy for anyone to pay her much mind and she ordered a second pot of tea after finishing the first one.

The light was breaking over the cramped streets of Dover when she paid her shot and headed for the establishment where she might find the men she needed to talk to.

"Smuggling isn't their only lay," Etienne had told her. "You'll find two of them down by the docks, where they make a decent show of running a string of crab pots. The third is a cobbler with a shop off the Marine Parade."

Serena decided to try the cobbler first. After all, a cobbler would have to keep regular hours. The other two might be out on the water for days plying their pots or nets.

Serena learned from a shockingly youthful postilion that the distance from Snargate Street to the cobbler's shop was only a few minutes' walk. People were moving around and already the fish sellers were setting up stalls when she reached the harbor. She was rather stunned to realize the cobbler was situated within shouting distance of the customs house. Wasn't that *odd* for a smuggler?

Serena did not like the look of the shop, which was dark-fronted and mean, its single window crowded with old shoes and a faded wooden sign. A dim light glimmered beyond the filthy, fly-specked glass, indicating it was probably open for business.

She entered to find a narrow room with a man at the far end. He appeared to be her age and looked up from a boot he was mending. "Aye?"

"I'm looking for Derby."

"Are ye?" He turned his attention back to the boot, filing something with a short rasp. "And who might choo bey?"

"Etienne Bardot sent me."

The dull rasping sound stopped. "Da!" he called out loudly enough to be heard at the customs house across the way. He resumed his filing.

The blanket shifted behind him and a hunched, older man came out. The two consulted with each other in low voices, eying her with hard looks. Just when she was beginning to wonder if she should leave and try one of the others on her list, the older man waved to her.

"Come on beck." He disappeared behind the curtain.

Serena swallowed; he wanted her to follow him in *there*?

The cobbler kept working on his boot, not paying her any mind. She did not want to go through a door covered with a blanket in a cobbler's shop that smelled of mildew and boot blacking, but what else had she expected?

She picked her way past piles of ragged footwear and gave the young man a wide berth. On the other side of the blanket was a cramped living space smelling strongly of cabbage and unwashed bodies. It was everything in one room—kitchen, scarred table covered with dirty crockery, two cots with twisted lumps of blankets, and a small coal fire that barely cut the damp.

The old man was already seated in one of the room's two chairs and motioned toward the other one.

"Bardot sint ye?"

It took her a moment to decipher his words, spoken with a Kentish accent that was even stronger than those around Rushton Park.

"Yes. I've come to warn you to abort your plans for the next shipment. You might know Mr. Bardot's last shipment was intercepted?" He continued to stare. "I believe two men died and one is in jail."

The old man smoked his pipe and regarded her through the smoke. His face like a mask of cured leather.

"And Bardot sint ye?"

Serena wondered if he'd even heard what she had just said.

She spoke more distinctly this time. "I am here to make sure none of you get caught by the excisemen. It is possible they might know of the shipment from the man they are holding."

He sucked the stem of his pipe.

Serena sighed and stood. "That is all I came to say. I wish you will tell your associates. I hope I have spared you some trouble."

She turned and walked back through the curtain. The young cobbler had gone, and a tattered yellow shade had been pulled down over the window. When Serena tried the door, she found it was locked. She pulled again, harder, thinking she must not have turned it the right way or pulled hard enough.

The scuffing sound of a boot on grit came from behind her, right before a bright light exploded, accompanied by a sharp pain and the sound of her own voice.

"What—" She wanted to say more, but that was all that came out.

The last thing Serena thought as she slid to the floor was that she should have told Gareth she loved him.

Chapter Nineteen

Gareth quickly realized he couldn't simply pack up Dec and leave. The man had been abusing himself for weeks. He was half-starved, weak, and had developed a terrible thirst for spirits. Without discussing the matter outright, the Irishman had tacitly agreed to the removal of anything stronger than the inn's homebrew.

The first night had been bad, but the next two had been even worse. By the fourth night Declan was able to sleep most of the night, even if Gareth was not.

The dream came to him almost immediately when he laid his head on a pillow. It had been years since he'd been tormented by it night after night. He'd been grateful that his yelling, which had woken him on two occasions, could not possibly be heard beyond the empty rooms that surrounded him. And on his other side was Declan's suite, and his friend was in no condition to hear anything beyond his own agony.

They spent most days playing cards, dozing, or reading. Only in brief catnaps did he find any sleep and rest. When he couldn't sleep, he worked the problems in the journal he'd brought with him. As Dec began to feel better, he spent most of the afternoon reading a cherished novel loaned to him by the innkeeper's wife.

By the fifth day without drink and with regular meals Declan was looking pink-faced and almost healthy. This morning the man who Gareth had engaged as a temporary valet had assisted the Irishman with a bath, a shave, and had given him an acceptable haircut.

A Figure of Love

He was dressed in a clean nightshirt and banyan, lounging in a chair beside the window, reading the wretched novel, *Emma*. He was enjoying the book immensely and had already interrupted Gareth a dozen times to read choice lines.

"Here, now, Gare—listen to this one: *Silly things do cease to be silly if they are done by sensible people in an impudent way.*" He laughed and slapped his thigh.

Gareth gritted his teeth and stared at the nearly blank page in front of him. While he was grateful for the book's capacity to entertain his friend and keep his mind off more destructive thoughts, he'd developed an abiding hatred for the relentlessly interfering Emma Woodhouse, her hen-witted friend who fell in and out of love more often than most people changed their stockings, and the fawning Mr. Elton, whose unrelenting obsequiousness only reaffirmed every suspicion Gareth had ever held about vicars and clergy.

Now that his friend appeared to have regained some of his health and good spirits Gareth no longer felt consumed by worrying over him every minute. Instead, he now had plenty of time to worry about his other concerns. While Declan slept and convalesced, Gareth increasingly thought of reasons why it was imperative he go back to Rushton Park. He told himself he didn't need any excuse—it was *his* house—but he hated to think how foolish he would look haring back after the letter he'd left her.

Remembering the letter made him grimace, although he reassured himself that he'd said nothing cruel or cutting in it. He tried to picture her kissing Bardot and generate some anger to excuse his cold missive. But he'd found the jarring mental image had dimmed the longer he'd been away. It had been replaced by more pleasurable images—the memory of her body sheathed by her wet, translucent chemise, or her arms above her head, her body vulnerable to his ravaging hands and mouth.

He closed his eyes in disgust when he realized he was, yet again, as hard as a pikestaff.

"Here, then, Gare. Isn't that one of your grooms?"

Gareth looked up. "What?"

Declan was leaning over and looking out the window, which overlooked the back of the inn.

"Yes, I swear that is the fellow called Timkins. And that looks like one of your new horses—the one the boy named Lightning."

Gareth came from behind the desk to look out the window. Yes, it was Timkins, and he was talking to the innkeeper and following him inside. What the devil?

There was a knock on the door a few minutes later.

Timkins and the innkeeper stood in the hall.

"Ah, Mr. Lockheart. This gentleman says he has a message for you. I thought I would accompany him and make sure it was—"

"Yes, he is my employee. Thank you, Mr.Trencher, come inside, Timkins."

Gareth closed the door on the innkeeper before he could recommence talking and turned to the young groom. "What is it?"

"Mr. Jessup sent me, sir." Timkins, familiar with his master's preference for brevity, handed Gareth a thick envelope.

He looked at his grit-covered servant and realized he must have started out quite early to have arrived here before noon. "Go see to your needs. I have engaged every room on this floor and those above, take one of them for yourself."

Timkins nodded and left without a word.

Gareth realized Declan had risen from his comfortable chair and was staring at the letter in his hand.

He opened it and found two separate sheets of paper. The first bore Jessup's elegant script:

"Mr. Lockheart:

This letter was found at first light by one of the servants, wedged between the main doors (the letter bore today's date) *and addressed to you. You will notice the word "urgent" written on the face of the message and your name. Given the nature of its unusual mode of delivery I thought it worthwhile to send Timkins with it first thing. I would have consulted with Mrs. Lombard, but she has made an unexpected journey to assist a sick friend in Dover."*

Respectfully,

M.J. Jessup"

A Figure of Love

Gareth's eyes snagged on the last sentence, which was glaringly un-Jessuplike. Why would he have consulted Mrs. Lombard about such a matter? The answer to that was simple: he would not have. Jessup did not speak of Gareth's business to anyone. He was a paragon of discretion. If he added this sentence, it was to indicate—in his inscrutable way—that something was not right.

Gareth looked up and met Declan's impatient stare. He handed him the letter and opened the second, smaller, envelope.

"To Mr. Garth Lockhart, he that is a sucksessful man of bisness. We have some one who is nown to You and are keeping her safe now, but cant promise she will keep being safe. If You are wanting to make shur of her good helth You will come with no heel dragging and bring £2000 as reward four owr hard work. Come only with Your Self to the Ship Hotel in Dover and tell the hed-drawer you want to by a grey horse. We will wait only until the new moon."

Gareth read the letter three times, but it still made no sense. The new moon was four days hence. He had four days. He looked up to find Declan holding the letter with a perplexed look on his face. His eyes drifted to the one in Gareth's hand. "Well?"

Gareth re-folded the letter. "I'm afraid it is a matter of some urgency. Mrs. Lombard's Italian marble has become mired in customs in Dover."

Declan's expression was comical. "Marble? All this about some rock?" Amazement vied with skepticism.

Gareth would have to tread carefully—yet another thing he was not good at—if he was to keep his friend out of this. "You are not a sculptor, nor am I. It seems, however, this is rather singular marble she has been waiting for. She's gone to Dover to try and sort out the problem, but they are proving. . . resistant. I will need to go and assist her."

"And what can you do?"

"They want to see the original paperwork. You know how these excisemen have become. Recall that trouble we had with the part we needed for the mill in Manchester?"

"But that was during the War—and from America."

Gareth tucked away the letter and shrugged. "What can I say, Declan, they will not release the marble until they have seen the documents." He turned toward the desk and began assembling his books and papers.

"I'll go with you."

Gareth grimaced at the desk. "That won't be necessary."

"Why not? Or don't you want me to come?"

He let out a slow breath before turning, his mind scrabbling for a convenient, convincing lie. Lying was yet another of his weak points.

So, he thought of the truth, and turned. "I hate to ask you, Dec—"

Declan's forehead wrinkled. "Hate to ask me what?"

"I wouldn't ask you, if I didn't think it necessary. But with Mrs. Lombard gone, there is nobody to supervise the thirty-odd men working on the grounds. Do you suppose you might stay for a few days—just until I return?"

"You want me to supervise your garden project?"

Gareth knew he would do it—wanted to do it—by the slight twitch at the corner of his mouth. It was always what gave Declan away at the card table when he had a good hand.

"It would only be for a few days."

Dec nodded slowly, chewing his lip as if considering the matter. "I'll admit I've begun to chafe at lying about all day." He glanced up and smiled, looking more like himself than he had since Gareth had arrived. He rubbed his stomach. "I'll also admit I've been missing your cook's excellent meals and too-tempting cream cakes."

Gareth forced himself to smile and act normally, even though inside he felt like he was crumbling.

***

The Dover road was as execrable as Gareth remembered. Even his traveling chaise, a conveyance of unparalleled quality and design, could not protect his body from the tossing and jolting.

He'd considered taking his curricle, which was lighter and faster, but he would not want to convey Mrs. Lombard back in that vehicle.

They'd stopped for new horses in Canterbury even though he'd changed once already in Sittingbourne and the distance between the two towns was not more than fifty miles. But Gareth was determined to make up for lost time and fresh horses were the best way to do that.

Hours alone in his carriage gave him far to much time to think.

Getting Declan to Rushton Park had been simple enough—his friend had had enough of Biddenden. But making arrangements for

Dover without tipping Declan to what was really going on had taken its toll on Gareth. If Dec had guessed what Gareth was really going to do, he'd have insisted on coming with him.

The strain of lying to a man who was not only his best friend, but adept at lying himself—and usually quite good about scenting out liars— was offset by the knowledge that Declan would remain at Rushton Park and keep Oliver safe.

Gareth had been stunned by the joy—yes, there was no other word for it—he'd felt at seeing the boy again. And when Oliver had hurled himself at his legs and hugged him, he'd not minded the personal invasion. In fact, he'd discovered his hand patting the boy on the shoulder before he even knew it.

Naturally Declan had watched all of this with a broad grin and wildly amused glitter in his eyes. His friend was aware of his lifelong aversion to being touched by others; Dec would know better than anyone what a radical shift was taking place inside him. Perhaps even better than Gareth, who simply pushed the matter aside. He had far too much to do to sit about pondering the uninteresting mysteries of his own mind.

So, he'd sent letters and received messages at all hours of the day and night, spent time showing Declan the plans Serena had drawn up and the current progress. He'd taken the time to walk to the new lake with Oliver, who'd been beside himself with excitement to be the first to show him. And finally, when he'd done everything he could think of, he made haste for Dover, taking only two grooms—Timkins and Butler— who both rode on the box, armed. Gareth was traveling with a good deal of money in his possession and the road was known to attract the wrong sort with its frequent mail coaches.

He arrived in Dover in good time even though the road was rutted and rough with dried mud. Gareth hated to think what it must have been like after the last rains.

The Ship Hotel was a fixture in Dover and doing a brisk business when Gareth arrived. He had to pay double the usual rate to engage two of the best rooms, but he believed it to be money well-spent. He could not imagine Serena's condition after almost a week in the hands of her captors, but she would wish for a bath and privacy.

At Ruston Park he'd gone to her room himself and packed her bag. He'd been shocked to see how little she possessed and hoped her wardrobe was so sparse because she'd left the bulk of her clothing in London.

But when he went up to Oliver's room later that night to bid him farewell, he'd noticed the boy's nightclothes were clean and pressed, but patched and washed thin with use. The realization had consumed him ever since; did she really earn so little money?

Gareth banished the thoughts. He was here, now, and he needed to keep his mind fixed on the problem at hand.

After a quick visit to his room he went down to the taproom, which was brimming with custom at this time of the evening, its clientele a varied mix of seafarers and travelers just arrived from the latest packet.

He made his way to the bar, where a surly looking brute with an eyepatch greeted him with a frown and asked him what he was having.

Gareth ordered a pint of house brew and when the man delivered it, he pushed a gold coin across the bar. "I wish to purchase a horse. A gray one." The effect on the man was miraculous. His one eye widened and the sneer slid away as he smiled, revealing a mouthful of black teeth that made Gareth shudder.

"Aye. A gray horse, ye say? I know a man what has a gray horse. Be waiting at the stone bridge on Folkstone Road at midnight." He turned and walked away without another word, but the coin was gone.

Gareth lifted the mug to his mouth and then noticed the greasy thumbprint on the cracked rim and put it back down without taking a drink. He looked at his watch: he had a little over two hours to wait. He went to the private parlor he'd taken and ordered a meal, hoping the cleanliness standards in the rest of the hotel were higher than those in the taproom.

***

Serena was cold, tired, scared, and hungry for something besides dried fish and bitter ale. But mostly she was just bored.

She'd lost track of the days in her dingy little prison, but thought at least five must have passed, based on the number of times they had fed her. They'd taken her satchel and shoes and cloak, making certain she would not get far even if she could escape.

There was at least a half dozen of them, although the only faces she ever saw were the two cobblers. The others stayed in the outer room and argued in hushed voices. She knew they were arguing about her.

The old man had come to her not long after they'd brought her here. She knew that because her head had still pounded and ached from the blow.

She'd been curled up on an uncomfortable cot, trying to sleep and having no success when the door opened and he shuffled inside.

Serena pushed herself up, wincing at the pain the movement caused.

"Sorry 'bout yer head, lass." He sat in a chair and smoked his infernal pipe.

"And I'm sorry I took the time, trouble, and money to come down here and warn you. I should have let you fetch the goods and gotten shot. I should have—"

"There aen't no shipment."

"What?"

Derby nodded. "And there weren't no arrest nor dead men."

"You are lying."

He shook his head, a glint of pity in his eyes.

Serena stared at him. "But why? Why would he tell me such a thing?"

"Don't know."

"So, if there was no arrest and no trouble, why have you brought me here?"

He shrugged.

Serena wanted to scream.

"Truth is, yer cousin is a wrong 'un. Rotted to the bone. Ee'd a pair o' hands waiting to take the ready from us but we sussed the lay and did for 'em. But we miss '*im* and 'e took to 'is 'eels."

Serena untangled the garbled speech slowly. "You mean he tried to cheat you?"

He nodded.

She laughed, an unpleasant sound with no humor. "Well, I assure you, I mean nothing to my cousin. If you are intending to ransom me back to him, you will be waiting a very long time."

"You've wrongtaken me, lass. It aen't 'im we're waitin' on."

Serena could only stare. Who else could he believe would pay for her? She had nothing on her to indicate any relationship to anyone. She only had the little bit of money and—

"Oh no."

He nodded. "Oh yes. Even such as we 'ave 'eard of Gareth Lock'art. One of the richest men in England." He paused. "An odd ' un, by what we could find. But a downy one by any man's measure."

"Just because you have found a bank draft from him does not mean he will ransom me. I am his employee."

That made the old man laugh. "Oh, aye, and a fine one you are."

Her face burnt in the cool, damp room. "I am *not* his mistress. I am his landscape gardener and sculptor."

"Oh, is that what the fancy folk be callin' it nowadays?" He chuckled in a way that made her wish for her largest mallet and one of her chisels.

Serena waved a hand. "Go ahead and laugh and wait. You will be waiting a long time."

He pushed himself to his feet, tapped out his pipe and ground it under foot, and left the room, still chortling to himself. The fool.

That was the last time anyone had spoken with her. But not the last time anyone had come into her room. The younger cobbler had come the third day, and he'd not brought food. She would have recognized the light in his eyes even if he hadn't begun unbuttoning the flap of his breeches as soon as he'd come in the room.

"What do you want?" she'd demanded, stalling for time even as her blood ran cold.

He'd laughed. "I want a taste o' a rich man's tart." His eyes had flickered jerkily as they swept her from her stocking-covered toes to her hair that had not been washed or combed for days. She could only imagine she looked—and smelled—appalling, but the bulge in his breeches convinced her he thought otherwise.

She backed up against the wall, her eyes darting around the room for something to hit, poke, or bash him with. But the only thing was the cot she was lying on and the old barrel chair that was almost too heavy to move.

"I'll scream," she threatened, as he came closer, his greasy, stained breeches falling open to reveal drawers even worse.

"Not with your mouth full, you won't."

Suddenly, it was 1806 all over again. It was winter, and she'd been hiding in Favel's house with two other women. They'd been eating what they could scavenge, avoiding any fires so they would not draw the notice of the men dressed as soldiers who'd been robbing and raping their own people.

She was coming back from the woods, where she had found a fat duck in some poacher's snare. It would be worth risking a fire to have some meat. She'd been rushing, so excited about her treasure that she had not been paying attention when she'd rounded the corner of Favel's abandoned stables and walked right into a hard chest. Etienne Bardot's chest, it had turned out. The leader of his small band of rapists and looters.

That had been the beginning of a nightmare that lasted five long months.

The young cobbler, she did not even know his name, came to the edge of the cot and dropped his filthy drawers.

"Be a good girl, now," he said, thrusting his hips toward her. Just like Etienne had done so many times.

She smiled and then opened her mouth as wide as necessary.

He was crying, his hands over his naked hips, blood leaking through his fingers when the men flung open the door. Serena had found strength from places she'd never even know it existed. Enough to lift the unwieldy chair and trap his body beneath the legs.

The men had lifted her bodily from the chair and put her on the bed. They'd leaned over the weeping, writhing cobbler and pulled away his hands, cursing at what they found.

"You'll have to take him to old Fletcher," one of the men said, both wearing the dark woolen face masks they must wear at night out on the water.

"Aye," said the other, turning to her, his eyes wide in the round openings. "You done him good, lass. But I reckon he earned it."

Serena was in the corner, her knees pulled up to her chest, shivering even as sweat stung her eyes. In her mouth she could taste blood and the room around her was same one she'd thought she'd escaped ten years ago.

Chapter Twenty

Gareth wasn't surprised when he felt the business end of a pistol touch the back of his neck. He'd heard the man coming through the trees, after all. He'd made more noise than a herd of horses.

"Don't try anything funny-like."

"I have nothing funny planned," Gareth said, telling the truth.

His captor grunted and searched his person, finding the packet of money quickly. Chalmers would be most displeased to learn Gareth had stored such a bulky object in his coat—one of Gareth's favorites, a dark green superfine.

He heard hushed voices behind him; so, more than one had come. The soft whicker of a horse told him they'd sounded like a herd of horses because they'd actually brought a herd horses. Not smart if they'd been sneaking up on a man who hadn't wanted to be captured.

After a somewhat heated debate, during which the pistol disappeared from the back of his neck, a second voice spoke up.

"I'm gonna tie a cloth over yer eyes and then ye'll get up on this pony. I've got 'is lead, mind, so you'd better not try escaping."

Gareth almost smiled. Escape? After he'd gone to so much trouble to be captured in the first place?

But the smell and texture of the cloth wiped any smile he might have had off his face. He swallowed at the sensation and had to force himself not to jerk away. The irony of him being more discomposed by a dirty cloth than a loaded pistol was not lost on him.

When the rag was secure hands touched his shoulders and pushed him toward the strong smell of horse. It was indeed a pony they had brought for him, one of the rugged mountain-going breed. His feet almost dragged on the ground the horse was so small. If given a choice, he would have walked and spared the poor beast, but they did not offer him one and he did not wish to argue. Or speak to them at all, really.

The pony turned and headed back the way it had come, or near enough. The sound of other animals came from in front and behind, so there were others and they'd not put him on a miniature horse merely to humiliate him.

He counted while they went, measuring the minutes. At approximately fifteen minutes he smelled the sharp tang of salt air just before they began a steep descent. He'd guessed they would have their lair somewhere near the water.

It took nine more minutes before the terrain leveled out. The sound now was of hooves on stone and he could feel the damp salt air. So, they were headed down the beach. But three minutes later they headed back up again and leaves and branches brushed his body. They stopped less than a minute after that.

"All right, down ye come." It was the first man and he took hold of Gareth's bicep, causing him to stiffen. "Easy there, now. I've got me pistol." He gave a rough yank and Gareth stumbled off the horse.

"Ye got a bit o' beef to ye—must be all that brass, eh?"

Coarse chuckles greeted this dull witticism, and Gareth judged there to be perhaps five men total. A barrel poked him between the shoulders.

"Walk."

They entered a dwelling of some kind, something with a wooden floor, which magnified the racket of booted feet all around him. Another low-voiced consultation and then fingers moving roughly at the back of his head.

He blinked his eyes in the dimness, vaguely making out at least four shadows hovering at the edges of what was a small, mostly empty room.

The smallest man, the only one without a hood, took a step toward him, the packet of money in his hands. "This aen't £2000."

"You are correct."

"The deal was for £2000."

Gareth quite respected the man's singleness of purpose.

"You will get the other £1500 when I see her."

His words caused grumbling in the ranks and one of the figures, limping badly, shoved past the smaller man, reaching for Gareth's neck.

"Stand down!" the leader shouted. For a small man he had an impressive set of lungs and a commanding tone. Even so, the much bigger man hesitated, and for a moment Gareth thought he might disobey. But his shoulders sagged and he dropped his hands, backing away with his odd, hunched over limp.

Another conversation ensued, this one louder, less careful—as if he were deaf as well as trusting, rich, and beefy of build.

As if he were a fool.

Gareth knew what he was destined for—the smuggler never would have let him see his face if he had any intention of letting him out of this shack alive. To these men, £2000 would be a fortune, even split among five. Not only did they discuss Gareth and their options, they also discussed their missing companion in crime, the fifth member, whose tardiness was causing some concern.

Gareth examined the mud on the toe of his otherwise glossy boot and frowned while his captors finally agreed there was no harm in letting him see Serena, since they'd be together soon, in any case. Gareth thought that had a menacing finality to it.

The short man approached and then gestured to the only door other than the one they'd used to come inside, and Gareth preceded him. There was a smokehouse lock on the door and the man fumbled with the key for a long moment until it gave a dull click. He removed it and pushed the door open.

***

There had been far more activity than normal outside Serena's prison over the past few hours. In her windowless room she could not tell if it was day or night, but they had last brought her what she was almost certain was her midday meal hours ago. Not that the substance of the meals changed—it was dried fish and ale, three times a day. She had asked one of her jailors for water some time ago, but they had ignored her request. They had ignored her request that they empty her chamber pot, until she had threatened to hurl it at the next person through the door. The biting incident had done one thing, at least, it had convinced them she could be dangerous.

She believed they were here to dispose of her. Serena was not stupid. She could identify the cobbler and his son. They would never let her go, even if Gareth sent somebody with ransom money. That thought had been hovering at the back of her mind for days, but this was the first time she had taken it out and looked it straight in the face: she was going to die. Either in this wretched little cell or with rocks tied to her ankles at the bottom of the ocean. The only thing she could take any comfort from was the knowledge Oliver would be well-cared for. Without her to blackmail any more Etienne would have no reason to tell the duke and duchess of his true heritage. Oliver would go live with his grandparents, just as they'd always wanted.

And even if the truth somehow leaked out, Gareth would take care of Oliver. She'd seen signs of his kindness all over his estate. He might not have cared for Serena, but she'd seen him with her son—had seen the way he'd lost some of his reserve in Oliver's company. Gareth would take of her son.

Accepting her fate had made her feel stronger, less alone, rather than more afraid. So, when she heard the lock rattle, she sprang to her feet, refusing to meet her captors crouching in the corner or cowering in bed.

The door swung open, but instead of a black hooded jailer, it was Gareth.

Serena thought he was a figment of her imagination. Tall, broad, stern-faced, dressed to perfection, and without a hair out of place. And so very still.

She took a step forward, her hand outstretched. "Gareth?"

A slight flush rose in his cheeks at the sound of his name and Serena launched herself at him. "You're real!" The words were muffled against his hard, muscular, wonderful-smelling, beloved-feeling chest.

His arms closed around her tighter than the metal rings on a barrel.

She felt the pressure of his lips on the top of her head. "Serena."

She looked up at the sound of her Christian name on his lips and he claimed her mouth, his kisses fierce, his hold so tight it hurt.

Hands came between them, as if to tear them apart. "That's enough," a voice commanded, while another set of hands pulled her away, or at least tried to.

"Christ! They're as tight as two sides of a bloody clam," another said, causing chuckles all around.

Cold metal rested against her temple and Gareth's arms released her. "All right, all right. Bloody touchin' that is. Now, about the rest o' the money."

Before Gareth could answer there were three rapid knocks, a pause, and then another.

The one holding the gun lowered his arm. "It's about bloody time. Open the door, Kedge."

Things became something of a blur at that point.

Gareth gave her a shove that launched her all the way back toward the cot while yelling, "Go!" as if she had any choice. He swung his right elbow and a resounding *clack* filled the small room, followed by an agonized roar as the man fell backward, staggering out of the room into one of the other men. Gareth slammed the door shut and slid the heavy chair in front of it just as a pistol shot rang out and splinters of wooden plank door showered the room.

Gareth's body landed on her and he dragged her down to the floor, covering her like a human shield while a second shot filled the air, this one sounding farther away.

"Stay still," he ordered, when she tried to push up and see.

It occurred to her he rather enjoyed giving orders, but she decided this might be a wise one to obey.

"It will be safe shortly," he told her, easing his weight on to one elbow so he didn't crush her. Which was too bad, actually, as she'd quite enjoyed being crushed. Although she supposed her current condition was an affront to a man as fastidious about cleanliness as he was.

"Who are they?"

"Excisemen, constables, and one Bow Street Runner named Steele."

***

Serena had to have two baths before she could wash all the dirt and smell away.

Just as Gareth had predicted, the fracas ended quickly and fatally for two of the smugglers. Serena could not say she was sorry to see that her would-be-rapist was among the two who had been shot. His father was still alive, but rather the worse for wear.

He had winked at Serena as the men dragged him off. "Sorry, lass."

Gareth's carriage was waiting at the top of a torturous climb, which she made on the back of a sturdy little pony. Her prison had been a smuggler's shack half-dug into the cliffside, not even a mile away from town.

Gareth himself had stayed at the bottom of the cliff when she left. "I need to stay and give details to the constable," he'd told her, no longer holding her now that she was wrapped in a cloak—one of her own—and wearing shoes, also her own. "Will you be all right for the ride back to the hotel? Timkins and Butler will be with you, and two of the excisemen."

Serena smiled. "It is less than a mile, I will be fine. Right now, I'm more afraid of my own smell than smugglers."

He'd not even cracked a smile at her weak attempt at humor, instead nodding in his abrupt way and turning back to the men who were waiting for him, as if that brief moment of tenderness in each other's arms had never happened.

That had been hours ago, and still he'd not come to see her—even though she'd heard him enter the adjoining room half an hour earlier.

She'd left her hair loose, hoping some of the heavy masses of curls would dry. Gareth had brought a nightgown and dressing gown, as well as an outfit suitable for a carriage ride. She'd sent the clothes she'd been wearing for the past week off with one of the maids, telling her to burn it. But dresses being worth what they were—even stinking, ragged, patched ones—she expected some happy maid to be sporting her best traveling dress on the streets of Dover tomorrow. And she would be welcome to it.

She paced restlessly without her sketchbook to occupy her or her small, cheap watch to tell her the time, as the thieves had relieved her of both.

Finally, when she could stand it no longer, she strode to the single door she knew separated them and flung it open.

He was bare-chested, lying on his bed, reading a book, the room blazing with light.

He lowered the book and gave her one of his Gareth Lockheart looks, the haughty-unreadable combination he did so well.

"You were *reading?*"

He arched his brows at her. "As you see."

"Were you just going to leave me stewing?"

He crossed his arms over his chest, the movement more than a little distracting. "I assumed you would be sleeping."

She just shook her head, too angry to do anything else. How could he read at such a time? They might have died! They might be—

He held a hand toward her. "Come here."

She thrilled at his tone, which her body recognized instantly, but she shook her head. "Do you always give orders?"

He appeared to consider her question, which any other man would have known was rhetorical. "Yes, as a matter of fact."

Serena's lips twitched to smile at his very Gareth Lockheart response, but she stopped herself in time, maintaining a scowl. With great difficulty.

And then she saw something on his face—a look she'd never seen before. It was a smile. A glorious, slow-growing, honest-to-goodness, teeth-exposing smile.

Serena stared.

He lifted his hand again. "I was just teasing. Will you *please* come join me in my somewhat lumpy but clean bed?"

She dropped her jaw and gave him a look that was only half mocking amazement. "Gareth Lockheart knows how to tease?"

He nodded. "He does."

"And Gareth Lockheart can say please?"

"Sometimes."

"And Gareth Lockheart has teeth. I know, because I saw them for the first time when he smiled."

"Yes, you are correct on all counts. But right now Gareth Lockheart is wondering why we are talking about him in the third person. Come here, please."

She went to him. How could she not?

As he lifted the bedding for her to join him she noticed the fine sheeting. "Is this *your* bedding?" She stood beside the bed.

"Chalmers always brings it for me when we travel. I found he had packed a set and the maid seemed happy enough to put them on.

Serena could imagine the girl had been thrilled—along with imagining herself in between them.

"I noticed my bed had none."

"I'd hoped your bed would be superfluous."

"And what do you mean by that?"

"Serena, my arm is about to fall off."

She climbed in beside him and he gathered her up, his body long, hard, delicious smelling, and naked.

"Mmmm," he nosed around in her hair. "You smell much better than you did earlier."

She laughed into the smooth column of his throat. "I have to admit I wondered how you managed to touch me."

His arms tightened. "I would have done the same had you been in that wretched hole twice as long."

Her throat tightened. "Oh? What about three times as long?"

He hesitated before saying, "Hmmm. Perhaps not."

She laughed, the tears spilling out before she could stop them.

He held her away and looked down at her, his handsome face suddenly reminding her of knights and their armor. His impassive expression was like a face plate on a war helmet. And tonight the plate had slid aside a little, allowing her a glimpse of an expression she'd never seen on his face before—tenderness mixed with confusion.

Serena did not think she could tell him the truth about why she was here. It would kill any chance of more looks like the one he was giving her.

"Why are you crying?"

"Because I'm happy."

He cocked his head. "I know I am a monumental dolt when it comes to reading other people, but aren't tears a sign of sadness?"

"Not for me," she said, following the words with a big sniff.

He made her cry harder by kissing away her tears. Oh, she could not bear it.

"Why are you being so nice to me? Why?" she demanded, thrusting him rudely away.

He leaned back and propped his head up with his hand, the action causing fascinating movements all up and down his naked torso.

"Why?" he repeated, mulling over her question in his serious, thoughtful way. "I cannot be certain, but I have come to believe the distracting emotions I've been experiencing lately might very well be that mythical thing called love." He capped off this very Gareth declaration with a second smile in one evening, this one self-mocking.

"Love?" It was all she could manage, and even that came out strangled and squashed, as though it had been run through a mangle before leaving her mouth.

He nodded. "Yes. I think Gareth Lockheart loves you."

***

Gareth was genuinely alarmed: Emma Woodhouse had *not* burst into tears when Knightly declared his love for her. This crying, unlike her earlier crying, came in the body-wracking sobs of a young child—or a person mourning something terrible, like a death. Gareth could do nothing or say nothing that seemed to help. So, he held her, his chin on her head while she burrowed into him and cried until his chest was wet. Finally, the sobs turned to little gulps, and then rather aggressive sniffing. When he thought it might have ended, he gently put her away from him to look for clues as to her next mood.

"Oh, don't," she said, burrowing back in before he could see much other than a red tipped nose. "I'm so mortified."

At least that was what he thought she said, although it sounded more like, "I'b zo bortivied."

"Ah . . ."

"Will you tell be what habbened."

Gareth deciphered this and assumed she meant this evening's events rather than his emotional metamorphosis and embarrassing declaration.

"Yes, of course. Your captors sent me a note indicating I might wish to ransom you."

She shifted at this information, but still did not show her face. "Did they say why?"

Gareth smiled to himself at the question. "No." He waited for more, but she was silent. "But I suspect it had something to do with your cousin."

That got her attention. She twisted, until he could see her face. She looked beautiful, even with puffy eyes and a red nose. The expression in her eyes was one he did not like to see: fear. So, he did what he could to alleviate it.

"I recalled your cousin had recently come from Dover but was on his way to London. I wondered if he had changed his mind and come back here. If so, perhaps you had come to render him some assistance."

Her body stiffened, but still she did not speak.

"I employ a Runner whose judgment I trust implicitly—Mr. Steele, whom you met briefly this evening. I sent him a message to find Bardot. I knew Steele would find him if anyone could. It turned out he *was* still in London." He cleared his throat. "I'm afraid the rest of what I have to say may not please you. Do you wish to hear it?"

She nodded, terror replacing fear in her eyes.

"Mr. Steele learned certain things in pursuit of Mr. Bardot, none of them particularly good. When he had a chance to speak to him in person—he found him gambling in a dangerous part of town—he spoke to him at some length, and great depth. One of the subjects he discussed was his association with you."

Serena closed her eyes.

"Serena."

She shook her head. "I'm so sorry. I lured you here, and to certain death if you had not had the foresight to know that—"

He took her chin in a gentle, but firm, grip and tilted it. "Please, look at me."

She did. "I am so very, very sorry, Gareth. I have been terribly foolish."

"No, you have been scared, and at the whim of a very unscrupulous man." He frowned. "I'm afraid Mr. Steele left Bardot rather the worse for wear, but he got me the information I desperately needed—both to rescue you, and to accept my feelings for you."

She pushed herself up onto the pillow, lifting her chest to his face in the process. Like most of her clothing, her nightgown had been washed and worn until it was thin; he could see her nipples, their delicate points against the fabric, just inches from his face.

"Gareth? *Gareth?*"

He looked up and encountered the woman who owned the nipples that were bewitching him. "Hmm?"

"I asked to know what he told you."

"What who told me?"

She sighed, looked down at her chest, and then pulled the covers up.

"Wait," he said.

"In a moment. First, can we finish this discussion?"

Gareth would have preferred otherwise, but he could see she might be a stickler on this point.

"Bardot told Steele how he'd found the letter from Lombard when he ransacked the chateau where you'd cared for him until he died. Bardot kept the letter, thinking the part about the child not being Lombard's might prove useful. After the War—when things had become too uncomfortable for him to remain in France—he came to England, recalled Lombard's letter, and sought you out. He's been blackmailing you ever since."

He realized she was still waiting and his eyes narrowed. "What else are you expecting me to say?"

She shook her head, but even Gareth could spot the telltale signs of her lie. He sat up, suddenly less than happy, although he could not say why.

"Is there something you have not told me?"

She flinched at the sharpness in his voice.

He began to push back the covers, but her hand stayed him. "Please, don't go."

"Are you his lover?"

"*What?* No!"

Gareth found the look of revulsion on her face more convincing than her answer. But still, there was something he needed to know.

"Then why were you kissing him?"

She shook her head, her brow deep with wrinkles. "Kissing him? I never kissed him."

"That night—the night he stayed at Rushton. I saw him leave your room. You called him back and then—"

She laughed, but when she saw his expression, she shook her head vigorously. "No, no, no. I'm not laughing at you; I'm laughing at what you think you saw. I'd called him back to warn him not to roam your house and steal anything because I would be watching. And *that* is when he kissed me." She made a moue of distaste. "I had to wash my mouth out a dozen times after."

Gareth fell back against the pillow, weak with relief.

She leaned over him, her hair a frilly curtain around them. "Is that why you were such a beast to me before you left?"

He felt his face heat.

She punched him in the arm. Hard.

He winced and rubbed his arm. "That hurt."

"You deserve that. If you'd been there when I woke up I would have used a mallet on you."

"I apologize."

She grunted.

"But you were telling me about Bardot."

"Do you recall what you said before?"

Gareth recalled everything he said, he always did.

"Yes," he said, hesitant. Should he ask for clarification? Or should—

"Did you mean it?"

"About apologizing?"

She hit him again.

"Ow!" He grabbed her wrists and rolled on top of her. "Perhaps I need to bind you."

The look of pure lust that flashed across her face at his words made his entire body hot. "I think perhaps I need to bind *you*," she said, leaning toward him and kissing his throat.

"I will have to consider that." He would have to give it a *lot* of consideration. "But quit trying to distract me. And hitting me. Tell me what thing you mean."

Her gaze flickered. "You know—about love."

"Oh. That." After her reaction he had hoped *she* might have forgotten.

234

"I'm sorry I cried. It was just that I felt ashamed."

Gareth's head began to get that heavy, stuffed feeling it did when he found himself confounded by obscure social conventions. "Serena—"

"I love you, Gareth. I love you until I hurt with it."

It was his turn to gulp. Several times before he could speak. But he was still confused. "Then why are you ashamed?"

She sighed and he rolled off her, taking her with him. "Tell me, Serena. You will always need to speak plainly and be direct with me. I am not good at guessing what you are thinking or why."

"I know. I'm not trying to be obscure on purpose. It is just—" She threw up her hands. "Bardot is Oliver's father."

Gareth felt like she'd just hit him again, but hard this time. "But you said—"

"I know what I said—he *wasn't* my lover." She rolled onto her back and shoved her hands through her river of hair, pulling so hard it made Gareth wince. "I don't know how to explain war to somebody who hasn't lived it."

He could have told her he knew a little about war, and someday he might. But not tonight. Tonight he waited, giving her time.

She heaved an enormous sigh. "Bardot led a band of criminals and they terrorized our small village. He came to the old chateau, found me, and raped me. Again and again for five months."

The word *rape* echoed in his head, over and over. Gareth's brain seized, the blood in his veins so hot it might have been boiling.

She shook his shoulder. "Gareth? *Gareth?*"

He saw her, but it was as if she stood at the end of a long, narrow tunnel. A red tunnel.

"Gareth, please, I didn't tell you so that you would be enraged. I didn't—"

"I'll find him and then I'll kill him." He did not recognize his own voice.

She flinched away, shaking her head. "No, please, let it end now."

"He is an animal—a mad animal that needs to be put down."

"Somebody will kill him, but it will not be you." She wrapped her arms around him, raining kisses on his ear, neck, cheek, and even his nose. "My love, my lover, please."

The words had a power he would not have imagined: he was her love.

She must have felt the tension go out of him because her own body relaxed. "I love you too much to risk anything bad happening to you, Gareth. Please promise me you'll forget all about this?"

"I promise," he lied. For her peace of mind he would let her believe he'd forgotten.

He saw she was waiting for him to speak. "Will you tell me how you got away?"

She nodded and lay back on her pillow. "There were always soldiers from half a dozen sides passing through our area. Robert Lombard was one example. He was a messenger to some general or other, and he wore the uniform of an officer. Even so, Bardot would have killed him. They caught him riding through the woods and shot him off his horse. They brought him back, thinking to make sport of him, but I convinced them he must be rich, that his signet ring bore the seal of an aristocrat. I told them that they should keep him alive and ransom him. So, they had Robert write a letter to the duke."

Gareth nodded, it was a clever plan.

"He lived for a few months, but he was badly injured—we wouldn't know just how badly until later. In the time while we waited, I began to know him. I did not love him, but I greatly admired him. He saw what Bardot did to me and despised him for it. It was he who came up with a plan. The priest in our village knew what went on at the chateau, but he was old and frail and could do nothing to stop the raping and stealing. But he did agree to write marriage lines for us, even though they would need to be smuggled from him to Robert and then back, so he could put his seal across our signatures.

"The letter Robert wrote to the duke went down in a packet, although I did not know that until later. But Bardot must have suspected something had happened and he was becoming restless as Robert became weaker and weaker. I think Robert knew he would die, although we always spoke of him getting better, of us escaping together. Not long after Bardot sent the second letter, Robert became very ill from something wrong inside him—something our village doctor could not fix—and he died. Bardot thought to keep up the fiction that he was alive long enough to collect the ransom." She stared up at the ceiling, lines of tension around her eyes as she recounted the story. "But real French troops arrived in the area—hundreds of them. They came while I was out with the priest waiting for him to finish the marriage lines. Word swept through the village that everyone at the chateau had been arrested for sheltering known deserters. Father Bastian gave me all the money he had, even the little he'd collected for the church. I left with only the clothes on my back, the money he gave me, and the marriage lines. Robert had written a letter for me that I'd hidden in the house—it would explain things to his parents if he could not." Her eyes were glazed with tears. "I could not go back for the letter, but Bardot did. You know the rest of it."

Gareth felt drained just hearing her story. It was no wonder her eyes looked haunted sometimes. He pulled her closer, holding her tight.

"You have nothing more to worry about. Steele made it clear to Bardot that his days of blackmailing you were over." And had driven the point home with his fists, according to the Runner's report earlier in the evening. Gareth could only regret he'd not told him to detain the man. Now they'd have to find him all over again. And what Gareth did to him this time would make the beating seem like a pleasant memory.

Serena yawned, hugely. She looked up at him and blushed. "I'm so sorry. I don't know why, but I'm suddenly dead tired."

Gareth knew why. She'd been carrying around her fear for years. It would not surprise him if she slept two weeks straight. He would make sure she got all the rest she needed.

He nuzzled her neck. "Go to sleep."

"But I want—"

"I know what you want. Trust me, you will soon be getting more of *that* than you will be able to bear." He pushed his hips against her to illustrate his point.

"But I want you *now*." The words were barely a whisper as one of her hands pushed between them, settling on his erection.

He sucked in a harsh breath. "My God, Serena."

She chuckled. "You feel so—" a yawn stifled whatever it was she was going to say and her grip became slack.

Gareth sighed and pulled her closer. "Shh," he whispered into her fragrant hair, kissing her lightly. "Go to sleep . . . my love."

Her breathing was heavy and deep before he'd even finished speaking. He relaxed into the bed although he knew he could never sleep with her. He would hold her for as long as he could, and then he would go sleep in her room. He hadn't felt it earlier, but he was exhausted now himself. He'd had the nightmare every night. He could only hope it had come because he'd been either worried about Dec or terrified about Serena for the last ten days.

Gareth kept telling himself to get up and go get some sleep, but he held her until close to dawn, until he could no longer see straight. And then, without making a sound, he got out of bed, covered her to her chin, extinguishing all the candles still guttering in their sockets, except the one in his hand, and went into the next room to sleep alone.

Chapter Twenty-One

For a moment, Serena thought she was back in her prison. But the soft, caressing bedding and enticing smell of Gareth relieved her of that fear. The room was still dark, although a bright yellow line showed where the drapes met, telling her the day was well on its way.

She knew the bed was empty before she even felt the empty sheets beside her. She tried to recall last night but could only remember one thing. He knew everything and loved her; she closed her eyes and smiled, clasping his pillow to her chest, inhaling the clean, intoxicating scent of him. But where *was* he?

Serena opened her eyes, pushed back the covers, and padded to the adjoining sitting room; it was empty. When she opened the door to the room he'd engaged for her she saw the bed had been slept in and the door to her own sitting room was open.

She found him at her writing desk, a neat stack of papers on one side and an unopened pile of correspondence on the other. He looked up at her, his eyes taking a moment to focus before they sharped.

"Ah, you are awake." He placed his quill in the holder and sat back. Although his face had not changed expressions, she now knew him well enough to realize he was pleased to see her.

Serena felt shy under his gaze, his gray eyes darkening as he swept her head to foot.

"I woke up to find you gone." She glanced at the papers. "You are doing work?"

"I brought some work with me, but some correspondence is from today." He turned and picked a letter from the pile. "Here is one from a mutual acquaintance."

Serena looked down at her son's writing. The letter was addressed to Gareth. She glanced up. "May I read it?"

He nodded. "It is for both of us."

She opened the single sheet, which was dated just yesterday and contained only a few large, looping sentences. And only the last one having anything to do with her.

Serena snorted. "What a cheeky thing he is, writing to ask you to bring him some piece or part that he needs. And with barely a word to spare for his mother except his wretched dog ate his sketchbook and will I buy him another." She shook her head.

Gareth chuckled and the sound was so unexpected—so sweet and boyish—Serena could only stare. He was quite blindingly lovely, even with dark smudges beneath his eyes. "Did you sleep in here, Gareth?"

He turned away at her question. "I did not wish to disturb your rest."

She shook her head, amazed he could be so smart, yet so ignorant in the ways of women—at least in the way of her.

She went toward him, pushing against his knees until he turned back to her and she stood pressed tight in the 'V' of his thighs. She placed her hands on his face, lightly skimming the skin beneath his eyes. A light flush spread across his high cheekbones and his eyes fluttered shut, long sable lashes fanning his cheeks. She could tell by the deepening of his breathing that he was not untouched by her actions.

She leaned down and trailed kisses up his jaw, until she got to his ear. "I *wanted* you to disturb me," she whispered, her face heating at her forward words as she stood up and looked down at him.

His eyes were open, pupils flared and he took her hips and pulled her against him, his head nestling between her breasts, his hands cupping her bottom with massaging fingers.

"Mmm." His growl rumbled through her chest and she closed her eyes. He felt so . . .*perfect,* so *right.*

He turned his head and gently bit the side of her breast.

She laughed. "Are you going to eat me?"

His hot mouth roamed her body above the thin gauze of her gown, nipping and sucking her until the fabric was damp.

"When we return to Rushton I am going to tie your arms and legs to the four posts of my bed—tightly, so you cannot move or squirm away. And when you are bound and spread for me, I will take my pleasure. And I will lick and suck and bite every part of you."

The words and the raw, confident desire with which he spoke them sent a crippling wave of lust straight to her core.

"You will?" Her heart pounded at the erotic picture he painted with only a few blunt words.

"Mmhmm." He held her tight, his tongue tracing a line straight down to her navel. "Pull up your gown."

Serena obeyed with alacrity, not caring if he said please or not.

He slid a hand between her thighs and entered her with his long middle finger. She shuddered, her body becoming boneless as he began to pump her with slow, rhythmic precision, his head pushing up under her loose gown and his hot mouth fastening on her breast.

"Oh, Gareth."

His mouth tightened at the sound of his name and a second finger joined the first as he shifted her with his free arm, positioning her bottom on one hard thigh.

"Wider." His mouth left her breast only long enough to move to the other nipple, while his pumping hand paused to nudge her thigh.

She opened her knees to him and he gave a smug grunt of approval, his lips and tongue sucking and teasing her sensitive nipple until she thought she would go mad; all the while his fingers were plunging in and out, his clever thumb circling her core until she arched back over his arm, crying out her pleasure.

He scooped her up in his arms and strode into the adjacent room. She watched him slit-eyed through a haze of pure contentment, laughing when he tossed her onto the bed and positioned himself at the edge. His face was hard and his eyes burning into her as he ripped open the fall on his breeches and freed himself. Serena was already inching toward him when he slid his hands beneath her thighs, jerked her toward him and lifted her hips off the bed, entering her with a savage thrust.

***

His famous self-control had unraveled and snapped. Looking up to find her beside him had made him realize—with blinding clarity—that she was *his*. He could look at her whenever he wanted. And the way she had come to him told him he could have her whenever he wanted—that she felt the same way, or at least something very similar.

She wrapped her legs around his hips while he drove into her, unable to get deep enough inside her.

Words from long ago, as insidious as serpents, invaded his passion and enflamed it—"You won't fall easily, Gareth. But you will fall hard when it finally happens." Venetia's words—a warning—and she'd been right.

He had fallen, but he hadn't been broken by his fall, as he'd always feared. Instead, loving Serena made him stronger, less hollow, and more of a human being.

He looked down at her face as he drove into her like a battering ram—her lush lips parted and slack, but still smiling, her skin mottled with passion, her heels digging into his ass as she tightened around him, pulled him in deeper—and then he exploded inside her with an intensity that left him blind.

He was still floating a few moments later, when she said his name.

He forced open his heavy lids. He was still buried inside her, his knees braced against the bed. She was smiling up at him, her hair a glorious tangle, her nightgown up around her neck, and her eyes filled with their usual, teasing mischief.

"Yes?" It was all he could do to squeeze out the single word.

"Can we go home?"

Gareth looked down to where their bodies were still joined, worry bubbling through the euphoria still clouding his mind. "You mean, right *now*?"

She chuckled. "I meant tomorrow. It is already too late today." She laid a hand over his and he looked up. "I miss Oliver."

Relief coursed through him. "So do I." He lowered her to the bed, the feeling of loss when he was no longer inside her wrenching.

"And I also want to get back home so you can do what you promised."

"Promised?" he repeated, probably looking as foolish as he sounded.

She nodded, squirming a little. "You know. . . the thing with your bed?"

Gareth thought he must be the stupidest man alive: Thing? With a bed?

And then it came crashing down on him and he stared into her wildly blushing, hopeful face.

"You are insatiable," he said, not bothering to hide his grateful amazement.

She covered her hot cheeks with her hands. "I know. Isn't it wonderful?"

Gareth couldn't help it, he threw back his head and laughed with pure joy.

***

They lounged the rest of the day away, ordering their meals brought to their room. They made love, ate some more, and Serena dozed. She woke up once and found Gareth watching her.

"Don't you ever sleep?"

He wound a strand of her hair around his finger. "You have lovely hair."

Serena gave a mock shudder. "It must resemble a bird's nest. It always does when I fall asleep with it wet." Gareth looked impeccable, even when lying naked in bed. *Especially* when lying naked in bed.

"How soon will you marry me?"

Her heart leapt at his words but she cut him an arch look. "Nobody has asked me yet."

He glanced up from her hair, his direct stare having the power to disconcert and strip her bare, even though they were naked in all other regards.

"Will you be my wife, Serena?"

She took the hand that was playing with her hair and brought it to her lips, kissing the smooth back of it, the gesture causing him to look ruffled. "I would be honored to be your wife, Gareth."

He claimed her with a deep, tender kiss, leaving her breathless, as always.

243

"How soon will you marry me?"

She laughed. "You are relentless. Is this how you accumulated all your wealth?"

As usual, he took her words at their face value. "Declan tells me I can be single-minded, and often he does not sound as if he means it as a compliment."

"Rest assured that *I* intended it as a compliment. You do have a rather singular ability to concentrate. I have seen some of that same characteristic in Oliver."

He nodded, again taking a thick curl and playing with it. "He is a very clever boy. His work on the automaton he is building is well-conceived and thoughtful." He glanced up at her. "Would you object to engaging a tutor for him?"

"I have wondered if I am doing him a disservice by keeping him close to me. His grandparents have offered to send him to school, but . . ."

"But you enjoy him too much to live apart."

He was right—but should that be the determining factor for her son's education? "What do you think would be best?"

He filled his lungs and let the air out slowly, his expression introspective. He was not a man to give quick, thoughtless answers to important questions, and her son was already important to him. Yet another thing she loved about him.

"I believe the benefit of such schools as Harrow or Eton is largely social. It is possible to engage tutors with far finer credentials than their poorly paid teachers. Your son would receive a better education at home, with us, but he would lack that ineffable *something* that binds the English ruling class together. You must decide if that quality—those connections—are worth doing without his presence in your life."

As usual, he was correct and to the point.

"You mention the ruling class—but their control is no longer inviolable—as you and Mr. McElroy and dozens like you give daily proof. Perhaps my son's association with *you* would benefit him more than antiquated bonding customs. Besides, he has his grandparents for that."

He turned on his side and propped his head in his hand. "You will not tell them the truth now that you no longer rely on them?"

"That is not why I did not tell them, or at least not the main reason." She traced the fascinating musculature of his stomach, smiling as his body jumped and tightened under her finger. He seized her hand and held it and she looked up into gray eyes that kindled.

"I would like to know this, Serena."

Serena did not know if she could make him understand, and even if he understood, would he believe her? She looked into his patiently waiting face and knew she owed him that much.

"At first, I needed their help desperately. I was a woman expecting a child in a new country with no home or family and very little money. As strange as it might seem, they needed me, too. I was the last person to have seen their son, even that little piece I had of him was more than they had. And of course they believed I was carrying his child. It did not eliminate their grief, but it eased it. And then after Oliver was born?" She let out a sound that was half-sigh, half-groan. "Then it became even harder—now my son loves these people and feels like he belongs. Now I would be hurting him if the truth were known—especially if he learned he was the bastard child of a deserter, thief, and rapist." Her mouth twisted with distaste. "Do you understand?"

Gareth still held the hand he had captured, and he was massaging it absently, which did not make his erotic stroking any less distracting.

He hesitated, and then nodded. "I understand."

"But you do not agree?" She could hear the reservation in his voice, but not outright condemnation.

"No, I do not agree. But then I look at the matter from a different perspective. I never knew either my father or mother and would give all the wealth and possessions I have for just a few moments to confront them." He looked and sounded as calm as ever, but the words made her soul ache for him. He gave her hand a gentle squeeze. "But that does not mean I think what you are doing is wrong."

The distinction he made was rather fine, but she could accept it. "Perhaps one day I will tell him. When he is older." She gave him a look from beneath her lashes. "When he has brothers and sisters of his own to call family."

That got his attention.

He took the hand he was holding and led it beneath the covers, until it rested on his hot, hard length.

She giggled. "Are we done talking now?"

"I am."

***

At first the sounds of distress were part of her dream, a low, desperate keening sound—somebody in distress, in pain. Serena ran through woods that became a house, the agonized sound getting louder, but no closer. She came to the edge, her arms flailing, launching her body upright in bed.

Her breathing was coming in short harsh gasps as the room materialized around her. It was Gareth's room—the bed with his sheets, a bed that was empty except for her. One candle guttered low on a table by the connecting door.

And then that sound—the one from her dream. She pushed herself from her bed, not bothering to find her robe, and ran to the source of the sound—the connecting door.

On the other side the room blazed and Gareth writhed in the bed. His rigid body was bent in half, almost in a ball. Sweat poured off him in rivulets and the horrible, gasping cry escaped from between his clenched jaws, his teeth chattering hard enough that she could hear them across the room.

She rushed to the bed but then hesitated, her hand inches from his shoulder. How to wake him without startling him? While she dithered, the moans came faster. She laid a hand as light as a feather on his shoulder.

His reaction was explosive, the word, "*No!*" tearing out of his throat so loudly the windowpanes rattled. His arm swung out and caught her in the shoulder, the glancing blow enough to throw her off the bed.

Serena scrambled back up to find him cowering on the far corner, his eyes darting like those of a trapped, terrified animal. He looked nothing like the man she knew, his handsome features distorted by sheer terror.

"Gareth, love. It is Serena. You are having a bad dream. It is only a dream," she soothed. "Gareth." She reached up and touched his foot. He jumped but did not pull away. Instead, his eyes settled on her, the irises bouncing wildly before settling, his pupils mere pinpricks.

"Serena." His voice was rough and hoarse, as if from prolonged yelling. "You shouldn't be here." He coughed after forcing the last word out, doubling over. She climbed up beside him and slid her arm around his torso, rubbing his back in firm circles, leaning close to kiss his head, which was soaked as if he'd been immersed in water.

"Of course I should be here," she whispered, holding his shuddering body tightly.

She held him like that while his breathing slowed and his shivering stopped, until he freed himself without looking at her and left the bed.

"Gareth?"

He stopped in front of the door to the other room, his back to her while he leaned forward and gripped both sides of the door frame, almost as if he were propping himself up. His head sagged and he shook it back and forth.

"I did not want you to see this. I do not want you to see *me* like this."

She shook her head. "See what? A nightmare? It is a normal part of life. We all have them now and then—"

"No, Serena, this is *not* normal, and it does not happen now and then."

"I don't understand."

"And I don't want you to. That is why I sleep alone."

"But I want to understand. I want to—"

He wheeled on her, his expression almost as horrifying as the one he'd worn during his nightmare, wild and frantic and half-mad. "I cannot speak about this. You must understand what I am saying. I do not wish to grant it that power—to give words and sound to it. It is bad enough when I am trapped inside—it is—it is—" He rammed a hand through his hair and wrenched it so hard Serena winced. "It has destroyed the night, but I will not allow it into my days." He stared at her, his eyes wide and entreating. "I cannot. I can*not*."

She nodded shakily, brushing tears from her cheeks. He crossed the room and grabbed her, his arms crushing her until she could not breathe.

Chapter Twenty-Two

They left at first light. The atmosphere in the carriage was somber, and Gareth knew she had not forgotten last night. He had cursed himself in the hours since; he should have locked the door. But he knew that was weak thinking. Serena was not the type of woman to accept locked doors, separate rooms, separate lives. If he had married a true daughter of the aristocracy, as he had once planned, he would have gone to her once a week and then returned to his own bed and none would have been the wiser.

He looked up from his thoughts to where she sat, facing the horses. She was waiting for him.

She slid to one side of the narrow seat. "Will you not sit beside me?"

Her words warmed him inside. "Will you not be cramped?"

Her eyes flickered over his body like a heat wave. "Yes."

Gareth moved across the short distance and lowered himself beside her, her body warm and soft along his side. She put her hand on his knee and he took it in his. They both stared down at their linked fingers.

"I have ugly hands."

Gareth spread her smaller hand open in his palm, turning it to view both sides. She had been working lately and there were hard callouses, a small slash on the pad of one finger, the skin chapped on the back, and the shape of her thumb proof of her hand's strength and skill.

He raised it to his mouth and kissed her palm.

"I like your hands."

She nudged him with her shoulder. "You are supposed to argue with me, Gareth, tell me how lovely and dainty and delicate they are."

His mouth curved into a smile, as it seemed to do so readily in her company. "I am not adept at flattery or flirtation, Serena. I can tell you they are beautiful hands to me, because they are yours and because they are capable and create art and because they give pleasure when they are on my body." Her cheeks flared at the last words, her eyes dropping shyly away. He tilted her chin, forcing her to meet his eyes. "You will find me a dullard, I am afraid. Laughter and smiles and jests do not come easily to me as they seem to with other men. Declan says that is because I do not exert myself, but that is not true. I have no capacity for poetry or flowery prose, anything so obscure tangles my thoughts. . . pollutes my reason." He turned and slid an arm behind and beneath her, lifting her into his lap, her hip resting against his arousal.

She gave him a smile of pure bliss, her emotions as easy to read for him as a book.

He kissed the tip of her nose. "I have very little experience with women, Serena. And I have only ever loved one."

She cupped his jaw and brought his face lower to kiss him. "I don't like to think of you with another woman. It makes me want to break things."

He brushed a kiss over her mouth, warmed by her possessive words.

"I fell in love with you the way you are, Gareth. You can say more to me with a look than most other men can say in an entire volume of poetry."

"I don't like to think of you with other men," he said, his words an echo. "It makes me want to claim you again—to take you and remind you that you now are mine."

She shifted in his arms, until she sat astride him, her eyes heavy and her smile lazy and hungry. "I have never made love in a carriage." Her dexterous hands were already busy at the closure of his breeches and he lifted his hips so she could pull them down. Her hand closed around him and a low grunt of pleasure escaped him.

She stroked him to slick hardness, her eyes never leaving his. "I will want to sketch you like this, you know."

He hardened even more at her words. "You have not paid me for my last sitting."

That made her laugh. "You are not a professional model, you should be grateful for the opportunity to become part of a great work of art."

Gareth thrust into her hand. "Even a novice should receive some payment." He lifted her skirt and petticoats to her hips, his cock pulsing at the unbearably erotic sight of her serviceable stockings and the plain garters that held them just above her knees, nothing but smooth, naked thigh above them until . . . His mouth flooded with moisture at the sight of her curls.

She lifted her eyebrows high. "Novice?" Her thumb swirled his hard, slick head and she grazed him lightly with her nails.

Gareth jolted under the intoxicating combination of pleasure and pain. "Dammit, Serena!"

"Language, Gareth."

He pushed away her hand and positioned himself at the hot, wet entrance to her body, bringing her down hard. They both gasped and then froze, reveling in their joining.

The carriage struck a massive rut or bump and she grabbed his shoulders to keep from falling off, her sheath tightening around him while her lush bottom bounced up and down.

Gareth groaned. "I love the road to Dover," he murmured, guiding them both to pleasure while her laughter filled the carriage.

***

It was barely light when they reached the long drive that led to Rushton Park.

Serena tucked loose curls beneath her hat and straightened her crushed, wrinkled clothing. Naturally, Gareth somehow managed to look cool and unruffled, even though she'd ridden him as savagely as any Ascot jockey.

"You know our arrival like this—" she gave a general wave to encompass everything, "alone and together in your carriage—will scandalize the neighborhood."

251

He cocked an eyebrow with puzzled unconcern. "Does that bother you?" The question showed even more than his expression that it did not bother him.

"I do try not to leave scandal in my wake. But, no, I cannot say I am terribly bothered."

"We will be married soon and people will forget all about this."

She smiled at his bland tone and impassive expression. She loved knowing that only she—out of everyone—saw the real, passionate man beneath his tightly controlled exterior. Her happiness dimmed slightly when she thought of the part of himself he kept secret even from her, but she had a lifetime to learn about him and help him overcome whatever made him sleep alone.

Gareth leaned forward, his eyes on the window, the skin around them tightening subtly.

"What is it?"

"I don't know. It looks like every servant on the property is out in front of the house."

"Perhaps Jessup has brought them out to welcome us?"

"Perhaps." He did not sound convinced.

Serena leaned across him to look as they pulled up to the house. Dozens of eyes stared back at her, none of them happy or welcoming.

Gareth opened the door and kicked down the steps before the carriage had even stopped moving.

Declan pushed through the crowd toward them as Gareth assisted Serena down from the carriage, her eyes already flickering through the assemblage, looking for one small figure.

Her heart staggered and beat so hard it felt it might knock a hole through her chest. Things slowed and sharpened and Serena felt as though she were moving through heavy air as her eyes swept back and forth ever more rapidly.

"Oliver. Where is Oliver?" The words were mumbled, as if her lips were numb. "Oliver."

"It's the boy," Declan said, his face like a wall of granite. "He has been taken. We found this only a quarter of an hour ago." He held out a grubby folded slip of paper.

Serena's arm wouldn't obey any commands of her brain so it was Gareth who opened the piece of paper. He looked down at her. "It's Bardot. He has taken Oliver and will not tell us where he is until I pay him £5,000."

Only when Gareth's arm came around her did Serena realize she was falling.

***

Gareth was not surprised Serena's mind had simply shut down. He knew as well as anyone how one horror heaped on another and another would eventually trigger the body's best response to save itself from madness. He had wondered at the fortitude she had exhibited after her escape from a week-long incarceration. Her face had been thinner, a sure sign of suffering even if her smiles and apparent strength might have led him to believe she was untouched. He knew she had believed she would die in that shack—and the guilt of leading him there to join her must have been overwhelming.

Her French servant, a hatchet-faced woman who appeared to give even Jessup reason to pause, had shooed him from Serena's room like a bothersome fly. "Go away. If you want to help her, bring back her son."

Gareth agreed, so he'd left. But part of his mind was still back in that room with her, when he needed all his wits with him now.

"I'm not alone in this. We'll be watching you closely, so don't attempt to send messengers to either the authorities or your man in London, Steele," the brief letter read. *"Tomorrow you may send one rider to withdraw the money from your bank in London. A messenger will arrive the following morning to tell you where to take the money. Once you have delivered it, another messenger will arrive to tell you where to find the boy. Do not deviate from these instructions."*

He looked up at Declan. "Tell me again what we know."

Dec nodded and took a deep breath. "One of the housemaids saw him arrive. He must have left his carriage or horse hidden somewhere and walked to the house." He scratched his head and frowned. "That was the first thing we did—look for any sign of him or any trace of a possible accomplice. We found nothing."

Gareth did not think that was surprising. The property was vast and there were hundreds of places a person could hide.

"Who was the last person to see Oliver and when?"

"The old nurse. She said he finished his work at three and said he was going down to the library to find some book he had been searching for over the course of the last few days."

Gareth nodded. Bardot had come into the house. "So, he has been gone . . . " he looked at his watch, even though he had looked at it so often he knew already what time it was, "perhaps four hours. Oliver must have gone willingly. I cannot imagine Bardot dragging a struggling ten-year-old down the drive without anyone noticing."

"Yes, that was our conclusion, as well. He could have gotten into the house through the sunroom, the orangery, the library itself, or any of a half-dozen other ways. He must have been fairly comfortable with the house."

Gareth thought of what Serena had told him. She might have stopped Bardot from roaming that night he stayed, but who was to say he did not come back some other time? He was a lifelong criminal who must be a master of escaping capture to even be in England after his actions during the War.

"I am going to assume he has conspirators. I am also going to assume they are watching our comings and goings. It is moonless, so we could not send anyone against his instructions even if we wished. With the servants all in position I believe we will see anyone before they can see us." As soon as it became dark enough, Gareth had positioned servants at various points around the house, including the roof. If anyone approached the house from any direction, they would be noticed.

"Have you considered this is all a ruse and he may have men waiting on whomever goes to collect the money in London?"

He had. "I think it possible. But part of me thinks they would not wish to have a solitary rider with so much money, a perfect target for thieves, unless they were planning to be those thieves. That is why I will go tomorrow." He could not send a servant into such danger.

"No, I will go."

Gareth opened his mouth, but Declan held up his hand.

"She will need you here, Gareth. And if something goes wrong—if *we* are wrong in thinking they will rob the courier. Or if the courier gets robbed by some other thief. . ." Worry twisted his harsh features. "You will need to help her and it might be you will have to make some difficult decisions."

Gareth knew he was right.

"Let me do this for you, Brother."

Who else could go? Who else did he trust more than Declan? Nobody.

He nodded.

"Good. I will leave at the first crack of daylight. I was thinking I might—"

Declan's voice faded away as the idea struck him. *Of course!* What a *fool* he'd been.

He stood and headed for the door.

Declan's chair scraped behind him. "Where are you going?"

"The dogs."

***

Serena resisted the pull toward consciousness, but she had to swallow the liquid or drown. She gulped convulsively and coughed—and then gulped again.

"*Bon,*" a voice said.

Serena was not dreaming, nor awake, but in some in between place. She was hiding. From something bad.

Oliver.

She sat up abruptly, frantic. "Oliver!"

"Shh, now, you are doing yourself no good." This in French, the words harsh yet still soothing. Nounou stood on the other side of the bed, her hands busy with a glass on the bedside table.

Serena shoved off the blankets, swung her feet off the bed, and promptly slid to the floor. She looked up to find the room tilting back and forth in a way that caused her gorge to rise.

"Nounou." The word was a hollow croak and her head tipped back, unwilling to stay upright on her shoulders.

Strong hands lifted her like a rag doll and laid her gently on the bed. A door shut, and somebody pulled the blanket up around her.

"Go to sleep, *mignon*. You can do no good in your condition."

"But—" Her mouth was thick and full of cotton wadding. "What?"

"A little milk of the poppy. Sleep."

She wanted to yell at her, but dozens of small hands clutched at her body and pulled her down, down, down . . ..

***

Gareth and Declan each held items of Oliver's clothing the Frenchwoman said he'd worn lately. The dogs followed Oliver everywhere now that they lived in the house. The only time he put them in the barn was when he had something to do and they could not go. There had been one or two accidents in the house and Serena had told him they must stay in their stall when he was not with them.

The dogs began whining and snuffling even before Gareth opened the stall door. They had been trained not to jump, but they were rambunctious and restless, waiting for permission to leave their stall.

Gareth squatted down in the clean straw and held out the cloth cap. The dogs went wild, leaping and sniffing and making sounds he could only assume indicated dog happiness.

"They certainly know his scent."

They took two lanterns in case they had to split up for some reason, but only lit one, and that one with its shutter lowered almost all the way and allowing a narrow circle of light that barely lighted the ground two steps ahead of them. They clipped leads to two of the hounds and turned the rest free.

The only sounds as they left the stables were the snuffling of snouts and stridulating of thousands of nighttime insects. They had both dressed in dark clothing and darkened any visible skin with ashes. Gareth hardly see his own hand.

The dogs ahead were invisible, but they stayed close enough to hear. The two they kept on leads pulled in the same direction, down toward the river.

Gareth briefly thought of the mine Oliver had led him to that day and could only be grateful he had sent workers to close the opening, especially as the dogs seemed to head in that direction.

They stumbled and cursed quietly behind them, Gareth's heart growing heavier as the dogs led them almost directly toward the mine.

But, suddenly, the two dogs on leads stopped and Gareth heard a distinct snarl and snap among the dogs ahead.

"What is it?" Declan whispered.

Gareth had no idea. This was the first time he had been with the dogs—or any dog, really—without Oliver's company. He knew his friend suffered from the same lack of canine experience. The place where they had grown up had no dogs—they were just another mouth to feed.

The dogs' growling became louder and almost savage sounding.

"Jesus!" Dec whispered, "if there is anyone out here they will certainly hear this. Can't you make them be quiet? What the hell is going on?"

Gareth realized his dog had begun to strain toward the river and the old mine. Dec's dog was pulling in the opposite direction.

He gave a soft snort. "They are having a dog argument. Look at them, Dec."

A moment of silence and then, "By God, you're right. What the devil do we do now?"

"We split. We've both got pistols and lanterns. It's obvious something happened here, enough to make the dogs think he went in two directions. The boy knows this area like the back of his hand. Perhaps he escaped Bardot and ran away? I don't know, but we split." He knelt on the grass to light his lantern.

"Do you think we will be able to split them?" Declan asked, crouching down beside him, his eyes barely a glitter in the low light.

"They seem to want to. Besides, Oliver has trained them to obey." He shuttered both lamps until they set out. "Do you think you are familiar enough with the layout of the property to find your way back to the house, Dec?"

"Yes, I've gone out every day while you've been gone and the boy took me down past the lake to where he found an old gamekeeper's shack. In fact, it occurs to me that might be the direction the dogs want to head. He spent a good deal of time there and even had a spirit lamp and made tea for us. There were several other items of his there and he told me he often takes naps and reads there. Possibly Bardot knew about it."

Gareth chewed his lip. He knew of the shack, of course. "Perhaps I should go with you?"

"I think we should follow both trails." He hesitated. "Do you think the dogs will start baying and making a racket if they catch scent of him?"

Gareth lifted the shutter on his lamp a hair and snapped his fingers and all nine dogs converged on them. "Sit," he hissed, pleased and surprised when they did just that. Eighteen canine eyes looked back at him. He could have sworn they knew this was not a game.

"Track now," he said, his voice a little louder. Of course the dogs made no comment, but he thought their bodies tightened in anticipation.

"Oliver took them hunting hares and used this command. I can only hope it will work to track their master." He dug his watch from his pocket. "It is seven minutes after ten o'clock. I think we should agree to meet back at the stables at a certain time, no matter what we are doing or what we have found."

"Agreed."

Gareth mentally made the journey to the game shack and back to the house on foot and added some extra time for a little exploration and perhaps some false trails. "Two hours. We should meet back at the stables at seven minutes past midnight."

Dec chuckled.

"What is so funny?"

A hand landed on his shoulder and gave a squeeze. "Nothing. See you back at the stables at seven minutes past midnight."

Chapter Twenty-Three

Serena woke up to a pounding head and mouth full of cotton.

Nounou sat beside the bed, mending some item of Oliver's clothing.

Serena's body sat up without any command from her brain. "Oliver!" The word came out a raspy whisper.

Nounou lowered her mending. "I hope you're not going to behave like a fool and begin running about achieving nothing."

Serena felt as though she'd been slapped in the face. She opened her mouth, prepared to deliver the set-down of a lifetime, but the older woman was not done.

"I suppose you believe fainting from exhaustion will somehow help find your son."

She met Nounou's dark brown gaze, her black slashes of eyebrows drawn down into a 'V.' And she shut her mouth.

"*Bon.* Now eat." She gestured to the bedside table, where a tray of bread, butter, and jam sat waiting, also a pot still puffing a little steam: chocolate.

While Serena tucked into the tray Nounou told her what had happened in the five hours she'd slept.

"There are eyes watching everywhere if anyone should come near. Somebody will leave at first light to collect the money." She shrugged, her eyes once again on her mending. Although she gave the impression of calm, Serena saw how the muscles in her neck were standing out, her shoulders bowed with tension. "I do not know who will go fetch that.

259

Right now," she glanced up and gave her a direct look. "Mr. Lockheart and the other one have taken the dogs to see if they can find Oliver's scent."

Serena looked at the window, but the drapes had been pulled. "Can they see tonight?" She had been locked in a hole for a week and had no recollection of whether there was a moon or not.

"Not very well. They took lanterns but cut them to barely a glow." She grinned up at Serena suddenly. "It reminded me of my childhood in Marseilles, with the *contrebandiers*."

Serena supposed she should be surprised the rather staid older woman had once engaged in smuggling, but people were never just what they seemed.

"How long have they been gone?"

Nounou glanced at the clock on the mantle, it was half-past midnight. "It must be well over two hours now."

Serena drained the rest of her chocolate and set aside the tray, expecting Nounou to stop her when she got out of bed. Instead, the other woman nodded to the foot of the bed, where laid out were a long-sleeved, dark green dress, fresh stockings, her dark blue pelisse, and her scuffed leather ankle boots—all clothes she wore to work.

"You might as well dress to be useful, if the time comes."

***

Gareth heaved a sigh of relief when he saw the entrance to the mine was still blocked with tightly packed stone. But his relief didn't last long when the dogs kept scenting a trail north, beyond the area he had explored with Oliver that day.

They led him around the stone face that held the old mine entrance, the going rough over an outcropping of rocks that must run east until they intersected the river. As he tried to find an area that was not so steep, he encountered a section of rock that seemed to have been hewn down to make a narrow pass, the dogs shot through it like water down a spout. Gareth followed more slowly, needing to carry the lantern directly in front of his body to fit through the narrow cut out.

There was an unexpected drop-off and he almost smashed the lantern on the rock as he skidded down some loose stones and landed with a hard thump on his arse. He paused for a moment to listen. There were no dogs nearby, nothing but insects.

"To me," he ordered in a low voice. Nothing.

When Gareth tried to stand, he realized the ground was still uneven. He had no choice but to shed more light. He lifted the shutter only a fraction of an inch but enough to see a few feet ahead. A drop of at least four feet and then what looked to be the other side of the stone face with trees growing snug up to the rocks. No sign of dogs.

He edged his way down the hillside in a shower of pebbles and dirt. When he reached the bottom he found trees growing close and hugging the rocky protrusion. A rough path had been hacked through the brambles where they met the trees and Gareth's breathing quickened.

He pushed through thorny brush that clawed at his boots and buckskins. Sounds of snuffling and whining came from around the corner of stone ridge he was following. His heart was beating with a combination of expectation and dread when he found the cluster of dogs running back and forth in front of an opening into the rock which had once been boarded up. All but the two bottom planks had been pulled from the wall in rotten pieces. The dogs were nosing at the remaining wood and dancing around, their bodies twisting with excitement. Something white caught his eye beside one of the chunks of wood and Gareth leaned down. It was a small scrap of paper, folded several times. He unfolded it slowly, his heart alternating between excitement and dread; he recognized Oliver's handwriting. It was part of a larger note, the words written with the graphite pencil Gareth had given him, the sheet of paper from the small pad of paper.

"Carry this with you," he'd said, giving the boy one of the same pads of paper he always carried. "When a good idea comes to you, you do not want to be without a way to record it."

Gareth thought the words were Oliver's notes to himself about the automaton he was making as a surprise gift for his mother.

He carefully re-folded the note and tucked it inside his coat. One of the hounds came near enough to sniff at his face and Gareth gave the animal a pat and then scratched between its ears, just the way he'd seen Oliver do a hundred times.

"He's in there, isn't he?" he asked the dog, knowing as he did so how ridiculous such a thing was. But the dog seemed to like it, wagging its tail twice as hard at the sound of his voice.

Gareth stood and approached the opening on feet that were heavier than blocks of lead. The brush had been trampled and then pushed back in a poor effort to cover the hole. Gareth lifted the light until it illuminated what lay behind the boards.

"Good God." He barely forced the words out through his frozen jaws.

***

"It is an hour after he said he would join you. We must do something." Serena told herself she had shown amazing restraint for the past thirty minutes.

McElroy looked up from the plan of the estate the draftsman had made. "He must have found something around here—this old chalk mine."

Serena stood at the edge of the desk where he was seated and looked at the map even though it was burnt into her mind.

"Gareth had the mine entrance closed up the very day he first saw it." She could not bear the thought of either Oliver or Gareth anywhere near the old mine, which the locals considered not just haunted, but terribly unstable in places. She had threatened Oliver to within an inch of his life if he was ever discovered poking around in the ruins, which Flowers, her construction foreman, said hadn't been used for hundreds of years.

"We used to dare each other to go in them, as young 'ungs. 'Twas stupid, but boys are stupid," he'd admitted when Serena voiced her concerns. "But Mr. Lockheart has closed up the last of 'em. The other openings either caved in on themselves or was boarded or rocked over years ago."

She remembered those words now.

"There are other entrances. Entrances that were closed up a long time ago."

McElroy regarded her with a steady look. When he wasn't smiling, he looked far older, deep lines carved around his overlarge mouth and dozens of smaller lines mapping the skin around his green eyes. "I know I have only my gut to go on, but Gareth must have found something. He is, as you might know, punctual to the minute."

Serena's mouth curled into a smile at the thought of him ordering her to meet him at the river in an hour and twenty-three minutes.

"You might have also realized he is also not fond of dark, cramped spaces."

She nodded, fighting down a flare of jealous anger that this man knew more about Gareth than she did. "I knew he didn't care for the dark, but I knew nothing about small spaces."

McElroy did not enlighten her. "I am going to take the dogs and follow the trail from where we split up."

"I am going with you."

He cocked his head as he looked up at her, and finally shrugged. "Fine. I don't have the time to argue with you and you have the look of a woman who will do whatever she damn well pleases."

Serena decided she liked the Irishman better and better upon further acquaintance. She turned away and headed for the door.

"I only need my cloak and I am ready."

***

The cavern beyond the entrance was far wider and taller than Gareth expected. It was certainly twice as spacious as the diagrams he'd seen of a Cornish mine that Dec had been keen on acquiring.

The lantern only illuminated a few feet around him, even though he had removed the shutter and set it ablaze. There was no way he could have entered this black hole without it. Even with the light, his insides churned and his hands trembled as he investigated what was essentially a big, winding cavern. No smaller tunnels led out from this one, which must have served as some sort of staging area in the distant past. No, there were only two ways out of this vast cavern that he knew of: the way he'd come in and the blocked-up entrance.

One of the dogs was on its hind legs, its paws resting on the top of the board he'd climbed over. Gareth looked at the anxious animal to avoid looking at what occupied the far end of the big cave: a hole that dropped straight down into Hell.

A choked laugh broke from between his chattering teeth. Even with his shriveled sense of humor he could appreciate the irony. A cave, with another, smaller, cave inside of that. All the situation lacked was crippling hunger pangs and a swollen, bloody back from Mr. Jensen's leather strap. Oh, and rats—he should never forget the rats.

There was no time for hysteria, and he knew it. At the very least, the note proved Oliver had been here. It might have been days ago, or he might be down there right now.

Gareth approached the hole and dropped into a crouch before leaning over the edge and lowering the lantern. Hand and footholds had been chiseled out of the rough wall and metal rungs set in the stone at widespread intervals. When he lowered the lantern into the shaft, he could see what looked to be dry stone floor far below.

He glanced around the cavern, looking for something that could be used to tie the lantern around him somehow. Unfortunately, he'd worn no cravat because he owned only white neckcloths.

But the cave only held the skeletons of small animals, twigs, branches, and more cobwebs than he'd ever seen in his entire life.

And then he remembered the dog lead. It had jerked out of his hand when he'd slid down the hillside. He went back to the opening to find all the dogs waiting, eerily quiet and expectant. He quickly removed the rope lead and tied it in a knot around the metal lantern handle and then tied a knot in the rope itself and looped it over his head. It hung down his back, heavy against his throat, but not enough to cause breathing problems.

He'd taken off his gloves, thinking it would be easier to gain purchase in the hand holds, but his hands—his entire body—ran with sweat, so he put them back on.

As he took another look down the shaft, he couldn't help being grateful he did not have a fear of heights, along with everything else. He took hold of the top metal rung and gave it a hard tug before turning his back to the hole. And then he began his slow descent into darkness.

***

Serena's heart was pounding and it wasn't because she'd just slid down a hillside on a wave of rocks, pebbles, and dirt.

"Are you hurt?"

McElroy leaned toward her, the cloud of dirt further obscuring the dim light from the lantern.

"I'm fine. Where are the dogs?"

He helped her to stand and then turned. The dogs were gone, but the trail they'd taken was clear.

"Gareth, or someone, has recently been this way," he whispered. "We will need to go single file or you risk being torn to shreds by the brambles. Hold on to the tail of my coat."

He held the lantern ahead of him and took small steps. She followed him, all but blind, shuffling her feet across the uneven terrain.

Serena told herself not to become overexcited. It was possible Gareth had come here and moved along. Although it was only a hunch, she just didn't think Etienne had ever left the property. As for co-conspirators, she couldn't imagine who he had left that he hadn't double-crossed or used so badly they were after him, too. He would be out of money and there was no inn or hostelry where he could take a struggling child. And Oliver would know enough never to follow him off the property. No, he was here, on the estate, and this was the best possible hiding place for a man with no other options but to kidnap his own son.

Low whines and snuffles snapped her from her daze and McElroy came to a halt. She peered around him and saw nine leaping dogs and a large opening in the rock face.

"Oh my God." She pushed around him and then realized she couldn't see without the lantern. "Quick, the light—right here."

He lifted the light over her shoulder as he followed behind her.

They stopped at the opening to the cave. "He must have gone in there." She began to lift her foot over the remaining wooden barrier, but his big hand on her shoulder stopped her.

She swung around, furious. "My son is in there!"

"We don't know that yet. And what are you planning to do?" He didn't wait for her answer. "Let us investigate this calmly."

Serena glared up into his face, prepared to fight him tooth and claw, but the worry she saw on his rugged face gave her pause.

"Very well, what do you suggest?"

"I will go in first and then open the lantern. Then I will look around, and then I will help *you* inside once I've determined it's safe."

She gave an abrupt nod, her stomach in knots as he disappeared inside and a few precious seconds passed before he opened the shutter, illuminating a surprisingly large cave.

"It's enormous." He turned to her. "You say this was an old chalk mine?"

"Yes, but not for hundreds of years." She looked over his shoulder. "What is that? Over there in the corner?"

The light moved to the far side of the cavern.

"It is a shaft of some sort," his voice was an eerie echo and she watched him bend down. "It looks to go straight down to some other level." He stood and came back toward her, his expression grim. "That shaft is the only other way out of here. The dogs wouldn't have been waiting outside the cave if Gareth hadn't gone down it. And that dark hole is Gareth's worst nightmare."

***

Gareth had been mistaken when he'd believed the shaft was his worst nightmare.

This was his worst nightmare.

The ceiling had already been coming down when he entered the biggest of the two corridors that led off the shaft, but the low, keening moan had convinced him he was heading in the correct direction. He stepped gingerly, as if that might keep the roof over his head. But he knew that was foolish conceit.

Fine dust obscured the tunnel ahead of him and worked its way into his nostrils and throat, until he had to pull his shirt up over his nose and hold it there in order to breathe.

He walked for less than a minute when he came to the source of the dust. A section of wall and ceiling had come down and closed off all but a small sliver of cave. A human hand lay beneath a large rock, the fingers not moving.

"Hello? Is somebody there?" a terrified, boyish voice called.

A wave of relief hit him so hard it left him woozy. "Oliver," he said softly. "It is Mr. Lockheart."

He heard a choked sob and his eyes followed the direction it seemed to be emanating from—above the slide of rock. He needed to keep the boy calm.

"Are you hurt, Oliver?"

Several loud sniffs and then, "A rock landed on my arm, but I don't think it's broken. But Mr. Bardot got caught beneath it. I told him we should go back when we saw the broken timber but he wouldn't listen. He became quite angry and shoved me over the rubble and before he could climb over it himself it came down on him. I tried to dig him out, but more of the wall kept—"

A sickening crack and then an oddly hushed roar cut off whatever he'd been about to say. Gareth jammed himself tighter against the cavern wall, as if that would save him as the ceiling came down with all the force of a huge foot, covering the place where Gareth had just been standing.

"Mr. Lockheart!" The boy's choked scream cut through the dust.

Gareth's throat was too filled with pulverized rock or chalk to speak but he lifted the light higher, scrambling up the rocks to get closer to the hole while he cleared his nose and mouth.

"Get away from the collapse, Oliver," he ordered hoarsly just as another section of ceiling and wall fell.

Something heavy and sharp landed on his right boot and he gave a muffled grunt of pain. It took a great deal of effort to free his foot from the detritus that poured in between the bigger rocks, much like the sand in an hourglass eventually filled the gap.

His eyes burned with grit, tearing and weeping as he blinked and tried to see. Not that he needed to make any difficult decisions, there was only one, get through the gap to the other side without bringing it all down on the boy.

"Oliver?" he croaked.

"I'm here."

Gareth closed his eyes at the sheer force of his relief. He cleared his throat several times, the lamplight illuminating the still shifting rocks and pebbles as they tumbled down the most recent slide.

"Don't touch the wall anymore or try to shift the rocks, Oliver, do you understand?" Gareth spoke as calmly as ever, not wanting to alarm the boy, but the words themselves sent a grim message.

"You think more will collapse, don't you, sir?"

Gareth ignored the question. "I'm going to pass the lantern up through the crack. I want you to take it." Gareth's teeth had begun chattering the moment the thought of parting with the lantern even entered his mind and he had to use every ounce of strength to force the words out. "You should be able to take it by the metal frame without burning yourself. When you have it, I want you to very carefully examine the rest of the corridor. I've noticed old square beams—look to see if any are fallen before you go forward. If so, stop and go no further. Do you understand?"

"Yes, sir. I will not go forward if I see any signs of instability."

Gareth smiled to himself. "Very good. I will wait here." *In the pitch dark.* He shifted as carefully as he could, but any movement seemed to send more rocks cascading. When he got as close to the top as he dared, he lifted the lamp and waited until he felt a light tug and then he released it, plunging himself into darkness as the light receded.

He swallowed and prepared himself for whatever came next, forcing down the taunting voice that accompanied the darkness. He concentrated on regulated his breathing, trying not to move or touch anything that might bring the rest of the ceiling down on his head. The blackness became blacker, solidifying into something cold, clammy, and alive. He fought the compulsion to make himself smaller, to disappear, to hide.

Oliver and Serena. He mined the words from beneath the fear and repeated them in his head, *Oliver and Serena.* The cold receded and he pictured their faces; he was here because of them. Because he loved them.

The thought was like an ember at first, glowing brighter as he held the image. He pictured what Serena had looked like when she said she loved him, or what Oliver looked like when he glanced up from some piece of work he'd done particularly well, seeking Gareth's approval, his eyes trusting.

A hundred years passed before Oliver's voice floated through the crack.

"The tunnel branches some distance ahead. One corridor is level but the other looks like it leads to a shaft."

The boy's voice woke him from his reverie and Gareth realized one thing immediately: he was no longer shaking.

"Do you judge it to be stable, Oliver?" He sounded calm and confident, like the kind of man a boy could trust.

"The wooden beams are still in place, although one is sagging. There are no piles of dirt and the air is cleaner where the corridors split."

Gareth was once again impressed by the boy's intelligence. "Do you think it is fresh air?"

"I think so, sir. I keep trying to remember where this part of the cave is . . . and I think it might be directly below the section you closed off."

Gareth had been thinking the same thing. This part of the corridor was doomed, it was only a matter of time. As if hearing him, a massive chunk sheared away somewhere close by and hit the cave floor with a giant *whumph!*

Thick, cloying chalk dust filled his shrinking grave.

"Are you all right, sir? Mr. Lockheart?" For the first time, the boy's voice held an edge of hysteria.

Gareth lowered his shirt, which he had pulled up over his mouth. "Oliver?"

"Yes, sir?"

"I'm going to try and widen the gap and come through." He stopped and coughed, choking on the fine dust before he could speak again. "I want you to take the lantern and go stand at the far end, near the fork." He hesitated, not wanting to scare the boy, but it needed to be said. "If something happens to me, do not come near this cave in. Mr. McElroy knows we are down here—or he will soon. Someone will come."

The answer took a long time coming. "Yes, sir."

"Good. Now go to the fork."

He counted to one hundred after his little prison had gone completely dark and then he reached into the blackness, in the direction of the hole.

Chapter Twenty-Four

"The tunnel is blocked by a cave in, and I could hear chunks still falling." McElroy's face was streaked with sweat and dust, his skin gray and white striped.

"Did you see—"

"I saw nothing other than rocks. The air is choked with a very fine dust. Chalk, I suppose."

Serena's mind skittered and shied away from the unthinkable. Instead, she nodded and clasped her hands together, as if that might keep her from flying apart.

"We must unseal the other entrance, the one we passed on our way here."

McElroy nodded. "I agree. However, we don't know if Bardot is down there, or even if Oliver is down there. The only thing we know for sure, thanks to the presence of the dogs, is that Gareth is down there. We need to handle this with secrecy or we risk alerting anyone Bardot might have set watching."

"Yes, of course. But what—"

He dug his watch out of his filthy coat. "It is almost four. We have been gone from the house three hours. I need to get back and be ready to go to London as planned."

Serena could see by his expression that leaving at a time like this was almost tearing him apart. She laid a hand on his arm and he gave her a grim, knowing smile.

"We will go back to the house and take the two biggest footmen. The opening has been closed with stone blocks, but two strong men will be able to move enough of them to get inside. Or to get out."

"That is a sensible plan. Except for one thing, I will wait by the entrance of the cave. An extra set of hands will not go unwanted." She smiled up at him. "And I know my way around stone."

***

Gareth felt as though he had eaten a pound of dirt and rock. He looked at the boy, who sat against the cavern wall, his small body tense as he watched him come awake.

"I'm sorry, sir."

Gareth could only lift his eyebrows, but it was enough.

"For disobeying you and coming back."

A gritty laugh forced its way out of his throat. "I'm glad you did."

Gareth had made it through the hole, but just as he was about to climb down to the floor of the cave a rock had clipped the back of his head and knocked him out. He'd woken up to find small hands wrapped around his, pulling him hard enough to yank his shoulder from the socket, but moving him inch by inch.

He pushed himself up, grimacing at the pain in his right foot and wiggling his toes. They hurt, but he didn't think his foot was broken. Every bone in his body creaked and ached as he lurched to his feet.

Oliver stood beside him. "You can lean on me if you need to, sir. I'm stronger than I look." He grinned up at Gareth, his teeth a startling white in his dirty face.

Yes, Gareth thought, *you certainly are. Just like your mother.*

They hobbled together toward the fork in the corridor. Gareth was astonished by how sound and clear the rest of the corridor appeared. The beams and their cross-pieces were old—ancient, he would guess. Numbers and letters were carved into them, leading him to believe they were part of some long-lost system. These caves often went for miles, like those at Chiselhurst, which were still being mined. They could wander for a very long time, but he believed Oliver's supposition was correct: they were somewhere below the opening he had sealed.

"Do you need to rest?"

Gareth realized his breath was coming in loud, sawing rasps and shook his head. "Just swallowed lots of dust, and perhaps even a rock or two." His lips twitched into a smile, which made the boy's narrow shoulders sag with relief. "Let's have a rest when we get to the bottom of that shaft."

"Is my mama angry?" Oliver asked, cutting Gareth a nervous look.

"Angry?"

"Doesn't she know I came into the cave with Monsieur Bardot?"

Oh, that. "No, we did not know where you had gone."

His answer seemed to make Oliver even more miserable.

"What is it?" Gareth asked.

"She is going to be very angry when she finds out I was in here."

Somehow Gareth thought she would forgive him. "She will be relieved you are safe."

"Yes, she will. But *then* she will be angry."

"Ah, is that how mothers operate?"

They came to a small semi-round room, just like the one at the base of the other shaft, and Gareth lowered himself to the ground, more grateful than he would have liked to sit for a moment.

The boy sat cross-legged beside him, close enough that one knee rested against Gareth's thigh. He understood the impulse to touch another person in a time of stress, but he was surprised he did not feel the revulsion that usually accompanied such human contact.

"I remember you grew up in an orphanage. Did your mama and papa die? My papa died fighting in the War. He was a hero." Pride tinged with regret colored his voice.

Gareth thought of the boy's real father—a blackmailing thief who would kidnap and ransom his own son—and suddenly understood why Serena was so reluctant to tell Oliver the truth about his parentage.

"Why did you and Mr. Bardot come down into the caves?"

"He told me he'd found something astonishing, and that it would make a nice surprise for my mama when she came back home." He shot Gareth a nervous glance. "When I told him I wasn't allowed in the caves he said it would be all right if he was with me." He chewed his lip, a gesture just like his mother's. "I don't think there was really anything down here. Do you?"

Gareth wondered what answer would make the boy feel least anxious or foolish. He finally shrugged. "I daresay there could be any number of interesting things down here. Unfortunately, they will stay buried; I expect it will never be safe to explore these caves."

Oliver nodded. "Still, it is rather a shame, isn't it?"

Gareth looked around at the small cave they were in and realized, with a shock, that he agreed with the boy. He couldn't have said when, exactly, he'd ceased to be terrorized by the darkness, confinement, and brooding pressure above his head, but he did know it had been banished. He hoped it was gone for good but was grateful it was gone for now.

***

Serena was in a half-dream, half-awake stage. The night was still velvety black, although it could not be much longer until dawn. She sat against the entrance to the cave, as if mere proximity to the stones would bring her closer to the man she knew was trapped below. She vacillated between wanting her son to be with him, and not wanting him to be facing such danger. Still, being with Gareth would be better than being with Etienne.

It was a struggle not to scream with frustration and pound her fists on the neatly stacked blocks behind her while she waited for the promised footmen to arrive. She told herself McElroy's caution was wise. To be rash and attract attention would jeopardize Oliver. But to wait? Every moment Gareth was inside these caves would be an hour for him.

She closed her eyes against the horror of her thoughts but that just created new, more insidious images: Oliver, trapped and alone; Gareth in the dark, his eyes burning with unspeakable despair. The thought that he'd gone into his very worst nightmare for her son made her love him even more—which she hadn't thought possible.

Serena bowed her head and prayed. *Oh, God, please don't let anything happen to either—*

"Oww!" A not insubstantial rock bounced off her dark bonnet and landed beside her.

"*Hello?*"

For a moment she thought the rock had jarred her son's voice loose in her head. And then she spun around and onto her knees, pressing her forehead against the cool, rough stone.

"Oliver?" She sounded utterly unlike herself.

"Mama!"

She didn't realize she was crying until a tear landed on her clenched fist. She gulped in air. "Is—" her voice cracked and she tried again, "Is Mr. Lockheart there?"

A muffled but precise voice came through the tiny gap in the stone. "I'm here, Serena. All is well, except for your cousin, Mr. Bardot, who I'm afraid was caught in the collapse."

Tears flowed freely now. "Oh, thank God! *Thank God!*"

***

Squeezing one's voice through a gap is one thing. Squeezing a boy and full-sized man through was quite another.

The two footmen arrived and began to remove the carefully placed rocks. Some of them, like the one Gareth and Oliver had managed to displace, were quite small. But many were more than even two big men could lift.

With the threat of Bardot gone, Serena ran back to the house to enlist more help. It was not until several hours later, when both captives had been freed, that anyone remembered Declan McElroy.

By then, Oliver had been welcomed back into the crushing—but not scolding—arms of his mother and Nounou. He was then thoroughly bathed, dried, fed, and ensconced in a warm bed. For once, he fell asleep before Nounou could complain about the light.

"He is exhausted," Nounou said, motioning for Serena to leave her vigil beside his bed. She had not left her son's side since pulling him from the hole in the cave. "Come, it is time you bathe and eat."

Serena closed the door with regret.

"I have just had a bath sent to your room."

Serena nodded. "Has the doctor been to see Mr. Lockheart?"

"Been and gone some hours ago. He will be fine and walk as normal in only a few days."

"Thank you, Nounou."

A Figure of Love

The French woman gave her a knowing look and snorted. "You look terrible. Go and bathe and put cucumber on your eyes. You won't wish him to see you this way."

Serena laughed. "For your information, he has already asked me to marry him, Nounou."

"Ha! He might change his mind if he were to see you now."

When Serena arrived in her room and had a look in her mirror she had to admit the older woman might have a point.

She would hurry and clean herself and then go and call on Gareth, no matter how scandalous such behavior might be. But when she lay in the steaming warmth of the tub, a powerful lassitude crept into her body. She would close her eyes. Only for a moment.

**

Gareth didn't care that the maid had squeaked and then scuttled through the still open doorway when strode into Serena's room.

She was not in bed and her sitting room was dark. "Serena?" he called, limping through her dressing room toward her bathing chamber. His breath caught in his raw throat at what he found.

She was asleep in her bath. Her hair had been washed and lay over the high tub back, puddled on the floor like chestnut-gold foam. Her arms floated by her sides and her full breasts rose above the water line, their nipples hard. Her body was covered in goose pimples, telling him the water had long cooled.

He crouched beside the tub, grimacing at the assorted aches and pains. "Serena, wake up."

Her eyelids fluttered and she regarded him with huge, unseeing pupils, her expression confused as she left sleep behind.

"Gareth?" Her hand rose from the tub, dripping water.

"Yes, it's Gareth." He let his eyes drop to her slick, bobbing breasts and the shadowy triangle beneath the water. "I think you must be clean now."

A slow, joyous smile spread across her tired but beautiful face and she held a hand up and examined it. "I am becoming a prune."

He stood and took one of the big Turkish towels from the pile, opening it and holding it out. "Come, I will dry you."

She rose from the water like a goddess from the sea and his body rejoiced at the sight of her water-slicked curves and rosy peaks and dark chestnut curls.

He helped her from the tub and then began to rub her dry.

"What time is it?"

"It is not yet six." He knelt on one knee and started with one foot while she held herself steady on the edge of the tub.

"Mr. McElroy—"

"He returned an hour ago." Gareth dried between each perfect toe, spending an inordinate amount of time on her elegant arch and ankle before moving up her calf.

"Mmm," she purred. "That feels good. Is Mr. McElroy unharmed?"

He forced himself to stop mid-thigh, afraid she might never get dry if he gave in to the distraction that lay at the top of her legs. "He is."

She laughed. "Really, Gareth. Must I pull each syllable from you?"

He found himself again at the top of a well-dried leg, his eyes at the perfect level. Perhaps only a little taste. A little lick. Just one suck . . .

"Gareth!"

He looked up from where he knelt between her thighs. The view of her breasts from this angle was lovely. So was her flushed face, which was looking down at him with an expression he believed to be equal parts amusement, asperity, and desire. He latched on to the desire.

"Hmm?" He caressed the skin that bordered her sex with his thumbs, gently opening her to his hungry eyes, his mouth watering.

"I'm cold." She shivered to illustrate and Gareth handed up the towel without breaking contact with her body. She slung it over her shoulders and gave a low laugh, which Gareth took to be encouragement.

He parted her folds and took her into his mouth, curling his tongue around her small organ. He massaged her rhythmically, until she became swollen and wet, her thighs spreading wider without any encouragement from him.

"Oh, Gareth."

He responded to her soft plea by sliding a finger into her slick, tight heat, pumping her while he continued to suck and tease. Her hands tangled in his hair and pulled hard enough to hurt. He reveled in the pain and worked her without mercy toward completion, only halting when he felt her knees sag, as if they might buckle. He gave her one last thrust and released her, lurching clumsily to his feet.

"Come," he said. He was too whipped to risk carrying her so he took her limp hand and tugged her toward her bed.

She followed unsteadily and he released her only long enough to pull back her bedding, slip off his robe, and pull his nightshirt over his head, almost howling with pain as he worked his sore muscles.

Gareth slid into bed beside her and took her into his arms, warming her still cool body with his hands. He kissed her damp hair and pulled her closer with one leg, until they were twined together like vines. "Declan sent a message to Mr. Steele when he made the withdrawal from the bank."

"Hmm? Declan? Oh. But what about—" she broke off, as if too embarrassed to articulate her wants. Gareth felt a grin tug at his lips.

"Oh, you wish to know what about the men who were supposed to be watching him?" he teased, knowing that was not what she wanted at all. "Well, his message told Steele of the situation and instructed him to lag behind a quarter of an hour."

Her cool, calloused hand slid between them and wrapped around his painfully hard shaft.

He gave a low, satisfied grunt of pleasure but continued his story, his voice only a little strained.

"As we suspected, he was set upon by two masked men in broad daylight, just to the south of Shooter's Hill," he said, naming the notorious lay of robbers and highwaymen, although not usually in the middle of the day. Her hand froze in mid-stroke and he realized he had better continue his tale. "The two men had just relieved him of the money and were heading off with his horse when Steele came over the hill with five of his fittest, most fearsome Bow Street compan—" He broke off as she began to work him in earnest, thrusting into her tight hand.

But then the vixen stopped.

"Please continue." Her voice was cool and toneless and if Gareth had been a more suspicious sort he might have wondered if she were mocking him.

He had to swallow several times and gather his scattered wits. "The Runners made short work of the robbers who, when their masks were removed turned out to be—"

"Sandford and Leeland." She had released him, her voice thick with disgust. "It was them, was it not?"

"Yes, you are correct."

She groaned and turned onto her back, covering her eyes with her hands.

"What is it?"

"I should have known. He came to me in London, furious and threatening. He thought I was the one who said something to you to get him discharged. He was in the process of making good on his threat when Miles, a very good friend of mine, interrupted and drove him off."

Gareth shook his head. "Why didn't you tell me this, Serena?"

"I could hardly say anything at the time, and it never occurred to me when we learned what Etienne had done. I should have known two such slimy characters would find each other."

"According to McElroy, who only stayed around long enough to watch Steele get the entire story, Featherstone went to Bardot. He claimed the Frenchman was desperate for money and told him I would likely pay money to protect you and the boy."

She turned to him and put a hand on his shoulder. "Oh, Gareth, I am so sorry you have been used this way."

"I am sorry I didn't have Steele keep Bardot when he had him the first time. None of this would have happened."

She slid a hand from his shoulder up his neck. "You couldn't have known."

He inched closer. "None of that matters now. What matters is that Oliver is safe. Fortunately Bardot never told them of his relationship to Oliver, so I suppose we can thank him for that." He rested a hand on her belly, which jumped and quivered at his touch. "The Featherstones are someplace they can never hurt either of you again."

Her body froze. "Gareth, you haven't . . . had them *killed?*"

The thought had crossed his mind, but he knew what killing another man had done to Dec, no matter how justified.

"No, Dec just sent them on a little trip." He stroked her stomach in ever growing circles, his fingers *accidentally* brushing her mound.

She shook her head. "I won't ask—I don't want to know."

He rubbed her in silence, until her legs spread a little.

Gareth accepted the invitation and entered her, thrilling as her sheath tightened around his finger.

"Ah." The sound accompanied a softening of her body, her core molten beneath his questing hand. Her hand caught at him. "I want you."

Her words enflamed him, but he shook his head, rising up on his knees and kneeling between her thighs, spreading her wider, his eyes flickering from his hand to her face.

"Not yet, but soon. You will come for me first."

She tightened at his words and her breathing quickened. He smiled down at her, pleased to know she was aroused by his command. And when she came, which she did far too quickly, he prolonged her ecstasy, teasing her climaxes out in waves.

He entered her in a long smooth thrust, taking his weight on his forearms while tasting her breasts, his hips driving into her in deep, hard strokes until he pushed them both over the edge.

***

He woke with a start beside her, his body rigid, his eyes wide.

"Gareth?" The candles had guttered low and darkness claimed all but the bed.

He was beside her, their bodies entwined. They'd both fallen asleep after their lovemaking, but something had woken her. She now knew it had been the tension in his body: he was having a nightmare.

"Gareth?" She slid a hand under his chin. "Are you awake?"

He gave a slight nod and his eyelids drooped as he exhaled slowly. "Yes, I'm awake."

She opened her mouth to ask about his dream, but then closed it. When he wanted to take her into his confidence, he would. Until then, she owed him love without reservation.

"Declan and I lived in the house of a Mr. William Jensen, a man who claimed to operate an orphanage, yet never placed any of the children he took in—at least not with families or legitimate employers." He turned onto his back and stared up at the darkened canopy above their heads. "There were those who stayed only a short time—comely girls and boys who would disappear after they'd been well-fed and their bones no longer showed. They would leave one day, dressed in new clothing, bound for some new life." He looked down at her, his eyes bleak in the low light. "Dec and I used to envy them. Before we knew better."

He slid an arm beneath her and pulled her close. "I can't remember a time I wasn't there. I've since concluded I might have been either Mr. Jensen's son, or perhaps some relative's child. He brought Declan home when he was perhaps six. Jensen had caught him picking pockets in a crowd outside the old Drury Theater. He was dirty and half-wild, but Jensen must have seen something in him." Gareth shook his head. "I don't know why Dec was alone. Perhaps he worked for one of the men who ran gangs of children to steal and work for them. Or maybe his family left or died or were arrested and he had to fend for himself. He's never said, and I have never asked him. Jensen kept us away from the other children, giving us a room together. There were never many children at his *orphanage*, but he didn't want us getting to know any of the others for some reason."

His hand traced idly up and down her arm, which had begun to sprout goose pimples, but this time not from the cold.

"We became a team, Dec and I. Jensen would host card parties—and parties for other activities, as we would learn eventually. He and his associate, a Mrs. Burgess, who did not live at the orphanage, but who must have served as a procuress, would set various traps for their guests." He paused and looked at her. "What I am going to say will be upsetting."

She nodded. "I understand."

"Dec and I were novelties. We would serve drinks and food and so forth. The whole time I would watch the cards and let Jensen know how to bid. Sometimes the men would take a break that lasted for a while. I know now that they went to the rooms prepared by Mrs. Burgess. Rooms where they could indulge in other tastes." He squeezed her tight.

"They sold children—virgins—to the men who came to play. I learned later they would blackmail their clients afterward."

Serena had seen terrible things during the War—and she'd suffered at the hands of such men herself. But raping a child was a level of darkness she'd never let her mind imagine.

"With my skill at cards, I was too valuable for such things but I'd noticed a change in Declan. He'd become sullen and withdrawn—even with me. Jensen punished him more and more, yet to less and less avail. You see, Serena, Jensen's punishment was to lock us in the old cellar under the building. Nothing but rubbish and vermin and damp rot and darkness. It had not taken many trips to the cellar to convince me I should *always* pay attention when Jensen was at the card table."

His hand dug into her shoulder so hard it hurt, but she just pushed closer to his body, which had begun to sweat in the cool night air.

"But Dec had a harder head. Or maybe he just liked it better in the cellars than he did in the rooms where Jensen sent him."

He took several deep breaths and Serena wanted to tell him he could stop—that she didn't want to know. The truth was, *she didn't* want to know. But he had to tell her, that much was painfully clear.

"One night one of the guests took a fancy to me. I must have been twelve, perhaps thirteen—I'm not sure when my birthday is and Jensen never mentioned such things. In any event, the man kept giving me coins with each little thing I brought. He seemed so . . . happy to give them to me. Jensen must have thought so, too. I don't know who the man was, but when he got up to take a stroll he asked me to join him. Declan was there. I believed he was sulking because of all the money I'd earned. Not that I would be allowed to keep any of it. But he jumped to his feet and shouted, *No!* as we were about to leave the room.

"The gentleman rushed me away but I could hear Jensen's voice, ordering Declan to his room and telling him he'd been a very bad boy. Jensen never ordered any of us to our rooms as punishment—it was only the cellar. He must not have wanted to do that in front of his customers, thinking to punish Declan after they'd all gone. Instead of going to his room Declan followed me and my new friend, who led me to a door that was always kept locked, a bedroom of a sort I'd never seen before. It was filled with tools for any perversion imaginable, and many that are not.

"He shut the door but did not think to lock it—after all, he must have paid a good deal of money to have me. If I wasn't there to count cards and help him, Jensen would likely be losing money. When the man asked me to sit on his knee, I knew I didn't want to be there. He was the sort of man who enjoyed rough play and he had me—a scrawny youth—pinned to the bed with one knee when the door flew open and a ball of rage descended on him."

"Declan," she breathed.

"The very same. Unfortunately, Mrs. Burgess must have been nearby. She came and pulled Declan off the man's ear, which he'd bitten hard enough that there was blood everywhere. She led the screaming man from the room and locked us inside. We were there for hours—long enough to placate their customer, get rid of the other guests, and then come back to deal with us." He shook his head at whatever was in his memory.

"Jensen had missed the fact we had both grown and were no longer little boys. Declan, in particular, had developed a good deal of brawn. Jensen entered the room and struck me across the face with his fist. I must have been dazed for a few moments because the next thing I knew, Declan was on top of Jensen, his hand holding a bloody knife. He must have struck Jensen just so, because he was dead within minutes."

"Oh, Gareth!"

He looked down at her voice, his expression bland. And that was when she realized how thick his mask was—and just how little it concealed when you came to know the real man beneath it.

"Mrs. Burgess had already left, no doubt believing Jensen had us firmly in hand—just as he had for years. We ransacked his study but could not get to the real money, which was in a safe in the wall. There were perhaps nine others in the orphanage—all chosen for their handsome looks—and we told them to take what they could find and run."

"Where did you go? You were only boys."

He shrugged. "We were safer away from Jensen. We hid with hundreds of others, down by the river, under bridges, wherever we could escape the weather or bigger, meaner thugs than ourselves.

"It was Declan who came up with the idea of making me look older and trying our luck at a gambling hell. He was smart and had learned from Jensen how to remove only the down from a duck and not leave it bare." His lips curved into an ironic smile. "Soon we had enough money to get off the streets. I knew a life at the card tables would never end well and when the little shop where we bought our victuals closed, we offered to invest our money if a look at the legers showed any chance of saving the business. It did, as they almost always do." He glanced down at her. "That was the beginning." He frowned and then raised a hand to brush a tear from her cheek. "Have you been crying again?"

She shook her head. "No."

"Don't cry for me, Serena. I am one of the lucky ones."

"This is why you wanted to marry well—to influence our government to do something about these horrid men?"

"Yes, that was one idea."

"I'm so sorry my reputation and connections will not bring you all the influence you hoped for."

"You don't understand, *you* will give me the strength I need to persevere. I don't need to marry an aristocrat's daughter; marrying to secure political influence is a coward's way." He turned her in his arms, until her breasts pressed against the sleek hardness of his chest. "Sleeping alone in a blazing room was another act of cowardice." He kissed her when she opened her mouth to demur. "No, do not argue and try to make me feel less of a fool. I cannot promise I will not wake you up with my shaking and yelling some nights, but I will not let the thought of it unman me—certainly not at the expense of doing without you in my arms." He covered her with kisses and she never wanted him to stop. But she still had one last thing to tell him.

"Gareth? Darling?"

"Hmm?" he murmured from somewhere near her right breast.

"You'll need to be extra gentle with them for a while, Gareth."

He stopped and his head pushed up from beneath the covers, a pucker of concern between his beautiful gray eyes. "Have I been too rough?"

She smiled and stroked his jaw. "No, they are just very sensitive right now."

His head cocked. "Is aught amiss? Should I call back Doctor—"

She laughed. "No, if I am correct it is nothing he can cure." She hastened to assure him when she saw the horror in his eyes. "It is nothing bad, do not look like that! It might be nothing at all, but I think—" she broke off, now wishing she had said nothing at all.

"What?   You   think   what?"

"It has only been three weeks but the last time they became this sore I was with child."

His expression was beyond comical. And he'd stopped breathing.

"Gareth? *Gareth?*" She shook his shoulder.

He blinked. "I'm going to be a father."

"Well, possibly. Probably, if I am reading the signs correctly."

"I'm going to be a father."

She laughed. "You seem to have become stuck in something of a rut."

"Oliver is going to have a little brother or sister."

"Well, those are the usual two options." She paused, drinking in the beauty and strength in his face. "I love you, Gareth."

His lips began to curve, not stopping until he was grinning. "You have made me a very happy man. I love you, Mrs. Soon-to-be-Lockheart.

"Oh?" she teased, as his rare and beautiful smile melted her heart into a puddle. "How much."

Still smiling, he slowly backed away, until he disappeared under the covers. And then he commenced to show her just how much.

Epilogue

Three Weeks and Two Days and Nine Hours Later . . .

Declan sealed the brief note with one of Gareth's wafers and propped the envelope against his inkstand, where he would be sure to notice it. He'd celebrated Gareth and Serena's wedding with true gladness in his heart. Even a blind fool could see the two were madly in love. But now he needed to take his misery and anger and burning desire for drink somewhere far away— someplace where he wouldn't taint his best friend's hard-earned happiness. His note said he needed time to himself, but he told Gareth not to worry and promised he would be here at Christmas.

He was making his way out of the vast library, which no longer blazed with half a hundred candles, when he heard a distinct burp, followed by a groan.

As usual, he let his curiosity get the better of his sense—he needed to be off, but he apparently needed to see who was in the library even more. He retraced his steps to the big desk and then to the long brown leather settee that faced the barely glowing hearth.

The Earl of Avingdon lay stretched out, a champagne glass balanced on his chest. His eyes swung lazily up to Declan.

"Champagne always gives me gas." The aristocrat swung his feet onto the floor and his body into an upright, if wobbly, position. He gave Declan an engaging grin. "Sit and have a drink with a man soon to be shackled?"

Declan laughed, he couldn't help it. People rarely surprised him, but this man had. An honest-to-God earl wanting a drink with the likes of him?

"Why not?" he said, even though he knew why—he needed to get the hell out of here.

The earl tried to push himself up but didn't have much luck.

"You sit, I'll pour." He went to the decanters. "I'm afraid there is no champagne."

"Thank God. Whiskey if he has it."

"Oh, he has it." Declan poured two glasses from a bottle he knew Gareth had paid triple digits for and carried both toward the other man. He handed him one and raised the other high, "To your upcoming nuptials, may they be as joy-filled as those we witnessed today."

Avingdon tipped his head back and poured the contents of the glass down in one big gulp. He grimaced as the liquid burned its way down, the expression in no way diminishing his perfect features.

Declan had always been secure in his ability to attract members of the opposite sex but the earl was the type of man to make other men feel like inelegant oafs and get every woman in the room swooning. Still, Dec couldn't help noticing his battered Hessians and threadbare coat. Everyone—even men who looked like this and had a title to boot—had their problems.

He glanced at the empty glass in the earl's hand. "Another?"

Avingdon reeled back a little. "No shank, er, *thank* you, I had better not."

Dec shrugged. "Suit yourself." He took the chair across from him.

"I don't know your friend well, but I believe they make a fine couple, don't you think?"

Declan agreed, although he hadn't always. Of course he now knew some of that was fear at losing Gareth's friendship, a foolish fear. "Yes, I believe they will rub along quite nicely together. What about your future wife?"

Avingdon blinked. "What wife?"

"I thought you said you were soon to be shackled?"

He watched with amusement as realization dawned slowly in the man's enormous blue eyes. "Ah. Yes. *That* wife. Well," he raised his glass and then saw it was empty. "I have not spoken the necessary words yet."

"Are you worried she will not have you?"

An expression of anger or something like it flickered across his face. "No, I'm afraid she will." He shook himself, as if he'd just heard what he'd said. He grimaced. "Dear me, that sounds quite dreadful. I'm afraid I may have given you the wrong impression. I have no particular woman in mind. You see, I have only recently come into my title."

Declan had heard the man's brother died unexpectedly not long ago. "I'm sorry for your loss." That's what people said, wasn't it?

The other man waved away his condolence.

"Bloody shame it was, although there are more than a few in my family who think he was damned lucky to get out of it." He burped. "'Scuse me. 'Course I planted the last bastard who said that a facer. Not good, not good. Not at a funeral."

Dec was beginning to wish he'd poured himself a larger drink. He'd had no idea aristocrats did interesting things like engage in brawls at funerals.

"Aunts, cousins, nieces, sisters, and even a brother. Every last one needs it."

"*It?*" Declan repeated.

He looked up and blinked, as if surprised to find he wasn't alone. "Brass. I need brass."

Ah, he was skint. Declan took a sip. "Well, I daresay the heiresses will be queuing up for a chance at being a countess." Not to mention for a chance to marry a man who didn't look like a bloated trout, which was what most of the aristos he'd met resembled.

His words seemed to depress the other man. "Ne—*hic*—never wanted to auction myself off like a side of pork."

Declan laughed and the earl scowled at him. "Whasso amusing?"

He shrugged. "You, I guess."

Avingdon flinched back as if he'd been slapped, and then he threw his head back and laughed—far louder and with more gusto than the small comment deserved.

"You're right," he finally said. "You're right. I'm bloody pathetic. Men of my sort marry for money all the time. All the bloody time." He nodded owlishly. "And what a bargain I'll be for some downy young miss, eh?" He stared through Declan, his eyes bleak.

The man was beyond foxed and blue-deviled to boot. He needed to go to bed and sleep it off. Not that it would be any better in the morning, of course. No, no matter how much you drank, you woke up with yourself—even after all that effort to leave you behind. Nobody knew that better than Declan.

He finished the little bit that remained in his glass and struggled against the pull to have another. And another. He put the glass down with a thump that made the other man look up.

"You off then?"

Declan nodded. "I am."

Avingdon peered at the windows, which were covered by heavy drapes, and then at the giant long clock, whose face was big enough for even a drunk to see. "Late for a ride, issnit?"

"Aye, but the moon is bright and the night is clear."

"Where you going?"

Declan smiled, "I have no idea." When the earl didn't answer Dec looked at him. He was sleeping, his mouth open. He stood and smiled down at the man. "Good luck, mate."

A soft snore was his only answer.

Declan had a feeling the handsome aristocrat would need some luck. But then again, who didn't?

Thanks so much for reading A FIGURE OF LOVE!

If you enjoyed reading about Gareth and Serena's world you can meet more of their friends in

THE ACADEMY OF LOVE series—seven romantic Regencies about out-of-work schoolteachers who are about to get some serious lessons in love!

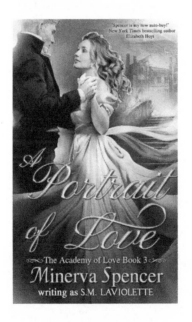

Here's an exclusive excerpt from
A Portrait of Love
BOOK 3 in
THE ACADEMY OF LOVE SERIES...

A Figure of Love

Chapter One

London
1803

Honoria ran down the stairs as if winged death was snapping at her heels.

It was ten minutes past noon; he would be here, already! She would have missed *ten entire minutes* of his company. Of staring at him. Of *worshipping* him.

She skidded to a halt outside her father's studio and checked her reflection in the shiny brass urn that sat on a plinth across from the door. A distorted, yellowed image of her face looked back at her. The belly of the vase stretched out her eyes and made them look long and exotic while shrinking her overlarge mouth into a prim, bow-shaped moue. Honey wished she looked like this imaginary girl instead of the pale, gangly, and big-mouthed reality that stared back at her.

She wrinkled her stubby nose at her brass reflection and hissed, narrowing her eyes and giggling at the evil image she'd just created. All she lacked to be truly horrifying was fangs.

He's in there, an unamused part of her mind pointed out.

Honey pinched her cheeks to give them a bit of color and pushed her waist-length and far-too-curly hair back over her shoulders. Her father would not let her wear it up until her next birthday, when she would be sixteen. For an artist Daniel Keyes could sometimes be a stickler for propriety and—

"Hello."

Honey jumped and yelped, no doubt resembling a huge startled mouse in her hideous brown painting smock.

Correction, a huge mouse with a red face.

She didn't want to turn around but she could hardly stand here all day. She swallowed noisily, as if her throat had rusted shut and slowly, ever so slowly, turned on one heel.

Eyes the color of hydrangeas stared down at her, their corners crinkling.

Lord Simon Fairchild.

Even his name was beautiful.

But nothing compared to his face and person. Not only was he beautiful, he was taller than her. At over six feet Simon Fairchild didn't exactly tower over her five foot ten-and-a-half inch frame, but it was near enough. And it made Honey feel—for the first time in her fifteen and three-quarter years—petite.

He was golden and broad-shouldered and graceful and he looked like a hero out of a Norse epic, all chiseled angles and fair perfection. His sculpted lips curved into a smile that released butterflies into her body.

"My lord," she croaked, dropping the world's clumsiest curtsey.

He grinned and took her hand, bowing low over it before releasing her. "Good afternoon, Miss Honoria." His voice was warm honey and it pooled low in her belly, the sensation . . . disturbing.

She blurted out the first words that leapt to mind—"You remembered my name"—and then wanted to hide.

His lips twitched and Honey only just stopped herself from smacking her palm to her forehead or crawling behind the big moth-eaten tapestry which covered much of the opposite wall. Of course he remembered her name, she'd only met him yesterday.

He clasped his hands behind his back, his gorgeous shoulders almost blocking the light from the cathedral window at the end of the hall. He was dressed for riding, which meant he would change into his portrait clothing once he entered her father's studio.

Thinking of Simon Fairchild changing his clothing gave her an odd, swirly, hot feeling and made her palms sweat. And she seemed to be salivating more than was necessary, as if her mouth were anticipating a delicacy.

Say something, you fool! Ask him something. Keep him here. Don't let him get—

"Are my sittings keeping you and your father in the city this summer, Miss Honoria?"

"Oh. No, we will stay here. We stay here most of the time."

He raised his eyebrows and nodded encouragingly.

"We rarely go into the country," she added lamely, unable to come up with anything better. And then inspiration struck. "Will *you* be going to the country, Lord Saybrook?"

"I no longer hold that honor, Miss Keyes," he reminded her gently.

Her face became hot yet again. "Oh, yes of course. The duke now has a son. You must be very . . ." Honey broke off—he must be very. . . what? Would a man be happy that he was no longer a duke's heir? She bit her lip.

Lord Simon grinned. "I'm very happy *and* relieved."

"You do not wish to be a duke?"

"No, I do not. Not only would it mean my brother's death, but the position entails altogether too much responsibility in my view. Besides, I have other plans."

"Other plans?"

"Yes, I wish to live at my country estate and breed horses."

Honey could not imagine the elegant man-god across from her rusticating and living the life of a mere country squire. She leaned against the doorframe to her father's studio, aware it was rude to keep a guest in the hall, but not wishing to share his attention with her father just yet.

"And you cannot do that *and* be duke?"

"Oh, I suppose the right kind of man could, but I wish for a quiet life, not responsibilities in Parliament and the management of hundreds of lives. No, the country life is the life for me. I'll be happy on my much smaller estate." He paused, his look speculative, as if he suddenly realized he—a man of twenty—was confiding his aspirations to a mere fifteen year-old. Honey had seen the look before—every person she associated with was older than her. She'd never gone to school, had no close relatives her age, and only socialized with her governess or her father's friends. Being young had never bothered her before—but, suddenly, it felt . . . limiting.

He bent low to catch her eyes, which had dropped miserably to his feet. "But you can't possibly find my boring plans of interest. While I'm off mucking about in my stables you'll no doubt be whirling around ballrooms and breaking young men's hearts."

Honoria could not think of a single thing to say that would not be humiliating.

So—" he said when she remained stupidly mute, his shapely mouth ticking up at one side, his eyes warm yet gentle.

It was impossible not to smile when he was smiling. "So?" she echoed as the two of them stood staring at one another.

He chuckled and shook his head, as if she'd said something amusing. He gestured behind her to the studio door, which she was blocking with her body.

"I'd better get inside. I believe I'm late and your papa is probably going to give me the raking I deserve."

Honey stepped aside, gawking like the smitten fool she was. He opened the door and again gestured. "After you, Miss Honoria. That is if you are going to join us again today?"

"Of course she is," Honey's father boomed from inside the brightly lighted room, where he was preparing his work area. His voice acted like a catalyst and Honey tore her eyes from Simon's perfect features and bolted into the room.

"Good afternoon, Papa."

Daniel Keyes gave her an approving smile as she went to her easel and then turned to Simon Fairchild. "My daughter will one day be England's premier portrait painter," he said, speaking with such certainty, pride, and love that Honey's heart threatened to grow right out of her chest.

Lord Simon cut her one of his devastating smiles. "So, you will be painting a portrait of me while your father paints his?"

"Yes," Honey said, pulling the cover off her much smaller canvas. She was glad to look away from Lord Simon's distracting person; her wits were already scrambled from their brief conversation in the hall.

Her painting was coming along quite nicely, not that she would show it to anyone until it was completed. And even then. . .

"Right now my daughter spends half her day studying to be a young lady and the other half honing her art. Once she is eighteen she will be free to paint at will," Daniel Keyes said as the younger man stepped behind the large screen in the corner of the room. To change his clothing.

Honey reminded herself to breathe and forced her gaze away from his head, which was visible above the screen. Her own face heated and she tried to control her breathing, which was sawing in and out just like their ancient butler Dowdle after he had climbed two sets of stairs.

"And will I get to see the portrait *you* are painting, Miss Keyes?"

Her head jerked up just in time to see him toss his waistcoat over the top of the screen. Which meant he was only wearing his shirt. His thin, fine, soft, muslin shirt. His eyes met hers as he did something behind the screen. Put on a coat? His other waistcoat?

Honey swallowed, but her father and Lord Simon were waiting with raised brows.

"I don't know yet," she mumbled.

"An artist's prerogative," Daniel Keyes said with a laugh. "She might not even let *me* see it, my lord."

Her father was right. There were plenty of sketches and paintings that were only for her eyes and she rather suspected this painting might be another.

***

On Lord Simon's fifth visit he asked her father if he could take Honey for a ride in his high-perch phaeton. Hyde Park was thin with people, but Honey still felt as if she were on the top of the world in his tall carriage with *him* beside her. It was the most magical afternoon of her life.

Until his next visit, when he took her to Gunters.

Miss Keebler, her governess, came along for that treat, but even the presence of her dour chaperone couldn't dampen the day.

All that month Lord Simon took her places or dined at her father's house and spent evenings mixing with the many artists and actors who comprised Daniel Keyes's social circle, which included Honoria, who'd been allowed to eat dinner with her father's guests since turning fifteen.

Part of her knew he was only spending so much time with her because London in the summer was devoid of most of his usual friends and entertainments. But she didn't care.

He took her on strolls after his sittings and they sat in the park together. Always with Miss Keebler nearby, of course. He told her about Everley, his home in the country, and what his plans were for new stables, improvements to the house which was Tudor and always in need of repair. He spoke of growing up with his brother on the great estate of Whitcomb and told her tales of ghosts in the castle and how he'd once dressed up in a sheet and terrified his nurse, earning the worst paddling of his youth.

Honoria told him about growing up surrounded by artists and how she'd pled with her father not to send her away to school. How she planned on taking over the management of the household when she was sixteen next year, and taking care of him. She shared her dreams that she might go to the Continent someday—when it was once again safe to travel—and see all the great art she'd only been able to read about.

Honey knew it was unheard of for her father to require so many sittings—in fact, he usually finished his portraits after no more than ten or twelve meetings. But, for whatever reason—maybe because he knew how greatly she enjoyed it—he had the young nobleman visit the house over a period of thirty-two blissful days and *sixteen* sittings.

Honey wished it would never end.

***

"Will you accompany me for one last ice, Miss Honoria?"

Honey looked at her father as she laid aside her brush and he nodded, the somewhat distracted look in his eyes told her he was still deep inside his work.

He turned to Lord Simon, who'd emerged from behind the screen, once again dressed in his street clothing. "Did you bring that yellow bounder today?"

Simon—Honoria thought of him by his Christian name, now, although only in the privacy of her own mind, of course—smiled and shook his head. "No, sir, I'm afraid it will have to be my brother's clunky old boat."

Daniel Keyes chuckled at this characterization of the ducal barouche, which Honey had ridden in once before. "Why don't we have a glass of something reviving while my daughter does whatever it is that women need to do before going out to eat ices?"

Honoria loved her Papa for many reasons, but especially for giving her this chance to change into the new dress she'd just had made—hoping for a day like today to wear it.

She rang for the parlor maid to help her change—she didn't have her own lady's maid—and was down in her father's study just as the men finished the amber liquid in their glasses.

They stood when she entered, and she wanted to weep with joy when Simon's eyes widened appreciatively at her new costume.

It was a crème silk with a dozen rows of tiny primrose ruffles around the bottom, a spencer in the same yellow. Matching silk lined her bonnet, the wide ribbon tied in a floppy bow beneath her right ear.

"You look lovely, Honoria," her father said, his eyes uncharacteristically serious, as if he knew how important this last outing was to her.

Not until they were seated in the big carriage, Miss Keeble beside her, did Simon speak.

"That is a smashing outfit, Miss Keyes. I'm glad it's such a clear, sunny day so we can show off both you and that very pretty bonnet."

Honoria tried not to preen at his words, but it was difficult to keep her smile from growing into a grin.

They spoke about her father's portrait, which he would deliver sometime next month.

"I daresay my brother will plan some party for the unveiling. You will come with him to Whitcomb, of course?"

Had she heard him correctly? Was he inviting her to his family's home? "I—I shall have to ask my father," she said in a breathy voice that was likely inaudible above the street sounds.

"When you visit we can ride out to Everley, which is not far from the duke's home."

"That would be lovely." It was all she could force out, her mind being too busy imagining herself mounted on a magnificent horse beside him, galloping across a stark, dramatic moor—which she knew very well did not exist in East Shropshire.

He spoke of his home and family on the brief ride and his words were like a siren's song that held her entranced.

When they arrived outside the confectioner's carriages lined the street both ways. Clearly they weren't the only ones to have such an idea on a beautiful day.

"It will be stuffy inside and the tables outside are taken," Simon said. "Shall we enjoy our treat in velvet-lined comfort?"

Honey and Miss Keeble agreed and Simon gestured to one of the waiters. Once they'd placed their orders they sat back and watched the fluctuating crowd, many of whom seemed to know Simon. Honoria was deep inside a fantasy where she and Simon were married and leaving for their country home tomorrow, only stopping to take leave of their many, many friends when Simon uttered a word—just one single word, but one that pulsed with more emotion than she'd heard from him in an entire month.

"Bella!"

Simon's enraptured expression sent her plummeting back down to earth. He was gazing at three women who'd stopped beside the carriage. To be precise, he was only looking at *one* of the women, and with his heart in his eyes. She—Bella—was the most beautiful woman Honoria had ever seen.

"Hello, Simon." Bella smiled up at him as he scrambled down from the carriage. Her cherry red lips parted slightly to reveal dazzling, white teeth. She had skin like proverbial porcelain and navy blue eyes. Her hair was brown, dark enough to look black, the ringlets glossy and luxurious beneath her tiny straw hat.

Simon's face was hot and eager and he wore an expression she'd never seen before—an expression he'd never worn for her.

Honey felt something crack inside her chest: Simon loved this beautiful creature.

"Bella, Agnes, Mrs. Frampton what are you doing in Town at this time of year?"

His words seemed to come from the bottom of a very deep well, and it was all she could do to remain upright inn her seat.

The older woman—Mrs. Frampton—Honey supposed, answered him, "Agnes is getting married next month and we needed a few last minute pieces of this and that." She was speaking of one daughter, but her eyes were on the other—the one who looked like an angel come to life—right before her faded blue gaze flickered to Honoria. The gesture was minute, but Lord Simon had impeccable manners. Usually. A flush covered his beautiful, high cheekbones when he realized he'd neglected his hosting duties.

"Mrs. Frampton, Miss Arabella Frampton, and Miss Agnes Frampton, I have the honor of introducing you to Miss Honoria Keyes and her companion, Miss Keeble. Miss Keyes is Daniel Keyes's daughter."

Nods and smiles all around, but Honoria could hardly take her eyes off Bella Frampton long enough to even remember what the other two women looked like. Either could Simon.

A waiter appeared with their ices.

"Would you care to join us?" Simon offered, blissfully unaware that his six words were like an ax to her heart.

"Yes, please do," she said mechanically when four pairs of blue eyes turned her way.

The women did a very unconvincing job of demurring and Simon opened the barouche door and gestured inside. "Please. You shall be a bit cozy but I'm sure Miss Keyes will not mind?"

Nobody noticed that her smile was more suited to a death mask and Honoria soon found herself staring across at two of the newcomers, Mrs. Frampton wedged beside her.

The strawberry ice she'd ordered tasted like ashes and Honoria wanted to be back at home, in her room, in her bed with the blankets pulled over her head. And never come out.

Later, she couldn't recall a single word that was spoken, her only memory Simon's expression and the way his eyes had lingered on the dark-haired beauty every chance he got.

She slept very little that night, her once vibrant world suddenly gray and colorless.

The next day was his final sitting and Honey had planned to remain in her room and avoid seeing him—hopefully ever again. But her father put an end to that hope at breakfast.

"You look as though you didn't sleep well, Honey. What is the matter?" he asked when she joined him in the sunny breakfast room that overlooked the back garden.

Honey usually had a very healthy appetite and her father would have been suspicious if she'd refrained altogether so she served herself the smallest possible portion of everything from the sideboard.

"Just a bit of a headache, Papa."

"Hmm." He laid aside the newspaper he had been reading and gave her a piercing look, his eyes so similar to hers it was like looking into a mirror. "I know you've grown to like young Fairchild, my dear, but—although you do not act it—you are a girl of fifteen and he is a man of almost one-and-twenty. He is a good and kind young man so I've given you more latitude than a wise father probably would have." He frowned. "I often regret not sending you to school and giving you an opportunity to mix with young girls your age. Perhaps—"

"Please, don't Papa." She laid down her fork and knife and met his worried gaze. "Don't. I would have been miserable if you'd sent me away. I would have missed you and you know that painting is everything—"

"No, my dear, not everything. Don't forget about life. About love. About experiencing joy—what you have been doing recently. Without experience in love, loss, pain, joy, and *life* one cannot make great art."

Honey didn't tell her father that after yesterday she now had far more familiarity with pain than she would have wished for.

***

Honoria jerked her gaze from The Most Perfect Man in Britain to the clock: it was almost two-thirty. Soon it would all be over. Soon her father would lay down his brush for the last time and say—

"Well, my lord, it appears I have captured enough of you to satisfy even *my* exacting mistress." Daniel Keyes laid down his brush.

Simon, who'd been telling them about his plans for the remainder of the summer, smiled at Honoria. "You mean your daughter, sir?"

Daniel laughed. "I meant my muse, Lord Simon, but you might have something there." He looked over at Honey and raised his eyebrows. "Well, are you going to put poor Lord Simon out of his misery and show him his portrait?"

Before Honey could answer there was a sharp knock and the door opened to reveal their ancient butler, his face red with exertion.

"Good Lord," her father paused in the act of wiping his hands on a turpsy rag to frown at his servant. "Have you been *running*, Dowdle?"

The old man was too occupied gasping for breath to answer. Instead, he held up a rectangle of cream-colored paper.

"For me?" Daniel Keyes took a step toward him.

"A chaise waiting outside," Dowdle gasped before lurching across to the younger man and handing him the letter. "For Lord Saybrook,"

Honey was surprised at their butler's slip with Simon's title; Dowdle was usually such a stickler for propriety.

Simon tore open the letter and Honey watched as every bit of color drained from his face. He swallowed hard enough to be heard all the way across the room and then looked up.

"You'll have to excuse me, sir. It's. . . well, It seems my . . .my nephew developed a chill and a cough and—" He waved his hand in a churning motion, as if he were stirring the very air around him in the hope it would stimulate the correct words. His face was stiff and his eyes wide with horror. "My nephew, the young Marquess of Saybrook, has died. I must leave immediately for Whitcomb."

Chapter Two

Thirteen Years Later
London

"Hello? Are you there, Honey?"

Honoria startled at the sound of her name and turned.

Her friend and housemate Serena Lombard stood in the open doorway, a puzzled expression on her face. "Is anything amiss, my dear?"

Honey realized she was standing in the middle of the room staring at the letter. She held up the ivory paper with the black wax seal.

"What is it?"

"A letter from the Duke of Plimpton."

Serena's eyebrows rose. "Hmm, Plimpton—didn't your father once paint him? Or was that his brother, the marquess—Saybrook, isn't he?"

A roaring sound pounded in Honey's ears at the sound of his name: the first time she'd heard it spoken aloud since that day.

Serena's forehead creased with concern. "You *are* feeling ill, aren't you? You are as pale as a ghost. What is it?"

Honey turned away and folded the letter with jerky, clumsy hands.

"Honey?" Serena's fingers landed on her shoulder.

"I'm fine," she squeezed out between clenched jaws. "Just a bit light-headed. I-I'm afraid I missed breakfast this morning," she lied. It took three swallows to get rid of the lump in her throat and she forced her face into some semblance of self-possession before turning to her friend.

"Shall I ring for tea?" Serena asked in her slightly accented voice.

"Tea sounds perfect. And perhaps even some of Mamie's butter biscuits. After all, one does not receive a piece of mail from a duke every day. I shall meet you in the parlor in ten minutes and tell you all about it," Honoria promised, giving her friend what she hoped was a calm, encouraging smile.

"I'll round up everyone and send for tea."

The door shut behind her and Honoria's brain spun like the colorful little wooden whirligig Serena's young son had made for their back garden. The Duke of Plimpton—after all these years? She had not thought about the duke for a long time. But his brother Simon was a different matter. *He* still managed to escape from the Newgate-like prison she'd constructed in her mind just for him. It didn't matter how thick she made the walls or how small the gap between the bars, he always found a way to escape and come find her.

Honey's feet took her in the direction of her private storage closet, which she kept locked at all times. She stood on her tiptoes and felt for the key on top of the smallish wardrobe. It had been some time since she'd unlocked the door.

There wasn't much inside, in fact the armoire wasn't anywhere close to full. Four canvases leaned against each other, protected by old sheets.

The first was a painting of her mother. Although Honey had no memory of the woman on the canvas it was her father's work and his love for the subject was evident in every stroke. It was his finest work, in her opinion. She knew it was wrong to keep it hidden in the dark but it was her *only* reminder of both her parents and that somehow made it intensely private.

The second portrait made her smile. It was the first painting she'd ever done. She could not have been older than five. It was, of course, a portrait of the person she loved most in the world: her father. It bore a striking resemblance to Daniel Keyes and it brought to mind his reaction the day she'd painted it. Joy and love and pride had shone brightly from his handsome face, so strong that even now the memory warmed her like a comforting blanket.

The third was a portrait of her. Her father had done many of her over the years—over a dozen, several of which still hung on walls of their house. But this one? Well, this was special. He'd painted it not long after finishing Lord Simon's portrait that summer.

Daniel Keyes had been a self-absorbed man in many ways, but not when it came to Honoria. He'd known it would have been unbearable to expose her unrequited love to questions, but this painting was proof he'd felt every ounce of her suffering in his heart. Just looking at the pain in her eyes was enough to make Honey's throat tighten

She was beautiful in the portrait—far prettier than she was in life— her eyes like shards of broken ice, haunted, turned in on an internal landscape that was pure pain.

The portrait reminded her how her fifteen year-old self hadn't believed her bleeding heart would keep beating. Yet here she was: hearty and hale all these years later.

Her hand shook as she pulled the sheet from the fourth painting and looked into the smiling hyacinth-blue eyes of Simon Fairchild, now the Marquess of Saybrook.

As it always did, the portrait froze her breath in her lungs. Honoria had painted many portraits in the past thirteen years but in none of the others had she captured the pure light and human essence of one of her subjects as she had in this one.

Her technique was far superior now to what it had been over a decade ago, but she'd never painted anything better. The laughter in his eyes was so vivid she could hear its echo.

Honey shook her head and dropped the cover back over the image that had haunted her far too often over the years. He wasn't the only man she'd been fond of, of course, but no other man had inspired such depth of feeling in her heart.

She knew he'd gone to war because she'd read his name in the paper—when he'd returned. But what had happened to the young woman—Bella—and his plans of a life in the country?

Honoria locked the door on that question and dozens of others. She went to the small mirror beside the door and inspected her uninspiring reflection. Her heavy hair had come loose from its severe moorings and long tendrils wafted around her narrow face like a dun-colored gloriole.

A Figure of Love

To be honest, her narrow and freckled face with its pale gray eyes were significantly more appealing with disheveled locks as a frame, but it did not suit a woman of her age and position, so she did her best to tidy the loose strands without actually unpinning and re-braiding it all. The result was good enough for an afternoon tea with her housemates, who were spinsters like Honoria.

A diminutive garden packed with blooms separated her painting studio from the small house where she'd spent her entire life. After her father died she'd chosen to set up her painting studio in the carriage house, rather than his studio. It was foolish, but she'd left the studio untouched, not a shrine to him, but a place so full of his essence that she could not bear the thought of dismantling it.

As Honoria traversed the narrow walk that led to the back door of the house she noticed that Freddie's peonies—the size of cabbages—had bloomed and died. It would be another summer of her life, her twenty-eighth summer.

That notion was vaguely depressing but she was in no mood to ask herself why that was, not today.

Freddie—Lady Winifred Sedgwick—glanced up from the small writing desk in the corner when Honoria entered the parlor.

"Serena will be here in a moment. She has become embroiled in a battle of wills."

"Ah, a skirmish between Mamie and Una?"

"Who else." It was not a question. Their cook and housekeeper were both the best of friends and the worst of enemies, depending on the day.

Honey dropped into her favorite seat, a battered green leather wingchair that had been her father's favorite. She swore she could still smell the unmistakable combination of turpentine and bay rum she associated with him even though he had been gone six years. He'd died not long after her twenty-first birthday, passing away in his sleep—a quiet death utterly unlike his passionate, flamboyant life.

The door to the parlor swung open and Honoria's mouth curved into a genuine smile. "Hello, Oliver. Have you escaped your lessons?"

Serena's ten year-old son dropped a creditable bow. "Mama said that I might come down for tea."

"And Mamie's biscuits?" she teased. He smiled and came to sit beside her. Honoria ruffled his messy brown curls. "What have you been working on? I haven't heard any explosions lately."

"Mama said no more experiments with the electricity maker." He sounded rather mournful about that.

"How do you manage to entertain yourself in the face of such deprivation?"

"She gave me an automata." His grin was blinding.

"Ah. And have you taken it apart yet?"

He gave her a look that told her what he thought of such a foolish question.

Freddie came to join them after depositing a small pile of correspondence on the salver by the door. "He is making his own automata, aren't you, Oliver?"

"*Oui, Tante.*"

Oliver called them all "aunt" and spoke a fluent mix of French and English that was beyond charming.

The door opened and his mother, accompanied by Una with the tea tray, entered.

"Thank you, Una," Honey said to the tiny housekeeper.

Her dour servant just grunted and bustled from the room, no doubt headed back to the kitchen and a resumption of hostilities.

Beside her, Oliver's stomach grumbled and Honey gave him a look of mock, open-mouthed shock.

He flushed. "*J'ai faim.*"

"English today, Oliver," Serena reminded her son. "I wish Miles were here," she said to Honoria. "But he won't be back from the country for at least another week."

Miles Ingram was a friend of theirs who'd been the dancing master at the Stefani Academy for Young Ladies, where they'd all taught before the school closed last year. There'd been seven teachers and they'd grown as close as siblings over the years they worked together. And now they were scattered to the four winds: Portia gone to teach music in the wilds of Cornwall; Annis living with her Grandmother in the tiny town of Cocklesham; and Lorelei with her brother and his family at a vicarage. Only Honoria, Serena, Freddie, and Miles remained in London.

Freddie busied herself with distributing tea, small sandwiches, and biscuits.

"Well?" Serena demanded. "Will you put us out of our misery, Honey?"

"Perhaps she would like to wait until we've finished eating?" Freddie murmured.

"Oh, bother waiting," Serena said.

Honey laughed at her friend's impatience. "Very well, I shall read it to you." She opened the one page letter and read it out loud:

"*Miss Keyes,*

I am writing you at the recommendation of Viscount Heath, whose wife's portrait you painted this spring. I have seen the painting and found your rendering of the viscountess to be accurate without any evidence of flattery or over-indulgence."

Honey couldn't help chuckling at that. "Perhaps I should print that on my calling card—*Accurate portraitist not given to flattery or over-indulgence?*"

"Keep reading, my dear," Serena urged.

"*I would like to engage you to paint Her Grace and my daughter, who is sixteen and—*"

Serena clapped her hands and bounced up and down on the settee, jostling Freddie beside her. "Oh, Honey, that is marvelous!"

"Does he mention his terms?" Freddie asked, ever the practical one.

"He asks that I respond with *my* terms and the earliest date I will be available." She placed the letter in Serena's outstretched hand.

"When will you go?" Serena demanded, looking up from the letter, which she was cradling as if it were spun glass.

"Goodness, I've only just learned of it. I've not even decided if—"

"*Pffft!* Don't be coy. You know you will do it. How could you not? A duchess and her daughter. His Grace is quite well off, isn't he?"

Honey's friends did not know of her girlhood infatuation with the duke's younger brother. Why should they? Who told their friends such embarrassing things? She shuddered at the thought of disgorging such a pitiful confession.

"Honey?"

Serena and Freddie were watching her with expectant expressions.

A slight knock on the door made her jump.

It was Madame, Oliver's nurse/governess.

Serena smiled at her son. "You may take some of Mamie's biscuits up to the schoolroom."

Oliver—who'd been behaving with remarkable composure for a little boy in the middle of a tedious adult conversation— rose from the sofa with alacrity, dropping a gentlemanly bow before following the French woman from the room.

Honoria waited until the door closed before clearing her throat and asked Freddie the dreaded question. "What do you know of the Duke of Plimpton and his current household?" Winifred Sedgewick made her living as a matchmaker, even though she despised the term, and there was very little about society she did not know

"I know His Grace has been married for almost twenty years and that his wife was Devonshire's youngest. She is delicate and cannot have more children. I believe the daughter is their only surviving child."

So, the duchess had never had any more children.

"The duke's younger brother, Marquess of Saybrook, is his heir presumptive," Freddie continued, unaware of the chaos the name caused in Honoria's breast.

"Ah, yes," Serena said in between bites of biscuit. "He was at Waterloo." She paused and frowned. "Was there not something odd about his return?"

"Yes," Freddie said, "he was not found until after three days on the battlefield. I have not seen his name this past Season, so I daresay he is still mending."

Honoria knew all of this, of course. She'd followed the story of his return like a woman obsessed. She took a sip of tea and saw her hand was white from squeezing the cup's handle.

"I cannot imagine what he must have endured," Freddie said, shaking her head.

"Do you think he lives with his brother?" Honey forced the words through numb lips.

"That I do not know. Why do you ask? Oh," Freddy's eyes widened slightly. "I recall, now. You know him—the Marquess of Saybrook— don't you, Honey?"

"Her father painted his portrait," Serena supplied before Honoria could answer.

Freddie was the most perceptive person Honey had ever met. Luckily, she was also the most private and always kept well away from probing into other people's lives.

Serena did not. "What was he like?" she demanded, dipping a biscuit into her tea and then popping the soggy mess into her mouth, licking her fingers.

Honey bit back a smile at her friend's free and easy ways. She could hardly imagine the scandal the voluptuous Frenchwoman must have cause during her brief sojourn among the *ton*.

"It's been a long time since I last saw him, Serena." Thirteen years, one month, one week, and three days. Not that she was counting.

Serena gave one of her very French shrugs. "You must remember something about him?"

Honey sighed—why bother lying? "He was the most gorgeous man I've ever seen."

Serena's biscuit froze an inch from her open mouth.

Freddie looked down at her folded hands.

"Surely he is not more handsome than Miles?" Serena demanded.

Honey's face heated.

The Frenchwoman chuckled. "Ah, that must be a rare sight to see."

Honey turned away from her knowing look and fussed with the handle of her teacup.

"I believe he stayed with his brother when he first returned," Freddy said, mercifully changing the subject. "But he does have an estate of his own."

"Yes, Everley." Honoria's voice was barely a whisper. She set down her cup and saucer with steady hands and then looked at her friends. Freddie's beautiful, inscrutable face remained expressionless but Serena met her gaze with a bold, challenging stare.

"Well?" The irrepressible Frenchwoman broke the uncomfortable silence, her brown eyes sparkling. "When will you leave?"

Chapter Three

Simon was flying.

Or the very next thing to flying.

The sorrel stallion with its flaxen mane and tail was not only beautiful, he was also as enamored of speed as his master. Bacchus was his name but Simon would have done better to name him Mercury he was so fleet.

When they approached the end of the path that opened onto the long and somewhat hilly drive leading down to Whitcomb Simon gave the horse his head. Bacchus knew the road well and his powerful muscles exploded. The wind was so fierce Simon swore he could hear it whistling past the scarred remnants of his deaf ear.

His muscles bunched and stretched like that of his mount, the damaged skin of his face, throat, and torso burning. The pain was almost cathartic and it reminded him he was alive, something he needed to tell himself at least a dozen times a day.

"I'm alive," he whispered.

The wind ripped away his words but they pounded through his mind and body. He *was* alive.

Thundering hooves and blurring trees cocooned him. *Alive.*

He crested the ridge—and almost collided with a post chaise that was ambling down the center of the road.

"Holy hell!" His voice was so loud it caused the big stallion between his thighs to startle.

A Figure of Love

Life shrank to a fraction of a second as he shifted his seat and tightened his thighs, sending Bacchus charging toward the slight gap to the right of the carriage.

He was vaguely aware of the postilion using his entire body to wrench the chaise and four to the left. The carriage skittered sideways and the wheels rolled into the soft, damp soil beside the drive.

Simon thundered past without slowing, his heart pounding louder than the wind. He laughed, the sound mad to his own ears.

He was alive.

***

Honey looked out the window just in time to catch a glimpse of the most beautiful man she'd ever seen. And then the chaise lurched to the side, throwing her, her book, and her cloak to the floor.

Luckily the cloak went before she did and softened her fall so she was more startled than hurt when she landed on her knees. She held onto the seat as the carriage bounced over rough ground, waiting until the vehicle began to slow before pushing herself up until she could grasp the leather strap beside the door.

Her heart pounded like a drum in her ears, and not just because of the scare.

He was here. She closed her eyes and relived the lighting-fast image of a Norse god on a magnificent mount. The image—no matter how fleeting—had shown him to be just as beautiful as before.

Simon was here.

The chaise shuddered to a halt and shook her out of her stunned reverie. So he was here? What difference did that make? She'd known it might be the case. She'd prepared herself for seeing him again. Or at least she'd thought she had.

Honey grimaced at her pitiful dithering and released the strap, collapsing back against the squabs as the chaise shifted on its springs.

The door opened and the burly groom appeared in the opening. "You alright, Miss?" His homely face was creased with concern.

"Just a little shaken up. What happened?"

His expression shifted from concern to disgust. "Naught but a lunatic, riding hell-bent for leather. Beggin' your pardon, Miss." He pushed back his hat and scratched his head. "He came out of nowhere and went past in a blur—riding the damned finest piece of horseflesh I've ever seen," he said with grudging admiration, and then grimaced, "Beggin' your pardon, Miss."

Honey wanted to roll her eyes; men and their horses. "Are we close to Whitcomb House?"

"Aye, naught but ten minutes away."

She smoothed her navy blue traveling dress over her lap with shaking hands. *Good God. She would see him again.*

"Alright then?" the groom asked.

She mustered a smile and nodded. "Yes—yes of course. I am fine and ready to resume the journey."

He closed the door and within moments they were rolling.

She stared out the window and tried to sooth her jangled nerves, but the beautiful profile and flash of golden hair was stuck in her mind's eye—a problem with artists. She would have known that classical profile—distinct enough to grace a coin—anywhere. Hatless with buckskin breeches, black clawhammer, and tall leather boots completed the brief picture. He'd looked vital, not damaged at all. He looked like a Corinthian—or at least that is what she imaged they looked like, those men who relished their own physicality: bruising riders, crack marksmen, determined pugilists, and other such overtly-masculine foolishness.

Her stomach quivered at the image her mind would not relinquish. How could she endure the proximity of such a beautiful, vital, distracting man. It was simply too—

She shook herself, her anxiety all of a sudden annoying rather than crippling: she was eight-and-twenty, not fifteen! So what if he was here? She wasn't painting *him*, she was painting the duke's wife and child. She was here to work, to build her reputation as a portraitist and a commission for a duke was a powerful thing—could be a powerful thing—if she concentrated and did her best.

You are a woman grown—no longer a tall, skinny, gangly fifteen year-old, the logical, soothing voice in her head reminded her.

Honoria snorted at the thought. No, she was now a tall, skinny, gangly twenty-eight year-old. Good Lord! Hadn't she learned anything in thirteen years?

The racing of her heart told her she'd not learned much—at least not when it came to Simon Fairchild. She took control of her thoughts and bent them to her will, crushing the hopes, dreams, fears, and yearnings of her younger, infatuated self into a small, harmless cube and then placing it into a the prison in her mind with all the other dangerous thoughts, and then locking the door .

The chaise crested the ridge and Honey gasped. "Oh my goodness." Her eyes darted wildly as she tried to take it all in. Massive oaks flanked both sides of the drive at regular intervals, allowing glimpses of rolling parkland beyond. This was no house, not even a mansion—it seemed to stretch for miles and resembled a mediaeval township, but with different architecture. The drive led to a massive gatehouse that must have been part of the original edifice, its lines soaring and imposing.

Honoria had heard Whitcomb compared in size and character to Knole House and now understood why it was considered a national treasure. Her fingers itched to sketch it and she knew she would need to come back to this vantage point and indulge her artistic curiosity sooner rather than later.

The sun was already low in the sky when the carriage rolled onto the cobble drive that curved in front of the massive entrance. A woman in black, accompanied by two liveried footmen, waited at the foot of the shallow stone steps that led to arched doors at least fifteen feet at their peak, the heavy, weathered wood bound with intricate iron strapping. Over the entrance the dragon and greyhound of Henry VIII supported the Royal Arms of England.

One of the footmen came forward to offer his assistance as Honey descended from the carriage, her body sore and aching from the last eleven hours.

"Welcome to Whitcomb House, Miss Keyes. I am Mrs. Constable." The older woman gave her a perfunctory, but not unfriendly smile as she dropped a slight curtsy. "I daresay you would like nothing more than a cup of hot tea and an hour to rest?" She gestured toward the house, not waiting for an answer. "His Grace will see you in the library before dinner. But come, I will show you to your rooms."

Honoria followed the shorter, bustling woman into a hall that was straight out of a Shakespearean play. Her jaw sagged as she tilted back her head and gazed up at the four-centered-arch ceiling.

"This is the Great Hall and was built in the 1490s," Mrs. Constable said, not slowing. "The older parts of the house are not used as much as the South Wing, which was added in the 1740s and affords far more convenience and comfort. The family dines in the smaller dining room when not entertaining. His Grace has requested that you dine with the family." Her tone said the request was not really a request.

They ascended ancient flagstone steps that turned twice at ninety degree angles and opened onto yet another long hall, this one heading back in the direction they just came.

"This may seem a rather odd way of reaching the South Wing," the housekeeper said, as if reading her thoughts, "But it will make more sense shortly."

They passed through a lengthy wood-paneled hall, the dark wood floor covered with an ancient carpet runner that muffled their steps. Heavy iron sconces lighted their way at intervals and a massive rose window at the far end added an almost religious air. The housekeeper turned down a hallway on the right before they came to the spectacular window, leading them down an almost identical corridor.

"Is it only the duke and duchess and their daughter who live here?" Honey asked as they ascended what felt like a half story, entering a much wider and airier hall that was illuminated by cathedral windows with intricate tracery.

"His Grace's mother, the Dowager Duchess of Plimpton and his brother, Marquess of Saybrook, also live at Whitcomb." The housekeeper took yet another right, this hallway narrow and windowless.

Lord, she was so lost she could wander for weeks.

"The only one of the family to keep chambers in the East Wing is his lordship."

Honey blinked at the disapproval she heard in the woman's voice. So, the marquess was . . . difficult? Or was this merely the opinion of a servant who did not appreciate the extra work that must be entailed with serving two wide-spread wings of the house when one would have been more convenient.

They turned yet another corner but this time she staggered to a halt.

"Goodness," she murmured, vaguely realizing the woman she was following had not stopped walking.

"This is the older of the two portrait galleries," Mrs. Constable said, her increasingly distant voice causing Honey to resume walking, her head swiveling wildly to take in the almost suffocating number of portraits that covered the high, paneled walls, jammed together so tightly that some frames touched others.

Good God—she recognized the unmistakable style of Holbein. *Holbein!* She made an undignified squeaking sound. Her portrait would hang in a collection which counted one by Hans Holbein?

"Miss Keyes?"

Pulling her eyes away from the portrait—the subject a middle-aged man with no great physical beauty, but with a countenance so. . . *knowing* that Honey felt as if *he* were looking at *her*—was like pulling a heavy wagon from deep, sucking mud.

"Yes?" she said dazedly, turning her head and blinking, as if she'd just been blinded by a lighthouse lantern.

"It is just a little further, Miss." The woman's tone said she was a busy woman with no time to spare for goggling at fripperies like pictures.

Honey hurried after her, pointedly keeping her eyes from the flow of portraits that assaulted her peripheral vision. Later, she would come back later. This gallery would be reason enough to learn the layout of the maze-like house.

Something the housekeeper said dug through to the surface of her mind like a mole.

"Did you say this was the *old* gallery?"

"Yes, the new gallery is on the first floor. That is where the newer portraits hang."

Like her father's portrait of Simon Fairchild.

Honey's heart beat like a young girl's facing her first assembly: Simon *and* more paintings.

315

They ascended yet one more set of stairs, these wooden and carpeted with a rich maroon and gold pattern that seemed to levitate above the floor. Honey felt almost guilty stepping on such lovely, intricate work. She had never seen its like.

"And here we are," Mrs. Constable said, flinging open the first door on the right.

Honey gaped. She was vaguely aware that she was spending far too much time with her mouth hanging open and shut it.

The sitting room was a cream and lemon yellow shade that felt crisp and cool. Delicate, spindle-legged chairs and a low-slung settee were arranged in front of a massive fireplace with a cream marble mantle and surround.

"Through this door," the housekeeper opened a door to the right, "Is your dressing room." The room was monstrous and Honey's paltry collection of dresses would scarcely fill a corner of one of the huge armoires. A washstand, dressing table, clothing chest, several chairs and damask covered chaise longue, and large bathing tub near a fireplace weren't enough to make the room feel crowded.

"And here is your bed chamber." This last door opened to the most opulent room of the three. A monstrous four-poster bed held pride of place, curtained and canopied in the same lemon yellow and cream, but with hints of gold in the floor coverings and rich velvet drapes that covered the floor to ceiling windows that made up part of one wall.

Honey saw that Mrs. Constable was waiting for some reaction. "These rooms are lovely and quite . . . spacious."

"This is the family's section of the house. This room used to belong to His Grace's grandmother."

"Why, how kind of the duke to treat me with such generosity and condescension."

She made a sniffing sound that led Honey to think she agreed heartily with this assessment. The door opened and a footman entered with her portmanteau. "Ah, there is your baggage. I've taken the liberty of ordering a light tea and I will send up a maid to assist you."

"You're most kind," Honey murmured.

"The duke's study is at the other end of the Old Gallery. Ring the bell and a servant will escort you. His Grace will expect you at seven."

A Figure of Love

"Thank you." Honey didn't bother telling the other woman that she'd be able to find her way back to those portraits asleep and in the dark.

***

Honey was ready a full fifteen minutes before her meeting. Rather than sit in her room staring out at the view—admittedly quite a remarkable one that provided a sweeping panorama of the topiary and past that, the deer park—she made her way to the old gallery.

The wide, black and white tiled corridor was partly illuminated with windows set high above, perhaps thirty feet. The angle of the light such that it would never touch directly on a painting.

She noticed she was actually walking on tip-toes as she made her way down the length of the hall, as if approaching a holy relic. Well, for her this *was* the equivalent of a holy relic.

Her gaze flickered greedily across the collected booty of centuries. She dazedly registered styles, names, heroes: a Van Dyke, a Devit, a Seymore—complete with trusty steed, a Dance-Holland, a—she gasped and lurched toward a portrait slightly smaller than those beside it—a *Hogarth*! The subject, a beautiful woman whose eyes and expression invited the viewer into her boudoir, indeed, who promised and *enticed*—

A door down the hall swung open so hard it crashed against the wall hard enough that she could feel the vibration in her feet.

"You can go sod yourself, Wyndham!" The roar filled the hallway, although its owner was still inside the room.

Honey had never heard the voice pulse with so much rage when she'd known him, but she recognized it all the same.

Instead of simply scurrying away—as she should have done—she stood motionless, her eyes riveted on the gaping doorway. A soft murmur broke the silence—the person who was currently being yelled at, she supposed.

"Ha!" The word dripped with loathing and fury. "I don't bloody *care*, haven't you been listening? The whole place can go to the devil and you along with it. I'm telling you for the last time, Wyndham—do *not* meddle in my affairs ever again or I swear that you shall live to regret it." The enraged speaker catapulted out of the open doorway.

Even though Honey was frozen he must have noticed something out of the corner of his eye because he stopped and whirled around to face her.

She gave a small, nearly inaudible, gasp of surprise. *Good Lord!* What had *happened* to him?

He surged toward her with an odd, lurching gait that drove her back a step, raw rage rolling from him like waves of heat. "Who the *devil* are you? And what are you doing lurking about and listening at keyholes?" He kept walking, driving her back and back, until she hit the wall and felt something sharp jab her in the hip. The thought that she might have damaged a priceless painting was even more horrifying than the furious man stalking her. She turned to look over her shoulder and nearly fainted with relief when she saw it was only the corner of a plinth bearing a marble bust.

A hand grabbed her arm ungently and swung her around. The face that looked down on her was not far different from the beautiful portrait she had painted all those years ago—on the right side. But the left side had been vandalized with angry red scars—slashes and gashes and pits that bore the slick sheen of recently healed wounds— that had destroyed the smooth, high-boned beauty of one half of his face. His magnificent golden-blond hair had been cropped brutally close, doing nothing to hide what remained of left his ear or the deep horizontal groves that began at his jaw and deeply scored his cheek. He glared down at her with the same beautiful blue eyes, but the left eyelid was pulled down at the outside corner, the stretched skin giving the eye a perpetually sinister cast. He'd been tall and lithe when she'd known him but now his broad shoulders were powerful and substantial rather than graceful.

It was Simon, but it was not Simon.

***

Who ARE Minerva Spencer & S.M. LaViolette?

Minerva is S.M.'s pen name (that's short for Shantal Marie) S.M. has been a criminal prosecutor, college history teacher, B&B operator, dock worker, ice cream manufacturer, reader for the blind, motel maid, and bounty hunter. Okay, so the part about being a bounty hunter is a lie. S.M. does, however, know how to hypnotize a Dungeness crab, sew her own Regency Era clothing, knit a frog hat, juggle, rebuild a 1959 American Rambler, and gain control of Asia (and hold on to it) in the game of RISK.

Read more about S.M. at: www.MinervaSpencer.com

Made in the USA
Las Vegas, NV
26 November 2024

12686784R00194